I0561080

Kingdom of Magicians

Book One of The War-Torn Kingdom

by Timothy L. Cerepaka

An Annulus Publishing Book

Annulus Publishing, Cherokee, Texas, 2016

Published by Annulus Publishing

Copyright © Timothy L. Cerepaka 2016. All rights reserved.

Contact: timothy@timothylcerepaka.com

Cover design by Elaina Lee of For the Muse Design

ISBN-13: 978-0692707685

ISBN-10: 0692707689

Acknowledgements

I would like to thank my uncle, James Wilhite, for helping me get this manuscript into publishable shape. I'd also like to thank the rest of my family for supporting me while I wrote this novel. You guys rock.

Chapter One

KEO OF THE SWORD did not expect to have to fight a demon today on his way back home from running errands in the nearby town of New Ora. Nor did he expect this same demon to announce to Keo that he was but the first of many demons and that all of Lamaira was going to fall underneath their power, and from there, the rest of the world.

It all started earlier that day, when Keo—a young man with short dark hair and skin tanned from spending his days working and training in the sun—was walking through the Low Woods, a large forest located in the southern region of the former Kingdom of Lamaira. He was heading back from New Ora, where he had bought bread, milk, and other supplies that his master and mentor, Tiram of the Blade, had asked him to buy.

This was normally an easy task, even though Keo disliked having to go into civilization for any reason. All he had to do was walk into town, go to the merchants in town, stare at all of their wonderful wares (including one merchant who claimed to sell genuine Dracone talons and scales, although Keo thought that they were probably fake and so didn't buy any), buy what Tiram had asked him to buy, and then leave. He never really talked to anyone because he didn't know very many people in New Ora, even though he had lived in the forest near the town for years. He hated being around other people anyway, except for his mentor and his friend Nesma, although he had not seen Nesma since she joined the Magical Council—the ruling party of South Lamaira—a year ago.

So Keo was usually in and out of town very quickly, and thus was walking along through the Low Woods taking a familiar rough path he had walked upon many times during his life. The trees around him were large, tall, and thick, their leaves and upper branches providing relief from the hot summer afternoon sun. Cheep-chirps—a small, red-colored bird common in Low Woods—sang somewhere above him, but no matter where he looked, he could not see their red plumage or any sign of them. But he liked to listen to their musical chirps, as it was a comforting sound he had always associated with peace and solitude since his childhood.

The air in the Low Woods was also cool and easy today, as the sun's rays could not penetrate through the thick canopy above to warm it. Still, Keo could feel the cool air already starting to fade and he knew that within the next hour the Low Woods would be not quite as hot as the town of New Ora, but warm enough to make outside chores uncomfortable. And he had many outside chores to perform back at the cabin that he and Master Tiram shared. He wasn't looking forward to it.

As he walked, Keo kept his eyes and ears open for any sign of the various dangerous creatures that lived in the Low Woods, such as the mammoth bears and knife-tooth wolves. They rarely attacked, as most of the animals in the Low Woods feared humans, but every now and then a particularly hungry or crazy beast would assault travelers through the Woods and kill them.

Keo rested his hand on Gildshine, his magical sword, which

was sheathed at his side. He rarely had to use it due to the fact that most of the creatures in the Low Woods knew to avoid his master and him, but he was always prepared to wield it just in case. And he knew how to use it well, too, otherwise he would not be known as Keo of the Sword. Master Tiram had taught him how to use a sword well, so Keo was confident he could defend himself with Gildshine should he be attacked.

But today seemed like a slow, idle summer day. The chirps of the birds above seemed lazier than normal and even the merchants back in town who hawked their wares with the fervor of preachers had seemed a little more reserved than usual. It was probably because it was the height of summer and the summer heat always had a sleepy effect on everyone exposed to it, including Keo himself, even in the cool air of the Low Woods.

That was when Keo heard the crunching of leaves and branches nearby. His first thought was that it was perhaps a mammoth bear walking nearby, probably not going to attack him based on the easiness of its pace. Still, Keo kept one hand on the hilt of Gildshine, just in case he was wrong and the bear attacked.

But then Keo noticed that the cheep-chirps had stopped singing and he immediately stopped. He listened for the birds' tune, but no matter how hard he listened, he heard nothing.

Cheep-chirps only stopped singing at night, when they slept … or when there was danger and the cheep-chirps were trying to hide from predators. Of course, what Keo had discovered from living in the Low Woods for his whole life was that anything that threatened a cheep-chirp could often threaten a human being as well.

Keo listened for anything that should not be. All he heard was the same sound of fallen leaves and branches being crunched underfoot. It seemed like the cheep-chirps had silenced themselves when they heard those same sounds that he did. He didn't know for sure, of course, because there were many predators of cheep-chirps in the Low Woods that were far quieter than whatever was walking around nearby, but without hearing anything else, he had to assume that that was the case.

Then that sound of the creature walking also stopped, but not before Keo realized that the footsteps of the creature belonged to no Low Woods beast that he knew. It sounded almost like the footsteps of a human, which was possible, but unlikely. As far as Keo knew, the only humans in the Low Woods were Master Tiram and himself. Of course, the Low Woods were located near the southern border of South Lamaira, near the country of Hasfar, and so travelers from that country often passed through the Low Woods on their way to other parts of South Lamaira. Just the other day, in fact, Keo helped a Hasfarian traveler lost in the forest find his way to New Ora (although it was hard at first because the Hasfarian tongue was very different from Lamairan and the Hasfarian himself only knew a few Lamairan words whose pronunciation he butchered).

But this part of the Low Woods was never traveled by anyone except for Keo and Tiram, and Keo knew that Tiram was currently at the cabin back home resting, which he did more and more in his old age. That meant that there was something else nearby, but what it was, Keo didn't know.

Keo lowered his bag of goods onto the ground and drew Gildshine. He contemplated using the sword's magical power, which would require him giving up half his energy to make

Gildshine capable of cutting through anything, but decided against it. The thing he heard might not require Gildshine's magical power. In fact, Keo had only ever used Gildshine's ability a handful of times over the years and both times left him too exhausted to do anything for nearly a week, which was why he didn't want to use it here in case the creature avoided his attack.

So Keo listened again, but now it seemed like the source of the footsteps had vanished into thin air, because he could not hear it. The silence and stillness of the Low Woods was normally a comfortable thing, but right now it was unnerving and tense.

Then Keo heard breathing. It was slow and wet, like someone breathing through a dampened rag. It was coming from his right, behind a grove of trees that he had passed by many times over his years of traveling on this road. Keo slowly turned to face the grove, but did not yet move closer to it. He tried to see if he could spot anything in the branches and shadows, but the trees grew together so thickly that it was impossible to tell for sure what might have been hiding behind it.

"Who's there?" said Keo. "Are you a traveler? Are you lost? If so, I can help you."

No answer.

Keo tensed. He considered whether or not to step forward and decided that that was the best action to take. So Keo raised one foot and then put it back down on the ground.

As soon as Keo took that step, something large, furry, and loud burst forth from the trees with astonishing speed. The creature barreled toward Keo like lightning, but Keo jumped out of its way, just barely dodging it. As the creature passed, an awful stench like mud and blood followed the creature, making Keo gasp and cough as he walked backwards away from the creature, which came to a stop on the other side of the path and then turned to face him.

Keo had never seen anything like this creature in his entire life. It was large and round, almost like a ball, with two stout but strong legs and large fists with claws that gleamed like metal. The creature had a furry face with human-like features, but there was nothing human about the bloodlust in its red eyes. And it was large, easily twice as large as Keo, who was not a small man by any means.

Keo tried to remember if Master Tiram had ever described such a creature to him before, but he kept drawing a blank. This thing looked like it had stepped right out of his worst nightmares, but Keo did not run or show fear, because he had a feeling that this thing, whatever it was, would tear him apart if he showed even the slightest hint of fear in its presence.

But one thing Keo did notice about it was the sheer aura of evil that radiated from it. And 'evil' was the operative word, because Keo had never felt such a mighty aura from any creature dwelling in the Low Woods before. Most animals in the Low Woods were too mindless to have any conception of good or evil, but somehow Keo could tell that this thing was smart enough to tell the difference between the two concepts and had already made its choice about which one it supported.

And that, more than anything, was what made Keo afraid of the creature and what it wanted.

"What are you, creature?" said Keo, never lowering Gildshine. "Another inhabitant of the Lost Woods that I was unaware of until just now?"

The creature hissed loudly, but then Keo realized that it was simply that monster's way of chuckling. "No, human, I do not live in these pathetic woods. But I will rule them soon, as my master promised me."

Keo raised an eyebrow. "Who is your master? Is he like mine?"

"I know nothing of you or your master, but I will say that my master is the greatest of them all, much greater than any human master," said the creature. "Unfortunately, my master is unable to do anything in his present state, but worry not, because I will be the one to free him and when I do, your country will fall."

"What are you even babbling about?" said Keo. "You still have not even told me what you are."

The creature looked at Keo with glee in its eyes. "The true name of my people is unpronounceable in your mortal tongue, but you know of us in legend as the demons."

Keo's eyes widened. "Demons? But demons are a myth, a scary story told to scare young children into obeying their elders. You cannot be a demon."

"Whether you accept my existence or not, I don't care," said the demon, shaking its head. "All I care about is freeing my people and my master. They are rising, becoming more and more powerful with each passing day, and you humans are too stupid and divided to do a thing about it."

"How do you know if the demons are rising?" said Keo. "What does that even mean?"

The demon hissed again, this time actually hissing and not simply chuckling in a demonic way. "It means that, exactly six months from today, the Kingdom of Humans will end. It was a terrible age, one which I will be happy to see come to an end."

Keo had no idea what the demon was even talking about. "If the Kingdom of Humans is about to end, then what will replace it?"

"The Kingdom of Demons, of course," said the demon. "The rivers of your land will run red with your peoples' blood and there is nothing you can do to stop it."

None of this made any sense to Keo, who had always grown up believing that demons were myths and nothing more. Still, he recognized a threat when he saw it and this demon was by definition a threat, whether there was any truth to what it said or not. That meant it had to be stopped, and right away.

"I don't know how much of what you say is true and how much isn't," said Keo, "but I do know that you tried to kill me and are probably planning to kill other people. And I cannot allow that."

The demon shook its ugly head. "When did I express a need for your approval, human? The invasion will start in the heart regardless of whether you like it or not."

Keo took a fighting stance. "I didn't say I would stop this 'invasion' you speak of. I was just going to stop *you*."

Keo dashed toward the demon, Gildshine gripped firmly in both hands, and swung his blade at the demon. The demon blocked the blow with its claws and tried to swipe him, but Keo jumped back out of its range and stabbed at the demon.

The demon blocked the block with both of its claws and then charged at Keo with the speed of a rampaging ox. Keo dodged it by jumping to the right, but he also took advantage of its speed to slash it as he passed him.

Thus, Keo was shocked when his sword bounced off its hide. He was so shocked that his grip on Gildshine loosened and the sword flew out of his hands and landed on the ground several feet away, leaving Keo defenseless.

The demon turned to face Keo, a malicious grin on its awful face. "Surprised that your pitiful human blade failed to cut my skin? We demons have skin as hard as iron. Your puny human weapons cannot even scratch us."

Then the demon barreled toward him again, but Keo, as before, avoided it. He ran over to Gildshine, grabbed its hilt, and held the sword before him defensively as the demon stopped and turned to face him once more.

"Still going to try to hurt me with your sword?" said the demon. "Weren't you listening to what I just said about how useless your humans weapons are?"

Keo did not respond. He just looked at the demon defiantly, silently challenging it to attack him if it felt so brave. Of course, deep down, Keo was afraid of the demon because, if he could not harm the demon with Gildshine, then his chances of winning this fight fell close to zero. He seriously considered using Gildshine's magical ability, but at the moment he wasn't sure that he would get a chance to use it before the exhaustion kicked in and rendered him utterly defenseless.

I need to get close enough to the demon to cut it, Keo thought. *But its fighting style makes it impossible to get close. It attacks quickly, forcing me to dodge, and then stops well outside of the range of Gildshine before it attacks again. I need to get it to stop near me somehow.*

The demon shook its head. "Never mind. I will just tear you

apart piece by piece anyway, regardless of whether you own a dinky human weapon like that."

The demon reared back, but instead of barreling toward Keo at high speeds, it launched itself through the air at an astonishing speed. Keo realized that he needed to duck to avoid it just in the nick of time, but the demon still slashed at him with its claws as it passed by overhead and cut deeply into his right shoulder, causing him to cry out in pain as blood shot out from the wound.

Staggering forward, Keo glanced at his torn-open shoulder, which stung in the cool air of the Low Woods, and then looked over his shoulder to see that the demon had landed on one of the trees. The demon clung to the tree like some kind of bizarre, monstrous spider and its head turned almost all the way around to look at him. With a chilling smile on its lips, the demon raised its bloody claw and licked the blood off of the tip of its claw.

"Delicious," said the demon with a sigh. "It has been so long since I feasted on human blood. Maybe I will drain you of your blood first before I tear you apart, because all of this fighting has made me very thirsty."

Keo had no response to that, because his wounded shoulder made it impossible to talk without screaming from the pain. He stepped backwards, but even he knew that there was no running now. The demon was still as strong and fast as ever, which meant that Keo had to end the fight now if he hoped to survive.

But he's still nowhere near me, Keo thought, wincing at the blood running down his arm. *And I'm wounded. Wounded and alone. Not even Master Tiram knows that I'm under attacked, so I can't rely on him to save me.*

That was when a new thought occurred to Keo, a new plan for

dealing with the demon: He would make the demon come to *him*.

Gritting his teeth, Keo raised Gildshine and said, "Come on, demon. Hit me with your best shot, if you think you're so strong."

The demon looked genuinely surprised for a moment. "You mean you *aren't* going to fall down on your knees and beg me to spare your pitiful life? All of the tales I heard said that humans are cowards who break down at the slightest sign of death."

"Looks like someone lied to you," said Keo. He wanted to scream, wanted to move, but he stayed where he was because if he moved, then his plan would fail. "We humans are a lot stronger than we look."

The demon shrugged. "Oh well. Whether you die fighting like a soldier or on your knees like a slave, it will be very bloody and painful for you and great fun for me. Now die!"

The demon launched itself off the tree toward Keo, this time faster than ever. At the same time, Keo focused on Gildshine. Feeling his bond with his sword, he told Gildshine to take half of his energy so that it could cut anything. And Gildshine, as always, immediately complied, but Keo did not yet feel exhausted beyond help.

Instead, Keo felt Gildshine become stronger in his hands, saw its blade sharpen. And that fact made him smile, which the demon flying toward him must have noticed, because a look of confusion spread across the demon's features as it hurtled through the air toward Keo.

With a roar, Keo slashed Gildshine down on the demon when it was within his reach. In the brief second before Gildshine's enhanced blade made contact with the demon's face, Keo almost believed that even Gildshine's magic would not pierce the demon's skin and that all of his striving would be for nothing.

But in the next second, Gildshine cut straight through the demon's face and body. Both halves of the demon's body passed by Keo without touching him, although the black demon blood splattered over him anyway. The two halves of the demon crashed to the ground behind Keo, but Keo still turned around to make sure that the demon was not going to rise again.

To his astonishment, the demon's halves immediately started crumbling, turning into a sand-like substance, which sank into the earth rapidly until soon there was not even a hint that the demon had been there. It was like the demon's halves had been drawn into the earth by some unseen force, although that may have simply been the way that demon bodies decomposed after death.

In any case, Keo was glad about his victory only briefly, because a second after the demon's halves vanished, a sudden, heavy exhaustion fell over Keo. Then the pain in his shoulder became white hot and he staggered forward, barely able to remain standing.

Must ... get ... back ... to ... Master Tiram, Keo thought, his eyes heavy and his mind sluggish. *Now ...*

Keo managed to walk back over to his bag of goods, but before he could pick it up, he fell face-first onto the ground. The blood loss and exhaustion from using Gildshine were too much for his body to handle and he soon lost consciousness completely.

Chapter Two

K EO," SAID A FAMILIAR, harsh older voice above him. "Keo, you damned fool and son of a woodpecker, wake up."

Keo's eyes flickered open. At first, his vision was fuzzy and all he could make out was a blurred, gray shape above him. He almost thought that it was the demon again before his vision cleared and he saw who it really was.

It was the face of an older man in his sixties, with a short gray beard covering the lower half of his mouth. The old man's eyes were sharp and intelligent, but also judgmental, like the old man was judging the way Keo opened and closed his eyes. Tiny, minute scars ran along the old man's forehead and cheeks, barely visible in the light of the cabin, which seemed to be coming from a nearby fireplace, based on the crackling flames he heard.

"Master … Tiram?" said Keo. He tried to sit up. "Where am I? What happened? How—"

Tiram pushed Keo down with surprising strength for a man his age. "Lie back down, you damned idiot. Your shoulder is still healing. Unless you want to end up like One Arm Ramas, you should lie down and rest. Doctor's orders."

Keo rolled his eyes. "You're not a doctor, Master. You're not even much of a healer."

"Even though I've bandaged and fixed many of your injuries

over the years?" said Tiram with a snort. "Ungrateful brat."

"It was just a joke, Master," said Keo, hoping he did not offend Tiram. "Really, you're a great healer even if you haven't received formal training in the subject."

"I know," said Tiram. "But I really don't think now is the time to joke, especially after I found you half-dead in the forest covered in someone else's blood. And it wasn't even human blood, either."

Keo looked down at his body. He was lying underneath a wool blanket, but he could tell that his old clothes had been stripped off him, probably to be cleaned. He was wearing some pants, but had no shirt on, and the reason for that was obvious: His right shoulder was heavily bandaged to the point where he could barely move his right arm.

"Tell me," said Tiram as he sat back. He folded his large arms over his chest. "What happened out there? Mammoth bear? Knife-tooth wolf? Really angry cheep-chirp? The footprints and claw marks I found in the ground and trees looked nothing like any animal I know of in the Low Woods, so what was it?"

Keo tried to remember, but it was difficult for some reason. He suspected that the blood loss and exhaustion must have messed with his memory, but soon he remembered the demon's smiling face and shuddered.

"I was attacked by a creature," said Keo.

"Very specific," said Tiram. "I can see that all of my years of showing you how to identify the various animals of the Low Woods have paid off well."

Keo scowled, but continued speaking. "I mean, it was a creature that claimed to be a demon."

Tiram's smirk immediately vanished underneath his beard. "Continue."

Keo did not like Tiram's sudden change of tone. That always meant that Tiram knew something that Keo did not, something that wasn't good. He wasn't so sure that he wanted to keep talking now, at least until Tiram explained why he suddenly looked so serious, but Keo remembered how Tiram never explained himself unless he wanted to, so Keo continued his story.

"I was walking along the path home after I left New Ora after buying the things you asked me to get," said Keo. He put one hand on his forehead because his head was starting to hurt for some reason. "I was walking by myself when this strange creature that looked like a furry ball with a head and limbs jumped me. It claimed to be a demon and tried to kill me."

"Is that all it said?" said Tiram. His tone was dead serious now.

"No," said Keo, shaking his head. "It told me that its fellow demons were going to rise out of the 'heart,' whatever that is, and that the Kingdom of Humans is about to end and be replaced by the Kingdom of Demons." Keo looked at Tiram curiously. "I didn't think much about it, but now I wonder what it meant by that."

Tiram stroked his beard. Keo suspected that Tiram knew exactly what the demon meant by all of that, but he was obviously not going to share what he knew with Keo, at least not yet.

"How did you kill the demon?" said Tiram. "Or did it run away? I didn't see it anywhere when I found you."

"I killed it," Keo said. "I used Gildshine's magical ability to cut it in half."

"Gildshine is a pretty sharp sword by itself," said Tiram. "Any reason you had to use its magical ability? That seems pretty foolhardy to me, especially in your wounded condition."

"I had no choice," said Keo, shaking his head. "The demon's skin was impervious to Gildshine's normal blade and the demon claimed that normal human weapons can't hurt demons. I was forced to use Gildshine's ability just to survive."

"Ah," said Tiram. "Now I understand."

Keo raised his head and looked around the cabin room, searching for Gildshine. He saw the sword in its green leather sheath leaning by the front door, which made him sigh in relief, as he had worried that Tiram might have left it behind. He then lowered his head back onto his pillow and looked at Tiram, who now seemed lost in thought, looking more like a Monk of the Old Order at the moment than a master swordsman living by himself in the Low Woods.

"Master, you know what that demon was talking about, don't you?" said Keo.

Tiram looked at Keo suddenly. "What?"

"I said, you know what the demon was talking about," said Keo. "You didn't say that the demon was fake or that demons are just scary stories meant to frighten young children. You know that demons are real, don't you?"

Tiram looked highly reluctant to talk about this subject. Keo could tell because Tiram rested his hands on his knees and was looking around the room, which was a habit of Tiram's that Keo had come to recognize as what his master did whenever someone asked him a question about a subject he didn't want to talk about. That habit always contrasted sharply with Tiram's usual confident and tough self, which was why it always stood out to Keo whenever Tiram did it.

Finally, Tiram said, "I have heard … legends of the demons. My own parents, well before you were born, told me stories about the ancient times of Lamaira, about the times before the rise and fall of the Lamairan Royal Family, and before the Restorationists, Divinians, or Magicians existed. They said that in those days, demons ravaged Lamaira, stalking the land, killing humans and Dracones and any other species they found. Their power was unmatched and no one could stand against them, at least not for very long without suffering a horrible death."

"I have never heard those stories before," said Keo. "You told me the ones about the demons scaring little children, but never those ones about the past. Why didn't you ever tell me about them?"

"Because I never believed them and didn't think they needed to be remembered," said Tiram. He shuddered. "The stories my father used to tell me were always bloody and horrific. While I've never tried to hide the ugly side of life away from you, Keo, these stories were awful. They always ended with the demons brutally slaughtering—and in some cases even raping—their human victims. Just awful stuff, even for a hardened swordsman like myself."

"But what happened to the demons?" said Keo. "How were they defeated, if they were so powerful?"

"Well, according to my father, the demons ruled Lamaira until a human known as the Good King arose and challenged their rule," said Tiram. "He was the first human to kill a demon, and he did it using a powerful sword known as Shadowbane. This demon's death shocked its fellow demons and created hope in the hearts of every other human and Dracone in Lamaira. The Good King taught these humans and Dracones how to make their own demon-killing swords and soon rebellions rose up all around the kingdom, with demons dying in droves every day at the hands of the people they had oppressed for so long, despite the demons' best efforts to crush the rebellions before they got too big."

"So the demons were eliminated, then?" said Keo.

"A good chunk of them, according to the story I was told," said Tiram. "But then the Arch-Demon, also known as the King of Demons, rose from the very depths of the pit that the demons were said to have come from and fought against the Good King in an epic battle that was said to have lasted seven whole days. The two fought to a stalemate because the Arch-Demon's armor and strength matched the Good King's own, so the Good King, in a final act of desperation, cast a spell to banish the Arch-Demon and what remained of his followers back into the pit from which they came. Thus, all of the demons were banished from Lamaira, supposedly for good."

"What happened to the Good King after that?" said Keo. "Did he die of the injuries he sustained from the fight?"

"No," said Tiram, shaking his head. "The story goes that the Good King was the first King of Lamaira. He founded the Kingdom of Lamaira and his line ruled for one thousand years until the recent death of King Riuno, which as you know splintered the kingdom into the three warring factions that fight over it now."

"And the demon said that the demons were going to rise again," said Keo. He sat up, wincing at the pain in his shoulder.

"Then we have to stop them."

Tiram's old but firm hands grabbed Keo's chest and shoved him back down again. "Sorry, kid, but those legends are just that: Legends. They don't mean anything. They're probably cobbled together by bits and pieces of other stories and history and likely don't have more than an ounce of truth between the whole lot of them."

"But this thing was an actual demon," said Keo. "It could not be harmed except by Gildshine's magical power and it claimed to be a demon. I think that means that the legends you just told me are true."

"They may have some truth to them, but I don't think they are true overall," said Tiram. "Besides, you are getting too excited and you need rest if your shoulder is going to heal."

"The demon said that its brothers would rise in six months," said Keo. "That means that the demons are close to breaking free again."

"The legends also state that demons are liars who are not to be trusted," Tiram said. "Even if this creature that attacked you was in fact a real demon, it might have just been saying that in order to scare you."

"I don't think so," said Keo, shaking his head. "You weren't there when it spoke to me. It sounded confident that its fellow demons were going to rise in six months. And it said they were going to attack all of Lamaira and attempt to destroy it."

"But why?" said Tiram. "Why are the demons rising again, if that is indeed the case? The seal that the Good King was said to put on them was supposed to be unbreakable. How did this demon escape?"

"Who knows?" said Keo. "Maybe the seal is weakening and this demon managed to slip through. Or maybe there is someone else in Lamaira who let it out somehow. All I know is that we must stop them before it's too late."

Tiram laughed. "By 'we,' do you mean you and me? Because the two of us, even together, aren't much against an army of demons, you know."

"No," said Keo. He looked at the ceiling. "The two of us by ourselves are too outnumbered to fight off the demons. But maybe, if we had an army of our own, then we could defend Lamaira against them."

"And just where do you intend on finding an *army*, of all things?" said Tiram. "They aren't exactly sold at the market in town, you know."

Keo thought about that for a moment. He hated to admit it, but Tiram had a good point. It would not be easy to find an army, but then, perhaps Keo did not need to make his own. An idea occurred to him that he decided to share with Tiram.

Looking at Tiram, Keo said, "Master, I think that if the three factions were united under one banner, with all of their armies and resources working together, then we could defeat the demons before they become too powerful or at least be prepared to fight them ourselves if they rise again."

Tiram slapped his knee and laughed again except this time it was a much longer and harsher laugh. Keo felt flustered, but he didn't think that it was a bad idea and he didn't understand why Tiram apparently thought it was so dumb.

"What's the problem?" said Keo, as Tiram continued to laugh like he had heard the funniest joke in his life. "Don't you think that could work?"

It was a couple more minutes before Tiram managed to get control of his laughter, although he still chuckled every now and then. "In *theory*, maybe, it would work. The three factions, taken together, certainly do have enough power to form a formidable army. No doubt there."

"Then what is to stop us from informing the factions about the demons so they can get prepared for the attack?" said Keo.

"The three factions hate each other's guts," said Tiram. "They've been at war for a little over twenty years now, which is about as long as you have been alive, and every attempt at establishing peace between them has completely and utterly failed. I thought you'd know that by now."

Keo frowned. "Well, it's not like I keep careful track of national politics. That was Nesma's job, before she left."

"But you understand why your plan won't work," said Tiram. "Right? You would need to convince the factions to put aside their differences and reunite after twenty years of separation and war. That's about as likely to happen as the Dracones returning to Lamaira."

"But it's also our only option," said Keo. He tapped his forehead. "As far as we know, no one else in Lamaira knows that the demons are about to return. Therefore, it is up to us to spread the word as far and wide as possible so that everyone will know and have time to prepare for the attack."

"I'm still not convinced that this 'attack' is going to happen or that the demons are actually going to return," said Tiram, shaking his head. "Even if you were in fact attacked by an actual demon, that doesn't mean anything. Maybe the seal isn't perfect and so the occasional demon is able to slip out into the world. Doesn't mean that any other demons are going to start following it through."

"Unless the seal breaks," said Keo. "What if there are multiple demons that have escaped and are working together to free their brethren? The demon didn't mention any other demons working with it, but I think it's possible that it wasn't alone, otherwise it wouldn't have acted so confident that its brothers would rise."

"Well, that would certainly be kind of those demons to save their friends, but I consider it unlikely," said Tiram. He scratched his chin. "And anyway, that still won't make it easier for you to convince the three factions to work together. You're not exactly a well-known or respected figure in Lamaira, you know. They'll just see you as a kid from the middle of nowhere who is saying crazy things that may or may not be true."

"You're right," said Keo. Then he brightened up. "But what about Nesma? She went to go work for the Magical Council, the leaders of the Magicians. She's my friend. She'll listen to me and help me get my message to the Magical Council itself. And from there, it should be easy to get audiences with the leaders of the other two factions."

"You haven't spoken with Nesma in a year, though," said Tiram. "Right? How do you know she will listen to you? What if she's too busy?"

"Nesma is my best friend in the world," said Keo with a huff. "Of course she'll listen to me and do whatever she can to help me get my message in front of the people who need to hear it most. I just need to travel to Capitika and find her there. She'll be happy to see me, especially since it's been so long since we last spoke."

"Capitika is a long ways away from here, though," said Tiram.

"Not to mention that I still haven't given you permission to go."

"Permission?" said Keo. He propped himself up on his elbows and looked Tiram in the eyes. "Master, I am an adult. I don't need your permission to do anything. And besides, I won't be gone forever. I'll be back by next month, after I convince the three factions to unite against the demons."

"That's incredibly optimistic," Tiram observed. "You do realize that convincing sworn enemies to put aside their two decades of accumulated differences will probably take more than a mere month to do, right?"

"You don't know that," said Keo. "I just need to visit Nesma and let her know and then she can let the leaders of the other two factions know, too. And I am going whether you approve or not."

Tiram clearly did not want Keo going anywhere, but he stopped arguing the point. He just shook his head, muttered something too low for Keo to hear, and then said, "All right. Do what you want. I'll hold the fort back here while you are away. But don't leave until your shoulder is healed, at least."

"I won't," Keo promised. He winced at the pain in his bandaged shoulder. "But I still have to leave as soon as I can. There's no time to lose."

"Right," said Tiram. "I'll help you get your supplies ready so you can be ready to go as soon as you feel better. For now, you should rest."

Keo nodded, even though he wanted to keep talking. Still, he was starting to feel drowsy again and so closed his eyes and drifted into sleep then and there, although he was still making plans for his journey to Capitika even as he fell into a deep sleep.

Chapter Three

IT TOOK KEO'S SHOULDER a week to recover, mostly because the cut had done a lot more damage than he had thought. Thus, Keo spent most of his time in bed, letting Tiram bring him meals and allowing his master to change his bandages once a day. It was frustrating because Keo wanted to leave right away, but it was always unwise to travel long distances with a wounded shoulder and so Keo did not want to lose the use of his right arm just because he was too impatient to wait for it to heal. Tiram certainly didn't seem to mind the fact that Keo could not go anywhere right away, but that was obviously because Tiram did not want Keo to leave.

Keo understood why. Aside from Keo, Tiram lived entirely alone in his little cabin in the Low Woods. Although Tiram had raised Keo ever since he found Keo abandoned as a baby on the now-overgrown road in the forest, Tiram had no other family or relations that Keo knew of. Tiram didn't even have any friends. Anytime Keo asked Tiram about his family, Tiram would always change the subject or give exceedingly vague answers that always left Keo wanting more.

As a result, Tiram had grown to rely on Keo for many things, such as running errands in town and the like. Keo was aware of the rumors from the people of New Ora who liked to paint Tiram as some sort of crazy hermit who hated people and ate children, but he knew those were false. Master Tiram could be eccentric and cranky, sure, but he was a good man at heart and an even better swordsmen, having taught Keo everything he knew about swordsmanship, as well as giving Keo Gildshine in the first place.

No doubt the reason Tiram wanted Keo to stay was so that Tiram would not have to do as many chores about the cabin or run errands into town. Keo did not mind doing these things for Tiram, who he saw as both a mentor and father figure, but right now Keo had far more important things to do than split wood for the winter or buy supplies in town, and he hoped that Tiram understood that, even though Tiram still seemed skeptical of the possibility that the demons were going to rise again.

At the end of the week, when Keo's shoulder had fully recovered from the wound, Keo slung a pack full of food and water over his shoulder and attached Gildshine and its green sheath to his side on the front steps of the cabin. Tiram stood in the doorway of the cabin, of the only home that Keo had ever known, watching him with annoyance and worry in his old eyes.

"Are you sure that you still feel all right?" said Tiram. "That shoulder wound was very deep and bloody, even after I cleaned it. If you want to stay and rest a little while longer—"

"No," said Keo, shaking his head as he stood up, having finished tying the laces of his old hunting boots. He then patted his shoulder, which no longer hurt. "It feels fine. You know I'm a quick healer, master. That sort of injury might have incapacitated a normal person for a month, but not me."

"I know," said Tiram. "Still, Capitika is a long way away from here. Are you certain you'll get there in a week, like you said?"

"Yes," said Keo. "I know the way there. I'm going to go stop by New Ora, pick up some supplies there, and then take the old roads to the city. If the ancestors are feeling kindly toward me this week, then I should hopefully avoid any bad weather that could delay me or even force me to stop for a few days."

"But you've never gone farther than New Ora before," Tiram said. "Are you sure you will be able to get all the way to Capitika before the demons return?"

"Yes," said Keo. He gestured at the path leading from the cabin to the woods surrounding them on all sides. "Lots of people go from New Ora to Capitika and back on a regular basis without any trouble. Besides, I know some shortcuts that some of the merchants in town have told me about, so I can use those to cut down on traveling time. Maybe I will even arrive early. You never know."

"Well, I'll be asking our ancestors to protect you anyway," said Tiram. "Just to be safe."

"I appreciate that, master," said Keo. He readjusted the straps of his pack one more time, just to make sure that it would not fall off, and said, "Well, this is good bye, then. I will see you in a month, master. Take care."

"You, too, Keo," said Tiram, waving at Keo. "Just don't do get yourself killed, all right?"

Keo nodded, turned, and walked down the steps toward the forest. He didn't make it very far down the path to the woods before Tiram called, "Keo?"

Stopping before the old wooden gate that separated the cabin from the rest of the forest, Keo looked back at Tiram, who still stood in the doorway with his own sword, Soulheart, sheathed at his side.

"Yes, master?" said Keo. "What is it?"

Tiram bit his lower lip and looked like he had a lot to say to Keo, but then he shook his head and said, "Nah, never mind. I just wanted to tell you not to be an idiot, but I figured you already knew that. Just leave and stay safe."

Keo could tell that Tiram wanted to say something else, but whatever it was, Tiram apparently thought better of it. Keo was tempted to go back and ask Tiram what he really wanted to say, but then he remembered that he only had slightly less than six months left before the demons returned, which meant that he had no time to lose if he was going to get to Capitika and find Nesma in time for the Magical Council to stop the demons in time.

So Keo simply nodded, waved good bye at Tiram one last time, undid the hatch on the front gate, and soon was gone, heading into the Low Woods, fully intending to get to New Ora before lunch, because it was early morning at the moment and it would take him a few hours to get there from here, assuming that he did not run into any obstacles along the way.

As Keo expected, he ran into no major issues on the way through the Low Woods to New Ora. Still, he kept his eyes and ears open at all times as he walked, expecting another demon—or maybe the same one from last week, if the demons could return from the dead, as he suspected they could—to attack him to try to end his quest before he got a chance to tell anyone about it. But he was not attacked by any demons along the way, although he did run across a wounded wood wolf that he had to put out of its misery.

Despite that, Keo did not feel safe until he emerged from the

Low Woods and onto the main path leading to New Ora, which was located in a nearby valley. He could even see it from his current position, a town of about one thousand people and a few hundred houses and buildings. Rising from the center of the town was a Magician's Tower, where the local Magician lived. It was the fanciest building in the town, with its silver rooftop and golden exterior, but Keo did not consider stopping by to speak with the local Magician, a grumpy old man named Skran, who he had never gotten along with and who had always distrusted Tiram and him whenever they entered town anyway. Besides, Keo knew that Skran would never believe his story about the demons or help him get to the capital, which was why Keo had to go to Capitika and tell Nesma about it himself.

So Keo went down the road into the valley and soon came upon the walls surrounding the town. The gatekeeper, a portly but strong man named Kima, sat in the guard tower near the gates, looking a little tired, as he always did, because Kima usually got the night and morning shifts. Still, Kima had always been a lot politer and friendlier to Keo than most of the inhabitants of New Ora, so Keo did not feel any reservations as he walked up to the gates.

"Good morning, Mr. Kima," said Keo, waving at the guard as he stopped in front of the closed iron gates. "Can you let me into town? I have to pick up a few things and I would like to do it right away."

Kima peered out the window of his guard tower at Keo, a frown visible under his silver mustache. "Back again? Weren't you just here last week? I thought you only came to town once a month."

"Yes," said Keo, nodding. "But I'm back again because I am going to Capitika and I need to pick up a few supplies before I head out. It's going to be a long trip and I just want to get some bandages and medicine so I can treat any injuries I might get on the way there."

"Capitika?" Kima repeated, sitting back in his chair inside the small tower. "Why are you going all the way out there by yourself?"

Keo considered telling Kima about the demons, but he did not want to worry the old man unnecessarily, nor did he want any rumors to spread about something even he didn't quite understand all that well.

Keo simply said, "I'm going to visit a friend of mine who moved there a year ago. It's been a long time since I last saw her and I miss her greatly."

"Ah," said Kima, nodding in understanding. "I got some friends in Capitika, too, who I haven't seen in years. Would love to visit 'em, but I'm not as young as I used to be, so I can't. Well, anyway, if you're going to come into town, you have to give me your weapon."

Keo frowned and glanced at Gildshine, which was sheathed securely at his waist. He already knew about this law that Skran had enforced on the town. Skran had decreed that anyone traveling into New Ora had to relinquish any and all weapons they carried—ranging from tiny daggers to huge broadswords—to the gatekeepers for the duration of their stay in the town, unless they were soldiers in the army or were granted a written exemption from Skran or Magical Council.

While Keo always complied with the law, he didn't like it

because he always felt a lot less secure without Gildshine. True, Master Tiram had taught him some hand-to-hand fighting techniques in the past, but the fact was that a sword was almost always a better weapon for self-defense than a fist. Of course, most people in New Ora were friendly and Keo had never actually been attacked while unarmed in town, but he still didn't like giving up his most prized possession, not even just for a few minutes.

But Keo knew there was no way he could get into New Ora without first relinquishing his weapon, so he nodded with reluctance, detached the sheathed Gildshine from his waist, and handed it to Kima. Kima took the sword gently and carefully and then placed it out of sight below his desk, where he kept all relinquished weapons until their owner returned to retrieve them.

Then Kima pulled a lever and the gates creaked open, allowing Keo to enter. Keo nodded at Kima in thanks and then passed through the open gates into New Ora itself.

As it was now mid-morning, most of the inhabitants of New Ora were awake and walking around the town, going about their daily work or running errands. Most paid him no attention, which was fine because Keo did not like it when strangers stared at him. And most of these people *were* strangers to him, even though he visited New Ora fairly often, because he didn't interact with most of them very much except for business purposes. He passed by a couple of kids playing some sort of game with rocks and sticks, several older men arguing about some of the finer points of magic, and a messenger—identifiable because of the red cap he wore securely on his head—who flashed past Keo on his way to deliver a message to someone.

Keo had one destination in mind: The open air marketplace, where he would buy some bandages and medicine to take with him on his journey to Capitika. While Tiram had provided him with some medical supplies before he left the Low Woods, the truth was that Keo believed he would need a lot more than what Tiram had given him, so he was going to get what he could afford here and then leave. He did not intend to stay very long. If possible, he would be in and out of Capitika in under an hour, if not quicker.

Thus, when Keo arrived at the marketplace located in the center of the town, near the Magician's Tower, he was surprised when he saw a huge crowd of people gathered near one of the stalls. They were all shouting and cheering, their shouts occasionally punctuated by the sounds of metal clanging against metal. The crowd was too thick for Keo to see through, but he knew that he would have to pass through them because the merchant he was thinking of who sold medical supplies always set up shop on the opposite end of the marketplace. Keo dreaded going through the crowd, though, because he hated having to push past other people, despite being a fairly big guy himself who was stronger than most people.

But a part of him was also curious to learn about what the crowd was watching, so he walked up to the back of the crowd and stood on his tiptoes to see over the heads of everyone else and find out what was going on. Unfortunately, he could not see much except that there were two people facing each other in the center, so he asked one of the people in the back of the crowd, "What's going on?"

The person he asked—a teenager with a sack full of beets

slung over his shoulder—turned to look at Keo and said excitedly, "There's a duel going on between this Wanderer from out of town and Merchant Yasfa. It's pretty amazing so far."

Keo knew who Yasfa was. Yasfa was an immigrant from Hasfar, which was south of the border and beyond the Low Woods, who sold Hasfarian goods to the people of New Ora. Keo had bought a few things from Yasfa in the past, but he had never thought of the merchant as being particularly violent or prone to dueling.

So Keo asked, "Why is Yasfa fighting the traveler? Did the traveler attack him?"

"No," said the youth, shaking his head. "I only just got here, but I heard that the Wanderer insulted Yasfa's wares and insulted him. Yasfa challenged him to a duel and the traveler accepted. It started just a few minutes ago."

"But how are they fighting if you aren't allowed to carry weapons beyond New Ora's walls?" asked Keo.

"Yasfa's got this weird stick he's using as a weapon," the youth explained. "You know that walking stick he always carries? He's treating it like a spear and a club combined. And the Wanderer doesn't have any weapons, but he's pretty skilled with his hands, so he's been getting some good hits with his fists."

Keo was about to ask who the traveler was when he heard a sudden *thump* from the fight and the crowd started shouting and chanting again. From what Keo could tell, the crowd was divided between those who supported Yasfa and those who supported his opponent. That was not too surprising, however, because while Yasfa had been a regular seller of Hasfarian goods in New Ora for some five years now, there were still many who did not like him due to his contempt for the native Lamairans, who he tended to treat as inferior despite having moved to the country a long time back, although he was always happy to take their money in exchange for his goods, of course.

But despite Yasfa's arrogance, Keo had always liked him, because Yasfa's Hasfarian wares were always of interest to him. He decided to find out just who this Wanderer was who was fighting Yasfa, which he would have to do anyway if he was going to reach the merchant who sold medical supplies.

So Keo pushed through the crowd until he got to the front, where he saw that a large space had been cleared out so that the two fighters could have space.

Yasfa stood closer to Keo, his short, ratty hair hanging down on his shoulders as he held out his staff in a defensive position. Yasfa had dropped his usual green Hasfarian robes in favor of wearing nothing but his brown pants, displaying his shirtless chest for all to see. Although Yasfa was older than Keo, the man looked just as fit as a man half his age, which surprised Keo because he had never thought of Yasfa as being a very fit man. Then again, he had not thought that Yasfa could fight, either, so there were clearly many things that he did not know about Yasfa.

Standing opposite Yasfa was a man who Keo had never seen before in his life. The man looked to be between Keo and Yasfa in terms of age, although his hardened and battle-scarred face made him look older than he probably was. The man wore a worn-looking leather jacket and a black tunic underneath, and he, too, had taken up a defensive position, holding his fists up before him like a trained fighter. The man had red eyes, an unusual sight if Keo ever saw one, because most of the people in New Ora had either brown or black eyes, sometimes green. The man looked much like a Wanderer, which was a type of person in Lamaira who had no home and belonged to no faction, simply drifting from place to place without any thought as to where he was going.

In any case, both Yasfa and the Wanderer were panting. Sweat gleamed off of Yasfa's chest, while sweat disappeared into the headband around the Wanderer's head. Even though the two of them had not been fighting for very long, it was clear that they had been going at it with everything they had. The Wanderer's right arm had the impression of Yasfa's staff on it, while Yasfa had a fist-shaped bruise in his face.

Nonetheless, it was clear that neither one was going to back down, despite the beatings that both of them had taken. Keo looked around, but did not see any of Skran's Enforcers around to break up the fight, although that did not surprise him because Skran around here typically did not break up these kinds of fights or duels because of his contempt for the commoners unless the fight turned into a riot of some sort.

"Well, well, red-eyes," said Yasfa suddenly, speaking in that same Hasfarian accent that made his speech hard to understand at times. "Ready to give up yet or do you want another beating?"

"I don't know," said the Wanderer. His voice was a lot softer than Yasfa's, but that did not make him look any weaker or less dangerous in Keo's eyes. "How much more can Hasfarian sand crawlers like you take?"

Half of the crowd gasped and looked around at each other when the Wanderer said that, while the other half laughed. While Keo was no expert in these issues, he knew that 'sand crawler' was typically considered a derogatory term for Hasfarians. And while Keo was rarely one to take offense for other people, he found himself liking this Wanderer far less than he had before.

Yasfa scowled and spun his staff. "Sand crawler? That is as much an insult to my god as it is to me. But I will take that as a 'yes,' so prepare for a beat down, you pale-skinned freak."

Yasfa charged toward the Wanderer, swinging his staff at him. The Wanderer, however, did not move. He simply stayed where he was, watching as Yasfa drew closer and closer to him, which made Keo wonder if the Wanderer was just going to stand there and let Yasfa beat him or if he had a plan to defend himself.

Right when the large tip of Yasfa's staff was only inches from the Wanderer's head, the Wanderer ducked, allowing the staff to go sailing across the space where his head had been. Then, taking advantage of the opening that Yasfa had left, Wanderer struck Yasfa's jaw with an uppercut from his right fist.

The blow connected squarely with Yasfa's jaw and Yasfa immediately staggered backwards, dropping his staff as he did so. The Wanderer, however, was not finished with Yasfa yet. He kicked the staff away, where it rolled several feet away outside of Yasfa's reach, and then advanced on Yasfa as swiftly as a snake approaching its prey. Yasfa, who looked dazed from the blow to the jaw, tried to punch the Wanderer, but it was clear that he had no training in fisticuffs, because his punch missed and the Wanderer responded with another devastating punch that almost knocked Yasfa off his feet.

Then the Wanderer unleashed a flurry of fast punches that Keo could barely follow. Every blow struck Yasfa in the face or chest and they came so fast and so hard that Yasfa was unable to mount a defense against them. There was no hesitation or slothfulness in the Wanderer's attack. Although the Wanderer could not have had more than half a second between each punch, it was clear that he put a lot of strength into each one in order to maximize the pain. Keo did not know as much about fisticuffs as he did about sword-fighting, but even he could tell that this Wanderer was no amateur, which made him wonder where this guy had gotten his training.

But that didn't matter to Keo at the moment because he could tell that the Wanderer was going to kill Yasfa if someone did not intervene. And while half of the crowd was clearly on Yasfa's side, they must have had the same realization as him regarding the obvious skill of the Wanderer, because no one looked like they were going to try to stop him and there was not a single Enforcer in sight to break up the fight.

I should just go and get the medical supplies I need, but Yasfa has always been fair to me, so I should help him, Keo thought. *I'll break up the fight and then go on my way.*

With that, Keo ran out into the circle of the fight, ignoring the calls from the people in the crowd to stay out of it. The Wanderer didn't seem to notice Keo coming, probably because he was too busy beating the spirit out of Yasfa, whose face was now bloody and broken from the repeated blows from the Wanderer.

"Hey!" Keo shouted as he ran up to the Wanderer. "Stop this! You're going to kill him if you—"

Keo was interrupted when the Wanderer whirled around like a tornado and slammed his fist into Keo's gut. The blow was like getting hit by a raging ox, sending Keo staggering backwards, the breath knocked from his lungs. He managed to regain his balance and his breath, however, and looked up to see the Wanderer had returned to beating on Yasfa as if Keo had not tried to interrupt him at all.

Scowling, Keo stood up, ignoring the pain in his gut from where the Wanderer's fist had struck, and walked back up to the Wanderer and said, "Hey, I said—"

Once again, the Wanderer whirled around to punch him, but this time Keo saw it coming. He caught the Wanderer's fist and twisted it, but then the Wanderer's other fist flew toward him out of nowhere and he had to let go and jump back to avoid getting socked in the head. This time, the Wanderer did not return to beating on Yasfa, who had by now fallen over onto the ground unconscious from the repeated blows to the face.

Instead, the Wanderer faced Keo, looking at Keo as if he had just rudely interrupted him while he was doing something important. "Just who the hell are you, kid? Friend of this sand crawler?"

"One of his customers," said Keo, holding his own fists up to protect himself in case the Wanderer decided to attack again. "I just didn't want to see him murdered in cold blood."

The Wanderer snorted. "I wasn't going to *murder* him. Cripple him, yes, beat him to within an inch of his life, of course, but murder? I am no murderer. Never have been, never will be."

"Could have fooled me," said Keo. "Why don't you pick on someone who can *actually* fight back equally, like me? I'm a trained fighter and so are you, clearly, so maybe you should try to take me on instead."

The Wanderer smirked. "Kid, you haven't insulted me like this dumb sand crawler has, but that's all right. You managed to catch my fist, which I will admit is impressive because very few have the reflexes for that, but I can also tell that you are a complete amateur when it comes to fisticuffs. I can beat you in two minutes, tops."

"Or perhaps we could not fight at all," said Keo, looking around the area briefly but seeing no one but the crowd of spectators who had been watching the fight. "Magician Skran's Enforcers will probably come by soon and throw us both in jail if we fight. Promise to leave Yasfa alone and leave New Ora within the next hour and I promise not to tell the Enforcers on you."

"I've tangled with law enforcement before and always won," said the Wanderer. "But I still hate dealing with 'em, so I'm going to knock you down and leave. Always hate these small towns anyway, 'cause they're full of arrogant kids like you who think that fighting a childhood bully is the same as fighting a trained adult fighter like myself."

With that, the Wanderer charged toward Keo like a wood wolf. Keo charged toward him and swung his fist at the Wanderer's head, but the Wanderer ducked and hit Keo twice, once in the gut and once in the chest.

The Wanderer's blows knocked the breath out of Keo's lungs again. Nonetheless, Keo still tried to stand and hit the Wanderer, but the Wanderer dodged it as casually as if going for a stroll in the Low Woods and then struck Keo in the face.

That blow was enough to knock Keo flat on his back. He hit the street hard, his head spinning, making it impossible for him to get back up and continue to fight. All he could make out was the Wanderer standing and smirking above him.

Then the Wanderer glanced at the watch on his wrist. "Fifteen seconds. A new record for knocking down ignorant kids like you.

My previous record was sixteen point two seconds, and that was against a guy much skinnier than you. What a—"

But then a solid *thwack* interrupted the Wanderer and he fell to the street unconscious. Keo looked up to see Yasfa, his face still bloody and his nose broken, standing right behind where the Wanderer had stood, panting as he held his staff before him. He was looking down at the Wanderer with savage glee in his eyes.

"Take that, you arrogant thug," said Yasfa. His words were even harder to understand than normal due to the fact that some of is teeth had been broken and his face was swollen in several places from where the Wanderer had hit him. "How do you like that?"

Just then, a loud whistle screeched through the air, which Keo recognized as the whistle that Skran's Enforcers always blew whenever they were coming. Three such Enforcers then emerged from the crowd, wearing gray iron armor with the symbol of the Magicians—a flaming staff—on their chests. They made their way over to where Yasfa stood over the Wanderer and Keo, grim expressions on their faces as they approached.

"What is going on here?" said the lead Enforcer, who was probably the Captain (although Keo was too dazed at the moment to recall the Captain's name), to Yasfa, who had lowered his staff and was now leaning on it like he always did. "We received reports of a fight starting over here. Were you involved in it?"

"Yes, Captain sir, I was," said Yasfa. He pointed at the Wanderer. "This man savagely attacked me for no reason. I was merely fighting in self-defense."

"I see," said the Captain. He glanced at Keo. "And what about this young man here? Did he attack you as well?"

"No, sir," said Yasfa, shaking his head. "He tried to save me, but was knocked down by this vile Wanderer."

Keo smiled. He had worried that Yasfa might not come to his defense, but apparently Yasfa valued Keo's patronage of his business enough to make sure that the authorities understood that Keo had done nothing wrong.

"I see," said the Captain again. "Well, self-defense is legal, so we're not going to take you to jail." He gestured at the Wanderer and Keo. "Instead, we'll haul these two to jail until we can determine an appropriate punishment for the laws they so flagrantly broke."

"What?" said Keo. His head still spun, but he managed to sit up anyway. "But I was trying to *protect* Yasfa. How is that against the law?"

"The law states that attacking innocent people is illegal," the Captain said. "It is also illegal for someone to start a fight with another person. Based on what I have heard and seen so far, you initiated a fight with the Wanderer even though he was attacking Mr. Yasfa here and not you."

Keo looked at Yasfa. "Yasfa, you don't actually *agree* with this, do you?"

Yasfa shrugged. "Your laws are not my laws, so who am I to argue with your Enforcers? I need a doctor, anyway, to look at my face and heal it. I have no time to waste arguing with the Enforcers over the finer points of the law, seeing as I am not a lawyer myself."

Keo could hardly believe Yasfa's treachery, but before he could yell at Yasfa for it, the other two Enforcers grabbed the Wanderer and him, propped them on their feet, and then shackled them with thick and heavy iron cuffs.

"All right, now," said the Captain. "Take those two to the jail and lock 'em up tight. I'm going to help Mr. Yasfa find a doctor, as well as ask the witnesses what they saw for the report."

"Yes, sir," said one of the Enforcers, a young man who didn't look much older than Keo.

Thus, the two Enforcers forced Keo and the Wanderer—who had now returned to consciousness, although he seemed dazed and hardly in any position to attempt to escape—away and through the crowd, which parted to let them through. Keo, however, glared at Yasfa one last time before they left, but Yasfa was already being tended to by the town doctor, who had apparently been one of the spectators of the fight.

But what made this worse was that Keo had no idea how long he would be in jail. Or how he was going to escape.

Chapter Four

KEO AND THE WANDERER were taken to the town jail, a small, square-shaped building located on the south side of the Magician's Tower. Here they were stripped of whatever possessions they had—including things that could not be used as weapons, such as Keo's food for his trip to Capitika—and tossed them both in one cell together, but without removing their shackles. The Enforcers warned the two not to try anything funny and that they had full permission from Skran to beat them if they tried to escape.

Once the Enforcers left, Keo looked around at the tiny cell that he and the Wanderer shared. It was half as large as the cabin back home, with only one measly window several feet above Keo's head that was blocked off by three thick metal bars. The wooden floor was dirty and cracked in several places, while the one cot built into the wall looked like it was about to fall off. The place smelled of urine and excrement, which made Keo wonder how often the Enforcers bothered to clean this place out. There was also what looked like a dried bloodstain on the wall, which didn't make Keo feel any better about this place.

The Wanderer, on the other hand, didn't seem terribly worried about being tossed into such a disgusting place. He took a seat on the cot, which creaked under his weight, and looked around at the cell like he had expected better of it.

"What a shitty jail," said the Wanderer. He grimaced and rubbed his head. "And, god, does my head hurt. That scrawny sand crawler can really hit hard with that piece of wood he calls a staff. I'll be better, though."

"You seem awfully relaxed about being tossed in jail, with no idea of when or if we will ever be released," said Keo in annoyance, folding his arms across his chest as he looked at his cellmate. "I shouldn't even be here. This is ridiculous."

The Wanderer shrugged. "I've been in worse. Once I was thrown in a cell that I couldn't stand up in. For three weeks."

"Wait, so you've had run-ins with the law *before*?" said Keo.

"In different places, yeah," said the Wanderer, although again he seemed pretty at ease. "One of the perks of being a Wanderer is that I have seen the interiors of many jails. And this is one of the worst, the 'too small for me to stand up in' one notwithstanding."

Keo groaned and walked over to the bars of the cell. Wrapping his hands around them, Keo looked up and down the hallway outside, but it was empty. There was a large iron hook on the opposite wall where the keys were probably kept most of the time, but at the moment it had nothing on it. Keo recalled seeing the jailer with the key ring attached to his belt, which meant that it was impossible for Keo to get the keys and use them to escape right now.

Sighing, Keo pulled his hands off of the bars, walked over to the wall on the right side of the cell, and sat down against it. He looked at the Wanderer again, who still seemed pretty content despite the situation they were in. He was even humming a tune that Keo did not recognize.

"I don't even know your name," said Keo. "What is it?"

The Wanderer looked at Keo and said, "Call me Dlaine of the Fist. You?"

"Keo of the Sword," said Keo.

The Wanderer raised an eyebrow. "Oh. So *that's* why you were such a terrible fist fighter. You're probably more used to fighting with swords than with your fists."

"I am," said Keo. He sighed. "But I had to leave my sword with the guard when I entered town. And I will probably never see it again unless Skran decides to let me out."

"What the heck's a Skran?" said Dlaine. "Sounds like a disease."

"The local Magician who runs the town," said Keo. He pointed at the window above their heads. "He lives in the big Tower in the center of New Ora. The Enforcers work directly for him and he's the guy who makes the laws around here."

"Let me guess," said Dlaine, gesturing at the cell they were in. "He's not exactly a fair or just leader, is he?"

"He's not tyrannical, but he is usually too eager to jail people for the smallest offenses, especially people from out of town like you and me," said Keo, nodding. "But it doesn't matter whether he's a just ruler or not. What matters is that I am stuck in here and this will mess up all of my plans."

"What are your plans?" said Dlaine. He cracked a grin. "Got a date with a cute girl tonight?"

Keo looked at Dlaine in annoyance. "No. I was going to Capitika to see a friend of mine, but now I will probably never see her again because I'm stuck in here."

"Capitika?" said Dlaine. He rested his chin in his shackled

hands. "What a coincidence. I was planning to head there myself after I got done with my business here."

"What do you want to do in Capitika?" said Keo, tilting his head to the side.

"None of your business," said Dlaine. "Anyway, you seem like a good guy, Keo. I apologize for punching you in the stomach. I tend to be a 'punch first, ask questions later' kind of guy. Nothing personal."

Keo winced at the pain in his stomach, which had subsided since they had been taken to jail, but which was still hard to ignore. "I noticed."

"Anyway, how long are criminals kept in jail around here?" said Dlaine, glancing around the cell.

"It depends," said Keo. "Depending on whether you actually committed any crimes and how serious those crimes were, you might be behind bars for a long time. If you haven't committed any crimes, though, they usually let you out after a day or two."

"Then why are you so worried about not getting to see your friend in Capitika?" said Dlaine. "After all, you didn't commit any crimes, right?"

Keo thought about whether to tell Dlaine about the demons. But he decided against it because he did not yet trust Dlaine with that information. Dlaine certainly seemed like a friendly guy, at least now that he wasn't punching Keo in the stomach, but that did not mean that Keo could trust him with this information just yet.

So Keo lied and said, "I told my friend that I would be there in three days, so if I am here for even a day, that will make me late and she will probably get angry at me for it."

"Then let this be a lesson that you shouldn't make promises

you can't keep," said Dlaine, shaking his head in disapproval. "But anyway, I can't be in here for a long time. I also have a deadline for getting to Capitika and I can't waste even one second inside this musty old jail cell."

"How do you intend to escape?" said Keo. "Are you a Magician?"

"Nope," said Dlaine, shaking his head. "Magic is inborn and I was never born with even an ounce of magic in my blood, so I'm not a Magician."

"Oh," said Keo. "So do you have a lock-pick or something that you can use to escape?"

"Again, nope," said Dlaine. "The Enforcers took most of my stuff from me when they patted us down, including stuff I could have used to escape."

"Then how do you intend to escape at all?" said Keo. He glanced at the heavy lock on the cell door. "Because I'm no master thief, either, and have never been put in jail, so I don't know any techniques we could use to escape."

"I have a friend on the outside who can get us out," said Dlaine. He glanced up at the window. "Don't see her yet, but I'm sure she'll show up pretty soon. Then again, she can be awfully lazy when she wants to, although she's bound to the same deadline that I am, so she doesn't have any excuse not to bust her ass trying to save me."

"Who is your friend?" said Keo. "I didn't see anyone with you when you were fighting Yasfa."

"She was there, but you just didn't see her," said Dlaine. "Which is for the best, since her presence would have drawn too much attention to us, and attention is the last thing that we want."

"Why?" said Keo. "Because you're a couple of outlaws?"

"There's that, but there's another reason why we prefer to stay under the notice of the law," said Dlaine. "Sadly, I think I might have slipped up by letting my anger get the best of me when I fought that Hasfarian guy. My friend keeps telling me that my temper is a problem, but I just never believed her until now."

Keo wasn't sure that Dlaine thought his temper was a problem because he certainly did not sound worried about it. The Wanderer only sounded concerned that he had let his temper get him into trouble, although Keo didn't worry about that because it made no difference to him whether Dlaine realized that his temper was a problem or not.

"How good is your friend at breaking people out of jails?" said Keo.

Dlaine chuckled. "Let's just say that she is one of only two people to escape from the Dark Prison and leave it at that."

Keo's eyes widened. The Dark Prison was supposed to be the most fortified prison in the entire country, said to be impossible to escape from due to the spells cast on it by the Magicians. It was controlled by the Magicians, who put their worst criminals in there. If Dlaine's friend could escape from the Dark Prison, then that meant that she was probably an extremely powerful Magician herself. It made Keo wonder if he had ever heard of her, but when he thought about it, the only female Magician he knew of was his friend Nesma, and even then he only knew of her because she had been his childhood friend. Then again, Keo knew of very few Magicians outside of Skran and Nesma, so that was probably why he did not know about her.

Keo was eager to ask Dlaine more questions about his

mysterious friend when Dlaine suddenly looked up at the window of the cell, smiled, and said, "There she is. You might want to move your head."

Keo frowned and looked up at the window, but he did not see anything except for the small, thick bars that were too close together for even his hand to fit through. "Move—?"

As soon as that word left Keo's mouth, the bars detached themselves from the window and then fell down directly on his head. The fall was not actually that great, but when the bars hit him on the head, it was still painful and made him cry out in pain.

"Ow," said Keo, rubbing his head with his shackled hands as he looked up. "What the heck?"

Dlaine did not seem to notice the pain that Keo was in. He just stood up from the cot and said to the window, "Jola, are you there?"

There was no response, but Keo thought someone must have been there, because Dlaine smiled and said, "Well, then get us out of here, girl! It took you long enough."

More silence, and then Dlaine, with a puzzled expression on his face, said, "What? Why not?"

Keo looked up at the window again, but still saw nothing. He wondered if Dlaine had lost his mind, but Jola had to be there, because how else could the bars have removed themselves from the window, seeing as neither Keo nor Dlaine had magical powers themselves?

Then Dlaine suddenly nodded in understanding and said, "Okay, I get it now. But don't wait too long. Remember the deadline. We can't be even a day late, do you understand?"

There was no response, at least not one that Keo heard. A

second later, the bars flew back up to the window and repositioned themselves where they had been a moment before, looking like they had never been removed at all.

Keo—whose head still hurt from when the bars had fallen on it—stood up and then looked from the window to Dlaine. "What was that all about? Was that your friend? The one who broke out of the Dark Prison?"

"The one and the same," said Dlaine. He sat back down on the cot.

"Why is she just leaving us here?" said Keo. "I thought you said that she was going to help us escape. Yet all she did was knock down the bars, somehow talk to you without me even hearing her speak, leave, and replace the bars."

Dlaine yawned and then lay down on the cot like he was going to take a nap. "Jola thinks this is a bad time to try to free us. It's day time, which would make it hard for us to sneak out of the town, and even if it wasn't, that window is too small for either of us to sneak through right now."

Keo sighed in frustration. "Then when *will* she save us?"

"Tonight," said Dlaine. He yawned. "Meaning that you and I are going to spend the next several hours in this cramped little cell trying not to breathe up each other's air."

"Tonight?" said Keo. "That can't be right. Are you certain that she can't get us out of here before then?"

Dlaine shrugged. "*I'm* certain that she could, but Jola most certainly isn't. And I tend to trust Jola's judgment on these matters, so we're stuck here until then."

"But you also have a deadline to meet," said Keo. "Doesn't it bother you at least somewhat that you are going to have less time in which to meet it?"

"Yeah, but what can you do?" said Dlaine with another yawn. "Anyway, I've spent the last few nights camping in the wilderness. This cell is hardly what I'd call a fancy hotel suite, but at least it isn't exposed to the rain and cold. So I'm just going to rest for a while so I'll have energy for tonight's escape."

With that, Dlaine closed his eyes, turned on his side, and soon was snoring deeply.

Seeing Dlaine sleeping so peacefully made Keo angry, but he also knew that there was no way that he could get out of here on his own. Only this Jola girl, whoever she was, could save them now, and she would not be able to do that until tonight.

That meant that Keo had as much to do in here as Dlaine did. So, grumbling under his breath, Keo sat down against the wall again, except this time he sat against the wall on the opposite side of the room so that those bars would not fall on his head again. Even so, Keo found it impossible to sleep because he was so worried about the possible demon invasion that was going to happen in six months.

Nonetheless, after a while, Keo succeeded in drifting off to sleep, although his dreams were punctuated with nightmarish visions of the demon he had fought back in the Low Woods, a whole army of such demons in fact, ravaging New Ora and the entire country of Lamaira. It was a dark dream indeed.

Chapter Five

H EY, KEO," SAID DLAINE'S voice somewhere above him, sounding like a whisper. "Keo, are you awake?"

Keo slowly rose from the deep slumber that he had fallen into. Blinking, he looked up and saw Dlaine standing over him. The mysterious Wanderer still had shackles around his wrists and ankles, but he looked awake and alert now, like he had gotten a good night's sleep. The cell itself was dark, save for candlelight from somewhere outside the cell and the stars and moon visible through the open window above. The cell was chillier than normal, too, even though it was a summer's night.

Yawning, Keo said, "Dlaine? What's going on? Is Jola—"

"Shhh," said Dlaine. He glanced over his shoulder. "Don't mention her name. We have to be very quiet if we're going to get out of here tonight."

Blinking again, Keo looked over at the source of the candlelight. One of the guards was sitting at a table near the cell, but he was lying there with his head on his arms, snoring softly and occasionally muttering things in his sleep that Keo could not understand. The guard seemed to be alone, but that did not surprise Keo, because the Enforcers usually only left one guard to watch over the prisoners at night anyway.

Keo looked up at Dlaine with a questioning gaze and whispered., "Is Jola nearby?"

"She should be," said Dlaine, his own voice so low that Keo had to strain to hear it. "I woke you up so you could be ready to leave at a moment's notice."

Keo rubbed the sleep out of his eyes and took a deep breath before exhaling it silently, a technique that Master Tiram had taught him that would allow him to wake up quicker. In seconds, he felt quite awake, although he could not suppress a yawn that escaped from his lips.

"Did Jola say how she'll get us out?" Keo whispered.

"No," said Dlaine, shaking his head. "But I know she'll be here soon. Just gotta trust that she knows what she's doing."

Keo was not sure that he trusted this Jola, but on the other hand he did not know her well enough to distrust her, either. Dlaine certainly seemed to trust her, but Keo barely knew the mysterious Wanderer as it was, so he did not know if he trusted him, either.

But then Dlaine held up a finger and said, "Shhh," again, even though Keo had not said anything, and then Keo saw one of the strangest sights of his life: The key ring around the guard's belt carefully removed itself and then floated over to the door of their cell.

Keo was not exaggerating. It was exactly what it appeared to be. The key ring floated through the air, like a leaf on a river, over to their cell, its keys clinking together quietly as it did so, until it stopped right in front of the door. Then the keys started to sort through themselves, as if they were trying to decide which one of them was supposed to be the key that would open the door.

"Is this a dream?" said Keo, looking up at Dlaine. "You also see the floating keys, right?"

Dlaine nodded, but he was smiling. "This isn't a dream, kid. That's Jola. She can turn invisible."

"So she's a Magician?" said Keo.

"Of a sort," said Dlaine. "Anyway, looks like she's found the key. Get up. We're heading out as soon as she opens the door and frees us from our shackles."

Keo scrambled to his feet as best as he could with the shackles around his wrists, while at the same time Jola inserted the correct key into the door and then opened it. The door to their cell creaked open rather loudly, but the guard did not yet wake up, although he did snort and mutter something about needing to oil some squeaky hinges.

Then the key ring floated in, although Keo of course now understood that to be Jola walking in. Dlaine held up his shackled wrists, which Jola then unlocked with another key on the ring, and then Jola made her way over to Keo, whose shackles she also unlocked with a key. But both Dlaine and Keo were careful to lower their shackles to the floor of their cell very quietly so that the guard would not be awoken by the sound of metal shackles falling to the floor. After they did that, Dlaine led the way out of the cell, with Jola in between them (although it was hard to tell due to her invisibility, with the only clue hinting to her position being the key ring floating between Keo and Dlaine).

They walked silently past the guard, who still seemed to be in a deep sleep. Even so, Keo thought that any moment now the guard was going to wake up, notice their escape, and sound the alarm, at which point every Enforcer in town would be after them and their great escape plan would be ruined. That was probably a paranoid thing to think, especially since the guard was clearly sleeping too deeply to even notice the large, hairy spider crawling along his arm, but Keo could not help but think it anyway—especially when Jola replaced the key ring in the guard's belt loop, which she did so expertly that she did not disturb the guard even slightly.

After that, they made their way through the small town jail's dark hallway, Jola in the lead to scout ahead and make sure there was no other guards in the jail. Again, every moment Keo expected the guard they left behind to wake up and start chasing them as soon as he noticed their escape but, as before, all he heard behind him was the snores and grunts and mutterings of the sleeping guard. It made Keo question how these guards managed to keep *any* criminals in New Ora under control, but then he remembered that New Ora was a fairly peaceful town and that most of the criminals were not invisible Magicians (or whatever Jola was) who had broken out of the most secure prison in the country, and so stopped questioning their easy escape.

Upon leaving the prison, Keo and Dlaine looked around. The town was dark, with only very few lights lit such as at the ramparts, which the gatekeepers were likely using to help them see any possible threats to the town. The light of the moon and stars in the sky above also illuminated New Ora, but they showed that the town's streets were totally deserted and the windows and doors on every house and building were closed shut. A scrawny-looking cat shot across the street, but it was the only living thing that seemed to be awake tonight besides Keo, Dlaine, and Jola.

"Weird," Dlaine muttered. "Why is everyone asleep?"

Keo looked at Dlaine in confusion. "Why *wouldn't* everyone be asleep? It's night time. Normally even I would be asleep at this time."

"I grew up in a big city, so I'm used to the night being the time when everybody comes out to have fun," said Dlaine. "But hey, this works out for us. The more people sleep, the less likely they will spot us and alert the guards to our escape."

"Right," said Keo, nodding. He then suddenly patted his clothes. "Hold on. I need to get my sword."

Dlaine looked at Keo in annoyance. "Why? Can't you buy a new one in the next town?"

"You don't understand," said Keo. "My sword is a one-of-a-kind magical sword. I left it at the town gates because that's the law. But if I am going to escape, then I need to get my sword first."

Dlaine shook his head. "No way, kiddo. If we try to get your sword back from the gatekeepers, we risk being caught. Better to let Jola show us the way out. You can get another sword later."

"You still don't understand," said Keo in annoyance. "My sword is a part of me. I don't know if you have ever owned a magical weapon before, but it is pretty clear to me that you have not. Otherwise, you would understand why I need to get my sword back."

Dlaine threw up his hands in exasperation. "Fine. Go and get your sword. Jola and I are going to leave and continue our journey to Capitika without you. Not even sure why I'm even wasting me time with you, considering how we aren't even friends."

"I guess this is where we go our separate ways, then," said Keo.

"I guess it is," said Dlaine. He briefly saluted Keo, an odd good bye gesture that Keo had never seen before. "See ya later, kid. And try not to get caught again."

With that, Dlaine turned and ran into a nearby alley between two buildings. And, although Keo did not hear her, he figured that Jola had likely gone with Dlaine. That meant that he was now on his own again.

Keo just shook his head and then turned and went in the opposite direction. Of course, he had to walk silently and in the shadows of nearby buildings, but that was not difficult to do, because years of training in the Low Woods had taught him how to traverse along almost any surface silently. Even so, Keo felt a little bad about separating from Dlaine, because he would liked to have had a traveling companion for his journey to Capitika.

But Dlaine had a point, Keo thought as he walked. *We're not friends. Just a couple of guys who happened to work together to escape prison. I doubt I'll ever see him again.*

Thus, Keo made his way through the sleeping town of New Ora, his eyes on the light from the back gate where he had entered the town. Gildshine was still there—his connection with his sword allowed him to feel it—and he was going to do his best to get it back, no matter who was currently guarding it.

Upon reaching the guard tower, Keo approached it with caution. There was a fire burning inside the tower, which was visible through the hole in the door. He did not see whoever was guarding the gates tonight, but he doubted it was Kima, because Kima never took the night shift due to his old age. That was a fact that Keo had learned during one of his many trips to New Ora, because the older man had mentioned it to him for reasons that

Keo could not recall.

In any case, Keo approached the back door to the guard tower as carefully as he could and then peered through the hole. He immediately spotted the guard—a man in his thirties wearing a hodgepodge of various bits and pieces of armor from wherever he could find them, probably because the town of New Ora was too poor to give their guards proper equipment. The guard was sitting with his back to the door, his eyes focused on the darkness just outside the town. Like a good guard, he obviously expected New Ora's main threats to be external, which was good for Keo, because it meant that he did not expect someone from inside the town's walls to pose a threat to him.

The only question now was how to take him out. Keo considered throwing open the door and charging in and tackling the guard to the floor before he could react, but rejected that idea, partly because it was bound to be too noisy and thus awake the people in the nearest houses and buildings, but also because there was no guarantee that Keo could knock out the guard before he sounded the alarm and woke the whole town up. The guard was even armed with an ancient green blade tied to his waist, which appeared to be one of the old blades from the time of King Riuno, which meant that if Keo did not knock him out quickly, then the guard would have a significant advantage over Keo in combat.

I need to lure him out, Keo thought. *Then, when he comes out to check on the noise, I'll take him out before he even knows what happened.*

So Keo bent over, picking up the heaviest stone off the street that he could find, and then, after securing it in his grasp, knocking rapidly and loudly on the door while saying, "Guard!

Guard! Help! Someone is trying to harm me! Please save me!"

It worked. Keo saw the guard stand up and turn around, but that was all Keo saw, because he then stepped outside of the guard's view. A second later, the door opened and the guard stepped out, saying, "Don't worry, citizen, I—"

Keo immediately brought his heavy stone down on the guard's head. A sharp *crack* emitted from where the stone struck the guard's head and the guard immediately collapsed, although thankfully he appeared to be unconscious rather than dead.

Tossing the rock aside, Keo entered the guard tower, which was rather warm due to the fire burning in the center, and then dragged the guard inside as quickly as he could. The guard was heavy, but Keo was a strong man and soon had the guard inside. He then closed the door and turned to look at the guard tower's interior, which he had never been inside before in his life.

It was a fairly small space, with enough room for one person to sit comfortably in a wooden chair facing the open window that displayed the darkness just outside of the town's borders. The ceiling was high above Keo's head, but even so, he felt cramped in here anyway, like he had been put inside a tiny glass jar. It reminded Keo of why he liked the outdoors better than the indoors.

But then Keo spotted a rack along the left wall where all of the weapons that travelers to the town had to give over to the gatekeepers were kept. On the rack were four weapons: An ax, a long knife that looked more like a carving knife than a dagger, a spear, and a sling plus a bag of rocks that hung with it.

Where's Gildshine? Keo thought as he walked up to the rack to look at it more closely, in case he had somehow overlooked his sword. *It should be here. Where is it?*

Unfortunately, even up close, Keo could not find his sword. He pushed aside the ax and the spear, but did not find Gildshine behind the other weapons either. That was curious indeed, because Keo had been quite sure that he had left his sword at this specific guard tower. Granted, he knew that sometimes weapons left at the guard towers would be transported from guard tower to guard tower if the traveler left from a different gate, but as Keo had been arrested, there was no reason for them to move Gildshine anywhere.

Then again, I am technically a criminal, Keo thought. *They must have some rule that states that any traveler arrested within New Ora's walls loses all rights to their possessions, including any weapons they bring with them into the town. That means that my sword is either back in the prison or—*

"Right here, young man," said a scraggly, ancient, yet sinister-sounding voice behind him, causing Keo to whirl around to see who it was.

Standing before Keo was an elderly man in black robes, pointing the tip of Gildshine's sword against Keo's throat. The elderly man had gray hair and a gray beard, making him look similar to Master Tiram, but he was scrawnier than Tiram and had far more vindictive eyes.

"How did you know what I was thinking?" said Keo. "And who are you, anyway, old man?"

The old man scowled. "Old man? Old man? I am not merely an 'old' man. I am your elder and I shall be referred to as such. But as for who I am, I am surprised that you do not recognize me. I am Skran, the Magician of New Ora, and I am making sure that a criminal like you does not get ahold of a dangerous magical weapon like this."

Skran gestured at Gildshine, which had not wavered in his hands. "Much too dangerous to be in the hands of a common crook. I should take it as my own, as I am the only person in this dumb town who knows how to use this weapon without killing myself."

"Hold on," said Keo. "You are *the* Skran? Why are you here? I thought that your job was to *rule* New Ora, not to catch common criminals like myself."

"I have taken up the habit of prowling the streets at night, using the shadows to conceal myself, in order to make sure that the guards are doing their job," said Skran. "I don't trust most of them, as the people of this town are simply incompetent, but the guards generally do an adequate job. That's how I noticed you escaped, because I saw you making your way here and so I followed you without you ever being the wiser."

"Then why didn't you call the other guards?" said Keo. "Why not have your Enforcers apprehend me?"

"Do you think me a fool?" said Skran. "Of course I have summoned my Enforcers, but they are slow to rise at night even in an emergency like this. Still, they will be here and once they are, they will put you back where you belong, like the criminal you are."

Keo bit his lower lip. He had heard many stories about the power of Magicians like Skran. Some said that Magicians could make thunder clouds appear in the sky and lightning strike whatever target they pleased, while others said that Magicians understood the secrets of the universe. In any case, Keo did not know what kind of powers that Skran had exactly, as he had never met the Magician before and had never bothered to ask anyone else, but he knew that Skran could easily take him out no matter what Keo chose to do.

But Keo could not simply go quietly back to jail with Skran. He had to get to Capitika. He had already wasted far too much time in New Ora as it was. If he could not get to Capitika and find Nesma before the demons rose again … well, he did not know exactly what would happen, but he knew that it would not be any good. He would have to convince Skran to let him go, even though the Magician was probably not going to listen to him.

"Magician, you must return my sword to me and let me go," said Keo. "It is urgent that I leave for Capitika right away."

"Capitika?" said Skran. "Why do you want to go there? Hoping that maybe my superiors won't just ship you back here, to prison, where scum like you belong?"

"That's not what I expect to happen at all," said Keo, shaking his head. "You see, I have recently learned that the demons of old are rising again and will return to destroy Lamaira in six months. I have to go to Capitika to convince the Magical Council to ally with the other two factions in order to form a united kingdom against the demon menace."

Skran looked at Keo like he had completely lost his mind. "The demons? You mean the ones that the Good King was said to have banished ages ago, before the founding of Lamaira? Do you honestly think I am dumb enough to believe such a tall tale?"

"But it is the truth," said Keo. He pointed behind himself, in the general direction of the Low Woods. "Just last week, when I was traveling through the Low Woods, I killed a demon that attacked me. It told me all about how its brothers were going to rise again, which is why it is urgent for me to get to Capitika as quickly as I can."

"You truly are a foolish boy," said Skran. "I can tell a lie when I hear it. The demons of old, if they even existed at all, are forever banished from Lamaira. It is impossible for them to return. The Good King made sure of it."

"I am not saying that the Good King did not do his best to banish them, but the fact is that the demons are rising again, whether you want them to or not," said Keo. "I don't know why the Good King's seal is starting to weaken, but I do know that all of Lamaira needs to be united to stand against the demons."

"This is the most silly and inane story I have ever heard from a criminal attempting to convince me to let him go," said Skran. "And that is saying something, as I was once told by a criminal that he needed to leave because he was in fact a guardian spirit taking physical form and that he needed to be let free so he could bring gifts to all the good little boys and girls around the country. How stupid."

"But this is the truth," said Keo. "Ask the townspeople if I've ever lied to them. They know I'm honest."

"The townspeople have told me that they don't know you very well at all," Skran pointed out. "You come in, buy things, and leave, often without speaking to anyone. I doubt anyone in New Ora could confirm your wild story to me."

"Then ask my mentor, Master Tiram," said Keo, pointing toward the open window of the guard tower. "He knows that I speak the truth. He can back up my every word."

"You mean the crazy old hermit who lives by himself in the

Low Woods?" said Skran. "Who raised you from infancy, if I am not mistaken? Yes, he will most certainly be an objective witness to your story. Of that, I have no doubt."

The sarcasm in Skran's voice was so palpable that Keo could practically see it. Still, Keo knew better than to let his anger get the best of him, because Magicians like Skran were known for their skillful manipulation of the emotions of others. Even so, when Keo spoke, his voice was tight, because he had a great difficulty in keeping his temper cool in the face of this willful obstinacy.

"Listen, Magician, I am not lying," said Keo. He nodded at Gildshine, which Skran still held up to his neck. "Can't you feel all of the enemies that Gildshine has vanquished? I know that Magicians have a different relationship with magical weapons than we non-Magicians do. So can't you feel that Gildshine has vanquished a demon?"

Skran shook his head. "Naive boy, that sort of magic requires specialized skill on the part of the Magician in question. I have never bothered to learn the art of speaking to weapons, as it has always seemed more like a neat parlor trick than a useful application of my immense power. Besides, I bet you tricked it somehow, as you seem like the kind of person to do that."

"How could I, a non-Magician, trick a magical sword into believing that it had slain a demon?" said Keo.

"I don't know," said Skran. "But I do know that I have seen far stranger things in my long life. Anyway, I am done talking with you. Lower your hands and allow me to shackle you so I can return you to where you belong without trouble."

Keo was tempted not to, because he knew that he needed to

leave more than anything. Yet as far as he could tell, there was no way that he could fight Skran and get control of his sword back from the Magician. Skran may have been a frail, old man in appearance, but Magicians often controlled powers that dwarfed mere physical strength, so Keo doubted he could beat Skran even if Skran hadn't had him immobilized with his own sword.

So Keo lowered his hands and said, "All right, Magician Skran, you win."

Skran smirked. "I guess there is a brain in that thick skull of yours after all. Now, why don't we—"

Without warning, the flames from the burning torch reached out and slashed at Skran's hand. The Magician cried out in pain and surprise, dropping Gildshine to the floor as he staggered backwards, clutching his now-burnt hand. This sudden turn of events almost caught Keo off guard, but he knew an opportunity for success when he saw it, so Keo charged forward at Skran.

Skran looked up just in time to get punched in the face by Keo. Skran's face felt soft and fragile under Keo's fist as the Magician collapsed onto the floor on top of the guard who was still unconscious, but Keo did not let his guard down just yet. He picked up Gildshine and pointed it at Skran, but when the Magician did not get back up, Keo knew that he was out for the count.

Keo suddenly realized that he had no idea why the fire had attacked Skran. He looked at the burning flame, which had returned to its original size, but saw no hints to indicate what had caused it to increase in size the way it did. He almost wondered if he had imagined it before he heard a voice outside of the guard tower window say, "Hey, kid, over here."

Keo looked toward the guard tower window and saw Dlaine's familiar aged face in the light of the flame. He was leaning on the window's sill, an urgent look on his face as he gestured for Keo to come over.

"Dlaine?" said Keo, turning to face the Wanderer, although he wasn't sure if he was happy or annoyed to see him. "What are *you* doing here? I thought you had left town already."

"Jola convinced me that we should help you," said Dlaine. "She also made that fire burn Skran. But it doesn't matter why I'm here. Just come on and go. The Enforcers are on their way and Jola has done all she can to delay their arrival. We need to leave now."

Keo frowned and glanced over his shoulder at the door to the guard tower. "But what about buying supplies for the trip?"

"We'll survive," said Dlaine. "Now come on. Don't you have to be at Capitika or is that demon invasion you mentioned to Skran not actually going to happen in six months?"

Keo's eyes widened. "You heard me mention that?"

"Yeah, and I have a lot of questions about it, but for now we need to get gone," said Dlaine, nodding his head away from the town. "You got your sword, and Jola stole the rest of our supplies from the prison, so we have no time to lose."

Although he was thankful that Dlaine had saved him, Keo still was not sure he trusted the Wanderer and his strange, invisible friend entirely.

But when Keo realized that it was either escape with Dlaine and Jola or wait until the Enforcers arrived and dragged him back to jail, Keo dashed over to the window and crawled out as quickly as he could. Once his feet touched the ground, he and Dlaine ran into the darkness away from New Ora as fast as they could, with Keo hoping that the Enforcers would be too frightened by the darkness of the night to chase Dlaine and him.

Chapter Six

KEO, DLAINE, AND JOLA (who Keo still could not see) ran through the darkness into the wilderness surrounding New Ora until the lights from the village were lost completely. The only lights now were the illumination of the moon and stars above, but Keo, Dlaine, and Jola still needed to find a place to rest for the night.

Jola found them a small cave just off the road that they could hide in. Its entrance was blocked by trees and bushes, which meant that it was unlikely that anyone would see it from the road, even if they looked directly at it. In fact, Keo would not have realized that there was a small hidden cave there if Jola had not led Dlaine and him to it.

The cave was indeed small, far too small to stand up in, so Keo, Dlaine, and Jola had to sit in it. Keo did not mind this too much, because they had been running hard for what felt like miles and Keo was more than ready to sleep the rest of the night. Keo may have been in good shape, but he still got just as worn out from nonstop running as anyone else, especially after such an intense confrontation with Skran.

Leaning against the stone wall of the cave, Keo looked at Dlaine. The Wanderer appeared to be listening for anyone outside the cave, but then he nodded and said, "Okay, Jola, you can go and be our lookout. If you see anyone or anything coming this way, just tell us, okay?"

Keo heard and saw nothing from Jola, but based on Dlaine's smile, he assumed that Jola must have answered in the affirmative. Then he heard some movement outside, bushes rustling, but Dlaine's calm expression told him that that was simply Jola going out to take her watch duty, thus leaving Keo and Dlaine alone in the cave together.

"Thank you for saving me back there," said Keo. He wiped some of the sweat off of his forehead. "I thought for certain that Skran was either going to chop off my head with my own sword or drag me back to prison himself."

"Don't mention it," said Dlaine, waving off Keo's gratitude like it was nothing. "I've never liked those self-important Magicians, anyway. And besides, I didn't think it was right to let a kid like yourself get thrown back into jail not more than an hour after you escaped."

"Well, thanks anyway, regardless of your reason for doing that," said Keo. "I deeply appreciate it, because your actions may have very well helped save Lamaira as a whole."

"Right," said Dlaine. He leaned forward, a serious look in his eyes. "That reminds me. You mentioned something about the demons of legend rising again when you were talking to Skran. What were you talking about?"

Keo bit his lower lip, because he did not want to speak about this with Dlaine. But he now knew that there was no hiding the truth, so he told Dlaine all about his encounter with the lone demon last week, what that demon had told him, and what he planned to do. Dlaine, at least, did not interrupt his story, listening as intently as if listening to a ghost story around a campfire in the middle of the night.

"And that is why I need Gildshine," said Keo, patting the flat of his sword, which leaned against the wall next to him where he could easily reach it if necessary. "I am hoping to deliver it to my friend, Nesma, who can read weapons and tell who their last victims were. By having her read Gildshine, she can then confirm the existence of the demon and hopefully convince the Magical Council to prepare for the demons' rise."

Dlaine stroked his chin, a thoughtful look on his face. "Well, that is the wildest story I've ever heard in my life. I grew up listening to those stories and legends about the demons—my older brothers loved to scare me with them—but I never thought they had any truth to them. And frankly, I am still not sure I believe it, because you don't have any actual proof that these demons really exist or that they are rising to kill us all."

"I'm not asking you to believe me," said Keo. "I'm only explaining to you why I'm trying to do what I'm trying to do. As long as you don't try to stop me, then I won't object to your skepticism."

"Well, I certainly have no plans to stop you," said Dlaine with a shrug. "If your story is a lie, then no one will believe you and nothing bad will come of it. But if it's true, then Lamaira itself might be saved … or what's left of it, anyway."

"Thank you," said Keo. "Now, Dlaine, since I have told you my reason for going to Capitika, what's yours? You mentioned having to meet a 'deadline' earlier."

Dlaine suddenly looked away from Keo. "When did I ever agree to tell you all of *my* secrets?"

"It's only fair," said Keo. "I told you my story. Now you tell me yours. Or else I will knock you out and return you to New Ora to be jailed, just like you deserve."

Dlaine laughed. "Kid, you couldn't beat me if your life depended on—"

In a flash, Keo had the tip of Gildshine at Dlaine's throat. He didn't even have to move much because they sat so close to each other. Dlaine's terrified eyes glanced down at Gildshine's sharp tip.

"You forget that I am a swordsman," said Keo. "I may not be a match for you in fisticuffs, but since I now have Gildshine, I'd say that equals things out a little between us, wouldn't you agree?"

Dlaine looked like he was still going to deny telling Keo anything, but then he sighed and said, "All right. I'll tell you my reason for going there. But put down the sword, all right? I don't like talking with a sword up against my throat like this."

Sensing that Dlaine was telling the truth, Keo lowered Gildshine and lay the sword across his legs. "Then start."

"All right," said Dlaine. He looked out the cave, like he was afraid of someone eavesdropping on their conversation, before looking back at Keo. "Jola and I have to be at Capitika in three weeks' time. That's the deadline I was talking about earlier. As for why we have to be there in the first place … my daughter is dying."

"You have a daughter?" said Keo in surprise. "You don't seem like a father to me."

Dlaine scowled. "Well, I am one, albeit not a very good one. Anyway, my daughter is dying of a deadly disease that no one has been able to cure. And Jola and I are supposed to deliver a potion that could cure her, which we received from … a friend, who said that the potion should be able to cure my daughter of her illness as long as we get it there in three weeks."

"Who is this friend of yours?" asked Keo.

"None of your damn business," Dlaine said, folding his arms over his chest. "All you need to know is that I trust him more than anyone else in the world, so if he says that the potion I carry in my bag will cure my daughter of an incurable disease, then I believe it."

Dlaine patted the bag sitting at his side. He flipped open the top and pulled out a tiny vial containing a deep blue liquid, which he showed to Keo for a moment before placing it back inside the bag, which he then put on his lap and held like it was his firstborn. Just as Dlaine closed the flap, Keo thought he saw darts in it, but because Dlaine closed the flap quickly and it was so dark, Keo decided that he probably had seen something else.

"That's what we're doing," said Dlaine.

"I see," said Keo. "Well, that is definitely what I would call a noble quest. I hope you succeed in saving your daughter's life."

"Thanks," said Dlaine. Then he smiled. "But why do you have to 'hope' I succeed when you can *help* me succeed?"

Keo frowned. "I don't understand where you are going with this."

"Come on," said Dlaine, pointing at Keo and himself. "You and I both need to go to Capitika for various reasons. We even have a similar deadline. And we seem to get along reasonably well. Why not travel together at least until we reach the city? After that, we can go our separate ways, but until then, we could be travel companions, if you want."

Keo considered the offer. "Well, I have to admit that that is a tempting offer. I have never traveled farther than New Ora in my whole life, so the trip ahead of me is vague. And it is always safer to travel in groups than by yourself."

"Exactly," said Dlaine. "The three of us can keep each other safe, particularly with my knowledge of the country that you lack. It's why Jola and I are always together. So what do you say? Want to give this a shot?"

Although Keo still did not know as much about Dlaine or Jola as he liked, he decided that he knew enough to decide whether to trust them. And seeing as he thought that a father trying to save his daughter's life was a noble thing indeed, that decided it for him.

So Keo nodded and said, "All right, Dlaine. I'll travel with you and Jola until we reach Capitika."

"Excellent," said Dlaine. He held out a hand. "Let's shake to seal the deal."

Keo reached out and took Dlaine's hand, which felt hard and scarred, and shook it.

After that, the two of them decided to go to sleep and head out first thing tomorrow morning. The small, cramped cave was not very comfortable, especially with the cold night air, but Keo eventually succeeded in finding a position that was less uncomfortable than the others and soon drifted off to sleep, wondering what the next day's adventures would bring them and hoping that he, Dlaine, and Jola would be able to get to Capitika as quickly as possible.

At the crack of dawn, Keo awoke to the smell of freshly-cooked bacon and biscuits. He saw Dlaine sitting in front of a small fire that he had apparently made himself, over which a small frying pan was suspended that contained bacon and biscuits. Dlaine looked up when he heard Keo moving and waved at him.

"Morning, kid," said Dlaine. "Want some fresh bacon? It's my specialty."

Keo blinked and yawned. The air in the cave was a lot warmer now, but the cold stone beneath him still felt cold, although it was warmer than before. "I didn't know you could cook."

"I *have* to know how to cook because of my wandering lifestyle," said Dlaine. "Jola doesn't even know how to make a sandwich, so I pretty much do all of the cooking."

"Okay," said Keo. He glanced at the cave entrance. "Say, where is Jola? Is she coming in for breakfast?"

"She's probably already eaten," said Dlaine. "She prefers to hunt and kill her own food. It's disgusting, but she says it keeps her in shape and that my 'awful cooking'—her words, not mine—isn't much different from eating raw meat anyway. She still doesn't think I've improved as a cook, even though that was years ago when she first told me that."

Dlaine sounded quite disgruntled when he said that, like Jola's criticism of his cooking still annoyed him. Keo, however, thought that the bacon in Dlaine's pan looked and smelled delicious and didn't care what Jola thought about it.

So Keo and Dlaine had a quick but filling breakfast of bacon and biscuits, along with some water that the two of them carried in their own flasks. Once they had their fill, the two of them repacked what little they had taken out of their packs and then crawled out of the cave into the morning air.

Standing up and stretching his limbs, Keo looked toward the road, which was empty at the moment. Even so, he did not walk onto it just yet. He looked at Dlaine and said, "Did Jola see anyone last night?"

Dlaine looked at the top of the cave, where Jola apparently was, and said, "Hey, Jola, anyone we should avoid travel on the road while we slept?"

As usual, Keo heard nothing, but Dlaine appeared to hear her, because he nodded and said, "Nothing, huh? That's lucky."

"Not necessarily," said Keo. "The people of New Ora consider it bad luck to travel at night. They think that there are vengeful spirits in the darkness that will kill any travelers who trespass upon their territory. The Enforcers probably believe that as well, which is why they did not come after us."

"Will they come after us now?" said Dlaine.

"Most likely, unless Skran told them otherwise," said Keo. "But that's why we have to keep walking. If we leave now, we should hopefully be able to outrun them."

"Do they have horses?" said Dlaine. "Because if they have horses, then we're screwed."

"They do have horses, but it usually takes them a while to get saddled up," said Keo. "I think that it's unlikely they'll send horses after us anyway, because they don't have many and they wouldn't want to accidentally lose or injure any of them. Still, we should travel as quickly as we can just to make sure they don't catch us."

"That was my plan in the first place," said Dlaine. "Let's go."

So Keo, Dlaine, and Jola walked onto the road and started heading down it as quickly as they could. It was still early morning and so the first rays of the sun were just starting to rise over the hills and trees around them. As a result, the air was quite cool, but not freezing due to the fact that it was currently summer. Keo glanced over his shoulder every now and then to make sure that no one was following them, but the road behind them was as empty as the road before them, for which Keo was quite grateful.

As they walked, Keo looked at Dlaine and said, "What's the next town between New Ora and Capitika?"

"Torgan," said Dlaine, nodding at the road ahead. "It's larger than New Ora, but it shouldn't take us long to pass through it. After that, we'll take a detour through the Silver Falls, which will take us to Carrk, and then after that is Capitika."

"And how long should that route take us?" said Keo.

"Depending on how fast we walk, what the weather is like, and so on, about a week and a half," said Dlaine. "But don't quote me on that."

"A week and a half?" said Keo. He groaned. "I knew it was going to be a long trip, but I didn't know it was going to be *that* long."

"Sorry, but there's not much we can do to improve our speed at the moment," said Dlaine, shaking his head. "We could get some horses in Torgan, maybe, but they can be expensive to rent and money is frankly one of those things I don't have a lot of these days and you don't exactly look like you were raised with a silver spoon in your mouth, either."

Keo frowned. "What if we found a Magician who could teleport us there?"

"Magicians can't teleport, though Jola can do it across very limited distances," said Dlaine as he kicked a stone out of their path. "That's a myth. I have a Magician friend of mine who told me that. They do have ways of traveling over long distances that we don't, but that's not one of them."

"What are their other ways of traveling long distances?" said Keo.

"No idea," said Dlaine with a shrug. "My friend said it was a trade secret. You know how Magicians are. Never tell you a thing and when they do it never makes any sense."

Keo nodded. "Right." Then he looked around them. "Where is Jola? Can I see her now?"

Dlaine shook his head suddenly. "No. Jola doesn't like to reveal herself to people who aren't me. She's not exactly shy, but she doesn't really trust people in general. It's nothing against you. She's just had some bad experiences with others and so prefers to stay invisible."

"Then how do you communicate with her?" asked Keo. "I have never heard her talk, and since she's invisible, you clearly can't see and read her body language. Does she have some sort of magical way of communicating with you or something?"

"We know how to talk," said Dlaine simply. "And anyway, I don't see why you need to know it. We may be fellow travelers right now, but that doesn't mean I need to tell you every little thing about me and Jola. I've refrained from asking you personal questions about yourself—such as where you got that neat little sword you got there—because I frankly don't need to know it."

"Well, if you want to know where I got Gildshine—" Keo began.

Dlaine cut him off. "I said, I don't need to know it. And if I do, I'll let you know, okay?"

Though Dlaine's tone was not mean, it was very clear that he considered the matter of revealing their personal histories to each other to be a closed matter for now. Keo may have been young, but even he knew what point Dlaine was trying to get across, so he did not utter another word about it.

In fact, the three of them walked in silence for the next couple of hours as they walked across the foothills and trees of the area between New Ora and Torgan. They ran into no other people, which made Keo wonder why the roads were so empty this morning, but then he recalled that few people traveled to New Ora from Torgan anyway, despite the proximity of the two towns. He considered it a good thing that there were fewer travelers on the road today, as that meant they would reach Capitika much more quickly than they otherwise would.

It wasn't until well after lunch that Keo noticed Dlaine's eyes darting to either side of the road. They were walking down a particular stretch of road that was bordered on both sides by tall, thick trees which had massive branches. The trees' branches provided some relief from the hot summer sun, yet Dlaine did not seem to relax underneath them the way that Keo did. He looked like he was looking for something, but what, Keo did not know.

"What did you see, Dlaine?" said Keo as they followed the road, which now curved slightly to the right. "You seem nervous."

"Nothing," said Dlaine. "But this particular part of the road is dangerous."

Keo raised an eyebrow. "Dangerous? How so?"

"Brigands and robbers are known to hide out here and rob any unwary travelers," Dlaine explained, gesturing at the trees on either side. "The trees provide excellent cover for them, which allows them to watch anyone traveling this road without ever being seen until they want to be seen."

"Has Jola seen any brigands or robbers?" said Keo. He rested his hand on the hilt of Gildshine, intending to draw his blade if necessary.

"She hasn't, but even Jola doesn't know about everything," said Dlaine. "I just think that we should be very careful. Lots of people have been robbed going down this road, including myself once several years ago."

Keo considered asking about the circumstances of that particular robbery before realizing that Dlaine probably filed that under 'personal information you do not need to know,' so he did not.

Instead, Keo said, "Is there any particular band of brigands we should look out for or—?"

"Nah," said Dlaine, shaking his head. "They tend to rotate because it is such a good robbing spot that they keep fighting over it. It's possible even that there aren't any here at the moment, but I doubt it because this spot is simply too good for any self-respecting brigand to leave alone for any period of time."

Keo looked around at the trees on either side of the road. They were indeed quite difficult to see through due to their thickness, which Keo figured made it easier for a thief or brigand to spy on them without any of them ever being the wiser. He tried to listen for any unusual sounds in the trees, but all he heard was the chirping of birds and the rustling of the leaves as the afternoon wind blew through. The entire place seemed deserted to him, but even so, Keo kept his hand firmly on Gildshine's hilt as they walked through the small forest.

Then Keo heard the *twang* of a bow and looked to his right just in time to see an arrow flying at his face.

"Get down!" Dlaine shouted as he grabbed Keo and pulled him down to the road as fast as he could. The arrow flew by overhead, but then Keo heard someone scream in pain and looked to the other side of the road in time to see a man stagger out from the trees and fall to the road with blood leaking out of his chest, the arrow from before sticking out of his chest.

"What the hell—?" said Dlaine, but he was interrupted by the sudden twanging of several bows going off at once and dozens of arrows flying from the left side of the road into the trees on the right side.

The arrows disappeared into thé thick leaves and branches of the trees, but Keo heard more than a few cries and groans of pain and someone fall through the trees, but he could not see anyone on the other side. He did, however, see another volley of arrows fire back in retaliation from the right side.

These arrows fell into the trees on the left side of the road, their iron tips digging into the trees, but this time Keo did not hear anyone fall down or cry out in pain, which probably meant that no one had gotten hurt.

But then another dozen arrows flew out from the left side, except these ones were larger and faster than the first volley. But Keo did not get to see where these arrows landed, because Dlaine grabbed him by the back collar of his shirt and said, "Come on, kid, get up! We're not going to get stuck in the middle of whatever this is. Come on!"

Dlaine pulled Keo up to his feet and the two of them dashed down the road, keeping their heads low even though the arrows overhead were too far above them to even touch them. But they did not get very far down the road before a dozen men—armed with swords and clubs—burst out of the left side of the trees, matched by an equal number of armed men emerging from the right side. The men charged at each other and started fighting, swinging swords, bashing clubs, and screaming and yelling all the while. And volleys of arrows kept firing back and forth between the two sides of the trees, although many of them were now aimed at the battle below as the archers of each side tried to take out their enemies.

Keo and Dlaine skid to a stop before the battle, watching in surprise as one man stabbed another man, only to get the back of his skull bashed in by the club of yet another man who was apparently an ally of the stabbed man. Then an arrow flew out of nowhere and struck the club-wielding man in the head, causing him to collapse into a bloody, still heap on the road.

That entire sequence happened in less than a second, but it was a good example of the ferocity and confusion of the battle raging before Keo and Dlaine. Even worse, there was no way for them to go through the battle without getting caught up in it.

Nonetheless, Dlaine grabbed Keo and dragged him to the shelter of several nearby trees, where they hid behind a particularly large tree that kept them separated from most of the fighting. Dlaine did a quick check to make sure there were no brigands hiding nearby and then turned to look at Keo, an annoyed expression on his face.

"See?" said Dlaine. "What did I tell you? There's a reason this place is known as Lethal Road and it's not because of the hungry bears."

"What the hell is all of that?" said Keo, peeking out from around the tree to see the two sides still battling each other like wild beasts. "Magician soldiers?"

"Nah," said Dlaine, shaking her head. "If I had to guess, it's two groups of brigands who both want this road for their own business. As they clearly don't know the first thing about the fine art of negotiation, they have resorted to all-out warfare and don't seem to care who gets caught in the middle."

"How do we get past them?" said Keo, looking at Dlaine again. "Could we go through the trees?"

"And risk getting filled with arrows from one side or the other?" said Dlaine. "No way. Getting shot with arrows hurts like hell. Especially in the behind. Trust me, I know what I'm talking about here."

The implications of Dlaine's statement made Keo wish that Dlaine followed his own 'as needed' policy as strictly as he expected Keo to, but before Keo could respond, a brigand with a large sword lunged out of the trees toward them.

Keo and Dlaine jumped apart as the brigand's blade struck the tree they had been hiding behind. He must have put a lot of effort into his attack, because the brigand's blade sank deeply into the tree, forcing him to pull hard to get it free.

Taking advantage of this man's predicament, Keo drew Gildshine and slammed its flat into the brigand's face. The blow instantly knocked out the brigand, who collapsed into a heap on the ground, his broadsword still stuck in the tree.

Still holding Gildshine out, Keo said, "Any ideas about how we *can* get out of here without becoming target practice for one side or the other, then?"

"Jola's searching for a way to get around this," said Dlaine. "I told her to hurry, so she should be back soon to let us know."

"I hope she is," said Keo, glancing around the tree at the battle, where now several men from both armies lay on the road dead or wounded (it was hard to tell which from here). "Because I'm not feeling very confident about our survival here at the moment."

"Don't you worry," said Dlaine. "Jola always comes through, so—"

Dlaine abruptly stopped speaking. Before Keo could ask him why, Dlaine suddenly collapsed, causing Keo to shout, "Dlaine!"

Keo took a step forward before feeling something prick at his neck. He touched his neck and felt some kind of feathery dart before he collapsed just as suddenly as Dlaine, everything turning black around him before he hit the ground.

Chapter Seven

WHEN KEO RETURNED TO consciousness, the world was upside down.

This sudden change in perspective caused Keo to gasp and try to get up, but then he realized that he was not lying down at all. Rather, he was hanging from a thick tree branch, a thick rope tied firmly around his body, arms, and legs. His head was free, but that did not mean much to him because he could not free himself with his head alone.

Confused, Keo heard a groan next to him and looked to his right to see Dlaine hanging next to him in a position very similar to his own. Dlaine did not appear to be hurt, but he groaned anyway as his eyes flickered open. He looked at Keo, a confused look on his own face.

"Keo?" said Dlaine. He looked very strange hanging upside down. "What happened? Where are we?"

"I was about to ask the same question, actually," said Keo. He looked around and saw that they were in a small clearing, with muddy earth beneath them that was covered in footprints. "Last I remember is getting hit by some kind of dart and then completely losing consciousness."

"Same here," said Dlaine. "God, I have an awful itch behind my left ear. But I can't even reach it because of this damn rope."

"Is that really the most important thing to be worrying about at the moment?" said Keo in annoyance. "We need to figure out how we got here and how to get out of here."

"I know," said Dlaine, nodding. "But that doesn't change the fact that that itch is really bad."

Rolling his eyes, Keo looked around the small clearing again. "Where is Jola? Why hasn't she rescued us yet?"

"She might not know where we are," said Dlaine. "But I have no doubt that she's looking for us. She'll probably find us sooner or later."

"Will we even live long enough for her to find us?" said Keo. He looked down—or rather, up—at the ropes dangling Dlaine and him from the tree limb. "How much do you want to bet that one of the brigand bands captured us and is planning to kill us?"

"More lems than I have at the moment," said Dlaine. "Then again, if they wanted to kill us, why wouldn't they have done it already? Brigands don't tend to be very subtle. Or smart, for that matter. Otherwise they wouldn't be brigands."

"Then we need to figure out how to escape before they come back to finish the job," said Keo. "Does that branch look weak to you? Maybe if we combine our weight and swing back and forth as hard as we can, we could break the branch off and fall to the ground."

"Worth a shot," said Dlaine. "Okay, on the count of three, we start swinging. One—"

Dlaine was interrupted by the sound of a lot of people walking through the trees nearby, their large feet crushing branches and leaves underfoot. Then four people stepped out of the trees and into the clearing.

Three of them were big, burly men who made Dlaine look like

a walking stick. They were all identical in appearance, which made Keo wonder if they were brothers, aside from the tattoos on their faces and arms and the slight height differences between them. The men were also armed with short, sharp swords, which Keo was pretty sure that the men could cut up Dlaine and him with if they wanted.

The fourth person, however, was a woman, surprisingly enough. She was a lot smaller and thinner than the big men around her, but she had such a stern, authoritative look on her face that Keo immediately identified her as the leader. She carried a quarterstaff on her back and a bow slung around her shoulder, her hair done in elaborate braids that would have made her look pretty if not for the scars on her face. She looked older than Keo, but younger than Dlaine, but regardless of her age, Keo could tell that she was not the kind of woman you wanted to cross unless you were suicidal.

The woman and her bodyguards—which was what Keo assumed those three men were—walked toward Keo and Dlaine. The bodyguards did not have their weapons drawn, but that did not make Keo feel any safer around them. He looked at Dlaine, who looked just as uncomfortable around this woman and her bodyguards as he did.

"Any plans for taking 'em down?" Keo muttered low enough for only Dlaine to hear.

"Nope," said Dlaine, shaking his head slightly. "Except maybe hope that our combined masculine charm is enough to convince the lady there to let us go."

"So we're going to die, then," said Keo.

"Probably," said Dlaine.

The woman and her bodyguards stopped a few feet from Keo and Dlaine. The bodyguards wore the ugliest scowls on their faces, while the woman looked at Keo and Dlaine like they were something she found on the underside of a rock. Keo tried not to show any fear before them, but it was hard because of the sheer power disparity between the woman and them.

It was Dlaine who spoke first, saying, "Hi there, lady. I'm so sorry we interrupted your little land dispute with those other guys, but we didn't—"

"Silence," said the woman. Her tone—harsh and no-nonsense —was enough to shut up Dlaine. "I don't want or need your apologies for anything."

"Oh, well, that's fine, too," said Dlaine, whose attempts at affability were a clear example of a losing battle to Keo. "Since we agree on that, I think we can also agree that we didn't do anything to hurt you or your men, so you can let us go."

"The kid knocked out one of my men with his sword," said the woman, pointing at Keo. "And I do not appreciate anyone, especially kids, harming my men."

Keo gulped when he saw the bodyguards fingering their sheathed blades, like they were just itching to start chopping up Keo and Dlaine like beef. And Keo suspected that they would be just as likely to eat them as well.

Nonetheless, Keo said, "But your man attacked us first. We are just peaceful travelers who were on our way to—"

"Silence," said the woman again. Her tone made Keo immediately shut up. "I don't care who you are or why you attacked one of my men. All I care about is that you nearly cost me that battle against the Riders earlier, and that is unforgivable by every definition of the word."

"Riders?" Keo repeated. "Who are they?"

"The other group that wants to control this road," said the woman. She gestured at her bodyguards and herself. "We are the Gatherers. And we are so much better than the Riders that they are not even in our class."

Keo wanted to ask why they had not yet wrested control of the road from the Riders if they were so great, but because the woman looked like she was on the verge of ordering her bodyguards to slice up Dlaine and him like beef, he kept that thought to himself.

Instead, he said, "Why didn't you just kill us, then?"

"Because of that sword you carried," said the woman. "It's obviously a magical sword. I've seen its kind before. They are very rare and unusual, so I decided to keep you two alive until I could find out where you got it and if there are any more."

"You couldn't make us talk even if we wanted to," said Dlaine. "We'll never tell you a thing."

"Many men have told me that," said the woman. She smirked. "I find that threatening to castrate them tends to make them talk."

Both Keo and Dlaine winced at the mention of castration, but Keo was not going to tell this woman anything just yet. While she seemed tough and serious about carrying out her threats, Keo wanted to see if he could convince her to spare them.

"What is your name?" said Keo. "I noticed you didn't introduce yourself."

"Celeresis," said the woman. "But you can just call me Cele. It is what I am known as and I prefer it to my full name."

"Celeresis?" Dlaine repeated. His eyes widened. "*The*

Celeresis? Celeresis of the Quick Hand?”

“You know her?” said Keo, looking at Dlaine in surprise.

“Know *of* her,” said Dlaine. “She's a famous brigand. She hasn't been active for very long, but she's definitely earned a name for herself in this area.”

“Thank you for introducing myself for me,” said Celeresis, who sounded more annoyed than grateful. “It saves me the trouble of having to talk about my own accomplishments and skills.”

“What has she done that's so noteworthy?” said Keo.

“Slaughtered pretty much every rival brigand gang she's come across,” said Dlaine. “Quite brutally, I might add.”

“A necessary step if I am to become the strongest brigand leader in this country,” said Celeresis, pushing some of her braids behind her ears. “And I am nearly there now. I just need to take care of those pesky Riders and I will be the undisputed queen of this area and the road. But I think it would be easier for me to accomplish if I knew how to use your magical sword.”

“Why would I ever tell you what its ability is?” said Keo. “I'm not in the business of helping brigands like you become more and more powerful.”

“As I said, castration is a very effective way to make most men talk,” said Celeresis. She nodded at her bodyguards. “My men here are all very skilled in that area, seeing as I have given them plenty of practice. Granted, they don't use any pain relievers, but that's fine, because they know how to castrate a man as quickly and easily as any.”

Based on the way Celeresis's bodyguards smiled, Keo knew that Celeresis was telling the truth. Not that that made him feel any better about the situation, however.

"But I might convince them to spare your manhood if you would simply tell me what your sword does," said Celeresis. She folded her arms across her chest. "All I know is that its power must be great, as magical swords always have powerful abilities. But I am also not fool enough to test it out on my own, as magical swords tend to have debilitating side effects that can leave their users in serious condition if they are not careful."

"No," said Keo. His head was starting to hurt, probably because he had been hanging upside down for so long. "You need to let us go. It is of utmost importance that you free us."

"Why?" said Celeresis. "So you can take your sword and never return? I did not become the Queen of the Gatherers by letting my captives go, much less when these captives have a magical weapon that could be of use to me."

"The fate of the entire kingdom rests on our freedom," said Keo. He nodded at Celeresis and her bodyguards. "And that includes you and your men."

Celeresis laughed. "The fate of the kingdom rests on the shoulders of two Wanderers who look like little more than beggars? What a joke, but still not as funny as the man I captured who claimed to be the reincarnation of King Riuno and who threatened to have the armies of Lamaira kill me if I touched him. I haven't seen any armies of Lamaira since I removed his head from his shoulders."

Keo considered whether or not to tell Celeresis about the demonic invasion that was going to come. He did not trust Celeresis or her bodyguards, but at the same time he did not have any time to convince them through other means.

So Keo said, "The demons from the old legends are rising again and they will destroy Lamaira if you don't let us go. You must free us so we can go to Capitika and convince the Magical Council to act before the demons become too powerful to stop."

Celeresis laughed again, this time a short and harsh laugh that instantly told Keo that Celeresis did not believe him. "Oh, really? Those monsters that only exist in scary bedtime stories told to make children afraid of the dark? I am no naïve child who will believe whatever you tell her. But nice try. I needed a good laugh, since I haven't had one in a while."

Keo scowled. He had expected her to say that and now he was all out of ideas for how to convince her about the reality of the demonic invasion or at least convince her to let Dlaine and him go.

"Well, it now looks like we are at an impasse," said Celeresis, putting her hands on her hips and shaking her head. "You won't tell me what your sword does and I am not going to free you. Men, you know what to do."

Celeresis's bodyguards drew their short but sharp swords from their sheaths, their smiles growing wider. Keo gulped, but he knew there was no way he or Dlaine could escape before the bodyguards did the unthinkable to them. He only hoped that the castration would not be as painful as he imagined it would be, though based on how bloodthirsty the bodyguards looked, he had a feeling that it was going to be quite painful indeed.

But then Dlaine suddenly said, "Wait! Don't remove our manhood just yet! I have an offer to make you, Cele, one I think will benefit us all if you accept."

Celeresis, much to Keo's surprise, held up a hand, causing her men to stop before they got too close. She looked at Dlaine with a suspicious but curious look in her eyes. "What is this 'offer' that you wish to make? I am listening."

Dlaine looked relieved that she was going to listen to his offer, but Keo wasn't sure whether he should be relieved as well because he did not know what Dlaine was going to offer her. He just hoped that Dlaine had put some thought into it, at least.

"All right," said Dlaine. "So you have said that you are trying to destroy the Riders, right? They've been giving you grief for a while now."

"Correct," said Celeresis. "They are the primary reason I have not been able to secure control of this road. What of it?"

"What if we helped you defeat the Riders in exchange for our freedom?" said Dlaine.

Celeresis frowned. "Helped? Do you mean you wish to join the Gatherers?"

"Nope," said Dlaine, shaking his head. "Instead, we'd work as sort of independent contractors. You'd send us in to go and kill the Riders' leader, which would undoubtedly leave the Riders confused and easy for you to finish off once and for all."

"Can you two do that?" said Celeresis in a skeptical voice.

"Not us, necessarily, but Keo here can," said Dlaine, nodding at Keo. "All he needs is his magical sword—which you stole from him, by the way—and he can tear the Riders apart like old cloth. All by himself."

Keo looked at Dlaine in alarm. "Dlaine, what are you—"

"Really?" said Celeresis. Her eyes darted to Keo. "This kid is that strong?"

"Yes," said Dlaine, nodding eagerly. "There's a reason he's

known as Keo of the Sword. It is because of his amazing prowess with a blade. He can cut swaths through entire armies with his magical sword, Gildshine, which is one of the most powerful magical weapons in the entire world."

"Interesting," said Celeresis. She no longer sounded quite as skeptical as before, but neither did she sound like she was sold on Dlaine's offer yet. "I have heard many legends about the power of magical swords, so I don't doubt that his can do that. But if Keo is so powerful, then why have I not heard of him until today?"

"Because he always kills his enemies," said Dlaine. "And those few who survive lose their tongues or are so scared of him that they cut out their own tongues themselves."

Keo looked at Dlaine in confusion, wondering where in the world that he was coming up with all of this stuff, but he also kept his mouth shut. Dlaine clearly had a plan to save their lives and Keo was not going to mess it up by voicing his confusion or disagreement.

"That does make him sound like quite the swordsman," said Celeresis. Her eyes narrowed. "What is the catch?"

"Simple," said Dlaine. "If Keo kills the leader of the Riders, then you let both of us walk free. You also return everything you stole from us and we promise never to harm you or any of your men ever again."

Celeresis tapped her chin. She looked at the ground, like she was trying to sense any downsides to the deal, but after only a couple of seconds she looked back up at Keo and Dlaine and nodded.

"Very well," said Celeresis. "I accept the deal. Men, let down the one known as Keo, but if he tries to run, cut his head off."

Celeresis's bodyguards moved quickly over to Keo. One of them cut the rope holding up Keo, causing him to fall, but he was caught by the other two, who actually helped him into a standing position. Even so, they did not let go of Keo when he stood, probably to ensure that he would not run away.

"Now, then," said Celeresis. "Let us get you your sword and then send you to the Riders. But if you try to run away instead … you and your friend here will not live long enough to regret that mistake."

Chapter Eight

KEO WALKED THROUGH THE undergrowth of the trees as silently as he could, which was quite silently, as he had a lot of experience in making his way through the woods without making noise after living in the Low Woods for his whole life. At his side was Gildshine, which was currently sheathed, as he found it easier to travel through the trees without holding his sword. He kept his eyes and ears open for any Riders, even though Celeresis had assured him that her scouts had confirmed that this particular part of the forest was Rider-free.

It had been about ten minutes ago that Keo had left the Gatherers' camp and came here. Celeresis had personally returned Gildshine to Keo and had also informed him of the identity of the Riders: A blonde-haired woman known as Yuras, who was said to be almost as violent as Celeresis herself. According to Celeresis, Yuras rarely actually fought on the front lines with her men during battle. Instead, she stayed at the Riders' camp, making strategic decisions from there, and it was her generals who were on the front lines instead.

The plan was simple. While Celeresis led the Gatherers on a frontal attack on the Riders, Keo would slip into the Riders' camp —which was now less defended due to the fact that most of the Riders would be out fighting off the Gatherers—and kill Yuras. It certainly seemed like a simple plan, but Keo had the strangest feeling that it would not work out quite so simply, as most plans did not.

Keo stopped when he heard some voices and dropped down behind some bushes. Peeking through the bushes, he saw a couple of Riders run by, swords in hand, no doubt to go meet the Gatherers' assault that had probably started by now. When they were gone, Keo stood up again and continued making his way to the Riders' camp.

But Keo did not move quickly. This was partly because quickness often lead to noisiness, but also because he had severe doubts that he could pull this plan off. Yes, he wanted to save Dlaine and himself, yes, he had no love for Yuras or the Riders, but deep down he wasn't sure he could be an assassin.

After all, Keo had never killed another human being before, not even out of self-defense. Yes, he had killed that demon, but demons weren't human and so he didn't feel so guilty about valuing his own life above that of a vile monstrosity. The problem was that he did not know Yuras and he had no personal reason to kill her, because she had never harmed him, whereas Celeresis had.

Still, Keo had to go along with it, because the other alternative was to get castrated and killed and he had no desire to lose his life or his manhood anytime soon. If he had to play assassin, then he would, but a part of him wondered if he couldn't find another way to end this conflict and save his life and Dlaine's life that didn't involve murdering someone he didn't know. He figured that there had to be, but if there was, it was clearly not an obvious solution. He thought about trying to communicate with Jola, but he didn't know where she was or how to communicate with her anyway, and even if he had, it was too late to go back on his word.

My and Dlaine's lives matter more than Yuras's, Keo told himself as he walked from tree to tree in an attempt to stay hidden from any watchful eyes. *Yuras is nothing more than a gang leader who has probably robbed countless innocent people over her life. Dlaine and I, on the other hand, are trying to* save *innocent people, so if I must take the life of a common crook like her, then that is what I will do.*

Of course, Celeresis was also a crook who had killed and robbed lots of people, but right now Keo could not deal with her. Maybe he would later on, after the demons were dealt with, but for now he had to think about his and Dlaine's best interests, and right now that meant killing this Yuras woman. He suddenly realized why Master Tiram always told him that sometimes you were faced with two different decisions that were almost equally terrible and there's not much you can do about it except grin and bear it.

After a few more minutes of walking, Keo saw several tents in a clearing through the trees. Walking doubled over, Keo stopped at the treeline and then peered through the gap in the trees, using some of the growing bushes to help hide him from any Riders who might still be in their camp.

The Riders' camp was large, with about three hundred tents total from what he could see. Several large campfires, currently nothing more than large piles of ash, stood at various places throughout the camp, likely where the Riders cooked and ate their meals based on the scent of the smoke that was sent his way by a strong gust of wind. A few Riders patrolled the edges of the camp, mainly large men with muscles like boulders, who carried axes, hammers, and other weapons at their sides. But they appeared to be the only Riders there, which made sense, because the vast majority of their fellow Riders were probably out dealing with the sudden attack from the Gatherers.

According to the report from the Gatherers' spies, Yuras was based in the large tent in the center of the camp. Two guards stood in front of the entrance to the tent, no doubt there to protect Yuras from assassins who would want to kill her. That meant that Keo would need to figure out a way to get past those guards, although he wasn't sure how just yet.

I'll have to be very careful, Keo thought, gripping the handle of Gildshine. *If I'm spotted, I probably won't live long enough to regret it.*

As silently as possible, Keo dashed out from the trees and in between two empty tents. He actually dashed inside one of the tents, which was thankfully empty, and then stayed still, listening for any sounds from the guards that might indicate that they had seen him. When he did not hear any guards coming over to his tent, Keo sighed in relief.

He poked his head out of the tent's flap, did a quick survey of the area to make sure that the guards were not looking this way (they were not, as their attention seemed to be focused on the trees around the camp), and then dashed over to the next tent, and the next, and the next, making his way over to Yuras's tent as quickly and silently as he could. He kept expecting to accidentally enter the tent of a Rider who had not left for some reason, but every tent he entered was empty, save for one, which had a sleeping Rider who thankfully did not notice Keo when he entered nor when he left.

At last, Keo reached the tent nearest Yuras's. It was tiny and cramped, like most of the tents, but he did not care. He peered out from inside the hot and stuffy tent and saw the two guards standing before Yuras's tent. They were talking to each other, chatting about the sudden attack from the Gatherers, but they did not seem to notice Keo. Even so, Keo could not simply walk up to the guards and demand that they let him inside Yuras's tent. They were easily the largest Riders Keo had seen yet and both carried huge broadswords that looked like they could cut Keo into firewood if he was not careful.

Pulling his head back into the tent, Keo thought, *I need to figure out how to distract them from the tent's entrance. Lure them away. But how?*

Keo looked around at the interior of the tent, searching for anything that might help him figure out how to lure the guards away from Yuras's tent. He sat on a sweaty, dirty bedroll, with a pack right next to it. Keo started digging through the pack, pulling out half-eaten biscuits, empty water jugs, knives and brass knuckles, and several other things, none of which would be very useful for luring Yuras's guards away from her tent. Scowling, Keo stopped digging through the pack and then folded his arms over his chest.

Think, Keo, think, Keo thought. *You need a distraction.*

That was when Keo noticed a small, round red sphere in the bottom of the pack. He grabbed the red sphere, which felt heavier than it looked, and turned it over as he examined it. It was rather warm in his hand, which made him wonder for a moment what it was until he suddenly remembered something that Master Tiram had once told him about.

This is a bang sphere, Keo thought. He held out the sphere as far from himself as he could when he thought that.

According to Master Tiram, a bang sphere was a very dangerous and very powerful weapon. When thrown with enough force, the bang sphere would explode against anything it collided with. Depending on how big the explosion was, it could even kill a person instantly. Keo had never seen one in real life before, but Master Tiram had described them to him at one point and this red sphere resembled it to an almost uncanny degree.

A part of Keo wanted to put it back down immediately, because bang spheres were known to exploded if handled incorrectly and Keo was in no mood to lose his hand or half his face from a bang sphere explosion.

But then another part of Keo told him that this was exactly what he needed to lure the guards away from Yuras's tent. Of course, he would have to be careful about where he threw it, as he did not want the guards to notice where the bang sphere came from, but he had to use it.

So Keo crawled over to the tent flap and peeked out quickly to make sure that the guards were still there. They were and they were also still talking to each other, although they were now sharing rather bawdy jokes that must have been hilarious based on how hard they were laughing with each other.

Let's see how funny you find this, Keo thought as he prepared to throw the bang sphere.

As fast as he could, Keo threw the tiny bang sphere through the tent flap. It flew over the heads of the chatting guards, who thankfully did not seem to notice it, and went much farther than even Keo expected it to go. The bang sphere landed on a tent on the other side of Yuras's tent.

And … nothing. No explosion, no fiery burst of flame that distracted the guards. It was almost like Keo had not thrown the bang sphere at all, which frustrated Keo greatly.

Now *how am I supposed to*— Keo thought.

A huge, earsplitting explosion sent burning chunks of canvas flying everywhere. The guards jumped when they heard the explosion, but they must have had greater control over their nerves than Keo thought, because they immediately ran over to the tent, shouting for the other guards to come and help with what they believed to be an attack.

Now was Keo's chance. He darted out from the tent toward Yuras's tent, which was now completely unguarded. He pulled open the flap to her tent and rushed inside, drawing Gildshine from its sheath as he entered.

Then he stopped to see exactly where Yuras was. The tent he now stood in was much wider and bigger than the rest of the tents, at least as big as two tents put together. There was plenty of room for him to stand up in and the entire place smelled like it had been freshly scrubbed recently, although there was also a definite odor of sweat and dirt that he could not deny. A closed wooden chest sat off to one side, while directly before him sat Yuras herself.

As Celeresis had described, Yuras had blonde hair, similar in color and style to Celeresis's own, in fact. She even had similar facial features, such as her nose, which was almost an exact copy of Celeresis's nose, in fact. She looked slightly heavier than Celeresis, but not by much.

The leader of the Riders was sitting on her bedroll with what appeared to be a map of the area spread out before her, which she had apparently been studying before Keo barged in. But she froze now and was looking at Keo in shock and confusion.

"Who are you?" said Yuras. Her voice sounded similar to Celeresis's, though Keo didn't focus on that. "I have never seen you before. And what was that explosion I heard outside my tent?"

Keo gritted his teeth and held Gildshine before him. "Sorry, but I'm going to have to kill you. It's nothing personal."

Yuras raised an eyebrow. "An assassin, then? Well, I'm not going to ask how you got past my guards. I'm just going to show you why it is always a dumb idea to try to kill the Queen of the Riders in her own tent."

Queen of the Riders? Keo thought. *That sounds like Celeresis's 'Queen of the Gatherers' title. What a strange coincidence.*

Yuras stood up. As soon as she did, Keo charged at her, aiming the tip of Gildshine directly at her heart. He didn't want to spend a whole lot of time trying to kill her, so he was going to try to take her life in one or two well-aimed blows, and then get out of here as fast as he could.

But Yuras dodged his sword easily, despite the lack of room for her to maneuver around in. Moving as quickly as the wind, Yuras grabbed Keo's hands and twisted them. Although Yuras's hands were smaller and lighter than Keo's, she could still twist his hands in painful, unnatural directions that forced him to drop Gildshine, which Yuras then kicked away outside his reach.

Keo struggled to break free of Yuras's grip, but then the Queen of the Riders kicked him in the stomach, knocking the breath out of him with her thick, heavy leather boots. Yuras then let go of his hands, causing him to fall down to the tent floor on his hands and knees, gasping for breath.

Nonetheless, Keo reached for Gildshine, which was only a couple of feet away, before he felt the tip of a knife rest on the back of his neck.

"Touch your sword, assassin, and I will cut off your head without even thinking about it," said Yuras, her voice angry. "Not that I want to, because I hate getting blood on my things, but I'm not afraid of killing anyone who tries to kill me first."

"Why don't you just kill me outright?" said Keo. He did not look up at her because Yuras's knife was against his neck in such a way that if he looked up, he would likely cut himself accidentally.

"Because no one has managed to get this close to me before," said Yuras. She sounded impressed, despite her anger. "My men tend to stop any would-be assassins from getting even one inch within the camp. Besides, I am interested in learning which assassin's guild that you belong to. The Death-bringers? The Brothers White Blood? Or are you just a lone wolf hired by someone to take me out?"

Keo considered lying to her, but something in Yuras's voice told him that she would see through any lie he might tell her. That meant he had no choice but to tell her the truth, because he figured that she was going to kill him no matter what, so there was no reason to lie.

"I'm not even an assassin, technically," said Keo. "I'm a traveler from the Low Woods who got roped into the conflict between you Riders and the Gatherers without my consent."

"Did Celeresis send you to kill me, then?" said Yuras. Her voice sounded more annoyed than angry now.

"Yes," said Keo, still keeping his eyes on the floor of the tent.

"Why?" said Yuras. "It isn't like her to send an untrained assassin to attack me, not unless you are a distraction for her *real* plan, whatever that is."

"Because of my sword," said Keo. He gestured toward Gildshine with his hand, but still did not move his head or neck. "It's a magical sword. She promised to let me and my friend go— her men captured us—in exchange for me using my magical sword to kill you."

"She did?" said Yuras. "How do I know you aren't lying in order to make yourself look more like a victim?"

"Because I can tell that you are smart enough not to be fooled by deception," said Keo. "And my life is in your hands, so if I lied and you found out, you could kill me easily."

Yuras did not answer immediately. Keo wished he could look up at Yuras's face, but her knife was still held against the back of his neck, which made even the slightest movement of his neck deadly. He fully expected Yuras to chop off his head or at least slit his throat—or maybe summon her guards and have them do that to him, if Yuras truly hated getting blood all over her things, as she said she did.

Then Yuras finally said, "I can tell you are telling the truth. You are too naïve to lie like that, especially to someone like me. Besides, that sounds exactly like the sort of thing my dear sister would do."

"Sister?" said Keo. "You mean that Celeresis is your sister?"

"My twin sister, actually," said Yuras. "Of course, she likes to say that she is the older sibling because she exited our mother's womb five minutes before I did, but we are still twins whether she likes it or not."

Yuras sounded quite bitter about that, as if she and Celeresis had spent countless hours arguing over that minor point. It seemed rather irrelevant to Keo, but he decided that pointing that out to the woman who could take his head off was probably unwise right now, so he simply kept his mouth shut on that subject.

Still, Keo had a few questions, so he said, "But why are you two fighting each other, then? I thought that siblings loved and cared for each other."

"Tell me, traveler, have you ever had a sibling before?" said Yuras. "Do you have any at all?"

"No," said Keo, still without looking up at her. "I'm an only child."

"Then don't pretend to understand what it is like to grow up with a vile, conniving bitch like Celeresis for a sister," said Yuras. "We have never gotten along at all due to our contrasting personalities—"

Keo had to hold back a snort that would surely get him killed, because to him, Yuras and Celeresis had very similar personalities from what he had seen of them both.

"—and the fact that mother always seemed to love her more than me," said Yuras. "But it wasn't until five years ago, after our mother died, that we were forced to strike out on our own and fend for ourselves. Because we had never married, we went our separate ways, joining robber gangs and rising through the ranks until we got to where we are today."

"So you turned to crime because you two had nothing better to do, then," said Keo.

He felt Yuras's knife dig slightly into the back of his neck. He thought for sure that she was going to take his head off his shoulders now, but then she stopped, although Keo felt some blood leak from the wound in the back of his neck where the knife dug into it.

"We're not common criminals," said Yuras. "We each rule our own gangs with an iron fist. We are two powers struggling for control of this road and I will never give up until my sister's neck is under my boot and she is begging for mercy like the coward that she is."

Keo gulped. He considered saying something flippant, but with Yuras as violent as she clearly was, he decided to take the more diplomatic route.

"Listen, Yuras, I really don't care about your conflict with your sister," said Keo, keeping his tone calm so that he did not accidentally provoke her to anger. "The only thing I care about is getting me and my friend out of this situation alive. Right now my friend is back at the Gatherers' camp, where they will castrate and kill him if I don't kill you."

Yuras made a snort of disgust. "Celeresis always had a disturbing fascination with the balls of men. But why are you telling me all of this?"

"Because I am *not* your enemy," said Keo. "I have no dog in this fight. Killing me won't do anything for you because I don't even work for your sister. The worst that might happen is that your sister will lose my sword, which she wants, but trust me when I say that you don't want my sword, either, because it's—"

"Magical," Yuras finished for him. "Yes. I have a great distaste for magic of all sorts, but magical weapons especially.

Besides, I have enough strength and power to defeat my sister all on my own."

Keo blinked. He was about to say 'It's cursed' so he could scare Yuras from touching it, but Yuras's reasoning was better than his, so he decided to roll with it.

"So you don't have any reason to hold me hostage," said Keo. "I'm no threat to you or your men. I just want to take my sword and leave."

Keo did not like to hear those words come from his mouth, but he felt he had no choice in the matter. He knew that Celeresis would be furious if he returned without having killed Yuras, but he decided that he would figure out a plan to save Dlaine and himself between now and then, assuming Yuras chose to spare him. He thought about searching for Jola, even though he did not know where she was, because he believed that Jola's magic might be able to help rescue Dlaine and get away from both Yuras and Celeresis.

But then Yuras said, "Sorry, but—while I believe you are not an actual assassin—I will still kill you and have my men dump your body in the middle of the woods somewhere."

"What?" said Keo. "Why? Weren't you just listening to what I said?"

"I was," said Yuras. "But you have already caused severe damage to my camp, which is unforgivable, and you might be lying about wanting to walk away. Besides, while I have no interest in using your sword for myself, one of my Riders used to study magical weapons for a living, so I will simply give it to him and let him figure out what it does and how to use it. Good bye."

Keo felt Yuras's knife lift off his neck. He looked up, saw the cruelty in Yuras's eyes and her now-bloody knife rising above her head, and knew that he was going to die, because there was no way he could move fast enough to dodge her attack.

But right before Yuras could bring her knife down onto his face, there was another explosion from outside that caused her to look up and say, "What the hell was that?"

Keo—though just as surprised by the explosion as Yuras—nonetheless rolled to the side, grabbing Gildshine as he did so, and rose to his feet. He then slapped the knife out of Yuras's hand and, before she could react, placed the tip of Gildshine against Yuras's throat. Yuras froze, her dark eyes focusing on the sharp blade now at her throat.

But before Keo could say or do anything else, one of Yuras's guards staggered through the tent flap, shouting, "Queen Yuras! The camp is under attack! The Gatherers—"

The guard suddenly choked and gasped before he fell forward flat on his face, a dagger in his back, with blood flowing from the wound. And standing behind the guard was none other than Celeresis herself, already drawing another knife from her belt, this one sharper and more jagged than the last.

But Celeresis froze when she saw Keo holding Gildshine's tip against Yuras's neck. It was the first time Keo had ever seen Celeresis actually surprised, but she soon recovered and appeared as confident and in control as she did before.

"Ah, Keo," said Celeresis, a smirk on her lips. "I see you are already in the process of killing my younger sister. I thought for sure that Yuri had killed you, but I guess she was just too soft on a kid like you."

The look of loathing in Yuras's eyes was as deep as the pit, but

112 | TIMOTHY L. CEREPAKA

she did not utter a word, likely because she believed that Keo would kill her if she spoke.

"Celeresis?" said Keo. "What are you doing here? I thought you were going to wait back at the Gatherers' camp for my return."

"That was a lie," said Celeresis. "I was merely using you as a distraction. My hope was that you would be caught by the guards, who would then be too distracted by your appearance to mount an effective defense against my select team of Gatherers who would go in and burn the entire camp down. What makes this plan so great is that it doesn't matter if you successfully kill my sister or not, because either way I will destroy this place, kill my sister, and win this bothersome conflict once and for all."

Keo had to admit that that was a pretty clever plan on her part. He felt used, but at the same time, he also admired Celeresis for her cleverness.

"But it looks like I don't need to kill my younger sister myself," said Celeresis. "Remember our agreement, Keo. If you kill Yuras, then I will let you and your friend go freely. I will even let you keep your sword, which I will no longer need after the Riders are gone."

Keo bit his lower lip and then looked at Yuras. She was defenseless now and it would not take much effort to stab her in the throat and let her bleed to death. To a certain extent, he might even enjoy it, seeing as she herself had been just about to kill him not more than a few minutes ago. And if Celeresis was indeed telling the truth, that she would let Dlaine and him go without complaint or any fuss, then Keo had no reason not to kill Yuras here and now.

On the other hand, Keo still did not trust Celeresis. She had already expressed a deep interest in taking Gildshine for her own goals. If Keo killed Yuras, there was nothing to stop Celeresis from killing him, taking Gildshine, and then maybe later killing Dlaine, too. It would certainly fit with her bloodthirsty, deceptive character.

Yet Yuras seemed no better than her to him. If he spared her, Yuras would probably kill him as soon as she got a chance. Even if she didn't have a weapon visible, Yuras seemed like the kind of person to carry all sorts of weapons on her that she could use to defend herself.

I feel like I'm at an impasse, Keo thought, his free hand balling into a fist. *I don't want to help or hurt either of them. I just want to get out of here and continue my journey to Capitika.*

"Come on, Keo," said Celeresis. "Make your choice. Either kill my sister or allow me to kill you for breaking our agreement. Stop delaying."

Celeresis's pressure annoyed Keo, even though he agreed with her that he would have to make a choice sooner or later. And it would have to be sooner, because he could hear the explosions and fighting outside and Celeresis looked like she was going to lose her patience very soon if he did not come to a decision quickly enough for her tastes.

Looks like I have no choice, Keo thought.

Without making a sound, Keo lowered Gildshine and stepped back from Yuras. Yuras immediately jumped away from him, drawing another knife from her boot that she had hidden away, while Celeresis shouted, "Hey! What do you think you're doing?"

Keo looked at Celeresis. "Not helping you. I want nothing to do with this conflict. While I'm no fan of your sister, I'm not going to do your dirty work for you. You will have to do it yourself."

Celeresis scowled and stepped toward him, knife in hand. "How dare you. Do you really want my men to kill your friend? Because they will, especially now that you have broken the deal."

"Not unless I get back to the Gatherers' camp first," said Keo.

"What makes you think I'll just let you leave?" said Celeresis. She raised her knife. "I'll cut your throat and burn your corpse with the rest of this damned camp."

Celeresis took another step forward, but then Yuras jumped in between her and Keo. She slashed at Celeresis, causing her sister to step backwards to avoid getting cut.

"Yuras?" said Keo in surprise. "Why are you helping me?"

"Not out of the goodness of my heart, I can assure you," said Yuras, without looking at Keo. "I'm only giving you a chance to escape because your escape would anger my sister, although don't think I forgot about how you tried to kill me. Understand?"

Keo nodded, but then realized Yuras could not see him, so he said, "Yes."

"Then leave," said Yuras, still facing her sister. "I'll keep my sister distracted. Leave, and never come back here ever again."

Keo did not need to be told that twice. He turned to face the tent wall and then slashed at it with Gildshine, cutting a hole in it large enough for him to exit through, but before he did, he looked over his shoulder at Yuras and said, "Thank you."

Yuras did not respond. She just advanced on Celeresis, who now looked so angry that Keo would not be surprised if she burst into flames. The two immediately started slashing and stabbing at each other, blocking and dodging the other's attacks with surprising grace and fluidity.

But Keo did not stay long enough to see who would emerge the winner. He dashed out the hole in the wall, Gildshine at his side, hoping that he would be fast enough to get to the Gatherers' camp in time to save Dlaine.

Chapter Nine

THE RIDERS' CAMP NOW looked more like a war zone than a base camp for a marauding band of brigands. Tents were burning, dozens of Gatherers were running around setting more tents ablaze or battling with the few Riders who were protecting the camp, and the smoke in the air was so thick that Keo started hacking almost as soon as he stepped outside. It didn't help that the sun was high in the sky now, its rays falling hard and hot, but Keo had to ignore that so he could focus on escape.

Keeping his head low and covering his mouth and nose with one hand to protect them from the smoke, Keo dashed forward through the camp, running around or between ruined tents and the fires that ate at them. He jumped over the burned corpse of a Rider, his eyes focused on the trees surrounding the camp. If he could just make it to the trees, then he would be home free.

But when Keo was about halfway from the tent, he heard the *twang* of a bow and instinctively ducked. An arrow flew over his head, causing him to look in the direction from which it came and spotted an archer—probably a Gatherer, based on the fact that he wore a similar leather coat to the other Gatherers—standing not far from him.

This archer, however, was not content to remain at a distance. He quickly advanced on Keo, drawing and firing arrow after arrow from his quiver, forcing Keo to go on the defensive by dodging or deflecting arrows with Gildshine. The archer shot fast, which made it impossible for Keo to find an opening in which to escape, although he did have a moment in which he was amazed that the archer could apparently see him through the smoke and flame of the camp.

One of the arrows grazed Keo's shoulder, making him wince, but he managed to dodge the next one. The archer was now only a few feet away from him and had run out of arrows, but rather than run away, the archer threw his bow aside and drew a sword of his own from his belt and then charged at Keo with it held out before him.

Keo blocked the blow with Gildshine, but the archer—perhaps swordsman was a better description of him now—struck again and again. Keo just barely blocked each blow, which came at him so fast and so furiously that he was still on the defensive. He had no idea if the swordsman held some sort of grudge against him or if he simply thought Keo was another Rider, but in any case, Keo had no time in which to think about it because of the speed and ferocity with which the Gatherer struck.

But then the wind changed direction and suddenly the smoke was blown into the eyes of the Gatherer. The Gatherer ceased attacking and looked away from the smoke, which gave Keo the opportunity he needed to slash at the Gatherer. Gildshine cut through the Gatherer's chest without difficulty, causing the Gatherer to shout in pain, but Keo followed that up with a kick to the gut, sending the Gatherer sprawling to the ground.

Keo did not wait to see if the Gatherer would get up and continue to fight. He ran toward the trees again, gripping his grazed shoulder, his eyes tearing up from the smoke and his hacking and coughing becoming worse and worse. He expected the Gatherer to get back up and come after him, but he did not hear anyone chasing him, and soon he was back in the trees, running as quickly as he could, not bothering to be quiet or stealthy about it, mostly because the sounds of explosions and fighting from the camp masked whatever sounds he may have been making as he fled.

Keo did his best to get as far away from the Riders' camp as he could, but the combination of fatigue from his fight with the Gatherer, his bleeding shoulder, and the smoke that had gotten into his lungs forced him to find a place to rest for a while. He found a couple of trees that grew so closely together that their roots were intertwined and, after making sure that no one could see him from the other side of the trees, went and hid behind it. He slid to the ground, coughing and hacking, despite his best efforts to remain silent in case anyone was following him.

To deal with his shoulder wound—his most immediate problem—Keo ripped off a portion of his sleeve and wrapped it around his wounded shoulder as best as he could. It would not be a good, long term solution, but it would have to do until he could have an actual healer look at it. Besides, the wound he had taken was not that deep, nor had the arrow hit anything vital, so perhaps even without a healer to treat it, the wound would heal on its own if Keo gave it time.

It was the lung damage that might be the biggest problem. Although the air in the forest was a lot clearer here than in the camp, so clear that Keo's coughing and hacking was starting to subside, the fact was that Keo knew how badly smoke could damage someone's lungs. Once, a house in New Ora had caught fire while Keo was running some errands. The house had burned down, but its owner, who had been inside it at the time, had been saved, only to die shortly afterward due to all of the smoke he inhaled. Keo was now afraid of smoke himself because of that, as he had been there when the man died from the smoke.

Of course, I didn't inhale nearly as much smoke as he did, Keo thought. *So I am probably going to be okay as long as I don't inhale any more smoke. I should focus on getting back to the Gatherers' camp now and rescuing Dlaine.*

Keo forced himself to get up. He was just about to leave when he suddenly heard two sets of footsteps crunching across the leaves and twigs of the forest floor nearby. Not knowing who it was, but suspecting that it was either a couple of Gatherers or a couple of Riders, Keo gripped Gildshine in both hands and stood against one of the trees. He held Gildshine up, listening carefully to the footsteps as they came closer and closer to his hiding place.

When the footsteps sounded too close for comfort, Keo stepped around the tree and swung Gildshine as quickly as he could. But just as he did that, he saw Gildshine flying toward Dlaine's head, but it was too late for Keo to stop.

Thankfully, however, Dlaine was fast. He ducked, causing Gildshine to fly past his head, and then snapped, "Damn it, Keo, what was *that* for? Almost took off my head there."

Lowering Gildshine, Keo coughed hard for a moment before saying, "Dlaine? I thought you were back in the Gatherers' camp. I thought you were one of them trying to sneak up on me."

Dlaine, who had both his and Keo's packs strung over his

shoulders, shook his head. "I escaped. Or rather, Jola here saved me."

Dlaine gestured at a spot just to his right, but as usual, Jola was invisible. Still, Keo did see the leaves crunch where she stood, which was how he knew for sure that she was standing right there.

"Jola?" said Keo. He hacked loudly before regaining control of his throat. "Where was *she* while we were at the hands of a woman who threatened to take our manhood away?"

"Said she got confused and lost in that earlier fight between the Gatherers and the Riders," said Dlaine. "Said all of the noise scared her. But she managed to find me all on her own and even managed to retrieve our packs from the Gatherers' treasury. See?"

Dlaine hefted the two bags on his shoulders. "And they have everything in them still, too, including the potion I need for my daughter. Isn't Jola the greatest?"

"I have to admit, that is pretty good," said Keo. He patted his chest and coughed slightly. "Why did you come here?"

"Because Jola suggested we look for you, of course, after I told her where you went," said Dlaine.

"You mean you guys really care about me that much?" said Keo.

"Nope," said Dlaine, shaking his head. "Frankly, I just wanted to take my stuff and run, but Jola thought you might still be able to help us, so I agreed to go look for you and make sure that you hadn't been brutally murdered by the Riders."

Keo's shoulders slumped and thought, *Well, that explains why he didn't ask me why I'm coughing.* "Oh. Well, I guess that's better than leaving me to die, anyway."

"Right," said Dlaine. He suddenly ducked when an explosion sounded from the direction of the camp. "What was that?"

"Celeresis led a group of Gatherers to attack the Riders' camp while I was trying to kill Yuras," Keo explained. "I was just supposed to be a distraction for the actual attack, you see. It didn't really matter whether I actually killed Yuras or not."

"Figured as much," said Dlaine, shaking his head. "Celeresis didn't strike me as the kind of woman to rely on people she doesn't know to do her dirty work, at least not entirely. What's going on at the camp now?"

"The Gatherers and Riders are fighting each other to the death," said Keo. "So are Celeresis and Yuras."

"So that means we should get the hell out of here before any of them try to come after us," said Dlaine.

"Right," said Keo, nodding. "But aren't there any Gatherers coming after you already? I mean, surely they must know that you and Jola have escaped."

"I think they're too distracted by their fight with the Riders to even know I escaped," said Dlaine. "Granted, this one guy *did* notice, but we knocked him out and hid him in the bushes where no one could see him. But once he gets up, we'll probably have all of the Gatherers on our tail, so that's why I think we should leave as fast as possible."

"All right," said Keo. "Then let's go."

Chapter Ten

KEO, DLAINE, AND JOLA escaped the forest and were back on the road in short order. They ran into no Gatherers or Riders on their way out, although they heard the battle cries of the fighting brigands, as well as the clanging of metal against metal, and even a few explosions every now and then. It appeared that the Gatherers and Riders were indeed too preoccupied with their own battles to notice their escape. Even so, Keo kept expecting Celeresis to show up out of nowhere and try to kill all three of them, although he also hoped that Yuras would kill her or that maybe they both would kill each other, because he didn't like either of the twins very much.

Upon leaving the forest, Keo, Dlaine, and Jola ran as fast as they could through the countryside, trying to put as much distance between themselves and the warring brigands as they possibly could. They ran even when the sun set and darkness fell over the whole land, although they did eventually set up camp on the side of the road once they got too tired to keep running. As before, Jola stayed up to watch the road and surrounding wilderness in case of attack, which made Keo wonder if she ever actually slept, although when she used her magic to heal his shoulder wound, he decided not to question her too much.

In the morning after breakfast, the three travelers made their way through the winding hills of the southern countryside. There were fewer trees here, which made Keo feel far too vulnerable, because there were fewer places to hide in case of attack. And of the few trees that were present among or on the hills, they were smaller and thinner than the ones in either the Low Woods or the forest back where the Gatherers and Riders fought. Dlaine did not seem too bothered by the lack of trees, but then, Keo was under the impression that Dlaine was rarely bothered by anything, because he no doubt had seen many strange and exotic locations during his travels around Lamaira, although he remembered his agreement not to ask Dlaine questions about his past and so kept such thoughts to himself.

It was mid-morning before they crested a hill and saw a town sprawling out before them. It was larger than New Ora, but not by much, although the houses and buildings within it looked a lot nicer than New Ora's, as if the inhabitants of this town were wealthier, though the western part of the town did look rundown for some reason. Indeed, Keo noticed a large domed building on the west side of the town that looked like nothing he had seen in New Ora, as well as the Magician's Tower rising from the center. The town walls were high and thick, with armed guards patrolling them, guards who wore armor that looked a lot cleaner and shinier than the armor worn by the guards of New Ora.

"That's Torgan," said Dlaine, pointing at the town. "New Ora's sister town and our next stop."

Keo looked at Dlaine. "Have you ever been there before?"

"A few times," said Dlaine. "It's pretty nice. They've got a big theater there that puts on plays about once a week, although the price for tickets is pretty steep."

"Is Torgan richer than New Ora?" said Keo.

"Yep," said Dlaine, nodding. He gestured to the west. "There are some gold mines nearby that have provided them with their wealth, in addition to the theater, which draws people from all over the country to visit. They're not quite as rich as Capitika, but they are richer than New Ora."

"Who is the Magician in charge?" said Keo, pointing at the bone white Tower rising from the town's center.

"Magician Erawa," said Dlaine. "Granted, the last time I visited this place was a few years ago, so she might not be in charge anymore, but she was the Magician in charge last time I was here."

"Is she kinder than Skran?" said Keo.

"Yeah, but she was always … eccentric," said Dlaine. He scratched the back of his head. "It's kind of hard to explain, but she used to be a stage actress before she became the town's Magician, so she has some of that strangeness about her that most actors and actresses do."

"Is it a bad eccentric?" said Keo with a gulp.

"Not really," said Dlaine, shaking his head. "But it doesn't really matter. We're not going to stay here long anyway. We'll stock up on some supplies and then make our way to the Silver Falls to the east."

"Okay," said Keo. "Then lead the way."

So Keo, Dlaine, and Jola made their way down the hill toward Torgan's front gates. As they got closer, Keo saw two guards standing in front of the gates. They were two rather tall, large men with muscles like carved rock, armed with spears and shields that looked very fancy to Keo. They had a strange symbol on the shields—a flaming arrow—which made Keo wonder if that was the symbol of the town or not.

Dlaine approached the guards with confidence. He stopped before them and said, "Hi there. We're a couple of travelers who are just passing through. Mind letting us in?"

"State your names and your business," said one of the guards.

"I'm Dlaine of the Fist," said Dlaine. He nodded at Keo. "And this is Keo of the Sword. Like I said, we're—"

"Hold it," said the first guard, holding up a hand. "Did you just say that you are Dlaine of the Fist and your companion is Keo of the Sword?"

Dlaine nodded, looking rather annoyed at being interrupted. "Yes, I did. Why?"

Without warning, the second guard slammed his spear at Dlaine's side. The blow knocked Dlaine flat off his feet, but before he could get up again, the second guard pointed the sharp tip of his spear at Dlaine's throat.

Keo immediately unsheathed Gildshine, but as soon as he did, the first guard pointed the tip of his spear against his throat faster than Keo's eyes could follow. Keo froze, although he still held Gildshine in his hand.

"Don't make a move, criminal," said the first guard, his voice harsh and authoritative. "By the laws of the Council, we guards have the right to kill any criminals who resist arrest."

"Criminals?" said Keo, making sure not to move his head too much in order to avoid impaling it on the guard's spear tip. "What are you talking about? Dlaine and I have never committed any crime. Right, Dlaine?"

"Uh, right," said Dlaine, though he didn't say it very convincingly. "We're just peaceful travelers."

"Don't lie to us," said the first guard. "We received a message from Magician Skran of New Ora that two wanted criminals, Keo of the Sword and Dlaine of the Fist, escaped New Ora two days ago *and* assaulted Skran while they were at it. We were given orders to keep an eye out for them, but I didn't think you'd be so stupid as to walk right up to the gate and declare your identities to us like a couple of arrogant fools."

Damn it, Keo thought. *Should have seen this coming.*

"Now, Keo of the Sword, drop your weapon and allow us to arrest you peacefully," said the first guard. "We'll take you to jail and then ship you back to New Ora in the morning."

Keo bit his lower lip. He knew that there was no way that he or Dlaine could get out of this situation unharmed or even alive, especially when he noticed the guards on the ramparts coming down to aid their fellow guards in arresting the criminals. He hoped Jola would do something to help, but he did not hear or see Jola doing anything. He supposed that even Jola might not be able to help here, seeing as these guards certainly looked more than ready to kill Dlaine and him if they needed to.

But neither did Keo want to comply with the guard's orders. With the demons rising in only a few weeks, Keo could not afford to waste any time in a jail cell. Besides, he was getting tired of getting captured or arrested by now, although he still saw no way to get Dlaine and him out of this alive.

Just as Keo was about to lower his sword, someone behind him shouted, "Wait!"

That voice—which Keo did not recognize at all—made him look over his shoulder, despite the fact that the guard before him was still pointing his spear at his throat.

A woman was walking down the road, a woman who Keo had never seen before. She looked older than Keo, but not as old as Dlaine, and she wore a brown traveling cloak. Her hair was short, but streaked with red, like she had dyed it that way. She had a walking stick that looked like it had been elaborately carved by an expert carpenter and she moved quickly, like a mouse, and was almost as small as one, too.

"Don't arrest them!" the woman called as she approached the guards and Keo and Dlaine. "There's been a mistake!"

"Woman, just who do you think you are?" said the first guard. "State your name and your business."

The woman stopped a few feet away from Keo and Dlaine and looked at the guards without fear in her eyes. "My name is Sadia of the Foot. And I am here to enter Torgan and also stop you from making a terrible mistake."

The first guard and second guard exchanged puzzled looks, as did Keo and Dlaine. Keo hoped that Dlaine might know who this woman was, but Dlaine looked just as confused as he felt, which did not reassure Keo that this woman could be trusted, whoever she was.

"A terrible mistake?" said the first guard. "What do you mean?"

"I mean that these two men are not the dangerous criminals you suppose them to be," said Sadia, gesturing at Keo and Dlaine. "They are, in fact, innocent of any wrongdoing in New Ora or wherever else they may have been."

"Why should we listen to you?" said the first guard. "We received a report—"

"It was a mistake," Sadia said. "Magician Skran confused

these two men with a couple of other criminals who escaped that same night. Keo and Dlaine are, in fact, innocent men who were released from jail once it was clear they had committed no crimes, but there was a mix-up among the Enforcers and as a result you were given the wrong report."

That sounded like a far-fetched story to Keo, but the two guards looked at each other with doubt, as if they had experienced this sort of thing before.

"Well, the Enforcers at New Ora *have* been known to make that kind of mistake before," said the first guard, somewhat grudgingly. "Like the time they claimed that Manfa of the Bread was a dangerous murderer only for it to turn out that he was just a normal man unlucky enough to share a name with an actual murderer who escaped from New Ora. That was embarrassing."

"And the situation here is the same," said Sadia, folding her arms across her chest. "You must listen to me because I am a messenger sent from Skran himself, who told me to come here and correct the mistake before you arrested any innocent people."

The two guards again exchanged puzzled looks, while Keo and Dlaine kept quiet. Keo could not recall ever hearing about a woman named Sadia working for Skran, but then, it was often said that Magicians had many different servants working for them at any one time and that many of them worked behind the scenes where you could not see them. In any case, Keo decided not to utter a word, because if this woman could save Dlaine and him from being arrested and hauled back to New Ora, then he was quite content to let her talk.

"But they identified themselves as Keo of the Sword and Dlaine of the Fist," the first guard said. "And the report we received explicitly said that the names of the two criminals were Keo of the Sword and Dlaine of the Fist."

"Like I said, it was a mistake," said Sadia. "Whoever sent you that report must have mixed up Keo and Dlaine with the real criminals."

"And those would be …?" said the first guard with a skeptical look on his face.

"Ceo of the Knife and Flaine of the Hand," Sadia said. "I can see how you might confuse them, however, because their names are quite similar."

"Figures," said the second guard under his breath. "Skran's men always send us mixed up reports. Surprised the Council hasn't revoked Skran's license for being such a screw up."

"Well, now that you know, you can let them both go," said Sadia, gesturing at Keo and Dlaine. "Or into Torgan, as the case obviously is."

The two guards once again exchanged doubtful looks, but as Sadia had laid out her case rather convincingly, the two clearly had no reason to arrest Keo and Dlaine. So they removed their spear tips from the two, allowing Keo to step back, while Dlaine scrambled to his feet, dusting off the dirt on his clothes and glaring at the guards.

"You're lucky that I'm not going to tell Magician Erawa about how you assaulted a couple of innocent people," said Dlaine. "Otherwise, you wouldn't have a job in this town ever again."

The second guard merely glared at Dlaine, while the first guard said, "Well, since you two are obviously innocent travelers, we can let you into the town."

Keo looked at the guard in surprise. "You mean we don't have to give up our weapons?"

"Nope," said the first guard, shaking his head. "Magician Erawa has decreed that all travelers may carry their weapons into Torgan, but you are not allowed to use them except for self-defense and they can be taken away from you if you are deemed a threat to the public."

"Wonderful," said Sadia, who had appeared between Keo and Dlaine suddenly. She slipped her arms through their own and said, "Then why don't we enter together? It's almost lunchtime and I, for one, am very hungry."

The first guard nodded, while the second guard walked over to a lever and pulled it down, allowing the gates to creak open. As soon as they had opened wide enough for Sadia to enter, she pulled both Keo and Dlaine in with her, smiling all the while at the guards, while the first guard looked embarrassed and the second looked annoyed. And although Sadia was clearly not a physical match for Keo or Dlaine, she managed to drag them along with her anyway because they were too surprised by this strange turn of events to stop her.

As for Torgan itself, it reminded Keo heavily of New Ora, except the streets were wider and nicer, and the houses and buildings appeared cleaner. There were also a lot more people walking about, a few looking at Keo and Dlaine being pulled along by Sadia, but most of the townspeople seemed to mind their own business and paid the new arrivals little attention.

But Keo did not get to see much else of the town, however, because Sadia immediately dragged Keo and Dlaine into an alleyway between two houses, well out of the sight of the guards and the general public. She then let go of them and peered out into the street before pulling her head back in and turning to face the two of them again. Only now, her smile was gone, replaced by an annoyed expression that contrasted sharply with her earlier kindly demeanor and her hands were on her hips.

"You idiots," said Sadia. She shoved them both in the chest. "I should have just let the guards take you. It's what you deserve for being so goddamn *stupid*."

"Hey," said Dlaine, regaining his balance and glaring at her. "Just where do you get off calling us idiots? We don't even know you. Nor did we ask for your help."

"I agree with Dlaine," said Keo, folding his arms over his chest. "While we appreciate the help, we *don't* appreciate a complete stranger like you insulting our intelligence for no reason."

Sadia sighed and rubbed her forehead. "Let me state it plainly: When you are a wanted criminal whose name is known in every town throughout the general area, do you really think that it is wise to go up to a couple of big, beefy guards, and announce to them that *you* are the criminal that they were warned about?"

"When you put it that way, it does make us sound foolish," Keo said. "But how were we supposed to know that we're wanted criminals? Or that the Enforcers in New Ora are talking to the guards in Torgan?"

"You should have known because that's how the Magicians operate," said Sadia, as if it was the most obvious thing in the world. "If one criminal from their territory escapes, they immediately alert their nearest fellow Magicians about it. It's an effective system that makes it hard for your average criminal to simply move to a different town and try to lay low because there will already be a ton of people looking out for them no matter where they go."

"I probably should have realized that," said Dlaine, scratching the back of his head sheepishly. "In my travels, I've seen that same system in action myself more than a few times. It's why I've —eh, well, I know what she's talking about."

"Thankfully, they don't have any drawings of you two yet, so the other Magicians and their Enforcers in this area can't identify you guys by sight," said Sadia. "But I really don't think you two should stay in Torgan for even a day. The guards have to report everyone who enters or exits Torgan to Magician Erawa at the end of every day, and she's the kind of Magician to investigate people like me who claim to work for Skran or other Magicians."

"Wait, so you *don't* work for Skran?" said Keo. "Was that all a lie?"

"Of course it was," said Sadia, waving off Keo's shock like it meant nothing. "But it kept you guys from having to spend the night in Torgan's dirtiest jail cell tonight, so I think you should be thanking me rather than acting all high and mighty because I lied."

"Right," said Keo. "Well, if you aren't one of Skran's servants, then who are you? Why did you even help us?" He looked at Dlaine. "Dlaine, you wouldn't happen to recognize her, would you?"

"If I had, I would have mentioned it already," said Dlaine. "I've never seen this girl in my life."

"I guess it's safe to introduce myself," said Sadia. "First off, my name is indeed Sadia of the Foot. So you don't have to worry about that."

"I wasn't, but thanks for letting us know anyway," said Keo.

"Anyway, I saved you two because, well, I'm not a big fan of the Magicians, to be honest," said Sadia. She looked around suddenly again, like she expected to see someone eavesdropping on her, even though the alleyway in which they stood was quite empty. "I've been secretly fighting against the Magicians because I don't approve of their rule. Me and several others."

"Rebels?" said Keo. "I've heard stories of groups of Rebels fighting against the Council's rule, but I didn't think I'd ever get to actually meet one."

"Well, we exist and we're here and everywhere," said Sadia. "We have men in New Ora who learned of your predicament and spread word of your capture to the other Rebels in the area. We didn't actually know where you were going, but Torgan seemed like a likely location, so I came here to see if I could intercept you before the city guards arrested you, which they nearly did."

"Why are you helping us, though?" said Keo, tilting his head to the side. "We're not Rebels, you know."

Sadia sighed heavily, like Keo was starting to test her patience. "The reason I am helping you is because we Rebels don't want the Magicians to unjustly imprison innocent people like you two anymore. We know that you two didn't do anything wrong and that you two are certainly not dangerous criminals who should be behind bars for the rest of your lives."

"So you basically helped us because you hate the Magicians, is that it?" said Dlaine.

"More or less," said Sadia with a shrug.

"Do you expect us to join you Rebels or something?" said Keo.

"No," said Sadia, shaking her head. "We understand that you guys are trying to reach Capitika, so we're not going to ask you to join us. We just wanted to mess with the Magicians' plans by helping you guys get into Torgan without being arrested."

"Well, that's rather kind of you," said Keo. "I—"

Dlaine tapped Keo on the shoulder, causing Keo to look at him and say, "Yes?"

"Can we talk in private for a moment?" said Dlaine. He then looked at Sadia pointedly. "And that does *not* include you."

Sadia shrugged like she didn't care.

"All right," said Keo. "Let's talk."

Keo and Dlaine walked several feet down the alleyway, away from Sadia, who had her hands in the pockets of her robes and was looking around like she expected something to jump out and attack her at any moment.

Then Dlaine stopped and said, in a harsh whisper, "I don't trust her."

Keo glanced at Sadia, who did not appear to be trying to listen to their conversation. "Why? She saved us from being thrown in jail."

"Because she's a Rebel," said Dlaine. "Tell me, what do you know about the Rebels?"

Keo frowned, thinking about everything that Master Tiram and the other people from New Ora had told him about the Rebels. "I know they aren't very well organized and tend to strike anywhere they please. I also know that no one knows their true numbers, so the Magicians don't know how to deal with them."

"Yeah, but there's a lot more to them than that," said Dlaine. He also glanced at Sadia and then leaned in closer to Keo and continued speaking, but in a much lower whisper. "The Rebels are crazy. They've been known to start riots and brawls everywhere they go, and without any good reason. I got caught in one of their riots back in Takzo a few years back and nearly got burned down with the inn I was staying at."

"Oh," said Keo, putting a hand on his mouth, though he made sure to keep his voice low so that Sadia did not hear him either. "What are the Rebels trying to do, exactly?"

"Destabilize the Magical Council's rule," said Dlaine. "They consider it illegitimate because the Council asserted its rule over South Lamaira after King Riuno's death."

"What do they want to replace it with?" asked Keo. "Their own king?"

"They don't have any idea of what they want to replace it with, as far as I know," said Dlaine in disgust. "And that's the problem. They demand that things change, but they don't seem to know what kind of change they want. They could end up backing a would-be tyrant and they wouldn't care as long as he wasn't a Magician."

Keo glanced at Sadia again, who still didn't seem to be eavesdropping. "Okay, but what does that have to do with us? Sadia already said that she doesn't expect us to join them."

"Yeah, but if Magician Erawa learns that we were helped by a Rebel, then that's just going to make it that much harder for us to get to Capitika," Dlaine said, nodding at Sadia. "Remember, the Magical Council has given orders to all Magicians and their Enforcers to arrest any Rebels or anyone related to the Rebels that they find, which includes *us* at the moment, in case you didn't know."

Keo put a hand over his mouth. "Oh my god. What do we do, then?"

"Leave Sadia alone, get what supplies we need from here, and then leave Torgan and never look back," said Dlaine. "Right now, it seems like the government of Torgan doesn't know that Sadia is a Rebel, so we might be able to leave before anyone starts asking questions. Even so, every minute we spend in this town now makes it that much more likely that the government will arrest us, especially if they learn that we are indeed the Keo and Dlaine that Skran warned them about."

"All right," said Keo. "Sounds like a good idea. But why don't we say good bye to Sadia first? Just to thank her for getting us out of that tight situation."

Dlaine looked like he would rather that they did not, but then he shrugged and said, "You can do it if you want. As for me, I'm just going to wait here."

Keo nodded and then walked back over to Sadia, who had not yet moved from where she stood. She looked up at Keo as he approached and said, "Yes?"

"Sadia, I just wanted to thank you for helping us, but this is where we have to part ways I'm afraid," said Keo. "For safety reasons, you must understand."

Sadia nodded. "Oh, sure. I understand completely. Besides, I have some things I need to do as well, things that I need to do without you, so I was planning to leave you two alone anyway. But if you ever need help, just go to The Overflowing Mug."

With that, Sadia turned and walked down the alleyway back into the crowded street and soon vanished among the throngs of people. It was amazing how easily she vanished from view, almost like magic, even though Keo was quite sure that Sadia was not a Magician herself.

Shaking his head, Keo turned and walked back to Dlaine and said, "Where to next?"

"We find the marketplace, get whatever we need, and leave," Dlaine said. "And we do it quickly, before sundown. If we do, then by the time the Enforcers realize who we are—if they realize who we are—we will be long gone."

Keo nodded and soon the two were walking down the alleyway back into the streets of Torgan, except now they were heading toward the marketplace, which according to Dlaine was near the Torgan Theater, on the west side of the town. No one seemed to pay attention to the two of them exiting the alleyway, but they made sure not to draw any attention to themselves just the same.

Even so, Keo thought he felt someone watching them. He looked around and spotted an elderly woman standing in the window on the second floor of a nearby building, looking down directly at Dlaine and him. But then she backed away out of view, which made Keo wonder if whether she had backed away because she did not want to be seen by him.

But he did not mention it to Dlaine, because he figured that that was simply a strange older woman who likely lived by herself and was probably of no threat to him or anyone else.

Chapter Eleven

THE TORGAN MARKETPLACE WAS similar to the marketplace in New Ora, only much larger. There were dozens of stalls and an equal number of merchants hawking anything from weapons to vegetables to fruits to clothing and everything in between. Most of the merchants were natives of Torgan, from what Keo could tell, but he noticed a handful of Hasfarian merchants selling Hasfarian robes and jewelry, plus some foreigners that he didn't recognize at all. The smells of bread, oranges, apples, carrots, and various other types of food filled the air, along with the sounds of merchants hawking their wares, customers buying or trading for the things they wanted or needed, and the occasional loud argument between merchants and their customers over the correct price for this or that item. It reminded Keo of New Ora, except louder, larger, and slightly more chaotic.

The most striking difference, however, was the large Torgan Theater that towered over the entire place. According to Dlaine, the marketplace had been established outside of the Theater due to the Theater's popularity. The idea was that the merchants would try to sell their wares to people entering or leaving the Theater due to the Theater's high volume of traffic, which made sense to Keo, although he did wonder whether you could hear all of the noise from the marketplace from inside the Theater or not.

In any event, Dlaine seemed to take the noisiness and largeness of the marketplace in stride. He told Keo that they needed to stock up on meat and bread, so they walked to the nearest merchant who sold such things. Unfortunately, they were not the only people interested in buying meat and bread, because they found themselves standing in a rather long line of people who held baskets of meat and bread in their arms, waiting to pay for their goods. Dlaine picked out what they needed—mostly bacon and biscuits, which seemed to be Dlaine's favorite food for some reason—and they stood at the back of the line, which seemed to be moving rather slowly. Keo was restless, because he wanted to leave Torgan as soon as possible, but they could not do that until they had bought their supplies. Dlaine had also mentioned needing to refill their water thermoses as well, which made Keo feel even more impatient than ever.

As he and Dlaine stood there, Keo looked around the marketplace, hoping to find something he could focus on to relieve his boredom, as the line wasn't moving very quickly. Although there were a lot of interesting things on sale at this place, Keo had a hard time focusing on any of it because he was so impatient to leave the town and continue on their journey to Capitika. He did briefly wonder where Jola might be, as he had not heard anything from her since they entered Torgan, but he decided that Jola was probably all right, as Dlaine had not yet expressed any concern over her disappearance.

That was when Keo felt like he was being watched. He looked over his shoulder, toward the Hasfarian fruit stand where a Hasfarian merchant was haggling with a couple of Torganians over the price of his spiked pears. But he wasn't focused on the merchant or his customers.

Instead, Keo was looking at the old woman standing just to the side of the fruit stand. She had long gray hair and wore white robes and was staring directly at Keo like she was spying on him. She looked just like the woman he had seen in the window on the second floor of that building, but Keo was unsure if she was the same woman or not.

"Hey, Dlaine," said Keo, tapping Dlaine on the shoulder.

"What?" said Dlaine, glancing at Keo as he took a step forward, because the line was starting to move now. "Did you see something you want?"

"No," said Keo, shaking his head. He gestured toward the old woman, who was still staring at them. "That old lady is staring at us."

Dlaine looked over at the old woman and frowned. "What old lady?"

"That—" Keo stopped speaking when he noticed that the old woman was gone. He then looked around, but did not see her anywhere nearby. "Huh? Where'd she go?"

"Are you sure you saw an old lady over there?" said Dlaine. "Maybe it's just the stress of our encounter with the gate guards earlier getting to you. Or maybe you're just hungry. It's almost lunchtime, after all, and we haven't eaten yet."

Keo rubbed his belly, which ached with hunger. "I guess that might have something to do with it, but I don't know. I saw the old lady in the window of a building in town. She was staring at us even then."

"Why didn't you mention her before, then?" said Dlaine in annoyance.

"I didn't think that she was that important," said Keo. "So I didn't mention her."

"Well, even if she *does* exist, I doubt she's harmful," said Dlaine. "Probably just the town idiot. Every town has one, you know."

"I don't remember New Ora having one," said Keo.

"Well, I hate to be the one to break it to you, Keo, but if you don't know who the idiot of your town is, then that usually means that it is you," said Dlaine. He shrugged. "Not that I think you're dumb, but …"

Keo was about to snap at Dlaine for calling him an idiot when he felt someone tap him on the shoulder. He looked over his shoulder and saw, to his surprise, that it was the old lady from before. She was now standing so close to him that Keo could smell the stench of dirt on her, which made him step back in revulsion.

"Is that her?" said Dlaine, looking over Keo's shoulder at the old woman. "Huh. How'd she get over here so quickly?"

Keo was about to ask that same question before the old woman held out a hand and said, in a very ancient voice, "Please, kind man, could you spare me a penny? I am a homeless and poor old widow who must rely on the kindness of strangers to survive."

A part of Keo wanted to give her some of his money—even though he was hardly a rich man himself—but then he hesitated. He did not know or trust this woman. There was something about her that didn't seem quite right to him, although he could not place it. Perhaps it was the way in which she spoke, like she had memorized a speech that she was reciting. Of course, with her old gray robes, she certainly looked like a homeless widow who relied on the kindness of strangers in order to survive, but Keo was still unsure if he should trust her or not.

He decided that he could not trust her and thus said, "I am sorry, miss, but I, unfortunately, don't have a whole lot of money to share with you. I'm just a traveler passing through and not a very wealthy man myself."

The old woman lowered her hand, looking rather disappointed by Keo's answer. "Oh, well. I suppose I will go and find someone else who will be kind enough to spare some of their money with a poor, homeless widow like me. May the Good King's spirit bless you nonetheless."

With that, the old woman turned and left. Keo watched her go for a moment, still not sure what to make of her, but then shook his head and decided that she was simply a homeless widow who needed money. Master Tiram had often told him that those who lacked homes often suffered in ways that those who did have homes did not. It affected their minds and their souls, making them behave in odd—and sometimes even criminal—ways.

In any case, the woman was leaving, so Keo did not see any reason to continue to worry about her. He turned to face the rest of the line and rested his hand on the handle of Gildshine.

Or he would have, if Gildshine had still been there. His hand met empty air and he looked down to see that Gildshine—sheath and all—was completely missing.

"Dlaine," said Keo, tapping Dlaine on the shoulder. "Dlaine, have you seen Gildshine?"

"Isn't it sheathed in your belt?" said Dlaine without looking at Keo. He took another step forward as the line progressed.

"No," said Keo, shaking his head in frustration. "It's … it's *gone*."

"Gone?" Dlaine looked over his shoulder down at Keo's belt. His eyes widened when he saw that Gildshine was gone. "How the hell did you lose a *sword*, especially one as large as Gildshine?"

Keo shrugged helplessly. "I don't know. It was there when we entered town and it was also there when we entered the marketplace."

"Are you sure you didn't just drop it somewhere maybe?" said Dlaine.

Keo nodded. "Certain of it, in fact. Gildshine's sheath is always attached very tightly to my belt. There's no way it could have simply fallen off. I make sure it can't fall off easily."

"Then did someone steal it?" said Dlaine.

Keo looked around the marketplace urgently, saying, "Well, I'm not sure, but—Hey!"

A teenaged boy—probably thirteen or fourteen—was walking away rather hurriedly from Keo and Dlaine into the crowd of shoppers buying things. The boy held Gildshine in his hands, a surprising feat for such a young kid, but then the teenaged boy looked quite muscular for his age.

In any event, as soon as Keo shouted at the boy, the boy immediately broke into a run. Keo looked at Dlaine and said, "Stay here and pay for our food. I'll go after the little thief."

Dlaine looked like he was about to argue with that, but Keo did not stay to listen. He darted away from their place in the line, his long legs carrying him across the stone road upon which the marketplace was built. He saw the teenaged boy pushing his way through the crowd, earning a lot of surprised or angry looks from the shoppers, but the boy did not seem to care who he annoyed or angered. As a result, the shoppers did not slow down the boy very much, although Keo figured he could still catch up to the boy as long as he didn't slow down.

Like the boy, Keo also shoved past any shoppers in his way. He didn't want to, but he knew that if he lost Gildshine, then he would never be able to prove to Nesma that the demons were coming back, and then all of Lamaira would be destroyed. One old man who he pushed aside actually whacked Keo in the back with his cane, and the old man must have either been ridiculously strong or perhaps simply wielded a thick cane, because the blow almost knocked Keo's breath out. As a result, Keo briefly lost sight of the boy, but he ignored the pain in his back and ran as quickly as he could in the direction he'd seen the boy run.

Then Keo saw the boy dart out of the marketplace and toward the Torganians' houses. The boy was clearly trying to lose Keo in the alleyways of the town, and what was worse was that the boy had a real chance of doing that, because Keo did not know Torgan's layout as well as the boy and he might end up wasting a lot of time searching for the boy or maybe never even find him again.

But even when the boy disappeared into the alleyway between two buildings, Keo nonetheless followed. When he entered the alleyway, he spotted the boy at the end take a turn to the right, prompting Keo to run even faster to catch up.

Keo managed to keep the boy in sight at all times, which surprised even himself. He suspected that the boy, though obviously quick, was being slowed down by Gildshine's weight, which explained why he was having a hard time losing Keo. A part of Keo hoped that the boy would simply toss Gildshine aside and escape, but Keo knew that the boy was not going to give up his new treasure that easily.

At one point the boy knocked over a large garbage can in Keo's path, spilling out rotten fruit, bones, and other trash onto the street. But Keo leaped over it without trouble and resumed running after the boy when he touched the street again.

After several more seconds of chase, the boy suddenly darted into the interior of one of the buildings. Keo almost tripped over his own feet as he stopped and looked into the building, which from a brief glance, told him that it was empty. In any case, even if the building was full of people, Keo would have entered because there was no way that he was going to lose Gildshine to some little brat.

Keo dashed inside after the boy, but found himself in a dark room, although he heard the sounds of the boy running ahead and he simply ran as well, heedless of whatever was there.

Thankfully, Keo did not run into or trip over anything, and in another minute he burst outside onto the back streets again, only this time he had briefly lost sight of the boy. Looking around, Keo realized that he was standing behind the Torgan Theater and noticed the boy wrench open the Theater's back door and dash inside before Keo could shout at him to stop.

Again, Keo was hesitant about entering someone else's property without permission, but the only alternative was to turn back and never see Gildshine again. And if he never saw Gildshine again, then that meant that all of Lamaira was doomed to fall to the demons.

So Keo dashed down the street to the back door of the Theater. He wrenched it open and ran inside and found himself standing in a dimly-lit area. It was a narrow hallway, going both ways, though it was full of things like chairs, strange masks hanging on the walls (including at least one mask that looked like the tortured face of a dying child), and a bucket of water and a mop, like whoever cleaned up the place had left his things here for some reason.

Keo looked to the left and to the right, but he unfortunately could not see any sign of the boy. It was like he had vanished into thin air, which made Keo wonder if he would never see Gildshine again.

No, Keo, don't think such negative thoughts, Keo thought, wiping the sweat off his forehead, sweat he had accumulated from running around so much in the hot summer sun. *You just need to look around. The boy is probably still in here somewhere, most likely hiding.*

But Keo first listened for the sounds of any other people who might be in here. The Theater, however, was silent; perhaps there were no plays scheduled for today. That made Keo feel safer, because he did not want whoever owned or worked in this building to see him and think he was a thief of some sort and call the Enforcers to arrest him.

But the lack of sound was also a bad thing because Keo could not hear any sounds that the boy might be making. He again looked both ways, but he was still uncertain about which direction the boy might have gone.

The longer I stand here trying to figure this out, the more time that boy has to put distance between me and him, Keo thought.

And if I let him get away with that, then I can kiss Gildshine—and Lamaira as a whole—good bye.

That was when Keo heard the scuffing of a boot against the wooden floor. It sounded like it was coming from the left end of the hall, but he could not see anyone who might have made that sound. It didn't sound very heavy, however, so Keo assumed that it had been made by the boy, who was likely hiding somewhere nearby.

But I'm not going to let him know I heard him, Keo thought. *Instead, I'm going to sneak up on him and get him when he least expects it.*

So Keo slowly walked down the hall to the left, making sure that his footsteps were inaudible, but also avoiding the various props scattered around his feet. He walked only a couple of feet before he heard the scuffing sound again, and this time, he located its source more specifically: It was coming from what appeared to be a closet door on the left wall, about a dozen feet down from his current position.

There he is, Keo thought with a triumphant smile. *Got you, you little brat.*

Keo continued walking toward the closet, only this time he was a bit faster than before. He thought it was rather foolish of the boy to hide in that closet, which probably lacked any escape route, but then, young boys like him could be very foolish (Keo should know, seeing as Master Tiram had berated him many times for making similar mistakes when he was the same age as this boy).

Keo stopped in front of the door and listened, but did not hear any sounds from the other side of the door. Maybe the boy had heard him approaching and was keeping quiet so Keo wouldn't hear him.

Stupid kid, Keo thought. *Should have picked a better hiding place.*

Keo put one hand on the doorknob, which was wooden and old. He listened again, but still heard nothing. It was like the boy was not hiding in there at all, but Keo knew better.

Keo yanked open the door, shouting, "All right, kid, I got you! Now give me back my sword or I'll—"

Keo stopped speaking when he saw that the closet was completely empty, save for an old, dusty-looking broom that appeared to have been unused for quite a while. And the closet was too small for the boy to hide anywhere, which Keo confirmed by poking his head into the hot closet and looking around. He could barely fit in there himself, so he pulled his head out and stared at the empty broom closet in confusion.

"What the hell?" said Keo. "Where is the—"

Something solid and heavy slammed into the back of Keo's head, knocking him out instantly.

Chapter Twelve

KEO, WAKE UP," SAID a familiar voice above him. "Wake up, you damn idiot. Why are you lying in the street like a drunk beggar?"

Keo's head hurt and it hurt even more hearing the loud voice above him. He opened his eyes, but it was hard because it felt like someone had tied heavy sandbags to his eyelids. And when he succeeded in opening his eyes, his vision was briefly blurry, showing him only a mixture of blur and gray and brown that made no sense to him whatsoever.

Then Keo blinked several times and his vision cleared up. He was looking up into the face of Dlaine, who was frowning like he was upset about something, although Keo was not sure what had upset him.

"D-Dlaine?" said Keo. His head throbbed, causing him to grab it and wince. "What happened? Where am I?"

"Lying in the street like a beggar, that's where you are," said Dlaine, poking Keo in the chest. "And I don't know what happened. Jola just found you like this and led me to you, though I noticed that you've got a huge bump on your head."

Blinking again, Keo looked around at his surroundings. He was indeed lying in the street, as Dlaine said, lying in the street just outside the Torgan Theater's backstage entrance. As far as he could tell, he and Dlaine were the only two people in this particular street at the moment, although he figured that Jola was probably somewhere nearby as well even if he couldn't see her.

"Can you remember anything?" said Dlaine. "The last I saw, you were running off after that kid who stole your sword."

Keo tried to remember, but it was hard because his head hurt so badly. "I remember following the kid into the Theater. Then I thought he was in the broom closet, but then he wasn't, and someone hit me with something heavy and next thing I know I'm here. I don't even remember being dragged out here, even though that seems to be what happened."

"Sounds to me like the kid got the jump on you," said Dlaine, stroking his chin. "Or maybe that kid has a friend who got you. Maybe it was even that old lady from earlier. Remember, the one who begged us for money?"

"You think she's related to the kid?" said Keo, rubbing his head and frowning.

"Yes," said Dlaine, nodding. "I've seen these sorts of partnerships among beggars before. One of them comes up and distracts you by asking for some money, while her friend comes up behind you and takes your wallet while you're not looking. I've never heard of a beggar stealing a magical sword, though. That's a new one."

"You sound like you have personal experience in this," said Keo.

Dlaine scowled. "Let's just say that there's a reason I keep my money bag tied firmly to my waist at all times and leave it at that. Anyway, do you know where the kid might have gone?"

Keo shook his head. "No. Like I said, I was knocked out, so I don't know where the kid is. He might not even be in town anymore for all I know."

"I sent Jola to go look for him," said Dlaine. "She's currently searching the whole town for him and will report back to us by the end of the day with her results."

"What?" said Keo. "The end of the day? I can't wait until the end of the day to get Gildshine back. What if the kid leaves town before then?"

"Well, I don't have any better ideas for finding the kid," said Dlaine with a shrug. "I've visited Torgan before, but I still don't know it nearly as well as its inhabitants."

"There's got to be someone we can ask about that," said Keo. He sat up and groaned as the pain in his head spiked. "Don't you know anyone in town who might be able to identify the boy for us?"

"Nope," said Dlaine, shaking his head. "I don't know very many people here. Most of the time I just pass through, though once I did stay to see a play in the Theater."

"Really?" said Keo. "What was it called?"

"I can't remember," said Dlaine. "All I remember was being bored out of my mind. The seating was really uncomfortable, too."

"It doesn't matter," said Keo. "We need to find someone in town here who can help us find and identify the boy. Even if Jola is searching for him, I think we'll have a much easier time finding him if all three of us are working together to do it."

"Sounds like a plan," said Dlaine. "One question, though: Who can we ask about the boy?"

Keo thought about that. Neither he nor Dlaine knew anyone in Torgan, much less anyone who would be willing and able to help them find a sword thief. The question stumped Keo for a good few seconds before he remembered someone who might know.

"Sadia," said Keo, looking at Dlaine. "Remember her? She's a native of Torgan, isn't she? She might be able to tell us who that kid is, maybe even where he lives."

"Sadia?" said Dlaine. He frowned. "We don't know where to find her, so unless you happen to have some magical locating abilities that you conveniently forgot about until this very moment—"

"Actually, I know exactly where to find her," said Keo. He rose to his feet, still rubbing the bump on his head from where he had been hit. "Follow me. We're going to ask directions to a place."

After receiving directions from one of the merchants in the marketplace, Keo and Dlaine went to the west side of Torgan, away from the Theater, and soon found themselves in a quieter, dirtier part of the town. The buildings were grimy and old, with broken windows or doors that just barely stood in their frames. The scrawniest dog that Keo had ever seen in his life—which had been lying on the doorstep of an equally dismal-looking house— looked up at them as they passed. It stood up and barked at them loudly, but it did not actually chase after them, which Keo was grateful, because the dog's teeth looked as sharp as knives despite the dog's scrawniness.

"Keo, are you sure we should be going to this part of town?" said Dlaine. "This looks like the place where all of the town's local lowlifes come to hang out."

"Sadia said that if we ever needed help we should go to The

Overflowing Mug," Keo said. "And The Overflowing Mug, according to that merchant, is in this part of town. Because that's where we're going to find help, we should be here."

"I'm not sure that this is such a wise idea," said Dlaine. "You know how I feel about the Rebels. A bunch of idiots rebelling against an authority that they have no intention of replacing with anything better."

"You sure sound like a Magician loyalist when you speak that way," Keo said.

"I'm no more loyal to the Magical Council than they are," said Dlaine, stuffing his hands into his pockets and looking around the area, probably keeping an eye out for any criminals. "But unlike them, I lived through the collapse of the Kingdom back in the day and I don't want to live through another."

Keo looked at Dlaine in surprise, though in truth, he probably shouldn't have been. He pegged Dlaine at being in his fifties, which meant that it was no surprise he had been alive during the Kingdom's collapse some twenty years back. Master Tiram had told Keo many stories about the collapse of the Kingdom of Lamaira, how it had been a dark and bloody time, with many people dying as various factions fought for control over what was left of the Kingdom. There was still war today between the three factions that had arisen out of the ashes of the Kingdom, but Master Tiram always said that it wasn't as bad now as it was back then, though it still wasn't as good as the Kingdom had been either.

Despite that, Keo was still very curious about the Kingdom, so he said, "Where were you when the Kingdom collapsed?"

"Remember what I said about how there is certain information you don't need to know?" said Dlaine. "That's part of it. It's not even particularly relevant anyway. The past is past and right now we need to focus on getting your sword back."

Keo nodded, but he still wondered if he would ever learn the true story behind Dlaine. It must have been very interesting, but Dlaine was obviously not in any mood to discuss it. Keo wished he was, but he knew there was no way that he could make Dlaine tell him anything, so Keo decided to drop the subject for now and focus on finding The Overflowing Mug instead.

And soon enough, Keo saw The Overflowing Mug's sign, a wooden board with a mug of overflowing beer painted on it, with the words *The Overflowing Mug* written underneath the picture in bold lettering. Although the sign was clearly very old, Keo could tell that a great deal of effort had been put into it by whoever had designed it, which seemed at odds with the shabby and cheap appearance of the rest of this part of town.

Neither Keo nor Dlaine hesitated to enter the bar. As soon as they did, Keo's nose was assaulted by the combined stink of smoke and beer, causing him to cover his nose. He looked around the tavern's main room, trying to see if he could spot Sadia anywhere.

The Overflowing Mug was a medium-sized tavern with about a dozen tables scattered around and a bar at the back where a large man who was clearly the bartender stood. The bartender was reading some kind of book, which struck Keo as strange because he never thought of bartenders as being particularly literate (though he may have been basing that impression off of his experiences with New Ora's bartender, a dim-witted man named Kaff who nonetheless was very good at making beer).

As for the tavern's other patrons, there were only a few: A man in his thirties sitting by himself at one table, looking half-drunk already, two other men who looked closer to Dlaine's age discussing politics, and a woman sitting at the bar, again by herself, with her back to the rest of the bar. It seemed strange to Keo that a woman would be drinking by herself here, but Keo had a feeling that The Overflowing Mug was not quite like other taverns he had visited before.

In any case, no one seemed to notice Dlaine and him enter, so Keo simply walked up to the bar and took a seat, as did Dlaine. As soon as they were seated, the bartender looked up from his book at them, which appeared to have a lot of text in tiny print.

"Welcome," said the bartender, whose voice was very deep and jolly, again in stark contrast to the general griminess of the place. "What would you like to drink?"

"We're not here to drink," said Keo. "We're looking for a woman named Sadia. She said that we could find help if we came here."

"Sadia?" said the bartender. He scowled briefly before his smile returned suddenly. "Where did you meet her? You wouldn't happen to be a couple of … *Enforcers*, would you?"

The bartender said the word 'Enforcers' like it was some kind of awful racial slur. Keo didn't feel offended, however, because he didn't care much for the Enforcers himself.

"No, we're not," said Keo, shaking his head. "We're just a couple of travelers who Sadia saved from being arrested earlier when we came to Torgan. She told us to come here if we need help, and because we need some help, we decided to take her advice and come here, because we don't know anyone else in

Torgan who could help us."

The bartender eyed them both rather suspiciously, as if trying to detect any lies in Keo's story. That made Keo wonder whether the bartender was expecting Enforcers to show up and shut down his tavern, although Keo was not sure why, because as far as he knew taverns were perfectly legal to operate in Torgan. Of course, Keo was not an expert on Torgan law, so for all he knew the bartender might be up to something illegal, although he didn't really care either way.

Then the bartender nodded slowly and said, "I know Sadia. Very kind, always trying to help out others. And also really hates the Magical Council."

"We noticed," said Dlaine.

"As for help … I suppose if Sadia referred you, then I should help you," said the bartender. "Besides, neither of you look like Enforcers, so I can probably trust you."

Again that emphasis on the Enforcers. That pretty much confirmed for Keo that the bartender was definitely up to some less-than-legal business, or maybe it was the bartender's association with Sadia, a Rebel, that made him so paranoid about Enforcers walking into his tavern and talking to him. In any case, Keo was just glad that the bartender was going to help them.

"But I should introduce myself," said the bartender. "My name is Sherf, Sherf of the Tavern. What can I help you with?"

Keo was about to introduce Dlaine and himself to Sherf, but then Dlaine gave him a look that said that it would not be wise to tell Sherf their real identities after they had lied to the gatekeepers. It seemed unlikely to Keo that Sherf or anyone else here would tell Torgan's Enforcers about their lie, but then Keo realized that he did not know any of the people in the tavern, so he decided to keep their true identities a secret for now.

"Nice to meet you, Sherf," said Keo. "Anyway, we came here because we're looking for someone."

Sherf raised an eyebrow. "Who might this 'someone' be?"

"We don't know," said Keo. He gestured at his belt, where Gildshine was usually kept. "Earlier today, my sword was stolen by a boy of about thirteen or fourteen with short brown hair. I chased him down to the Torgan Theater, but then I lost him. We're trying to find out who he is so we can retrieve my sword."

"A boy thief, huh?" said Sherf, stroking his stubble-covered chin. "Why do you need the sword? Can't you replace it?"

"No," said Keo, shaking his head. "It's irreplaceable and we can't leave Torgan without it."

"I see," said Sherf. "Well, I think I know who you are talking about. You said the boy thief looked about thirteen or fourteen with short brown hair, right?"

"Right," said Keo. "That's what he looked like."

"Then I *definitely* know him," said Sherf with a scowl. "That's my son."

Keo and Dlaine exchanged surprised looks, but then Keo looked at Sherf again and said, "Excuse me?"

Sherf slammed shut his book and said, "Damn it, I *told* him to stop stealing things from strangers, but that boy likes to pretend he was born without ears. I don't know what's possessed that boy to do this, but I'm gonna give him a whipping next time I see him."

"Next time you see him?" said Keo. "You mean you haven't seen your son today?"

"I saw him at breakfast, but he left after I told him to pick up some groceries at the marketplace," said Sherf. He rubbed his forehead and sighed. "Should have expected him to try to steal something, I guess, but a *sword*? Now *that's* a new one. If I were a thief rather than a good father, I might be impressed."

"But why would you son steal from us?" said Keo. "Especially if you don't approve."

Sherf looked away. "Financial troubles. Kid knows we don't have a lot of money, so he steals valuables from travelers and tries to sell them to get some. He's just trying to help, but he always gets me in trouble. Last time he did this I gave him a good beating, but apparently there are just some things you can't beat out of a kid."

"But where is your son right now?" said Dlaine, looking around the tavern as if he thought he might see the kid. "Do you have any idea where he might be?"

Sherf tapped his chin. "Hmm … if he hasn't returned yet—and I doubt he will—then he's probably gone to Old Cyclops."

"Who?" said Keo.

"Oh, that's right," said Sherf. "You two aren't from around here, are you? Although …" Sherf looked at Dlaine more closely. "You look familiar."

"I've been through Torgan before," said Dlaine curtly. "Anyway, who is Old Cyclops?"

"A black market dealer," said Sherf. "He buys pretty much anything you bring to him, regardless of where you got it. And he can pay pretty good money for it, too, especially if it is something valuable like a sword."

"What does Old Cyclops do with the stuff he buys?" said Keo.

"I don't know for sure, but I've heard he sells it to the various brigands that roam around the countryside between here and New Ora," said Sherf. "And sometimes also to travelers from other parts of the country who don't mind buying illegal goods."

"So if your son sells my sword to Cyclops, then it might be gone forever?" said Keo.

"Well, in all of the years I've known him, no one has ever succeeded in retrieving their stolen things from Cyclops once he gets a hold of them," said Sherf. "So yes, if my idiot of a son sells your sword to him, there's a good chance you will never see it again even if you live to be a hundred."

Keo jumped off his bar stool and said, "Then we need to go to Old Cyclops' place right away. Can you tell us where it is?"

"It's about five blocks down the street," said Sherf, gesturing toward the door. "If you see a building with a door with one eye painted on it, that's the place. But I don't recommend you go there."

"Why not?" said Keo. "It's my sword and I cannot afford to lose it. In fact, *Lamaira* cannot afford for me to lose it."

Sherf tilted his head to the side when Keo said that, but he didn't say anything about it. Instead, he said, "Because Old Cyclops is a mean, nasty old guy and he has a bunch of bodyguards who don't take kindly to people trying to take stuff from him that he considers his own. You two look strong, but his men are ruthless. Don't mess with them."

"We'll just have to deal with them if they get in our way," said Keo. He looked at Dlaine. "Right?"

Dlaine sighed, but slid off his bar stool anyway. "Guess so, even though I've lived a good portion of my life avoiding this kind of trouble."

Sherf shook his head in disapproval. "All right, then, but don't come crying back to me after Old Cy's men knock your teeth in and leave you in the gutter like so much trash. But if you do see my son—his name is Naye—tell him to come home and that I want a word with him right away."

Although Sherf sounded like a stern father, Keo also noticed a hint of worry in the bartender's voice, like he was concerned that Naye was getting involved in something too dangerous for a boy his age.

So Keo nodded and said, "We'll tell him that if we see him."

Then Keo looked at Dlaine and said, "Now what are we waiting for? We have no time to lose. Let's go."

Chapter Thirteen

J
UST AS SHERF SAID, about five blocks down from The Overflowing Mug was yet another old-looking, trashy building, with a bloodshot eye painted on its surface. There were no people standing around outside it, but if Sherf was telling the truth, that meant nothing except that Old Cyclops apparently didn't see the need for outside guards.

Keo immediately walked up to the door and slammed his fist on its a few times. He was in no mood for niceties or pleasantries, because he knew that the consequences for losing Gildshine would be absolutely catastrophic.

"Hello?" said Keo. "Anyone in there? Let us in or else!"

A second after he said that, a silt in the door opened and two eyes peered out. The eyes looked angry and annoyed, but Keo did not back away.

"Who the hell are you?" said the eyes. "One of Cy's customers?"

"No," said Keo, shaking his head. "But I want to speak with Old Cyclops anyway. He might have something of mine that was sold to him."

"Lots of people fit *that* description," the eyes said. "But sorry, if you're not here to buy or sell, then you can just go and head on right back to where you came from, kid."

With a harsh laugh, the slit closed, leaving Keo standing there fuming.

Keo stepped back and said, "Dlaine, help me. I'm going to knock down the door and fight anyone who gets in my way."

But Dlaine grabbed Keo's arm and said, "Hold on, kid. That's suicide and you know it."

"Suicide?" said Keo, looking at Dlaine in annoyance. "What are you talking about?"

"Listen, kid, I know how these types of thugs operate, and believe me when I say that they don't take kindly to uninvited guests," said Dlaine, shaking his head. "They'll do more than just beat you. They'll kill you and hide your body. We don't even know how many guys Old Cyclops has anyway, although I can assure you that they are all probably armed and wanted for murder."

"But they have Gildshine," said Keo, wrenching his arm out of Dlaine's hand. "I can't just let them have my sword and sell it to the highest bidder. I need it to get it back and I need to get it back *now*."

"I'm not saying you shouldn't try to get it back," said Dlaine, holding up his hands. "But I *am* saying that you should be *smart* about it."

"What do you mean?" said Keo.

"We need to sneak in without them noticing," said Dlaine. "Then we locate Gildshine, grab it, and run."

Keo looked back at the eye on the door. Although it was merely the painting of an eye and not the real thing, Keo felt like it was mocking him, as if amused by his frustration.

So Keo said, "All right, then. But let's hurry, because we have no idea if Naye has sold Gildshine to Old Cyclops yet."

Keo and Dlaine found the back door of Old Cylcops' building, although it was locked. But then Dlaine picked the lock with a lock pick he happened to have on hand (which Keo did not question, as he knew it was another one of those things that Dlaine would not explain) and opened the door, allowing them to enter silently.

The two of them entered a dark backroom that was empty of other people. Keo found this odd because he thought that Old Cyclops would have guards everywhere, but perhaps he thought that the locked door would be enough to keep out any potential intruders. Of course, it was too dark to see if there was anyone in there with them, but considering how no one had jumped out of the shadows to attack them yet, Keo figured they were alone.

The only source of light came through the crack of another door, which Keo and Dlaine silently approached. Voices could be heard from within, voices that sounded like they were arguing over something. Dlaine gestured for Keo to be quiet and Keo nodded to show he understood. He pointed at the crack, trying to indicate that he was going to look through it to see who was talking, and Dlaine gave him the thumbs up to show that he understood.

So Keo walked up to the crack and peered through it. He could not see much due to how tiny the crack was, but he did see that it was a large living room, with a sofa and several chairs scattered around, plus a couple of bookcases leaning against one wall.

Then Keo saw four people in the center of the room. Two looked like Old Cyclops' bodyguards, because they stood behind an elderly-looking man who had only one bloodshot eye and a cane. The bodyguards were tall and large, with scars on their faces that made them look fierce and deadly. Both of them carried thick clubs at their sides, which looked heavy enough to turn a person's head into pulp.

As for the old man, he actually looked tougher than them, even though he was smaller and skinnier than them. As Keo had noted before, the man only had one bloodshot eye, with a black eye patch covering his other. Keo guessed that the man was Old Cyclops, mostly because of his one eye, but also because the man sat with an air of authority that was obvious even from a distance. Old Cyclops carried a silver cane in his lap that looked quite fancy and expensive, which made Keo wonder where he could have gotten it, because it looked even more expensive than the building they were in.

Sitting across from Old Cyclops was a teenaged boy who Keo recognized as Naye. The boy looked a little nervous, probably because of the way in which Old Cyclops was looking at him, but he also looked like he had been here many times before and so was familiar with the way things were done. The boy did look a bit like Sherf, except younger and with less hair and in much better shape.

But what caught Keo's attention the most was Gildshine. His sword lay on the table between Old Cyclops and Naye, still sheathed and apparently undamaged from what he could tell. Keo wanted to dash out, grab it, and run right away. Indeed, he almost opened the door before Dlaine grabbed his wrist, causing him to look at Dlaine.

"Don't," Dlaine whispered. "Not yet."

Keo bit his lower lip, but he nodded. As much as he wanted to grab Gildshine right away, he also understood that it would not make sense to show themselves just yet. While Keo could only see Old Cyclops' two bodyguards there, that did not mean there were not other men in the nearby rooms who would be more than willing to teach Keo and Dlaine a lesson about interrupting their employer's business deals.

So Keo listened to Old Cyclops, who had a deep voice like a well, as he spoke with Naye.

"So," said Old Cyclops, his one eye flicking between Gildshine on the table and Naye sitting before him. "Where did you say you got this sword from again?"

"I stole it," said Naye. His voice cracked, which made him sound even more nervous than he usually did. "Stole it from a traveler from out of town."

Old Cyclops reached over and lifted up Gildshine, which made Keo angry, but again he stayed where he was. He watched as Old Cyclops brought the sword closer to his eye, his veined hands wrapped tightly around its sheath and handle.

"Was he a *rich* man?" said Old Cyclops, turning the sword over. "Because this blade looks quite unique. Reminds me of the swords used by the Knights of the Old Kingdom."

"I don't know, but he didn't look rich to me," said Naye. "I think he was a bounty hunter or mercenary or something."

Old Cyclops pulled the sword out of its sheath partway and his one eye widened when he saw Gildshine's shiny surface. Then he looked up at Naye, suspicion in his eye.

"This doesn't look like the kind of sword that a mere bounty hunter or mercenary would carry," said Old Cyclops. "Looks like something that a Magician would use. And not just any Magician, but one of the members of the Magical Council."

"I'm telling you what I saw," said Naye. His voice kept cracking, like he was going through puberty there and then, though it was probably because he was afraid of Old Cyclops. "And he didn't look like much. He almost looked like a beggar, even."

Dlaine suppressed a chuckle, causing Keo to glare at him, but then he returned his attention to the business deal as Old Cyclops spoke again.

"Must have been a thief, then," Old Cyclops said. He sheathed the sword again and placed it back on the table. "Probably stole this sword from a rich person or maybe from a Magician. That means it's valuable. Intensely valuable, in fact."

Naye actually smiled when he heard that. "Really? How much will you pay for it, then?"

Old Cyclops rubbed his chin. "Thirty lems."

Naye's smile vanished. "Thirty lems? That's not much more than what you paid me for that box of old books I stole a week ago."

"And?" said Old Cyclops. "Why should I pay you any more than that? Thirty lems."

Naye reached for the sword. "Well, if you are just going to pay that much for it—"

A knife slammed on the table between Naye's fingers and Gildshine, nearly taking the boy's fingers off. Naye jerked his hand back and held it close to his chest as Old Cyclops—who had drawn and stabbed the knife into the table even faster than Keo's eyes could follow—snarled like a beast.

"Sorry, boy, but I want this sword and I will take it and you will accept my offer of thirty lems," said Old Cyclops. "Besides, I know how poor you and your father are. I don't think you have the right to be so picky about how much money you get."

"But thirty lems is hardly more than what my dad makes in a day at his tavern," said Naye. "It's almost nothing."

"I don't care," said Old Cyclops, shaking his head. "Besides, what are you going to do with that sword if you won't sell it to me? There's no one else in this town that is willing to buy stolen goods from snot-nosed brats like you except for me. Are you going to give it back to the man you stole it from and then get arrested by the Enforcers? Or perhaps you are thinking of starting a sword collection and you simply haven't mentioned that to me before?"

Naye licked his lips and stuttered, saying, "W-Well, I—"

"Thirty lems," Old Cyclops interrupted. "Take it or … well, actually, you don't have much of a choice in the matter, so just take it. Unless you'd like my boys here to escort you out, of course."

Naye bit his lower lip. He looked like he was agonizing over whether to accept the paltry amount of money that Old Cyclops was offering him or if he should reject it. Although Keo was still angry at Naye for stealing Gildshine in the first place, he had to admit that he felt a little sorry for the kid, given that he appeared to be in over his head.

Finally, Naye said, "Deal."

Old Cyclops smiled, revealing a bunch of old, rotting teeth that Keo was surprised still hung in his mouth. "Wise choice, kid. Give him the lems."

One of Old Cyclops' bodyguards tossed a small brown bag at Naye. The bag landed on the table right in front of Naye, who looked at the money with the most regretful expression on his face.

"Now take your money and go," said Old Cyclops. He pointed sharply out of Keo's view, probably toward the door. "Or else I will have my men escort you out."

Naye reached for the tiny bag of money, but then stopped.

"What are you waiting for, kid?" said Old Cyclops. "You got your money. Just take it."

Naye looked like he was steeling himself for whatever he was about to do next, and then he pushed the money bag back to Old Cyclops. "No. You take it back. I want the sword. I'll find someone else to sell it to and make twice as much from that sale as I could from you."

For a moment, Old Cyclops looked genuinely surprised. His mouth hung open and his one eye widened. Even his bodyguards looked surprised at this audacious act. And again, though Keo was still annoyed at Naye, he had to admit that the kid had balls.

"Kid, I don't think you were listening earlier," said Old Cyclops. He leaned forward, his one eye fixed on the kid. "So let me repeat that again in words you might understand: There is no one in town like me. Thirty lems is the most you will ever make from this sword."

"I heard you before," said Naye. "And I still don't want your money. I'll figure out how to sell it. Just you wait and see."

"Perhaps you also forgot what I said about you rejecting my offer?" said Old Cyclops. He nodded at his bodyguards. "They will be more than happy to show you the exit … by force."

Old Cyclops' bodyguards did not move, but Keo could tell that they were ready to drag Naye out of here and give him the beating of a lifetime for daring to refuse their employer's offer. And, while Naye may have been a brave kid, Keo knew that there was no way that Naye could hope to stand against Old Cyclops' bodyguards even in a fair fight, which this clearly was not.

"I remember," said Naye. "But I still don't accept. And you'll just have to live with that."

Old Cyclops slammed his hands on the table and actually stood up. He leaned across the table toward Naye and grabbed the collar of his shirt, his good eye bulging from its socket.

"Live with that?" Old Cyclops hissed. "No way. No one ever says no to my offers. Especially not stupid kids like you."

Naye was shaking, but he still said, "I-I'm not changing my mind. Sorry."

Old Cyclops growled, let go of Naye's collar, and then looked at his bodyguards. "What are you two waiting for? Beat the kid's head in and then dump his body behind his old man's tavern as a lesson to anyone who wants to even think about refusing my offers."

Keo and Dlaine exchanged alarmed looks.

Now? Keo asked through his face.

Dlaine nodded.

So Keo wrenched open the door to the living room, causing Old Cyclops, his bodyguards, and Naye to look at them in surprise. Old Cyclops and his bodyguards merely looked confused, while Naye seemed to recognize them, though he appeared too stunned by fear to move just yet.

"Who the hell are you guys?" said Old Cyclops.

"I'm the owner of that sword that you two were haggling over like a couple of Hasfarian merchants," said Keo, pointing at Gildshine. "And I'm here to take back what rightfully belongs to me."

"And I'm his friend," Dlaine added. "Not that that means much, but hey, at least you know who I am."

"See?" said Naye suddenly, pointing at Keo. "I was telling the truth. I really *did* steal that sword from a bounty hunter."

"I'm not a bounty hunter," Keo said. "I'm just someone who wants his sword back."

"Actually, I'd say he looks more like a beggar," said Old Cyclops. "I mean, just look at his clothes and hair."

"Yeah, I agree," said Dlaine, nodding. "Granted, I don't look much better, but—"

"Enough!" Keo shouted. "I am going to get my sword back now."

"Sorry, but the sword's mine," said Old Cyclops. "And I really don't appreciate it when people barge in on my business deals without my permission." He gestured at his bodyguards. "Boys, teach these two idiots what happens when you get on my bad side."

The two bodyguards nodded and drew their clubs. They then started walking toward Keo and Dlaine, looking eager to kill them.

"Can you distract them both while I try to get Gildshine?" said Keo to Dlaine, without taking his eyes off the bodyguards.

"Sure," said Dlaine. "But I don't want to, because they look big and their clubs look like they will hurt if they hit me."

"Do it anyway," said Keo. "All right?"

Dlaine sighed. "Okay. But next time we're in this situation, *you* distract the big guys with clubs, all right?"

Keo nodded. "Fine."

Dlaine then ran toward the bodyguards, swinging his fists at them and forcing the two bodyguards to hold up their clubs defensively.

Meanwhile, Keo went around the fight between Dlaine and the bodyguards in an attempt to reach the table where Old Cyclops and Naye sat. But Old Cyclops grabbed Gildshine and ran out of the room, causing Keo to run after him as quickly as he could. He didn't spare Naye—who was still sitting in his chair with a surprised look on his face—a second thought as he pursued the old man out of the living room.

Although Old Cyclops was clearly a very elderly man, he was surprisingly quick, managing to keep ahead of Keo as he ran up the stairs of his house to the second floor. Gildshine certainly didn't seem to be weighing down Old Cyclops, either, which meant that he was also a lot stronger than he looked.

Old Cyclops reached the second floor before Keo did and vanished around the corner. Keo jumped the final few steps onto the second floor, but then he saw movement out of the corner of his eye and had to step back to avoid getting his skull bashed in by another one of Old Cyclops' men who was stepping out of another room, a large, burly man who carried a large club, similar to the bodyguards below. The burly man had tried to bash in Keo's skull, but because Keo had dodged, the man's attack missed.

The man raised his club again, but Keo had no time to play with this man. He kicked the man in the gut, causing his opponent to gasp in pain and drop his club. But Keo caught the club before it fell and slammed it into the man's face. His enemy immediately fell over onto the floor, unconscious, but Keo did not stand around long enough to confirm that. He jumped over the man and ran down the hall in the direction that Old Cyclops had run, his enemy's club still in his hand.

He saw Old Cyclops reach the end of the hall, rip open a door, and rush inside, slamming the door behind him as he entered.

He's locking himself into a room on the second floor? Keo thought. *What an idiot. Does he* want *to be caught?*

Deciding that this was an opportunity not to be wasted, Keo reached the door, opened it, and dashed inside. The room was as black as night inside, but as Keo entered, he heard something flying through the air toward him and jumped to the side. He felt something cut through the air and heard an old man curse, which he identified as Old Cyclops' voice.

And then, by the light streaming in from the open door, Keo saw Old Cyclops had drawn Gildshine from its sheath and had tried to slash him with it. But before Keo could try to take the blade from Old Cyclops' hands, the old criminal raised Gildshine and pointed its blade at Keo's chest, too close for him to avoid without getting stabbed.

"Don't move," said Old Cyclops. His breathing was hard, likely because of the physical exertion of having to run and swing Gildshine. "Or I'll stab you through with your own sword."

Keo stayed still. Although he was younger and faster than Old Cyclops, the fact was that the tip of Gildshine's blade was too close to his chest for Keo to risk trying to disarm him at such a close range. Old Cyclops' grip on the blade's handle did not even shake under his grasp, even though Old Cyclops himself was sweating and panting rather hard at the moment.

So Keo, speaking as carefully as he could, said, "Listen, Old Cyclops, I just want my sword back. I don't care about whatever else you might be doing here. Just give me my sword back and my friend and I will leave you alone and never bother you or any of your men ever again."

Old Cyclops shook his head. "Never. I have been in the business of selling valuable items for decades and I know a valuable object when I see it. This sword ... it's special. It's a magical sword, isn't it?"

Keo froze. "How did you know?"

"Because I can feel the magical energy flowing through it," said Old Cyclops. "I have handled magical weapons before, although I don't know what this particular weapon's power is. Still, magical weapons are very rare and in high demand in the black market, so I would be a complete and utter fool to return it to you." He grinned. "Unless you'd like to buy it back, but you don't look particularly wealthy to me."

Keo could not believe what he was hearing. Old Cyclops offering to sell his own weapon back to him? That was the most audacious thing that Keo had heard in a long time. And he would have said so, but he was aware of how precarious his current situation was. If he said the wrong things, Old Cyclops might just impale him without another thought.

Instead, Keo said, "If you murder me, the Enforcers will find out and haul you to jail."

Old Cyclops chuckled. "The Enforcers? They don't care about me. If they did, they would have thrown me in the Dark Prison years ago. No, I sincerely doubt they will investigate the murder of a traveler like you. The Enforcers don't usually investigate the deaths of foreign travelers with any real effort."

Keo gulped. The idea of his murder being ignored by the Enforcers made him nauseous. He wished that Dlaine or Jola was here, but he could still hear Dlaine fighting off Old Cyclops' men below and Jola was still out in the rest of Torgan looking for Naye. By the time either of them got here, Keo would probably be dead.

"Now," said Old Cyclops, smirking, "it is clear to me that you are going to keep coming after me until you get your precious sword back. And as I dislike it when the original owners of my wares bug me about their stolen property, I think I'll just end you right here and now, with your own sword, you little—"

Old Cyclops was interrupted by the sound of someone dashing in from the hall into the room. Keo looked just in time to see Naye's young form barrel through the open door way, causing Old Cyclops to look as well and say, "What the—"

With a cry, Naye drew something from his belt—the knife that had belonged to Old Cyclops—and drove it into Old Cyclops' side with all of his strength.

Old Cyclops howled in pain, dropping Gildshine to the floor. He clutched his side and staggered backwards, yanking the knife out of Naye's hand, but Keo took advantage of this opportunity to punch the old criminal in the face. Keo's fist connected with Old Cyclops's jaw and the elderly criminal fell backwards onto the floor, where he lay still with the knife in his side and blood leaking from his wound.

Breathing hard, Keo picked up Gildshine (plus its sheath,

which he found lying on the floor nearby) and, sheathing his sword, looked at Naye. Naye, however, was looking at his hands, which had blood from where Naye had stabbed Old Cyclops. He was looking at his hands like he had never seen the blood of another man on them before.

"Are you all right?" said Keo.

Naye suddenly looked up. There was fear in his eyes, which reminded Keo far too much of how he had looked in his younger years when he had first killed a living creature. "Y-Yes."

"Good," said Keo. He looked around, but could not see much due to the darkness of the room. "We need to get out of here now."

"But what about Old Cyclops?" said Naye, gesturing at the old man, who looked almost dead now. "He's—"

"Not our problem," Keo interrupted. "Anyway, we need to find my friend, Dlaine, who was fighting Cyclops's men. Then we can leave."

Just as Keo said that, he heard the sound of someone running down the hallway outside and an instant later Dlaine stumbled through the door before he turned and slammed it shut behind him. He then locked it and turned to looked at Keo and Naye, though it was hard to see him in the low light conditions of the room, which were only somewhat alleviated by the sun light peeking through the curtain of the window.

"Old Cy's got at least a dozen men out there," said Dlaine, panting like he had just run a mile. "I just barely managed to distract 'em long enough to come up here and see how you were doing." Then he looked at the floor and noticed the unconscious Old Cyclops lying in an ever-widening pool of his own blood and his eyes widened. "What the hell happened here?"

"Naye did," said Keo, gesturing at the kid, who still seemed stunned by his own actions. "He helped me get Gildshine back, so I promised I'd help get him out of here."

Dlaine looked like he was about to yell at Keo for agreeing to help the kid who had gotten them into this mess in the first place, but before he could, the sounds of several men beating against the door behind him made him look over his shoulder in alarm.

"Get back here!" shouted one of the men on the other side of the door. "Let us in or else!"

Dlaine looked at Keo again. "Okay, the kid can come with us, but how the hell are we supposed to get out of here?"

Keo looked at Naye. "Do you know any way out of here?"

Naye shook his head. "N-No. I've never even been up here before, so I don't know if there's some way out onto the streets from here."

Keo scowled and looked around the room for a possible exit. Then he noticed the window, which was closed and covered by curtains, and he ran over to it. Pushing aside the curtains, Keo lifted up the window itself, which creaked from lack of use, and poked his head out of the window. The street below was empty of people, but there was nothing soft to land on to break their fall. Even so, Keo realized that it was the only possible avenue of escape opened to them right now.

Looking over his shoulder at Dlaine and Naye, Keo said, "I think we will have to either climb or jump down the building. It's our only chance of making it out of here alive."

"Is there anything soft to land on out there?" said Dlaine.

Keo shook his head. "Just the hard street."

Dlaine groaned. "Oh, these legs of mine are not going to like this. Are you sure there isn't another way?"

"I'm sure of it," said Keo. "Anyway, we don't have much time. Get over here. It sounds like the door isn't going to hold for much longer."

Keo was telling the truth. Although the door to the room held surprisingly well against the constant barrage from Old Cy's men, it was creaking and groaning, sounding like it was about to blow open at any second.

Dlaine looked reluctant to jump out the window, but he and Naye ran over to Keo anyway. Keo opened the window as wide as he could and then stepped aside to let them jump through.

"You two go first," said Keo, gesturing at the open window. He rested a hand on Gildshine's handle. "I'll go last. That way, if Cy's men break down the door, I'll fight them off with Gildshine."

"Gee, you're such a polite young man," said Dlaine sardonically, "letting your elders jump out windows first. Your father raised you well."

Naye said nothing, but he looked extremely worried about jumping into the hard streets below.

Nonetheless, he did say, "O-Okay, I'll jump first," and he stepped onto the window sill. He froze, however, probably worried about breaking his legs upon landing.

"Come on, kid, get moving," said Dlaine impatiently, glancing at the door, from which the sounds of dozens of fists pounding on it could still be heard. "We don't have time to waste."

Naye gulped, but then nodded and jumped out the window with a yell.

But before Keo could watch to see if Naye would land safely, the door burst open and half a dozen large men staggered into the room in confusion for a moment before one of them noticed Old Cyclops lying prone on the floor and shouted, "Boss!"

Half of the men gathered around Old Cyclops to see if he was all right, while the other half noticed Keo and Dlaine and the same guy who had noticed Old Cyclops shouted, "There they are! Get them!"

Dlaine raised his fists, but Keo grabbed Dlaine and shoved him toward the window. "Leave. I'll hold them off."

"But—" said Dlaine.

"Just go!" Keo shouted.

This time, Dlaine did not complain. He simply turned, climbed out the window, and jumped. Then Keo turned his attention back to the men who were now running toward him. He drew Gildshine from its hilt and took up a battle stance, holding his sword in both hands.

When the men were close enough, Keo slashed across at them. Two of the men dodged by stopping outside of Keo's reach, but the third was not so lucky and got cut straight across the chest by Gildshine's sharp tip. The third man yelled in pain and fell to the floor, grasping his now-bleeding chest in a vain attempt to stem it.

While his fellows checked on the man to make sure he was okay, Keo saw an opportunity to escape. Sheathing Gildshine, Keo turned and jumped out the open window, closing his eyes as he braced for the impact of the street below.

But then Keo landed on something solid but soft that was much closer than the street. The jarring landing shook his eyes open, allowing Keo to see that he was standing on air only a couple of feet below the window of the second floor of the building that he had jumped from.

"What the—?" said Keo, but then he looked around and noticed Dlaine and Naye sitting around him. Naye's eyes were wide and he looked just as frightened as ever, while Dlaine was smiling and even chuckling. "Dlaine, what happened? Why are we standing on air?"

Dlaine shook his head and pointed at the street. "We're not standing on air. Jola cast a spell and created a barrier to catch us."

Keo looked through the invisible barrier that they stood upon, but he still could not see Jola. He believed Dlaine, however, because it was the only reasonable explanation for this inexplicable turn of events.

"How did she find us?" said Keo, looking at Dlaine in surprise. "We didn't even tell her where we're going."

"Jola knows how to find me," Dlaine explained. Then he looked down at the street and shouted, "Jola! Lower us down, will you? You know how I feel about heights."

Without a word, the barrier started to lower. Keo was at first worried that he might stumble and fall, but the barrier was firm and wide under his feet, and soon he, Dlaine, and Naye stood on the street again unharmed.

"All right," said Dlaine. He looked up at the second floor of the building, from which the sounds of angry men yelling could be heard. "Think we should get out of here before Old Cy's men come after us?"

"Good idea," said Keo. He patted Naye on the shoulder. "We're taking you back to your father at the bar, all right? So you're coming with us."

Naye nodded, but he still looked too astonished to speak. "Was that ... was that really a magical invisible barrier we landed on a few seconds ago?"

"Yes," said Dlaine, nodding. "Now we need to stop asking questions and start running, because I doubt it will take Old Cy's men long before they come after us."

So Keo, Dlaine, and Naye turned and ran down the street in the direction of The Overflowing Mug, Keo hoping against hope that they would get away before Old Cyclops's men saw where they were going.

Chapter Fourteen

I T WASN'T LONG BEFORE they arrived at The Overflowing Mug again, but this time, the tavern was empty, save for Sherf, who stood behind the bar reading that same book from before. Keo guessed that, because it was after lunch, most of Sherf's customers had gone back to their jobs, wherever those might be.

But just as Keo, Dlaine, Naye, and Jola entered, Sherf's head snapped up and he looked at Naye instantly. He slammed the book shut and walked around the bar to the rest of the tavern, revealing that Sherf was even heavier and stronger than he had initially appeared, with a stained white apron tied around his waist and an angry and disapproving scowl on his face.

"Hello, Mr. Sherf," said Keo as the bartender approached them. He patted Naye on the head. "As you can see, we got your son back safe and sound and—"

"Naye, what the hell did you think you were doing?" said Sherf, stopping a few feet from them. He folded his arms across his chest. "What have I always told you about making deals with Old Cyclops?"

Naye looked down at his feet and rubbed his hands together, avoiding his father's gaze. "I—"

"Naye?" said a familiar feminine voice from the kitchen behind the bar. "Are you back?"

A woman stepped out from the kitchen, a woman with red streaks in her hair and a brown traveling cloak. She did not have her walking stick, but there was no mistaking the woman for anyone other than who she was. She smiled when she saw Naye. "Naye!"

"Sadia?" said Keo in surprise, watching as the woman walked over to them quickly. "What are you doing here?"

"Hmm?" said Sadia, looking at Keo and Dlaine. "Oh, it's you two. I'm Naye's older sister."

"You're his older sister?" said Keo. He looked at Sherf in surprise. "So that makes you her father, then?"

"Of course," said Sherf. "I guess I didn't tell you that earlier."

"Yeah, you didn't," said Keo. "Why?"

"Wasn't important," said Sherf as Sadia stopped next to him. Then Sherf looked at Naye hard again. "You know what I've told you about stealing from people and selling their things to that crazy old man. What do you have to say for yourself?"

Naye gulped, but still did not look at his father's face. "I … well, I just wanted to help out with the money problems we've been having. That's all."

Sherf sighed and rubbed the back of his head. "Naye, listen, I know you want to help and all, but stealing things from people and trying to sell them on the black market isn't helping. You're just making things worse for all of us by risking getting arrested or even killed. I don't want you ever doing this again, all right?"

"No need to tell me that," said Naye with a shudder. "I *can't* do it again, not if I want to live, anyway."

Sherf and Sadia exchanged puzzled looks and then Sherf said, "Naye, you don't really think I'm going to *kill* you if you do that again, do you?"

"He doesn't," said Keo, causing Naye, Sherf, and Sadia to look at him. He jerked a thumb over his shoulder. "What Naye means is that his deal with Old Cyclops didn't really work out. He stabbed Old Cy in the side with a knife and last we saw the old man was bleeding to death. He might even be dead now for all we know."

Sherf's eyes widened. "Hold on. *Naye* killed *Old Cyclops*?"

"He might still be alive," said Naye, though it was a weak defense. "We didn't actually *see* him die and his men came to his aid as soon as they saw him, so he might—"

"Gods, Naye, that doesn't matter," said Sherf, shaking his head. "Whether Old Cy lives or dies, the fact is that his men won't forget about it. They'll come and kill you and me and Sadia and then burn down the entire tavern to finish it. This is the absolute worst thing that could have come out of this."

"I take it that Old Cy isn't exactly forgiving towards his enemies?" said Keo.

"Of course he isn't," said Sherf. "He may not look like much, but he's got a mean streak a mile wide. He's been known to kill anyone who slights him and then pretend that he had nothing to do with it, but if he survives this, I doubt he'll even pretend to not be involved with slaughtering us like sheep."

"I'm sorry," said Naye. He gestured at Keo. "I was just trying to save Keo. I didn't mean—"

"Son, I know that you didn't mean for anything bad to happen, but the fact is that there's no way that this will end well for any of us," said Sherf. He rubbed sweat off of his forehead with the stained handkerchief in his pocket. "This is going to be really,

really bad."

"Is there anything we could do to help?" said Keo. "Maybe we could go to the Enforcers and tell them."

"Are you kidding me?" said Sherf. "The Enforcers of this town don't care to get involved in these sorts of disputes, which they just see as being a conflict between a bunch of criminals. And even if we did, we'd have to tell them *why* Naye was even in Old Cyclops's place at all, which probably breaks about a hundred laws all by itself."

"Can you fight back, then?" said Keo. "Get some friends to protect the place from Old Cyclops's men?"

Sherf barked a harsh laugh. "I don't have any 'friends' that would risk their own life for me like that. That's just not how things are done around here, no matter who you are. Around here, you only rely on family or yourself and no one else."

Keo looked at Dlaine. "Any ideas?"

Dlaine shrugged. "Nothing. I don't think there's much we can do to help, unless you really don't want to get to Capitika in any timely manner. If you want to stay and help, you can, but Jola and I are leaving as soon as possible."

Keo frowned. He wanted to go to Capitika, get there as quickly as possible, but at the same time he wanted to help Sherf, Naye, and Sadia with their problems here. He didn't like the idea of leaving them alone to defend themselves from Old Cyclops and his men, but neither did Keo like the idea of staying in Torgan any longer than he already had. It seemed like an intractable dilemma to him, one that did not have much of a happy ending for anyone no matter how he looked at it.

But then Sadia said, "Actually, I think there is a way we could avoid getting slaughtered by Old Cy's men."

Sherf looked at Sadia in surprise. "Really? How?"

"We can leave Torgan," said Sadia, "and go and join the Rebels in the countryside. It would mean leaving behind The Overflowing Mug and most of our possessions, but I can guarantee you that the Rebels would welcome us with open arms and defend us from anyone that Old Cy might send after us."

Sherf's expression changed from hope to despair in an instant. He gestured at the tavern as he said, "But this is my business. I've spent years of my life building this into something great, not just for me, but for you two as well. I can't just *abandon* it."

"The girl has a point," said Dlaine. "Listen, it's pretty obvious that Old Cy—or his men, if he dies—isn't going to leave you guys alone. And because you can't defend yourselves from him or tell the Enforcers, that means that your only realistic option for survival is to join the Rebels, like Sadia said. And if you really care about your kids' lives, which are far more important than your business, you should listen to her and join the Rebels."

Sherf rubbed his handkerchief against his forehead, an agitated look on his face. He looked at his tavern again and then at Naye and Sadia. He was clearly torn about whether to go along with Sadia's suggestion or not, which made Keo feel sorry for him, because, while Keo was not a parent and had never owned a business himself, he understood Sherf's dilemma just the same.

Finally, Sherf said, "All right. We'll leave within the hour. Naye, Sadia, you two pack up and take whatever you can carry. Sadia, you can lead us to the Rebels' base, all right?"

"Sure," said Sadia, nodding. She looked at Keo and Dlaine. "What about you two? Will you join us? The Rebellion could use people like you."

"Sorry, but we have our own mission," said Keo. "We're heading to Capitika, so our next stop is the Silver Falls."

"The Silver Falls?" Sadia repeated. She suddenly started digging through her coat's pockets. "Hold on. I have something for you guys to deliver there if you wouldn't mind."

"What is it?" said Keo.

Sadia pulled a white envelope from her pocket and held it out for Keo to take. "Deliver this letter to a man who calls himself the Fallsman. He's a friend."

Keo took the envelope, which felt light, save for the tiny bump in the center that might have been some kind of ring based on how it felt. He tucked the envelope into his bag and said, "Okay. But where would we find this 'Fallsman,' exactly, once we get there?"

"Just follow the signs," said Sadia. "You'll know what they look like when you see them."

"But—" said Keo, who wanted more information than that.

But Sherf waved a hand and said, "Look, I'm thankful that you two saved my son and I would normally give you guys some beer on the house as a reward, but we really don't have time to waste. I said we're leaving within the hour and that's what we're going to do. I suggest that you two do the same."

"Brilliant idea, Sherf," said Dlaine, nodding in agreement. "But next time we see you, we're taking you up on that free beer offer, all right?"

Sherf nodded. "Of course."

"Great," said Dlaine. He tapped Keo on the shoulder. "Now let's go. No telling how quickly those guys will get here, so we should leave while we can."

Keo still wanted to ask Sadia more questions about this 'Fallsman' character, but he realized that everyone needed to leave as soon as they could, so he nodded, albeit reluctantly, and said, "All right. See you guys later. Stay safe."

With that, Keo and Dlaine left The Overflowing Mug and made their way back to the main part of Torgan, walking as quickly as they could, keeping their eyes and ears open for any of Old Cyclops's men who might have been following them, though they did not see anything out of the ordinary as they drew closer to the town's marketplace.

Chapter Fifteen

KEO, DLAINE, AND JOLA left Torgan in a little under an hour through the eastern gate. They faced no trouble with the guards, who let them through after only minor interrogation, and soon were on the road again, Torgan becoming smaller and smaller behind them the farther they walked. They tried to put as much distance between themselves and Torgan as they could before sunset, and by the time the sun dipped behind the western hills, Torgan was no longer within their view.

Then they set up camp just off the side of the road, near a grove of trees that provided them some privacy, and rested without much conversation, because the events of the day had worn out both Keo and Dlaine too much to talk. The only one who did not sleep was Jola, who, as usual, kept watch, which made Keo wonder if Jola was some kind of spirit rather than a human being.

In the morning, Keo and Dlaine had a large breakfast of bacon, biscuits, and fruit that Dlaine had bought from the Torgan marketplace. They ate their breakfast quickly and soon were on the road again, heading east toward the Silver Falls.

As they walked along the road in the early morning light of the rising sun, Keo remembered the events of yesterday and looked at Dlaine and said, "That was unexpected of you."

Dlaine looked at Keo, looking a bit startled by Keo's

statement. "What was unexpected of me?"

"Telling Sherf to go and join the Rebels," said Keo, readjusting the straps of his pack as they walked, "which you told me that you hated."

Dlaine shook his head. "I'm still not much of a fan of the Rebels, but I'm a father like him and so I think you should always do what is best for your kid. And if that means taking refuge with the Rebels, then so be it."

"I wasn't criticizing you," said Keo. "Just making an observation is all."

"Well, maybe you should do a little less observation and a little more walking," said Dlaine. He pointed down the road. "We still have a long way to go before we reach Capitika, so let's focus on what's ahead of us and not what's behind us."

"I agree," said Keo, nodding. "But just what *are* the Silver Falls, anyway? Master Tiram once mentioned them to me a long time ago, but all I know is that they're a large waterfall."

"Biggest in South Lamaira," said Dlaine, nodding. "I've visited them before. They're so named because the water looks like liquid silver depending on how the rays of the sun reflect off of them. And they really do. It's a beautiful sight, definitely something you have to see at least once in your life."

"Are there any towns there?" said Keo. "Any settlements we might need to watch out for?"

"There used to be a big city, called Castarious, built right into it, back when King Riuno was still alive," said Dlaine. He frowned. "But after his death, the city was torn apart by civil war and everyone left because they completely wrecked the city and no one wanted to repair it."

"Why not?" said Keo.

"Because everyone believes that Castarious is cursed," said Dlaine.

"Cursed?" said Keo. "By who?"

"Some say that one of King Riuno's Magicians laid a curse on Castarious to prevent it from being livable, mostly as a way to get back at the King for some reason," said Dlaine with a shrug. "The fact that the Magical Council has repeatedly failed to rebuild Castarious to its original glory is proof of the curse, or so everyone says."

"Why do you believe that the Magical Council hasn't succeeded in rebuilding the city?" said Keo. "I mean, what do you think the *real* reason is, if it isn't cursed?"

"Me?" said Dlaine. He chuckled. "They're too busy focusing on the war with the Divinians and Restorationists to put any serious thought, effort, or manpower into rebuilding Silver Falls. If it won't help in the war effort, then it isn't worth focusing on, or so they think."

"I see," said Keo. He glanced at Gildshine. "I hope I can get Nesma to convince the Council to work with the Divinians and Restorationists against the demons. But if they're that focused on the war effort, then they might not even listen to her."

"The Magical Council doesn't listen to anyone except for themselves," said Dlaine with a snort. "I doubt your friend could get them to listen to her."

"But she's a member of the Magical Council, too," said Keo. "So why wouldn't the rest of the Council listen to her?"

Dlaine looked at Keo in surprise. "Hold on. Did you say that your friend Nesma is a member of the Magical Council?"

Keo nodded as he kicked a rock out of their path as the road inclined slightly. "Yep. The youngest ever, if I remember correctly. She's my age, so she's about twenty-three, though I think she's older than me by about a month."

"You're pulling my leg," said Dlaine, shaking his head. "No one that young could ever get a place on the Council. She could be an apprentice to one of the Council members, sure, but an actual, full-fledged member, with all of the power that title implies? Nah, that's impossible."

"But it's the truth," said Keo. "She joined the Council about a year ago due to her powerful magical abilities and deep understanding of magic itself. She earned her position, though I haven't seen her at all since then, so I don't know for sure how she's doing."

"Your friend must be something, then, if she's the youngest member of the Magical Council ever," said Dlaine. "But that story is almost harder to believe than your story about the demons."

"The demons are real, too," said Keo in annoyance. "You seem to have trouble believing my stories."

"Because you keep coming up with crazier and crazier ones every time I ask you about your life," said Dlaine. He chuckled. "I bet next you're going to tell me that you're actually half-Dracone, right?"

Scowling, Keo punched Dlaine in the shoulder. "Would you stop joking? This is all very serious. Nesma is the only person I know who has the power to do something about the demons. Whether or not you believe the demons exist or are coming back doesn't matter, because they are and I have to stop them."

"Okay, okay," said Dlaine, rubbing his shoulder where Keo had punched him. "You gotta learn to lighten up a little, Keo. Even if you're right and the demons are coming back, that doesn't mean you have to be so uptight about it, you know?"

"I know," said Keo. "But you didn't see that demon that almost killed me back in the Low Woods." He shuddered. "Creepiest thing I've ever seen, and its threat was even creepier."

"Sure sounds like it," said Dlaine as the road started to flatten out again. "Good thing I wasn't there to see it."

Keo nodded, but then a new question came to mind and he said, "You said you've been to the Silver Falls before. Did you see anyone there who went by the name Fallsman?"

Dlaine shook his head. "Nope. Totally unfamiliar name to me."

Keo glanced at the bag slung over his shoulder, where he had stored the letter that Sadia had given him yesterday. "You really have no idea who he might be?"

"None whatsoever," said Dlaine, "though if you ask me, I think he might be some kind of Rebel agent. That's the only reason I can think of why Sadia would ask us to deliver a letter like this."

"Well, I'm sure he's probably not a threat, whoever he is," said Keo. "I just wish that Sadia had given us more information about his identity, though, so we knew what to expect."

"I personally think that you shouldn't have accepted the letter at all," said Dlaine. "What if it takes us a long time to find this Fallsman guy? The Silver Falls are a large place, particularly the ruins of Castarious. He could be anywhere."

"But Sadia said that we could find him as long as we follow

the signs," said Keo. He frowned. "Then again, I'm not quite sure what that means."

"See? That will just delay our arrival in Capitika even further," said Dlaine. "Let's just go straight through and keep heading to Carrk, which is the next town after the Falls."

"No," said Keo, shaking his head. "I promised Sadia I would deliver the letter. After she helped us avoid getting arrested back in Torgan and her dad helped me find my sword, I feel like this is the least I can do for her."

Dlaine sighed. "All right. But let's not linger after we do that, because we really don't have all of the time in the world to do that. Both of us."

Keo nodded in agreement. "The fate of Lamaira rests on our getting to Capitika before the demons rise again. And the life of your daughter as well."

So the three of them traveled east to Silver Falls, eventually following the Hanuf River, which according to Dlaine would lead them right to Silver Falls. The Hanuf River was a large, wide River that was said to extend to the end of the world, although Keo did not know if that was true or not. All he knew was that the Hanuf River had sparklingly clear water, the cleanest water he had ever seen in his life, and that he appreciated having the chance to use it to refill their flasks and bathe.

It was a couple of days later that Keo first heard the sounds of a massive waterfall somewhere in the distance. Having never heard a waterfall before, Keo initially thought that the loud noises belonged to some kind of large beast, but Dlaine assured him that it was no massive beast at all, but rather the sounds of the Silver Falls. Keo tried to see if he could spot the Silver Falls from a distance, but because it was around night time when he heard the sounds, the darkness of the night prevented him from seeing very far.

It was in the morning, after breakfast, that Keo saw the massive Silver Falls in the distance, but it wasn't until after lunch that they reached the Silver Falls themselves. Even before they arrived at the Silver Falls, however, Keo was amazed by what he saw.

The Silver Falls were gigantic, towering well above even Magician Skran's Tower and the tallest trees in the Low Woods, which were the tallest objects Keo had see until today. It was almost as big as a small mountain, looking like the throne of a god.

Gallons and gallons of water crashed into the river below. The Falls shone in the light from the summer sun, looking just like silver liquid, as Dlaine had described them. And even from a distance, the Falls were deafening, like millions of buckets of water being poured all at once over and over.

But besides the Silver Falls themselves were what appeared to be the ruins of a massive city. The ruins started from the bottom of the Falls, went way up the massive cliffs on either side, and then stopped at two massive whitish-gray towers that looked like even larger versions of the normal Magician Towers. The two towers were connected by a massive bridge between them, a bridge that seemed to be holding strong despite its obvious size and weight.

"Wow," said Keo, stopping on top of the hill they had climbed, staring at the Silver Falls with his mouth hanging open. "I have never seen that much water in one place before."

Dlaine also stopped and looked at the Falls, though he didn't look nearly as amazed as Keo. "Yeah, they're pretty impressive all right. And those are the ruins of the city, Castarious, that I was telling you about earlier."

"And it is so loud even from a distance," said Keo. "It must be deafening up close."

Dlaine nodded, but then snapped his fingers. He looked down to his right and said, "Oh, right. Jola, the spell, remember?"

Keo was about to ask what 'the spell' was before he felt a sudden coldness seep into his bones. It made him shudder and hug himself, although the coldness vanished as soon as he felt it, leaving Keo feeling the same as he had before he felt the coldness.

"W-What was that?" said Keo with a shiver. "What did Jola do?"

Dlaine gestured at his ears. "She protected our hearing from the Falls. The Silver Falls are incredibly loud up close and, while they haven't been known to take away anyone's hearing, I want us to be able to hear each other when we go there. Just to be safe."

Keo rubbed his ears. "My ears don't feel any different."

"No surprise there," said Dlaine. "They aren't supposed to. But you'll notice the difference once we get to the Falls. Now let's keep going. I want us to reach the Falls before dark."

Keo nodded, and soon the three travelers continued their trek along the Hanuf River to the Silver Falls and the ruins of Castarious. It took them a couple of hours of walking across hills and the remains of what appeared to be a stone road that might have once connected Castarious to the main road before they finally arrived at the foot of the Silver Falls. By then, the sun was higher in the sky than before and hotter as well.

The path they walked upon took them to the walls of the ruins of Castarious, which, despite their age, were in very good condition. They appeared to be made out of brick and metal and were three times as tall as Keo. Their metallic plating was rusted in several places, probably due to the moisture from the nearby Falls.

Now that they were practically on top of the Falls, Keo listened hard to see if he could notice anything different. The strangest thing he noticed was that the Falls were unnaturally quiet despite their proximity, which he supposed was Jola's spell at work. Even so, now that he noticed it, he found it hard to ignore the nagging feeling that the Falls should be much louder than they were (but Keo decided not to get upset about it because he liked being able to hear Dlaine) because he knew that the loudness of the Falls would make normal communication between them impossible.

Keo, Dlaine, and Jola entered the ruins of Castarious via the gates, one of which stood open, while the other lay inwards like it had been knocked over by a giant. As they walked beside it, Keo looked at the gate and saw that it had an old rusted engraving on the front, an engraving of a dragon's head breathing fire.

"What happened to this gate?" said Keo as they walked past it. "Who knocked it over?"

Dlaine shrugged. "Who knows? I wasn't here when the city fell. Might have just been the people trying to escape."

"But it looks like it was knocked inward," said Keo. "Like someone was trying to get *in*, not out."

"There was a lot of chaos in the initial days after King Riuno's death," said Dlaine, scratching his chin. "Could have been a band of mercenaries and brigands that attacked the city. It was sacked several times, if I recall correctly, because the King's Army abandoned Castarious about a month after his death." He gestured at a broken sword lying on the street nearby. "See? That sword probably belonged to one of the brigands who attacked the city."

Keo nodded and did not say anything else, because when they passed through the gates, he looked around at the ruins of Castarious itself. He did not know what to expect.

The ruins of Castarious were some of the largest buildings Keo had ever seen; not quite as large as the two towers at the top of the Falls, but definitely bigger than anything you could find in New Ora or Torgan. Many buildings reached three stories high easily, while even the smaller ones looked grander than other buildings Keo had seen in the last two towns they had visited. The streets were wide and paved with cobblestone, giving plenty of room for the hundreds of people who had no doubt lived here to walk around in.

Yet despite the ruins' magnificence, Keo did not like how Castarious felt. It was hard to describe, but it was like they had walked into a city of ghosts. The streets were silent, with no life anywhere except for a rodent that darted across the street too quickly for him to follow. Aside from himself, Dlaine, and Jola, there were no other people in the city that he could see, yet he felt like someone was watching them at all times, like the spirits of the former inhabitants of Castarious were still here, watching the three strangers who had entered the city's walls. That parts of the city glistened in the sunlight, probably due to the water that fell from the Falls (droplets of which fell on Keo's head and shoulders, although it wasn't enough to annoy him), did not help; if anything, the glistening buildings and streets made him feel even less welcome here.

"Do you feel that, Dlaine?" said Keo with a gulp, looking around the wide streets of the ruined city.

"Feel what?"

"Like we're not supposed to be here," said Keo. "Like we've broken some kind of law."

"Rumor says that Castarious is haunted by the ghosts of the people who used to live in it," said Dlaine, gesturing at the towering buildings before them. "Some say that that's part of the curse put on it by the King's Magician, who bound the spirits of the people here to keep anyone from populating the city again. Some call them the black ghosts."

"*Are* there ghosts here?" said Keo with a gulp.

"I doubt it," said Dlaine. "I've passed through here a couple of times since its fall and I haven't seen even one ghost. I've met people who have told me that they have seen ghosts, but they're usually crazy, so I don't listen to 'em. Don't worry about it."

Keo nodded. "All right. But why are we even going through Castarious at all? Isn't there another way to Capitika that is a little less frightening?"

"There is, but this way is quicker," Dlaine said. He jerked a thumb over his shoulder toward the gates. "If we took the main road, we might run into some of the Road Enforcers, the guys who patrol the roads of South Lamaira. And since we're both wanted criminals, they would probably arrest us. Or, assuming they didn't recognize us, they would instead force us to pay a road tax to keep going."

"Road tax?" Keo repeated. "What's that?"

"'A voluntary fee that contributes to the betterment of our society,'" Dlaine said. He sounded like he was quoting someone, albeit mockingly. "The truth of the matter is that it's just a way that the Road Enforcers enrich themselves at the expense of the people."

"I don't understand," said Keo. "How?"

Dlaine stopped and turned to face Keo. "It's pretty simple. The Road Enforcers patrol the roads for any travelers they can find. When they do find potential victims, they tell them that they have to pay a 'road tax,' which allegedly goes toward maintaining South Lamaira's roads, or else."

"Or else?" said Keo, tilting his head to the side. "What does that mean? Do they arrest them and take them to jail?"

"Sometimes," said Dlaine. He looked up at the sky, as if remembering something bad. "Most of the time, though, they beat the hell out of them, take whatever money they have on hand, and leave them to die. Nearly happened to me once about five years ago, but I managed to defend myself."

"That's horrible," said Keo, shaking his head. "But how come I've never heard of these Road Enforcers before?"

"They tend to stick around the larger towns and cities, the ones that get the most traffic," said Dlaine. "It gives them more people to steal money from. They usually ignore little towns like New Ora or Torgan, especially the more crime-ridden parts of the country."

"And the Magical Council is okay with this?" said Keo. "*Nesma* is okay with this?"

"I don't know if your friend approves, seeing as the Road

Enforcers have been around much longer than her, but I know for a fact that the Magical Council doesn't care," said Dlaine. He scowled. "The Magical Council is supposed to get a cut of the 'tax,' so they probably encourage those damned Road Enforcers to take as much money from travelers as they can. Just to line their own pockets."

"I should bring this to Nesma's attention when we get to Capitika," said Keo. "If what you say is true, then these Road Enforcers need to be stopped right away."

Dlaine chuckled and turned around again. "Good luck with that. Even your friend might not be able to do anything about them if the rest of the Council doesn't."

Keo wanted to say that Nesma would be able to put a stop to it, but if Dlaine was telling the truth, then Nesma probably got a cut of each tax that the Road Enforcers collected as well. And considering she had been a member of the Magical Council for a year already and had apparently not done anything about it, then maybe she actually approved of it.

Or maybe Nesma doesn't know about what they're doing, Keo thought. *Nesma is the newest member of the Council, so maybe the other Council members haven't told her about that yet.*

Even Keo knew that that was about as likely as actual liquid silver flowing from the Falls. Yet the idea that his best friend in the world might be participating in blatant government corruption like that was simply too depressing a thought to think about.

I need to focus on the present right now, Keo thought. *Maybe I will talk to Nesma about this when we get to Capitika. For now, we must find the Fallsman.*

Aloud, Keo said, "Well, now that we're here, I think we

should start looking for the Fallsman."

Dlaine stopped again and looked over his shoulder, a frown on his face. "You mean you were serious about delivering that letter a couple of days ago?"

"Very," said Keo. He patted his pack where he kept the letter. "It's only fair. Sadia helped us and now we're going to help her."

"All right," said Dlaine, the reluctance in his voice obvious. He looked around at the tall buildings around them. "But where are we supposed to look? Castarious is a huge place, not even counting the half of the city on the other side of the Falls. This Fallsman character could be anywhere."

"Sadia said to follow the signs," said Keo. "You've been through here before. Do you know what 'signs' she might have been talking about?"

Dlaine shook his head. "No." But then he suddenly looked down to the left and said, "Jola, what is it?"

Keo looked at where Dlaine looked as well, but he still didn't see anything, nor did he hear Jola speak. That frustrated him. Keo didn't know why Jola still had not shown herself to him or why she never spoke to him directly. It was like Jola didn't trust him, which was not entirely irrational, seeing as she had not known him long, but Keo still disliked not being able to see or hear her.

Dlaine nodded once or twice and then looked up at Keo again. "Jola says she's been thinking about what Sadia said back in Torgan and thinks she knows what 'signs' Sadia was talking about."

"Really?" said Keo. "Well, that's convenient. Where are they?"

"Jola will show us," said Dlaine as he started walking up the street. "Come on. She knows we don't have time to lose, so she's says we've got to go quick."

Chapter Sixteen

HALF AN HOUR LATER, after walking through the magnificent ruins of Castarious, Keo, Dlaine, and Jola arrived in front of a massive statue that stood in an open square all by itself. The statue was made of marble and looked like it had stood twenty or thirty feet tall in its day, but now half of it lay on the street, with bits and pieces of marble around it. The upper half of the statue that lay on the street was of a man with a stern but kind face, who carried a large sword that had also been broken in half, likely upon impact. There was a crown carved into the statue's head, a crown with a dragon's head carved into the crest, which made the man look like a king. The lower half of the statue, which still stood, towered over both of them.

"Where are we?" said Keo, looking around the area before focusing on the broken statue lying on the street in front of them. "And who is this a statue of?"

"This is part of the old business district," said Dlaine, gesturing at the empty storefronts that circled the area. "Used to be one of the busiest parts of the city before King Riuno's death. And speaking of King Riuno, this is a statue of him and had been built in his honor."

Keo looked at the statue more closely. He had been born just after the King's death, so Keo had never seen Lamaira's Last

King, as Riuno was sometimes called, before. So he was eager to get an idea about what the Last King might have looked like.

Yet there was something familiar about the statue's face, like Keo had seen it somewhere before. He realized that the nose looked just like his nose, except slightly shorter, but he thought little of it, because Keo's nose was not exactly unique, because he had seen other people in New Ora with it.

But the statue's eyes, which stared lifelessly at Keo, now those seemed too familiar, even in their stone form. They were as round as Keo's, which he found interesting because few people had eyes like his. Even his hair looked similar, albeit longer than Keo's short trim.

Dlaine was looking between Keo and King Riuno's face, a puzzled look on his face. "Weird."

"Weird?" said Keo, looking at Dlaine. "What's weird?"

"Your face," said Dlaine.

Keo sighed. "Dlaine, if this is another one of your jokes—"

"It's not," said Dlaine, shaking his head. "What I mean is that your face looks like King Riuno's, except younger."

Keo, surprised, looked at the huge statue lying before him. "Are you sure?"

"Yeah," said Dlaine. "Seriously, you look just like him. It's freaky. You even have a sword."

Keo looked at the large sword that the statue carried and then looked at Gildshine, which was sheathed at his side. The two swords looked virtually nothing alike, aside from their general shape, but Keo wondered how much he would resemble King Riuno if he were to draw Gildshine right now and hold it similarly to how the statue held its sword.

But then Keo realized that that would be a waste of time, so he said, "So why did Jola take us here? I don't see any signs that could lead us to the Fallsman that Sadia told us about."

"Jola said that the last time we were here, she saw some strange paintings on the ruins that she thought didn't mean anything," said Dlaine, his old eyes scanning the area. "But now she thinks they might be the signs Sadia told us about, because they all appeared to be pointing in one direction."

Keo looked around the area as well, but he didn't see any paintings anywhere, whether on the streets or buildings. "Well, I don't—Ah!"

Keo said that because he was suddenly knocked off his feet by a force he couldn't see and landed hard on the street. At the same time, however, something flew past the spot where his head had been mere moments before and struck the street only a couple of feet away. A quick glance told Keo that he had just narrowly avoided getting hit in the head by a long, silver blade that was shaped almost like an arrow.

"What the hell?" said Keo. He looked around, but did not see the person who had thrown that knife. "Where did *that* come from? And who knocked me over?"

"Jola did," said Dlaine, who was now looking around the area as well, his eyes scanning the tall buildings all around them. "She saw the knife coming. But I don't know who threw it."

Keo scrambled to his feet and drew Gildshine. He also scanned the buildings around them, but the ruins of Castarious seemed as empty and dead as ever. He almost wondered if he had actually been assaulted by one of the ghosts said to live here, but then he realized that an actual ghost wouldn't have been able to throw a physical knife at him like that. Still, the fact that Keo had not even heard the knife coming meant that whoever had tried to attack Keo was just as dangerous as any ghost, perhaps even more so.

Then Keo saw movement from within one of the buildings. He looked in that direction just in time to see a man wearing black to dash out, carrying two swords in hand, moving with the speed of a rushing river.

Dlaine raised his fists, but Keo dashed forward, causing Dlaine to shout, "Hey, kid! What are you doing?"

"He's got swords," Keo shouted, without looking at Dlaine. "I can handle him better than you. Just keep an eye out for any allies he may have!"

Dlaine said something else, but Keo did not hear him because, in a second, he and the man in black were in front of each other, and the man brought his swords down on Keo's head. Keo blocked the attack with Gildshine, but his opponent was stronger than he looked, because the impact of the blow almost sent Keo to his knees. But Keo managed to retain his footing and even found enough strength to push back.

His opponent, however, merely jumped backwards in response and slashed at Keo with one of his swords. Keo blocked it with Gildshine, but his opponent's other sword flew at his opening, forcing Keo to duck to avoid losing his head entirely. Seeing an opening, Keo tried stabbing the man, but the man in black blocked Gildshine with both of his blades. Then the man shoved Keo backwards, sending him staggering, but Keo recovered fast enough to block another couple of blows from the man, although just barely.

Breathing hard, Keo held Gildshine in a defensive position, watching his opponent carefully, who was now swinging his swords around like he was preparing for another attack. Keo looked for any openings that he could take advantage of, but the man left nothing for Keo to exploit, which told Keo that this swordsman was no amateur.

Then, without warning, the swordsman dashed toward Keo. He swung his left sword at Keo, which Keo blocked, but then the swordsman tried to stab Keo with his right sword. Keo barely managed to dodge it, however, and responded by kicking the swordsman in his exposed gut.

Keo's foot connected and the swordsman was sent staggering, gasping for air from the impact of the blow. Keo advanced and brought Gildshine down on the swordsman's head, but the swordsman blocked it in the nick of time, catching it between both of his blades.

Yet Keo did not give up. He forced the swordsman to go down, putting as much of his weight onto Gildshine as he could. And to his relief, the swordsman was indeed going down, even though he was clearly struggling hard against Keo's weight. The swordsman was almost on his knees now, at which point Keo was sure that the fight would be over.

But then Keo heard Dlaine shout, "Keo, to your right!" and he looked to his right and saw another swordsman in black wielding duel blades running toward him. Keo removed Gildshine from his first opponent and managed to block the second assailant's attacks, but then his first opponent swung his swords at him again.

Again, Keo forced his second opponent back and jumped to

the side, the tips of the first swordsman's blades nearly cutting through his side. Keo staggered, but still held up Gildshine before him as his two opponents ganged up on him. Keo heard a shout behind him and glanced over his shoulder to see Dlaine fighting his own set of swordsmen, though he was even more defensive than Keo, having to jump around and dodge to avoid getting slashed or stabbed by the two mysterious swordsmen.

Yet there was nothing Keo could do to help, so he looked back at the two swordsmen advancing on him. He backed up as quickly as he could, looking for any openings he could take advantage of, but the two swordsmen advancing on him left no openings for him to strike. And Keo was already starting to feel tired and hungry, but he ignored his fatigue in order to focus on doing what he needed to in order to win.

Where's Jola? Keo thought, scowling as he looked around the area. *Why isn't she helping?*

Then, without warning, Keo's two opponents surged forward and starting slashing at him with their four swords. Keo blocked each blow as quickly as he could, but even Gildshine was not large enough to block every blow, forcing him to dodge just as many attacks as he blocked. He had no time to strike back and was becoming increasingly certain that he was going to die unless a miracle happened.

Eventually, Keo and Dlaine were driven back to back, with the four swordsmen on every side circling them like lions looking for an opportunity to go in for the kill. Both Keo and Dlaine were tired and panting, but their opponents hardly seemed fazed, as if this was merely a light training exercise rather than a battle to the death.

"Any ideas, kid?" said Dlaine as they watched the swordsmen circle them.

Keo shook his head. "No. Where's Jola?"

"No idea," said Dlaine. "But I know she didn't run away. She's not a coward. I can tell you that much about her."

Keo frowned. "If she didn't run, then what is she doing?"

"Like I said, I don't know," said Dlaine. "Don't know who these freaks are, either."

Keo shook his head. "Wonderful. Just—"

At that moment, a sudden cry of pain shot through the square, so loud that it even caused the four swordsmen to look around in surprise, as if they recognized it. Keo and Dlaine looked around as well, but did not spot anyone who might have cried out in pain until a figure staggered out of the darkness of a nearby building.

The figure was a woman with short, dark hair. Like the swordsmen, she wore a black outfit that covered up much of her body and face, and she also carried a sword at her side, although her sword was thinner and shorter than the swords wielded by her allies.

The odd thing about her was that her right arm was twisted behind her back and she looked like she was in great pain. Her fellow swordsmen looked torn between staying and fighting Keo and Dlaine or going and helping her, which made Keo wonder just who this woman was and what was so important about her. Was she their leader?

"Stop!" the woman shouted. Her voice was rather high, but there was a definite commanding tone to it, like she was used to issuing orders. "Stand down! Spare these two."

The four swordsmen all exchanged puzzled glances, but they

lowered their weapons anyway and stepped back from Keo and Dlaine without another word. Still, Keo did not lower Gildshine, nor did Dlaine lower his fists, because there was a good possibility that this was a trick and that the swordsmen would attack if they saw an opening.

Then the woman looked over her shoulder and said, "All right. I let them go. Stop twisting my arm."

There was no answer, although Keo was confused until Dlaine muttered, "Jola's my girl," which helped Keo understand that Jola was the one twisting that woman's arm.

The woman's arm untwisted and she immediately started rubbing it. Keo expected the woman to order her men to attack Dlaine and him again, but the woman instead looked around hesitantly, like she expected a monster to leap from the shadows and eat her, before she walked toward them. Neither Keo nor Dlaine let their guard down, however, even though it was now clear that the woman was not going to have her men attack.

"Who are you?" said Dlaine as the woman stopped just outside of the vague circle created by the swordsmen. "Are these your men?"

The woman regarded both Keo and Dlaine with severe distaste, as if there was something about their appearances that offended her. "No. I am their commander, but they answer to a higher authority than me."

"Who's that?" said Dlaine.

"The Fallsman," said the woman. "And you have intruded upon his territory, which is why I and my fellow Warriors of the Falls tried to kill you."

Keo's eyes widened. "The Fallsman? That's who you work

for?"

"Yes," said the woman, nodding. "Do you recognize that name?"

"Yes," said Keo, nodding himself. Although it was risky, he lowered Gildshine, opened his pack, and started digging around in it for the letter for the Fallsman. "I have a letter that we were supposed to deliver to him."

"A letter?" said the woman in surprise. "Who is it from?"

"A woman named Sadia," said Keo. He stopped digging through his pack and looked up at the woman with an inquiring expression. "Do you recognize that name?"

The woman's eyes narrowed. "Too well."

Keo did not know why the woman seemed so hostile toward Sadia, but he didn't ask why. He just fished out the letter from his pack and held it up for the woman to see. "Here's the letter from Sadia that I was telling you about."

The woman held out her hand. "Give it to me and I will make sure that the Fallsman gets it."

Keo was about to do that, but then Dlaine grabbed his arm and lowered it, causing Keo to look at him in surprise.

"No way, lady," said Dlaine, shaking his head. "We have no guarantee that you won't kill us the moment we give you that letter. We'll take it to the Fallsman ourselves and you will lead us to him."

The woman folded her arms in annoyance. "No one sees the Fallsman unless he invites them, and you have not been invited to his presence."

Dlaine snorted. "That's one heck of an ego your master has. What, is he the second coming of King Riuno or something?

Either take us to Fallsman and let us deliver the letter personally or we'll have Jola—you know, the spirit that twisted your arm—show you why you generally don't mess with the spiritual world."

The woman gulped and looked around, like she thought that the 'spirit'—obviously Jola—was going to appear out of nowhere and attack her again. Then she looked at Keo and Dlaine, again with that same distaste in her eyes.

"Very well," said the woman. "I will take you to the Fallsman. The Warriors will not harm you, but I must ask you to put away your sword. The Fallsman does not like to meet armed visitors."

Although Keo did not trust either the woman or the Warriors at all, he nonetheless understood that he had no real choice in the matter. So he sheathed Gildshine and expected the Warriors to fall on Dlaine and him in a frenzy of metal and blood, but the Warriors did not move an inch from where they stood, thankfully.

"Now, follow me," said the woman as she turned. "The Fallsman is not far from here, so we should get there quickly if we do not run into any delays. I cannot guarantee that he will be happy to see you, but I know he will want to see that letter, so we must go, and quickly."

Chapter Seventeen

THE WOMAN—WHO SAID that her name was Takan of the Snow—led Keo, Dlaine, and Jola through the ruins of Castarious without looking back to make sure they were following. That was probably because the four Warriors surrounded Keo, Dlaine, and Jola on all sides, so if those three tried anything, then they would be swiftly put to death by the Warriors. Or so Keo believed, because all of the Warriors looked rather annoyed at being denied their chance to kill Keo and Dlaine.

The path they took through the ruins of Castarious was winding and confusing, taking them through several backstreets and even a few empty houses and buildings. Keo was pretty sure that he would never have been able to find the Fallsman on his own if he had tried and likely would have spent weeks or even months searching the city's ruins for him. Thus, he was glad that they had found Takan and the Warriors, even though he still didn't trust any of them one bit.

It was about half an hour later that they emerged onto a street somewhere deep in the ruins and stood in front of the most magnificent house that Keo had ever seen in his life. It was tall and wide, its front made of white brick that looked good even despite its age. It had a couple of stories, making it one of the smaller buildings in Castarious, but it made up for size in appearance, with four windows on each floor shaped like crystals. A tall iron fence surrounded it on all sides and the large front steps ended at a tall door that appeared to be made of oak. Two large dragon statues stood on either side of the door. This house had clearly belonged to someone important back in Castarious's heyday, but who, Keo did not know. All he knew was that it must have looked even better in the old days, prior to the fall of the Kingdom.

Takan led them through the gate, which creaked open rather loudly, and across the path with overgrown grass on either side. They walked up the steps to the front door, which Takan pushed open with little trouble, and then they entered the house itself.

The house's lobby was fairly wide open and even well-lit due to the sun roof, which allowed light from outside to stream in. Two sets of stairs with elaborate gold railings went up to the second floors, while an entryway in between them seemed to lead to another room, but Keo could not tell what that room was (although he saw a sofa and several chairs in it). The collective footsteps of Keo, Dlaine, Jola, Takan, and the Warriors clicked loudly off the marble flooring, which was a lot cleaner than it should have been, which made Keo realize that the Fallsman must care a great deal about his house if he apparently had someone to scrub the floor for him.

Then Takan stopped and gestured for the others to do the same. She turned around and said, "I am going to get the Fallsman and inform him of your arrival and your purpose for being here. Please be patient."

With that, Takan turned around again and walked up the left flight of stairs to the second floor. Soon she was out of sight, leaving Keo, Dlaine, and Jola surrounded by the four Warriors. Keo rested a hand on the hilt of Gildshine, although he was uncertain if he would be able to draw it quickly enough to defend them in the event that this turned out to be a trap and the Warriors attacked.

A couple of minutes later, Takan appeared at the top of the stairs again and said, "The Fallsman is coming."

Before Keo or Dlaine could say anything in response to that, a man stepped into view at the top of the stairs. He was a tall man, much taller than Keo or Dlaine or anyone else in the room. He wore a practical gray jacket and a white tunic underneath, which made him look somewhat ghostly in appearance. He had a harpoon, of all things, slung over his right shoulder and his face was long and pointed, his black eyes glaring down at them. The man's age was difficult to tell, although if Keo had to guess, he would have placed the man's age somewhere just below Dlaine, but he would not have bet money on that.

"The Fallsman," said Takan, gesturing at the man. She pointed at Keo and Dlaine. "Fallsman, those are the two men I told you of, who have the letter from Sadia."

The Fallsman's eyes focused on the letter in Keo's hand. "Then get the letter and deliver it to me."

Takan moved to do so, but then Keo said, "No. You come down here and get it yourself."

The Fallsman looked surprised at Keo's words, as did Takan and the Warriors. While Keo did not want to offend the Fallsman, he still didn't trust that the Warriors were not going to slaughter Dlaine and him as soon as they got a chance. He believed that the Warriors would be far less likely to attack them if the Fallsman was right in their midst, although he had no idea if the Fallsman would actually go with his demands or not.

Then the Fallsman laughed and said, "A strong one, you are. Very well. I prefer to do things myself anyway."

With that, the Fallsman walked down the stairs, Takan following silently behind. Once he reached the bottom, the Fallsman strode across the marble floor toward Keo and Dlaine, a confident smirk on his face, like he wasn't afraid of Keo or Dlaine at all. Of course, with four large, well-armed men to defend him, the Fallsman certainly had reason enough to believe that he was safe from a couple of strange men he didn't know.

Up close, the Fallsman was even taller than Keo had first estimated. He held out his hand—large and wide—for Keo to put the letter in. Reluctantly, Keo placed the letter in the Fallsman's hand, which the Fallsman then took without another word.

Opening the envelope, the Fallsman pulled out a folded up sheet of paper and a small, silver ring. He glanced at the ring before depositing it into the pocket of his jacket and then he unfolded the letter and started reading. It was impossible to tell what was written in the letter, but the Fallsman seemed so focused on reading the letter's contents that Keo believed he could draw Gildshine and stab him in the chest there and then and the Fallsman would not notice until he finished reading the letter.

After a couple of tense moments, the Fallsman looked up from the letter. He didn't look angry, but Keo kept his hand on Gildshine's hilt anyway, just to be safe.

"Well," said the Fallsman, drawing out the word as long as he could, probably just to make Keo and Dlaine anxious. "I thank you, strangers, for delivering this letter to me from an old friend of mine. I was skeptical that it was actually from Sadia at first, but there is no mistaking her handwriting or writing style for anyone else's. Unless one of you happens to be a master forger, although I doubt it, because neither of you look clever enough for the job."

"Uh, you are welcome, Fallsman," said Dlaine. He scratched the back of his head and looked around. "Now, er, will you please let us go? We have places to be and we can't really spend a lot of time here talking with you."

The Fallsman handed the letter to Takan, who took it, folded it up, and placed it in her breast pocket without another word. "No."

"No?" said Dlaine. "Listen, Fallsman, you aren't our boss. You —"

The sound of swords unsheathing was followed by all of the Warriors pointing the tips of their blades at Keo and Dlaine's necks, immediately making Dlaine shut up. Keo's fingers wrapped firmly around the handle of Gildshine, but there was no way he could draw it out to defend them, not when in such close proximity to these Warriors.

The Fallsman's expression had not changed. "Takan told me that you two have a guardian spirit following you. She said that it twisted her arm and was the main reason she brought you two here. Is that true?"

Dlaine bit his lower lip, clearly thinking about what he should say, and then nodded and said, "Yes. Though she's not exactly a guardian spirit. More like a very talented Magician."

"Hmm," said the Fallsman. "Well, in either case, I think I could use some of your help."

"Why should we help you?" said Dlaine.

"Because my men would be more than happy to remove your heads from your shoulders if you say no," said the Fallsman. "I mean, I'm not much of a bloodthirsty warmonger myself, but I wouldn't stop my men from killing you, which is what you deserve for invading my territory."

"Invading?" Dlaine repeated. "Okay, now that's bull, and you know it. We didn't even *know* it was your territory."

"I don't care," said the Fallsman. "I will tell my men to spare you only if you agree to help me with a particular problem of mine that only magic can solve."

Dlaine looked like he was about to tell the Fallsman where he could stick that harpoon of his, but Keo quickly said, "Well, Fallsman, why don't you tell us a little bit about your problem first? We can't really help you if you don't tell us what your problem even is, after all."

The Fallsman looked like he was considering Keo's words, and then he nodded and said, "You make a good point. You see, there is a ghost in my city and I need you to slay it."

"A ghost?" Dlaine said. "Impossible. Ghosts don't exist."

"Tell that to the six men I've already lost to it," said the Fallsman in annoyance. "I'm sure they'd love to hear that they weren't actually viciously murdered by a ghost."

Dlaine looked ready to argue the point, but Keo said, "Fallsman, why don't you start from the beginning and explain to us what you mean; how it started, for example?"

The Fallsman folded his arms across his chest. "All right. Well, I moved into the ruins of Castarious about a year and a half ago, bringing my men with me. While I did not intend to turn these ruins into a bustling metropolis, I did intend to make this city my territory by taking advantage of all of the rumors and myths about it that scared off everyone else. Ever heard of the myth of the black ghosts?"

Keo shook his head, but Dlaine said, "You mean the story about the ghosts, said to be made of shadow, that slash intruders to death with their swords?"

"Exactly," said the Fallsman, nodding. He gestured at the four Warriors standing around them. "My Warriors' appearance is based on those myths, even though I have not seen any actual black ghosts in all of the time that I've been here. In any case, I like to send my Warriors out every now and then to appear before the superstitious idiots who sometimes come here, which causes them to flee and warn everyone else to avoid Castarious like the plague, which in turn helps cement my own control over the ruins. It's a brilliant plan, if I do say so myself."

"Yeah, sure," said Dlaine. "Are you getting to the point or not?"

"About a week ago now, one of my men reported seeing a large gray wolf wandering through the streets," said the Fallsman. "I thought it was nothing more than a lost animal, as sometimes wild beasts from the countryside will come in here to make it their home or in search of prey. But I knew how dangerous wolves could be, so I sent three of my men to kill it so it would not pose a future threat to me or my men."

"What happened?" said Keo, though he found it hard to pay attention to the story with the Warriors' swords still at his neck.

"The wolf slaughtered them all," said the Fallsman simply. "Quite brutally, I might add. We still haven't found all of their body parts. So I sent three more men to hunt down the creature and kill it, but they also ended up getting killed, so I decided to take matters into my own hands and hunt the beast for myself."

The Fallsman spoke rather casually about losing six of his men, yet at the same time, Keo sensed an undercurrent of anger in his voice, like he was angry at the fact that this wolf had slain so many of his men.

"I successfully tracked down the beast near the docks where the merchants used to come in through the Hanuf River to deliver their goods," said the Fallsman. He gestured at his harpoon. "And I tried to stab it in the heart, only for my harpoon to pass harmlessly through its body. The wolf likely would have killed me there and then, if Takan hadn't distracted it with a bright light and saved me."

Takan looked quite proud of herself when the Fallsman mentioned that.

"So I returned to my mansion here and have spent the last week trying to come up with a way to destroy a ghost," said the Fallsman. "Unfortunately, I haven't been able to come up with any, because neither I nor my men have any experience in battling the supernatural. Right now, I've kept my men from patrolling the city as they usually do, because no one knows where the ghost wolf is and I don't want to lose more men to it. I have set up watchmen on the key parts of the city to make sure it doesn't get too close to the mansion, which is how Takan and the others found you two, because one of my watchmen saw you."

"And almost killed us," Dlaine muttered.

The Fallsman apparently either did not hear or was ignoring Dlaine, because he continued, saying, "So far, the ghost has not been seen again, but I know it is still out there somewhere. I don't know where it came from or why it is here, but I do know that it poses a threat to everything I've been building in this city over the last year and a half. If it's not stopped, I will be forced to leave Castarious for good."

"Do you want us to kill it?" said Keo.

"More or less," said the Fallsman, nodding. "Or send it back to the astral plane or wherever ghosts are supposed to be."

"And you are sure that it's a ghost?" said Keo. "Not, perhaps, a Magician using some kind of spell to make himself look like one?"

"I am certain that it is a ghost," said the Fallsman. "As I said, my harpoon passed harmlessly through its body when I attacked it, which is how ghosts are supposed to be. And believe me when I say that I was a firm disbeliever in the existence of ghosts before this week. I believed that all of the rumors and myths about the vengeful spirits of Castarious were nothing more than stories, yet I have seen for my eyes that there is definitely something not of this world in this city. And I cannot deal with it by myself."

The Fallsman sounded ashamed of that fact, like he did not like admitting that he could not handle this problem that was harming him and his followers. Though Keo still did not remove his hand from Gildshine's hilt, because he still did not trust the Fallsman.

"And why do you think that we can kill it, if you cannot?" said Keo.

The Fallsman smiled. "Because I know that the sword at your side is a magical sword, and magical weapons are said to be able to slay ghosts. Plus, you have a guardian spirit, which gives you another weapon to use against the ghost."

Keo had not expected the Fallsman to know that Gildshine was a magical sword. Nor did he know how the Fallsman could have identified it as such, as very few people could accurately identify a magical sword at first glance. That meant that the Fallsman was quite a bit more knowledgeable than he first appeared, which made Keo wonder what else the Fallsman knew that he could use against Keo and Dlaine.

"Well, it's not like we have much of a choice whether to help or not," said Dlaine with a shrug. "You said you would spare us if we agreed to help you, right?"

"Correct," said the Fallsman. "You see, the reason I have controlled these ruins for as long as I have is because I have always been one to take advantage of whatever opportunities present themselves to me, regardless of what they look like. And finding a couple of travelers with a magical weapon and a guardian spirit is one of those opportunities that I would be foolish to let slip by me like that."

Although Keo was no fan of the Fallsman, he had to admit that he saw the logic in the Fallsman's plan. This way, the Fallsman did not need to risk his own life or the lives of his men to destroy the danger to his rule. And the Fallsman knew there was no way that Keo or Dlaine would reject his offer, because they both still wanted to live.

Despite that, Keo wanted to tell the Fallsman 'no' just the same. And indeed, the words almost escaped his lips before a sudden scream from outside of the mansion startled him and everyone else, making them look around in surprise for a moment before something large smashed through the front windows of the mansion.

The large thing slammed into the ground and rolled for a couple of feet until it stopped a foot or two away from the Warriors of the Falls, who drew their weapons in case it was some kind of attack. Keo had drawn Gildshine and Dlaine raised his fists, while the Fallsman and Takan had taken a couple of steps backwards, though the Fallsman did grab his harpoon anyway.

Then Keo noticed that the thing that had been thrown through the window was a man, one of the Fallsman's Warriors based on his dark clothing. His body was cut and full of glass from being thrown through the window, but even worse was that his head was completely missing. It was nothing more than a bloody stump, like it had been completely torn off by some vicious beast.

"What did that to him?" said Dlaine, staring at the corpse with horror. "It looks like he was mauled by a bear."

Before either the Fallsman or his servants could answer, a loud, demonic howl filled the air. And it was coming from just outside the window that the body had come from.

Chapter Eighteen

LOOKS LIKE OUR GHOST is here," said the Fallsman. He gestured at his Warriors and Takan. "Men, stand down. Our visitors will deal with the ghost, as per the agreement."

The Warriors looked relieved to follow the Fallsman's orders and quickly walked away from the corpse that had been thrown through the window, while Dlaine said, "What? No backup?"

"I already said that my harpoon failed to harm it," said the Fallsman as his Warriors assembled around Takan and him. "Considering that all of my men also have rather ordinary weapons, I doubt they would be of much help against them. Good luck."

With that, the Fallsman, Takan, and the Warriors ran up the stairs to the second floor of the mansion. Dlaine opened his mouth again, probably to yell at them for being so cowardly, but before he could utter another word, something huge and gray burst through what remained of the window and landed hard on four paws on the marble floor.

The creature resembled a wolf in its general appearance, but it was much larger than any wolf that Keo had seen. Its legs went up to Keo's chest, while its body was three times as thick as Keo's own. It had whitish-gray fur that contrasted with the shining blood on its lips and its dead red eyes. Its tail looked as thick as a log, while its entire form was shimmery in appearance, like a ghost, yet it must have been more solid than it looked, considering how it had smashed through the window mere moments ago.

"By the gods," said Dlaine. "Is that the ghost?"

Keo nodded, never taking his eyes off the massive creature. "Must be. It hasn't noticed us yet, but it will soon. You can run, if you want. I know you don't have any way to harm the ghost, so —"

"And let you and Jola have all of the fun?" said Dlaine. He shook his head and took a fighting stance. "Nah. I'll help however I can, even though I've never fought a ghost before. Should be fun."

Keo frowned, because he really didn't think Dlaine would be of much help against the ghost wolf, but before he could voice that opinion, the ghost wolf suddenly looked at Dlaine and him. The ghost wolf looked almost stunned, as if it had not expected to see them here, but then its stunned look turned to rage and it howled once more, letting out such a loud howl that Keo cringed.

But then the ghost wolf ceased howling. Keo expected it to charge at him, Dlaine, and Jola, but then, without warning, the ghost wolf growled, "Murderer! I shall avenge the one you have slain, for the honor of the Kingdom of Demons!"

Before Keo or Dlaine could respond, the ghost wolf charged at them as quickly as lightning. It leaped through the air toward them, causing Keo and Dlaine to separate. The ghost wolf landed hard on the floor where they had stood an instant before and immediately turned to face Keo, who was walking backwards with Gildshine held before him defensively.

"You called me a murderer," said Keo, trying to put as much distance between the ghost wolf and himself as he could. "And you mentioned the Kingdom of Demons. What do you mean by that?"

"Don't play dumb with me, human," the ghost wolf said. Its voice sounded like a wolf attempting to speak the human tongue, although there was no mistaking its occasionally mispronounced words for what they were. "We demons all know how you killed Hand of Blood a week ago. We demons are connected to each other and can sense when one is killed and who they are killed by. But I did not expect to see you myself so soon, nor get a chance to avenge my fallen brother."

Keo recalled that first demon he had killed back in the Low Woods a week ago (though he hadn't known its real name), but he did not drop to his knees and beg for mercy or forgiveness. Instead, he said, "Sorry, but you still won't avenge your brother. I have to get to Capitika as soon as possible, so I can't let you kill me."

"Oh, so you think to warn your fellow humans about the coming invasion and return of the Kingdom of Demons, then?" said the demon. It chuckled. "I have heard stories about how foolish you humans can be, but never thought they had any truth to them. But I suppose that your foolishness is understandable, because you have no way of knowing just how hopeless your little quest actually is."

"And what do you mean by that?" said Keo.

The demon smiled, flashing its bloodstained teeth. "Now, now, Keo of the Sword, I am not going to go and tell you that. Instead, I am going to banish your soul to the fiery pits where it belongs. Die!"

The demon dashed toward Keo, moving as silently over the floor as if it was an actual ghost. It snapped at him with its massive jaws, but Keo blocked the attack with Gildshine. He swung Gildshine at the demon's face, but the demon leaped out of the way, narrowly avoiding getting cut by his blade.

Turning to face the demon, Keo did not run to meet it. Instead, he took a few steps backwards. He remembered from his battle with the first demon—the one that the ghost wolf called Hand of Blood—that even Gildshine could not harm it unless he activated its special ability. But, while activating Gildshine's ability to cut through anything would probably help him defeat this demon, he had to be careful because if he used Gildshine's ability and missed, he would be too weak to defend himself.

I'll bait him into attacking me, just like I did to his fellow demon, and then strike when he least expects it, Keo thought. *It worked once, so I don't see why it couldn't work again.*

"Going on the defensive, murderer?" said the demon. It growled. "Not that it matters to me, because either way I will tear you apart and scatter your body across the face of this pathetic ruin of a city."

"Then come at me, demon," said Keo, waving Gildshine at him mockingly. "Or are you afraid of the human who killed your friend?"

The demon let out an awful howl before charging at Keo again. Keo took up a more suitable fighting stance to ensure he had proper footing and then focused on his bond with Gildshine again. He asked it to take half of his energy so that it could cut through any substance in the world. And, as always, Gildshine complied and Keo felt the blade become stronger and more powerful in his hands than it had been mere moments before.

Yet Keo did not signal this power-up to the demon. Instead, he raised Gildshine above his head, intending to bring it down on the demon's head and cleave into its head with one stroke of Gildshine's sharp blade.

Just a few more seconds ... Keo thought, watching as the demon drew closer and closer to him with every bound of its long legs. *One ... two ... three!*

At the very last second, Keo brought Gildshine down on the demon's head. He fully expected to see his sword cut through the demon's skull without issue and thus end the fight immediately.

But without warning, the demon vanished into thin air and Gildshine struck the floor, where it stuck hard and fast. Surprised, Keo looked around for a moment before sudden exhaustion set in and he almost fell to the floor. But he managed to lean on Gildshine for balance, although even that was a challenge.

Where ... where did that damn demon go? Keo thought, panting and sweating as he looked around.

Then the demon's tail came out of nowhere and struck Keo in the side. The blow was strong enough to send him flying. He soared upside down through the air, unable to scream, before he landed flat on his back on the marble floor. Normally he would have jumped right back up to his feet after a blow like that, but the side effect of Gildshine's ability had fully fallen over him by now like a heavy cloud and he could barely move a muscle due to the sheer exhaustion that had overcome his body. He could only gather enough strength to raise his head high enough to see the demon looking at him with a smirk.

"Foolish human," said the demon, shaking its head. "I am not Hand of Blood. I knew about the power of your sword and how it can kill us demons. I tricked you into repeating your tactics, which worked out well in my favor. Killing you will be so much easier now that it will be almost unfair … if I even cared about human concepts like 'fairness.'"

Keo could not answer that charge, mostly because he was too tired to speak. He tried to sit up, but he could not even manage that much. So he contented himself with glaring at the demon, which then charged toward him, its bloodstained lips twisted in a bloodthirsty grin.

The demon launched itself through the air toward Keo and Keo knew that it was going to crush him underneath its weight. He tried to move his body once more, but failed, and so could only watch as the demon fell toward him like a falling boulder from the top of a mountain.

Then Keo felt something grab him and he was suddenly whisked away from where he lay. A second later, the demon crashed into the spot of the floor where he had been lying, a stunned and surprised look on its face when it looked down and realized that Keo was no longer underneath it.

Keo was just as surprised as the demon. He looked at his right shoulder and could not see anyone there, yet he felt two hands grabbing his shirt and pulling him along like a sack of potatoes. Then Keo saw that he was being dragged toward Dlaine, who ran over to Keo and met him about halfway.

The hands then let go of Keo, while at the same time Dlaine bent over him and said, "You okay, kid?"

Keo shook his head and said, in a weak voice that was little more than a whisper, "What … was …"

"Jola," said Dlaine. "She grabbed you at the last minute, as you no doubt noticed. But what happened to you? Did the demon cast some sort of spell on you or—?"

"Gildshine," said Keo. Every word was pure torture to speak, but he had to speak if Dlaine was going to understand what happened. "Give up half of my energy to … to give it the power to cut through anything."

Dlaine's eyes widened. "Really? Damn, kid, why didn't you tell me about that before? That could have been pretty handy to know."

Then Dlaine looked up at the demon, which had gotten over its surprise and was now glaring at them both. His own face looked quite pale as he said, "And that … that thing is an actual *demon*?"

"Yes," said Keo, panting hard. "Do you believe me now?"

Dlaine stroked his chin, a look of fear in his eyes. "Well, I have never been one to deny the reality of what is in front of me. So I guess I do, kid. That's going to make it harder to sleep at night, though."

"Least of our problems," Keo muttered.

"So how do we beat it?" said Dlaine, looking at Keo.

Keo shrugged weakly. "Gildshine could do it, but I … I already used up its power for the day and don't have any energy left to use it again."

Dlaine cursed. "Well, can magic hurt it, then?"

"Not sure," said Keo. "Not much of an expert in demon-killing, despite my experience."

Dlaine looked to his left. "Jola, think you can deal with the demon while I make sure that Keo here is safe?"

Keo heard no words of affirmation from Jola, but a second later Dlaine said, "Thanks," looked down at Keo, and said, "All right. Jola's going to distract the demon."

"What are we supposed to do?" Keo asked.

"Get your sword back, for one," said Dlaine as he stood up and looked around the lobby. "That could be—"

A loud howl pierced the air again and the demon was loping across the floor toward them. But it didn't get very far before a burst of flame appeared before it, causing the demon to skid to a halt. It stepped backwards from the flames, only for some kind of strange black dust to appear out of nowhere and fly into its eyes. The demon let out a howl of pain and staggered backwards, rubbing its eyes with its front paws as best as it could.

Keo watched the entire scene with amazement, while Dlaine frowned and said, "Huh. Jola's going easy on this one. Guess she's trying to figure out what hurts it and what doesn't. Smart one, she is. Anyway, let's get you back to your sword."

Dlaine hauled Keo to his feet and wrapped one arm around his shoulders. Even with Dlaine's support, however, Keo couldn't stand very well. He tried, of course, but his legs simply refused to stand on their own. He nearly collapsed again, but Dlaine forced him to remain upright and started walking him toward Gildshine, which still stood in the marble floor where Keo had planted it. Meanwhile, the demon was still rubbing the black dust out of its eyes, but then the floor under its feet split and it tripped and fell on flat on its stomach, so Keo figured Jola had it covered for now.

"Okay, Keo, we just need to get your sword and we will be all right," said Dlaine as they slowly made their way over to

Gildshine step by step. "It's the only surefire way to kill demons that we know of."

"But its magical power ..." Keo coughed. "It's powerless until tomorrow. It's useless."

"Maybe, but I'd still feel better with a magical sword than without one," said Dlaine. "I don't think Jola will be able to distract it for long, much less beat it on her own."

Keo was about to ask how they were supposed to stop the demon if Jola couldn't and Gildshine was currently powerless, but he was too exhausted to ask such questions, so he simply let Dlaine lead him to Gildshine. Upon reaching the sword, Dlaine lay Keo on the floor and then grasped Gildshine's hilt with both hands before pulling up as hard as he could.

Unfortunately, Gildshine did not budge from its position in the floor, causing Dlaine to say, "Damn it. Keo, how hard did you stab this thing into the floor?"

Keo could not respond, so he simply shrugged his shoulders, although even that was a weak motion.

"Never mind," said Dlaine. "I'll just have to put some more effort into retrieving it, then."

But just as Dlaine redoubled his grip around Gildshine's hilt again, a loud howl caused Keo and him to look in the direction of the demon.

The demon had finally succeeded in wiping the black dust from its eyes. It looked around again before spotting Keo and Dlaine, and then a vicious scowl appeared across its lupine features.

"Do not flee from me, murderer," said the demon. "This time, there is no escape!"

The demon took a couple of steps forward before more black dust flew toward its eyes. But then the demon vanished, causing the black dust to miss and fall onto the floor. A second later, the demon reappeared a couple of feet from where it had stood and slashed at the air.

Somehow, the demon's paw struck something that Keo could not see. He heard what sounded like a small body hit the floor and rolled a couple of feet, but he did not understand what it meant until Dlaine shouted, "Jola!"

It was a useless shout, however, because the demon started running toward them again. This time, Keo knew that there was no way either he or Dlaine would survive. The demon had murder in its eyes and it wouldn't take it long to kill them. It might even kill them both in one hit, which was certainly possible, considering its massive size and incredible strength.

Dlaine, rather than run, started pulling at Gildshine again. Keo wanted to shout at him to forget the stupid sword and run, but he completely lacked the strength to even mutter that thought. All he could do was lie there and wait for the demon to kill Dlaine and him.

But then, Dlaine finally succeeded in pulling Gildshine out of the floor. Then Dlaine stood between Keo and the incoming demon, wielding Gildshine in his hands with surprising expertise, like he had handled swords before.

"Pathetic human!" the demon shouted as it ran toward them. "You think you can hurt me with that blade? Your death shall be as painful as torture!"

Dlaine, however, did not reply. He just redoubled his grip on Gildshine and ran toward the demon. Keo wanted to shout at

Dlaine to drop the sword and run, because there was no way that Dlaine could hope to even touch the demon, but again he lacked the strength to speak and so could only watch as Dlaine ran toward his death.

But at the last second, a cloud of that thick black dust that Jola had thrown into the eyes of the demon flew out of nowhere and struck the demon in the face again. The demon let out a yelp of pain and surprise, skidding to a halt and wiping at its eyes again, but Dlaine did not slow down. He pulled Gildshine back and stabbed it directly into the exposed throat of the demon.

And much to Keo's surprise, Gildshine's blade cut through the demon's throat, sending black blood gushing from its wounds. The demon let out a gasp of pain, but did not fight back. Dlaine just drove Gildshine deeper and deeper into the demon's throat before pulling the blade out and stepping back.

Black blood now flowed down the demon's chest. Nonetheless, the demon managed to look down at Dlaine with hatred in its eyes.

"Murderer's … friend …" the demon said, its words mangled due to the damage done to its throat. "Killers … both of you …"

The demon's eyes rolled into the back of its head and it fell forwards. As soon as it crashed to the floor, its body crumbled into that same sand-like substance that Hand of Blood's corpse had turned into, before it, too, disintegrated into nothingness, leaving not even one drop of blood to indicate that it had been lying there mere moments before.

Then Dlaine lowered Gildshine and started panting. He looked over his shoulder at Keo and said, "What? Never seen someone kill a demon before?"

Keo blinked. "How … did you …"

"Luck, mostly," said Dlaine, turning around to face Keo. "Jola told me that all magical weapons have residual magic on them after their ability has been used. I wagered that Gildshine had enough residual magic on it to make it strong enough to kill the demon … and I also wagered that the demon would not know that and therefore would not see my being armed with Gildshine as a danger to avoid."

"Amazing," said Keo. "And lucky."

"Very lucky, but you know what they say about luck," said Dlaine. "It's about preparation meeting opportunity, or whatever. I can't remember right now."

Then the sound of clapping hands filled the lobby and Keo and Dlaine looked up at the staircase leading to the second floor. The Fallsman, plus Takan and his Warriors, stood at the top of the staircase, looking down on Keo, Dlaine, and Jola, like they had been standing there for a while. Only the Fallsman, however, was clapping, while Takan and the Warriors merely stood around him in silence. The Fallsman then lowered his hands and started walking down the stairs, his boots loudly clicking against each stone step. Takan and the Warriors followed their leader, still saying nothing.

"Excellent, excellent, simply excellent," said the Fallsman, putting his hands in his pockets as he walked down the stairs. "You killed the demon in less than an hour. Quite incredible. You two—or should I say three, counting your invisible friend—would surely be a force to be reckoned with if you ever decided to get into the life of organized crime, that's for certain."

"Yeah, sure," said Dlaine. He looked down at Keo and said,

"Let me help you up so we can leave."

Dlaine bent over and helped Keo to his feet. Keo was starting to feel a little stronger, but he still needed Dlaine's help to stand and knew that he would not feel well until tomorrow at least. Dlaine, to his credit, seemed to be holding it together, even though the killing of that demon had clearly shaken him. Or maybe it was the revelation that Keo had not been lying about the demons' existence that had shaken him.

Then Dlaine and Keo turned to face the Fallsman, who was now walking across the floor toward them. The Fallsman stopped several feet away from them, smiling, though Keo noticed how his eyes kept glancing at Gildshine, which Dlaine still held.

"I thought for sure that the ghost would kill you three, since you had so little time to prepare, but apparently I was dead wrong," said the Fallsman. He put his hands together. "Tell me, Keo of the Sword, where did you get that magical sword?"

Keo had very little strength in which to talk, but thankfully he didn't need to say anything, because Dlaine spoke instead.

"Sorry, but my friend isn't in the mood to talk," said Dlaine. He gestured at the spot where the demon had stood. "Now, we killed your ghost. According to the deal we agreed to, you said you would let us go if we killed it."

The Fallsman looked disappointed at the change in subject, but then shrugged and said, "I cannot deny that. Yes, you three may leave. I presume you already know how to leave Castarious?"

"I do," said Dlaine, nodding. "I've been here several times in the past, so I know my way around. Well, unless you've done some serious redecorating since the last time I was here."

"Ah, Castarious is the same today as it has been ever since the Kingdom's fall two decades ago," said the Fallsman with a chuckle. "I don't even have enough men to make any massive, sweeping changes to the city's layout, anyway." Then the Fallsman suddenly stopped chuckling and he looked serious. "That ghost … it called itself a demon, did it not?"

The Fallsman's tone was hesitant and even slightly fearful, as if seeking reassurance that he had not heard what he thought he had heard. It made the Fallsman look much weaker than he normally did, though Keo couldn't blame him, seeing as most people feared the demons.

"That it did," said Dlaine. "That it did. What of it?"

The Fallsman rubbed his hands against each other, which seemed like a nervous habit to Keo. "But that was a lie, yes? The demons are merely legend, scary stories children tell each other around campfires at night in order to frighten each other. It wasn't *actually* a demon, was it?"

"It was," said Keo, causing the Fallsman to look at him suddenly. His voice was still weak, but he wanted to be the one to explain it to the Fallsman.

The Fallsman's eyes widened. "And you mean to say that everything it said—about the Kingdom of Demons, about you killing one of its brethren earlier, and everything else—was true?"

"Yes," said Keo, nodding weakly. "The demons are returning. It's why we have to get to Capitika fast as we can, so we can tell the Magical Council so they can prepare for it."

The Fallsman tapped his chin in thought. Behind him, his Warriors exchanged terrified looks with one another, while Takan shifted her weight from foot to foot, like she was unsure how to react to this news.

"I …" the Fallsman seemed at a loss for words at the moment. "What will happen if the demons rise again?"

"Likely what happened in the old stories," said Dlaine. "Lots of death and slaughter and war and chaos and that sort of thing. Fun stuff."

The Fallsman now looked like he was trying to figure out how he was going to use this new knowledge to his advantage, but Keo doubted there was anything the Fallsman could do to stop the demons.

The the Fallsman shook his head and said, "Please, why don't you two stay the night in my mansion? You seem too tired to make the trek out of the city on your own, particularly today."

Dlaine eyed the Fallsman warily. "What are you trying to do?"

"Think of it as a token of my appreciation," said the Fallsman. He gestured at the mansion's lobby. "There are many rooms in my mansion, so we shouldn't have any trouble finding you a room to sleep in. Besides, it is getting late and by the time you leave Castarious, it will be pitch-black. And if I recall my demon stories correctly, the demons were always more prominent and dangerous at night."

Dlaine looked at Keo with a questioning gaze. "What do you think, Keo? Should we accept his offer or not?"

While Keo still didn't trust the Fallsman very much, he knew that there was no way that he, Dlaine, and Jola could make it out of the city in Keo's current tired state. The thought of sleeping in a nice, soft, comfortable bed even for just one night, after spending the last several nights camping outside in the wilderness, was too tempting for Keo to resist. And besides, the Fallsman's offer seemed genuine, so he saw no reason to reject it.

So Keo said, "Yes. We accept."

"Very well, then," said the Fallsman. He gestured at Takan. "I will have Takan here show you to your room and then you may leave in the morning when you are ready."

Chapter Nineteen

T
HAT NIGHT, KEO SLEPT soundly due to the sheer
exhaustion from using Gildshine. He slept in a very
nice, soft bed, while Dlaine slept on the sofa in the room
they were given. In fact, Keo slept so soundly that he did not even
dream, which was a common side effect of using Gildshine's
ability.

In the morning, when Keo awoke, he felt rested and refreshed,
while Dlaine seemed groggy and worn out, probably due to the
stress from yesterday's fight with the demon. They did not make
their own breakfast this morning; instead, they were provided
with breakfast by the Fallsman's men, who said that the Fallsman
wanted to give them this meal as a final reward for their help. The
meal was good, but they did not spend a lot of time eating it
because Keo and Dlaine wanted to leave Castarious as quickly as
possible.

Thus, it was an hour later that Keo, Dlaine, and Jola stood
outside of the Fallsman's mansion, their packs slung over their
shoulders and Gildshine at Keo's side. They were about to leave
before a voice from the top of the front steps of the mansion said,
"Wait!"

Keo and Dlaine looked over their shoulders to see the
Fallsman standing at the top of the front steps, with Takan
standing silently by his side. The Fallsman looked like he had not

gotten much sleep last night. Even from a distance, Keo could see the bags under the Fallsman's eyes, as well as the silver ring from Sadia's letter, which was still wrapped around the Fallsman's finger. Keo did not know why the Fallsman had apparently stayed up late last night, though he decided not to ask any questions about it, because the Fallsman didn't seem like he would answer those questions.

"Yes?" said Dlaine with a yawn. "What is it?"

The Fallsman glanced at Takan, who nodded, and then looked at Keo and Dlaine again and said, "When will the demons rise again?"

Keo and Dlaine exchanged puzzled looks before Keo said, "In about six months, according to the first demon I killed."

"And where will they rise?" said the Fallsman.

Keo shrugged. "We don't know. That's why we're going to Capitika. If we can get the Magical Council to help, we might be able to locate the demons and stop their return before it's too late."

"I see," said the Fallsman. He sounded and looked troubled at that thought. "Well, Keo of the Sword and Dlaine of the Fist, I wish you both the best of luck in your quest. And if you ever need any help, do not be afraid to send me a message."

"All right," said Keo. Then he hesitated, and asked, "What will you do about the return of the demons in the meantime?"

The Fallsman shook his head. "Now, now, Keo, I cannot tell you about *all* of my plans, even if we are now allies. The only thing I *can* tell you is that I—and my men—will survive, one way or another."

That was infuriatingly vague to Keo, but then, he supposed

that he didn't really need to know what the Fallsman's plans were, because he was quite sure that he had nothing to do with them.

So Keo nodded once more and said, "All right. Well, this is good bye, then. May peace and luck be upon you and your men."

With that, Keo, Dlaine, and Jola departed, leaving behind the Fallsman and his stately mansion. Still, Keo did look over his shoulder one last time before they left, but when he did, the Fallsman and Takan were nowhere in sight. He wondered if they had gone back inside the mansion to prepare for the return of the demons or if they had gone back inside to do something else.

It took Keo, Dlaine, and Jola a couple of hours to reach the back part of the city, where the ruins of Castarious met the Silver Falls themselves. Here Keo discovered that part of Castarious had been built directly into the cliffs of the Falls themselves, which was how the top and bottom halves of the abandoned city were connected. According to Dlaine, the top and bottom halves of the city were connected through a series of roads and tunnels carved into the cliffs, along with an old lift system that could carry hundreds of people at once. Unfortunately, the lift system was currently out of order due to the fact that no one had kept it in working condition for years, so the trio were forced to travel up the roads and tunnels built into the cliffs' walls instead.

That journey took them roughly three hours, with a couple of breaks in between for lunch and resting, and it was one of the strangest parts of the journey yet. The walls, ceiling, and floor of the roads and tunnels were damp from the Silver Falls outside, making them slightly slippery. The light from the sun outside shone through the Falls, casting strange shadows and light patterns on the walls. Even the Falls themselves were not very loud, but that was probably more due to Jola's spell still being active than anything.

Once they reached the top half of the city, Keo got a good look at the two massive Towers he had seen yesterday when he had first seen Castarious from a distance. They were truly gigantic, almost like giants or gods rather than towers, and the bridge between them looked equally massive. According to Dlaine, these Towers had once been the most popular way for the inhabitants of the city to cross the river without needing a boat, although apparently boats had still been in use. They were called the Crossing Towers in their heyday, but nowadays were completely abandoned. It was a miracle that the Crossing Bridge had not yet fallen, which meant that it was either designed brilliantly or it was being held up by some kind of magic. In any case, Dlaine told Keo that their journey was not going to take them up and through the Crossing Towers, so they would not need to test the Bridge's stability. Keo was glad about that, because even though he was certain that the view of the Silver Falls and the surrounding area were fantastic from the Bridge, he really did not want to find out if the Bridge was still strong enough to carry the weight of even just a few people on its surface.

By late afternoon, the ruins of Castarious were far behind them and Keo, Dlaine, and Jola found themselves once more in the hilly countryside of South Lamaira. They kept walking until they found another road, which Dlaine said would take them to their next destination—a town called Carrk—if they followed it.

So they followed the road until late in the evening, after the sun had fallen, and thus they decided to rest for the night. They found a grove of trees just off the main road that kept them hidden from the road and decided to camp there for the night. It was hard to go from sleeping on the nice, soft, comfy bed of the Fallsman's mansion to the hard ground, but Keo was used to it, so he did not complain.

But as he and Dlaine lay down on their bedrolls, while Jola sat in the treetops somewhere above keeping an eye out for any possible threats to their safety, Keo found his mind wandering back to what the demon back in Castarious had said to him. He looked at Dlaine, who had pulled his blanket over his body and was already closing his eyes, and said, "Dlaine?"

Dlaine's eyes snapped open again and he looked at Keo in annoyance. "What is it? Can it wait until morning? I'm wiped out from today's journey."

"I know, but there's something the demon said to me back in Castarious that got me thinking," said Keo. He rested his hands behind his head and frowned. "It said that I have no way of knowing just how 'hopeless' our 'little quest' actually is. What do you think it meant by that?"

Dlaine rolled his eyes. "Just a psychological trick. Obviously the demon was trying to crush your morale by making you believe that our journey to Capitika is hopeless. I hope you know better than to believe whatever nonsense that demon is spouting."

"I do," said Keo. "But—"

"But nothing," said Dlaine. He turned on his side, his back toward Keo, and said, "Good night. We have a long day ahead of us tomorrow, so let's both get as much sleep as we can."

With that, Dlaine immediately started snoring. Keo wanted to keep talking about the demon's words, but he knew better than to wake up Dlaine when he didn't want to talk, so Keo just pulled his blanket up to his chin and stared up at the dark trees. Through the gaps in their branches, he could see the stars in the night sky, which looked much the same as the sky back home in the Low Woods. It was a clear summer night sky, but that hardly comforted Keo.

That demon seemed too confident that our quest would fail, Keo thought. *And I'm not sure it was just lying. What if there is something about our quest that we don't know of, something that will make it pointless, like the demon said?*

Keo knew that he should have ignored such thoughts and gone to sleep, but he found it difficult because the demon's words had burrowed into his mind and would not leave him alone. He figured that the demon probably meant that some of its fellow demons would come after him, Dlaine, and Jola at some point before they reached Capitika, although that didn't seem like the correct conclusion to draw from the demon's words.

Eventually, Keo drifted off to sleep, but this time he had terrible dreams, dreams about the demon's lupine face glaring at him from the darkness and going on and on about the sheer hopelessness of his quest.

That was why Keo was happy when Dlaine shook him awake early the next morning and made breakfast for them both. Dlaine seemed grumpy, like he hadn't slept well either, but Keo did not ask him why, nor did he offer to tell Dlaine about his nightmares. He decided that he was going to focus on getting to Carrk, and from there, Capitika, regardless of anything that demon had said.

After breakfast, Keo, Dlaine, and Jola continued on their journey to Capitika. They walked along the main road all day, taking only the occasional break to eat or rest, and did not talk much, because Dlaine seemed distracted by something and anytime Keo spoke to him, Dlaine would snap at him like he had insulted him. Thus, Keo was alone with his thoughts for much of the journey, although he occasionally found himself looking over his shoulder just to be certain that they were not being followed by any demon.

In the late afternoon, they crested another hill and this time saw another town, similar to New Ora and Torgan, but twice as large as either. Keo estimated that there were about a thousand buildings altogether in the town below, including the large Magician's Tower that rose from the center. High stone walls surrounded the town on every side, with several Enforcers patrolling the ramparts or guarding the gates. From the north came a thin but steady stream of travelers, although they were too far away for Keo to make out many details, except that some of them rode horses and others had large wagons that appeared filled with goods for commerce.

"That's Carrk," said Dlaine, pointing at the town below them. "It is overseen by Magician Enira."

"Is she a good Magician or a bad one?" said Keo.

"Frankly, I don't know," said Dlaine with a shrug. "Last time I was here, she was just put in charge after the last one had his title forcibly removed from the Council."

"Why did the Council remove his title?" asked Keo.

"I don't know all the details, because the Council doesn't usually like us peasants know their reasoning behind such decisions, but I heard that he was removed because he apparently had refused to do something they told him to do," said Dlaine with a shrug. "And then he disappeared, though where to, I don't know. But frankly, I'd rather not know."

Keo nodded. "Then let's keep going. I'm already tired of sleeping in the wilderness."

Keo only managed to take one step forward, however, before one of Dlaine's strong hands rested on his shoulder. He looked at Dlaine, who was looking at him in annoyance.

"What?" said Keo. "Why'd you stop me? Don't you want to get to Carrk as quickly as possible?"

"Yes, I do," said Dlaine. "But remember what happened in Torgan when we told the gatekeepers who we are? They nearly arrested us, and would have if Sadia hadn't intervened. And I doubt Sadia followed us all the way from Torgan, unless she's that obsessed with you."

"Why would Sadia be obsessed with me?" said Keo, arching an eyebrow in confusion.

"That's not the point," said Dlaine. He pointed at the guards at the town's front gates below. "The point is that the Enforcers of Carrk probably know about us and what we're wanted for. Therefore, we can't just march up to the gates, tell 'em who we are, and expect them to let us in without causing a scene."

"What should we do, then?" said Keo. "Go around the town and head straight to Capitika?"

"No," said Dlaine, shaking his head. "We need to stop in Carrk because there is someone there who I need to speak with."

"Who?" said Keo.

"An old friend of mine who I haven't spoken to in a while," said Dlaine, somewhat vaguely. "Won't be long. But if we're going to enter Carrk, then we need to come up with a convincing lie so that the Carrk gatekeepers won't realize who we are and arrest us."

"Just like in Torgan," said Keo. "What were the false names Sadia made up for us?"

"She didn't make up any names for us," Dlaine pointed out. "Remember? She convinced Torgan's gatekeepers that we were mixed up with the 'real' criminals, Ceo and Flaine, but I don't think that will work here because the Enforcers in Carrk are probably still looking for a couple of prison escapees named Keo and Dlaine."

"Then why not call ourselves Ceo and Flaine?" said Keo. "It would be easier than coming up with some new names, wouldn't it? It's not like the Carrk gatekeepers know what we look like, anyway. They wouldn't recognize us, so they wouldn't know we were lying."

Dlaine opened his mouth, like he was going to criticize the idea, but then he closed it and looked like he was thinking about it. Then he nodded and said, "Actually, that is a good idea. Wish I'd thought of it first."

"All right, then, Flaine," said Keo with a smile. "Why don't you lead the way to town?"

Dlaine nodded and then the three of them made their way down the path to Carrk's southern gates. Upon arriving at the gates, they were met by the gatekeepers, a couple of Enforcers who asked them to identify themselves and state their business. Keo and Dlaine identified themselves using the fake names that they had agreed upon and were let inside without any issue. Neither did the guards ask for Keo or Dlaine to give up any of their weapons, which was good because Keo did not like being separated from Gildshine for very long.

Upon entering Carrk, Keo looked around at the town. It was similar to Torgan in appearance, except there was a large water fountain in the center of the street they walked upon, a fountain in the shape of a massive flower. The fountain sprayed beautiful, crystal clear water in the air, while many people stood or sat around it, talking and socializing among themselves. Children tossed coins into the fountain, while nearby parents kept a careful eye on the kids to make sure they did not get into trouble or hurt themselves. The water looked nice and cool in the hot summer sun, especially with the way the sun's rays reflected off its surface.

The streets themselves seemed a lot wider than in Torgan or New Ora. They were flatter and better paved, but they also looked a lot more used, like they got a lot of traffic. In fact, Keo saw a horse-drawn carriage parked in front of one building and through the carriage's windows he could see boxes full of what looked like glowing stones, though he had no idea what those stones were or what they did.

And a large banner was strung across the street, depicting two Magicians dueling each other, though Keo was unable to read the large, glittery words written on the banner and so had no idea what it was advertising.

"So," said Keo as the gates closed behind Dlaine and him. "Where is your friend? The one you said we needed to meet?"

"Nearby," said Dlaine, who was now looking around Carrk like he was afraid that people were watching him, even though as far as Keo could tell, none of the town's inhabitants seemed to be paying any attention to them. "Come on. We won't stay here long."

Dlaine immediately started walking down the street to the right and Keo followed, saying, "Okay, but what do you want to talk to your friend about? Is it related to our quest to go to Capitika?"

"It's related to *my* quest to save my daughter's life," said Dlaine, glancing over his shoulder at Keo in annoyance. "And as I said, we won't stay for long. I just need to ask her one question and then we can head straight to Capitika, which should only take us a couple of days at most."

Keo nodded and then looked up at the large banner, which they passed underneath on their way down the street. "What does that banner say? It looks like an advertisement for something."

Dlaine looked up as well before returning his focus to the street before them. "It's advertising Carrk's Tenth Annual Magician Charity Duel."

"Carrk's tenth what?" said Keo, picking up his pace to keep up with Dlaine, who was walking rather quickly for a man his age.

"Carrk's Tenth Annual Magician Charity Duel," Dlaine repeated, this time without looking at Keo. "Clean out your ears so I don't have to repeat myself again."

"I heard you, I heard you," said Keo. "But what is this charity duel thing? I've never heard of it."

Dlaine sighed as they walked past a man sitting on the street, strumming a guitar, with a hat nearby that was clearly where you were supposed to put donations for him. "I keep forgetting that you haven't gone anywhere past the front porch of your house for your whole life. Well, the Magician Charity Duel is part-tradition, part-government-enforced entertainment."

"That doesn't really clear anything up," said Keo. "At all. If it's a duel, does it involve fighting?"

"Yes," said Dlaine as they stopped to allow another horse-drawn carriage to pass them before they continued on. "See, the people of Carrk have always loved duels, whether between normal people or between Magicians. In the old days, prior to the Kingdom's fall, Carrk was where all of the best duelists in the Kingdom would come to fight, including King Riuno himself whenever the dueling bug bit him. So about ten years ago the people of Carrk decided to put this reputation to use by creating the Magician Charity Duel, in which two Magicians are invited from different parts of South Lamaira to duel for the entertainment of the people in order to raise money for the poor."

"Is it to the death?" said Keo with a gulp.

"Death? Nope," said Dlaine, shaking his head. "It goes on until one of them is knocked out or gives up. But the duels can get pretty brutal, depending on what kind of spells the duelists use and how much they dislike each other."

"You also said that it is part-government-enforced entertainment," said Keo. "What do you mean by that?"

"I mean that the government of Carrk is in charge of running it," said Dlaine as they passed a shop that seemed to be selling carved statues of Magicians. "Originally it was just run by the citizens themselves, but then the Magical Council caught wind of it and demanded that the charity duel be handed over to the government of Carrk because those sorts of things are supposed to be overseen by them."

"Is that a bad thing?" said Keo.

"Sort of," said Dlaine. "While the charity duels haven't

exploded, the fact is that they aren't doing nearly as well as they used to. Then there's the fact that the Magical Council is taking part of the money received during the charity duels and using it to fill their own coffers, which I think is the main reason they demanded that the government of Carrk take over the event more than anything else."

"Oh," said Keo. "Where does the duel usually take place?"

"Usually in the town square, which isn't too far from here," said Dlaine, gesturing down the street. "But we don't have time to stay and watch a couple of Magicians beat the stuffing out of each other. We're here to speak with my friend."

"Why don't we split up?" said Keo. "I think the charity duel, government corruption notwithstanding, sounds like a great way to pass the time. You and Jola can go to your friend's house and talk to her, while I go and watch the duel. We can meet up at the northern gates and head to Capitika from there."

Dlaine frowned, clearly not enthusiastic about the idea. "I don't know. I don't like the idea of splitting up, even if no one here knows who we actually are. Too much could go wrong and I, for one, am tired of things going wrong."

"I think you worry too much," said Keo, shaking his head. "I promise not to get into any fights with anyone, nor will I reveal my real identity. I'll just watch the duel, and once it's over, I will immediately head over to the northern gates and meet you there. I promise."

Dlaine looked at Keo with skeptical eyes, but then he sighed and said, "All right. You go and do that, while Jola and I go to my friend's house. Just be careful, all right?"

Keo smiled and nodded. "Sure. Now where's the town square

again?"

Dlaine gestured ahead. "Just go left at the corner of that street up there and you should eventually reach it."

"Thanks," said Keo. "See you later."

With that, Keo dashed across the street, passing by a group of Hasfarians who were talking rapidly among each other in the Hasfarian language, and was soon on his way to the duel, leaving Dlaine and Jola behind and hoping that the duel would be exciting and interesting.

Chapter Twenty

A FTER A FEW MINUTES of running, Keo eventually stumbled upon a large, crowded part of Carrk. The street was full of hundreds and hundreds of people, more than Keo had ever seen in one place in his life, all of them apparently here for the charity duel. There were even merchants on the sides of the streets trying to sell things to the people, but Keo ignored them because he had no interest in buying anything at the moment. Instead, he wanted to find out if the duel had started yet.

So Keo walked up to one of the merchants—who seemed to be selling some kind of strange red fruit with a strong sweet scent that Keo had never seen before—and said, "Has the charity duel started yet?"

The merchant looked at Keo and said, "Not yet, good sir, though it will start in five minutes. In the meantime, would you be interested in buying one of my—"

"No thanks," said Keo, turning and walking away from the merchant without even thinking about it.

Keo pushed his way through the crowd of people, earning more than a few glares or annoyed looks for his rudeness, but Keo did not care. Despite his height, he could not view the duel from behind the crowd, so he was going to make sure he got a spot in the front of the crowd so he could see the duel.

When Keo finally reached the front of the crowd, he found long red cord separating the crowd from the town square. The square itself was wide open and completely empty, which told Keo that the two Magician duelists, whoever they were, had apparently not yet arrived. He saw hundreds of people on all sides of the square, chatting away among each other, while a few men and women went around with boxes in their hands into which the spectators tossed in lems. From what Keo could tell, those people must have been the ones who collected the donations from the spectators. He dug his hands into his own pockets to donate, because he could see one of the men coming his way, but at that moment someone dashed out from the crowd and stopped in the exact center of the open square.

It was a short man with long dark hair, wearing a nice-looking blue suit and the biggest and whitest set of teeth that Keo had ever seen on another human being. The man raised his hands, causing everyone to fall silent immediately, which Keo found impressive, because he did not think that one man could make so many people stop speaking at once.

"Welcome, welcome, one and all, to the Tenth Annual Magician Charity Duel of Carrk!" the man said, his voice loud and booming despite his short statue. "My name is Yanar of the Voice and, as usual, I will be your announcer for this year's charity duel!"

Although Yanar seemed nice enough, Keo found himself put off by the announcer's large mouth and self-congratulatory attitude. There was something about it that made Keo distrust the man, though he wasn't sure what.

"I am extremely pleased to see so many people here today,"

said Yanar, looking around at the assembled spectators. "We have people from Capitika, New Ora, Torgan, Freni, even from faraway and exotic places like Hasfar and its capital Ishver. I can guarantee to each and every one of you today that this duel will be the greatest one yet."

The crowd cheered when Yanar said that, and Keo joined them. He liked a good fight as much as anybody, and despite his reservations about Yanar's character, he saw no reason to doubt his word here.

"And as always, please make sure to donate whatever you can to the Collectors who are going around the crowds collecting money for our poor and needy citizens," Yanar continued. "Remember, how much you give to those who have less than you is the *true* measure of your greatness, whether you are a powerful king or a humble peasant."

A man holding a box—apparently one of the Collectors— came down the front of the crowd on the other side of the cord. A dozen hands deposited as many lems into the box, including Keo, who despite not having very much money of his own decided he could afford to give away at least one lem, even being aware of what Dlaine had warned him about the corruption in Carrk's government. Then he returned his attention to Yanar, who had continued speaking.

"And now, to the main event," said Yanar. "Our two duelists today, who are considered to be among the best duelists in the country today! Come on out and show yourselves to the generous people of this town and others!"

A huge burst of fire exploded several feet away from Yanar, causing him to jump and everyone else in the crowd to stand back. Yet the fire lasted only for a second and soon went out all by itself, leaving a large man, built more like a mountain than a human being, standing in its place. The man's skin was as dark as coal, his head almost completely bald. He wore a simple red shirt with torn-off sleeves and towered over almost everyone else in the vicinity. Keo caught a brief whiff of smoke from the large man's body, which made Keo wonder if the Magician was a smoker or if it was due to his fiery entrance.

Yanar, who looked taken aback by the Magician's entrance, recovered pretty quickly and, gesturing at the man, said, "Everyone, I am pleased to introduce Magician Kraggan of the Fire, known in magical dueling circles as the Ever Burning Flame. Aside from having won the Magical Dueling Championship last year, Kraggan is also a veteran of the wars with the Divinians and Restorationists, so he has already helped our great nation in ways that many have not."

Half of the crowd immediately cheered when they saw the Magician. Keo had never heard of Kraggan before, but he knew a warrior when he saw one. Kraggan had scars along his arms and seemed to be highly aware of his surroundings. For a moment, Keo thought Kraggan's eyes focused on Gildshine at his side, but then Kraggan looked away and Keo decided that the Magician had been looking at something else.

"Magician Kraggan, I just wanted to say that it is a huge honor to have you competing in this year's charity duel," said Yanar. "It is truly a reflection of your generous spirit." He gestured at the crowd. "Any words for the crowd?"

Kraggan looked out over the crowds. He seemed like a silent type to Keo, but then Kraggan held up one hand and shouted, in a deep voice, "Citizens of Carrk and visitors from other towns and lands! I promise to give you what you have come for, and so much more. I have always considered generosity toward the poor to be among the chiefest of virtues, and virtue should be rewarded, which I shall be glad to do by giving you the greatest duel that this town—that Lamaira itself—has ever seen!"

Again, the crowd went wild, throwing up their hands and screaming. One of the women even shouted, "I love you, Kraggan!" while a man clearly shouted, "Kraggan's the best!"

"Yes, yes, yes," said Yanar, waving his hands at the crowd to calm them down. "Magician Kraggan is almost unmatched in his generosity, having promised to give half of his yearly earnings from the Magical Dueling Championship to our charity drive after this duel is over. Truly indeed, he is almost too great for this bleak world."

Wow, Keo thought, although he did not join the crowd in the third round of applause and cheering that erupted after Yanar's praise of the large Magician. *He sounds like a pretty great guy. I wonder how well he fights, though.*

Again, Yanar waved at the crowd to silence them and then said, "And now, please get ready to applaud Magician Kraggan's opponent, Magician Maryal of the Wind!"

Yanar pointed dramatically to his left, drawing the attention of the entire crowd, including Keo, to the spot he was pointing at. Keo expected this Magician Maryal, whoever she was, to make just as dramatic and flashy an entrance as Magician Kraggan, perhaps creating a large tornado to carry her down from the sky if her title was a hint to her magical powers.

But nothing happened. The bit of street that Yanar pointed at remained empty and bare.

At first, the crowd seemed content to wait for Magician Maryal's appearance, but as the seconds ticked by, more and more people began to fidget, and soon grumble. One man even shouted, "Hey! Where is she?"

Yanar, who was now sweating, pulled out a handkerchief from his front chest pocket and, dabbing his forehead, said, "Ah, well, it appears that Magician Maryal is running a bit late today. But not to worry, I doubt it is anything too serious. I'm sure she'll be here any minute now."

Although Yanar's tone was apologetic and pacifying, more and more people in the crowd were looking around, grumbling, and shifting their weight impatiently. Even Kraggan folded his arms over his chest, tapped his foot against the street, and yawned. And there was still no sign of Maryal anywhere, which made Keo wonder if Maryal had decided to run away rather than face Kraggan in battle. Keo could understand that, because even he wasn't sure that he could beat a man as large and big as Kraggan.

"So, er, uh …" Yanar looked around and then suddenly pointed at one of the Collectors, a man standing near Keo. "You! Go to Magician Maryal's inn and find out what she is doing. And do it quickly, because—"

Yanar was interrupted by a gigantic gust of wind that tore through the area. Hats, papers, and leaves flew through the air as the powerful wind blew through the town square. Even Kraggan had to brace himself against it, because the wind was quite cold despite the hot sun above.

As the wind blew, a large shadow passed by Keo overhead, causing him to look up in time to see a woman gliding on the wind with wings. Then he blinked and realized that the woman was actually gliding using her robes, which were spread out to catch the wind.

By then, the rest of the crowd had noticed the woman and many people were pointing at her in surprise, likely because they had never seen a gliding woman before. The woman circled the crowd once before landing suddenly yet gracefully on the street, right where Yanar had been pointing mere moments ago. She then stood up and tossed off her robes, which fell into a pile behind her.

The woman was probably older than Keo, with short blonde hair that was messy due to the wind from earlier. Unlike Kraggan, her green tunic had sleeves, but they were loose and open, most likely to help her catch the wind. Yet despite her dramatic entrance, she looked more than a bit tired, yawning as she stood up and rubbing her eyes like she had just awoken a couple of minutes ago.

"Sorry I'm late," said the woman. She yawned again. "I slept in and forgot to set my timer. I got here as quickly as I could."

Yanar—whose own hair had been blown messily about by the woman's wind—nonetheless recovered from the shock of seeing the woman and said, "That is fine, Magician Maryal. We are just glad to see that you are here for the benefit of Carrk's poor and needy."

Keo was not sure that that was exactly true, because Yanar's tone sounded annoyed and agitated, especially when he brushed his messy hair back. The crowd, too, seemed more annoyed than happy at her entrance, probably due to the fact that she had sent many of their possessions flying out of their arms or off their heads. Kraggan merely smirked, a sign that he didn't take Maryal very seriously as an opponent.

"Anyway, for those of you who don't know her, this is Magician Maryal of the Wind," said Yanar, gesturing at her. "Like Magician Kraggan, she, too, has several notable accomplishments under her belt like … like …"

Yanar seemed to struggle to come up with any of Maryal's accomplishments for a moment before he snapped his fingers and said, "Oh, yes. Now I remember. Magician Maryal landed in fourth place in the Magician Duel Championship last year. And I believe she has a few fans around here somewhere who could probably tell us more about what she's done."

Keo looked around at the crowd, which had gone silent. Maryal looked rather embarrassed at her own lateness or maybe she was embarrassed at the icy coldness with which the crowd seemed to treat her. Considering how no one seemed to like her or know much about her, Keo wondered why Maryal had even been invited to the duel at all. He almost felt embarrassed for her, yet he said nothing because he knew even less about Maryal than most of the other people in the crowd did.

Yanar must have sensed the awkwardness of the moment as well, because he then said, "Well, anyway, now that everyone has been introduced to these two great Magicians, let us get the duel started. Magician Kraggan, Magician Maryal, are you two ready? Do you remember the rules?"

Kraggan nodded. "Of course. No killing, no harming any of the spectators, and keep all spells in the circle of the duel."

Maryal yawned again and said, "I'm ready if Kraggan is. Let's do this."

"Very well, then," said Yanar. "As soon as I step out of the circle, the duel will commence. Prepare your spells and may the best Magician win!"

With that, Yanar ran away from the two Magicians. Kraggan cracked his neck and his knuckles, while Maryal looked like she was still trying to wake up. If Keo believed in betting, he would have been willing to bet on Kraggan, mostly because of the man's obvious strength and skill as a combatant. Maryal gave off the aura of someone who didn't take fighting very seriously, though Keo recalled what Master Tiram had said about not underestimating others.

Yanar ducked under the cord on the other side of the square, stood up, turned around, and said, "All right! Let the Tenth Annual Magician Charity Duel of Carrk begin!"

As soon as those words left Yanar's mouth, Kraggan summoned two fireballs in his hands and hurled them both at Maryal. He did it so quickly that Maryal barely had time to respond. She raised her hands and unleashed a blast of cold air at the fire balls right before they struck her, instantly blowing them out, but as soon as her wind died off, Kraggan slammed his feet into the street. A line of glowing heat shot out from where his feet had hit the street, snaking toward Maryal, but the Magician jumped into the air right before the heat hit her. She jumped toward Kraggan and attempted to kick him in the head, but the larger Magician dodged it, causing Maryal to go sailing past him.

Kraggan, however, grabbed the collar of her tunic as she sailed past him and hurled her away. Maryal crashed into the street and even rolled a few times before coming to a halt. The crowd erupted into cheers at that move, including Keo. He was not much of a Kraggan fan, but even he could recognize a good fighting move when he saw it.

Kraggan waved at the crowd as Maryal got back to her feet. Her clothes were covered in grime and dirt now, while her cheek had a small cut on it. Keo was impressed that Maryal could get back up again so soon after that attack, because it had looked like Kraggan had thrown her as hard as he could. Perhaps Maryal was stronger than she looked.

"Do you want to give up now, Maryal?" said Kraggan, spreading his arms wide, a jeering smile on his lips. "Or do you want to keep fighting? It's your choice."

Maryal wiped some blood away from her chin. She looked far more awake now than before, but she still seemed tired, though that may have been because she had just been tossed about like a rag doll.

She shook her head and said, "Sorry, Kraggan, but I didn't get to fourth place in the Magician Duel Championship by giving up after a few weak hits."

Kraggan laughed. "And neither did I win the Championship by fighting weak opponents who gave up after a light beating. I am pleased to see that you are far stronger than you look." Kraggan's hands burst into flame. "Unfortunately for you, it takes more than endurance to beat me!"

Kraggan raised his hands, like he was going to throw more fireballs at Maryal, but then Maryal waved her hands at him. Without warning, Kraggan's flames immediately went out, causing Kraggan to say, "What the—" before he suddenly grasped his throat and started choking.

The crowd gasped, including Keo, but Maryal did not hesitate to run up to Kraggan and kick him in the stomach. Even though she was shorter and smaller than Kraggan, her blow was enough to knock him flat off his feet. The large Magician fell to the street on his back and he immediately stopped choking. Instead, he started gasping for breath and rapidly sitting up, coughing hard like he had been strangled by a giant.

"What …" Kraggan gasped. "What was that?"

Maryal smirked. "Fire needs oxygen to burn. Take away oxygen and you can't even light a match. So I took away your oxygen. For that matter, human beings can't live very long without air, either, so it worked out in two ways for me."

Keo had to admit that that was a clever move, and based on the impressed expressions on the faces of many people in the crowd, he wasn't the only one who thought that.

Still coughing and gasping, Kraggan got back to his feet. He looked far weaker now than he had even a minute ago and was eying Maryal like she was a real threat.

"Very neat trick, Maryal, I will admit," said Kraggan, his voice hoarse. "But not neat enough."

Kraggan lashed out with a punch, causing Maryal to jump backwards to avoid it. But then Kraggan stopped his own punch halfway through and swung one of his large legs at her instead. Maryal must not have seen that move coming, because she did not try to dodge it. Kraggan's leg struck Maryal in the side, the blow sending her flying. She landed on the street and rolled a few more times, but as before, she was back on her feet almost instantly. Even so, Keo could tell that Maryal was having a harder and harder time recovering from each hit and he doubted that Kraggan would need to land more than two more blows at most to take her down for good.

"For I have some neat tricks of my own," said Kraggan. He slammed his fists together. "Want to see them?"

Kraggan slammed his fists into the street. A hand made out of rock shot out from the street and wrapped around Maryal's waist, causing her to yell in pain as it tightened its grip around her.

"I can control rock as well," said Kraggan with a smile. "And I know that *that* can't be stopped by taking away air."

Kraggan's smile vanished, however, when Maryal waved her arms at him and a powerful gust of wind struck him. It almost knocked him off his feet, but he managed to retain his balance, although his concentration must have slipped because Maryal managed to force the rock hand's fingers loose and launch herself into the air again. She landed in front of Kraggan and lashed out with a kick, but Kraggan dodged it and tried to punch her, which she ducked to avoid.

Then, taking advantage of an opening Kraggan left, Maryal slammed her fists into his stomach. She also created a burst of wind that actually sent Kraggan flying through the air uncontrollably. He landed hard on the street and lay there for a moment, stunned, before he got back up to his feet again, a scowl on his face.

"All right," said Kraggan. He sounded almost out of breath now. "You've annoyed me more than enough now. Time to end this."

Kraggan snapped his fingers. A second later, a circle of intense flame appeared around Maryal, causing her to raise her arms, no doubt in order to summon a powerful wind in order to blow the fire away, but then Kraggan snapped the fingers of his other hand and a stone hand burst from the ground and wrapped so tightly around Maryal's waist that her gasp of pain was audible even over the roar of the flames.

Keo immediately understood what Kraggan was trying to do. He was going to use the flame to increase the temperature around Maryal while using the stone hand to make it impossible for her to summon wind to blow it away and save herself. Likely Kraggan hoped that the high temperature would eventually either knock Maryal out or force her to give up once the temperature became too much for her to bear.

Beside him, Keo heard one man mutter to his friend, "This is just what Kraggan did to win the Championship last year. He must really want to end this."

"Yeah, but didn't that move almost kill his opponent?" said the man's friend. "I heard that the smoke and heat nearly killed him because he couldn't speak and officially forfeit the match."

"I doubt that will happen here," said the first man dismissively. "Kraggan isn't a murderer. Sure, he can be tough, but you have to be in order to be the Champion Duelist in this country."

Keo listened to the conversation with worry. He looked back at the scene of the duel. Barely visible through the intense flames, Maryal was still struggling to break free of the stone hand, but she was sweating up a storm and seemed to be having trouble breathing. Meanwhile, Kraggan was smirking and did not seem concerned that he might accidentally harm Maryal too much. As for Yanar, he was talking with an attractive-looking Hasfarian woman, apparently no longer paying attention to the charity duel.

Keo bit his lower lip. *If Kraggan keeps this up, he will*

definitely kill Maryal. Someone should stop him, but maybe it won't be necessary. Kraggan might just stop on his own or maybe Maryal will pull a trick out of her sleeve and save herself.

But Keo knew that both possibilities were unlikely to happen. Kraggan seemed to have lost all sense of mercy now, probably due to his frustration at how long the duel had gone on, while Maryal was clearly too weak now to save herself. And none of the spectators looked likely to try to help her.

But Dlaine told me that we're not supposed to get into any trouble here, Keo thought. *We're just supposed to visit and then leave. Not get involved in conflicts that might delay our arrival in Capitika even more than we already have. It is probably illegal for someone to interrupt a charity duel, anyway.*

Yet Keo did not want to be the witness to a murder. So, deciding to handle whatever consequences awaited him, Keo ducked under the cord, ignoring some of the people in the crowd telling him to come back. He ran over to Kraggan, who didn't seem to notice Keo approaching him until Keo shouted, "Hey! Stop it! You're killing her."

Kraggan looked at Keo in confusion, though the fire circle and stone hand did not go away. "Who are you?"

"It doesn't matter," said Keo, shaking his head. He pointed at Maryal, who looked like she was about to lose consciousness any second. "You've clearly won. There's no reason to keep harming her like this. Let her go."

Kraggan raised an eyebrow. "And just why should I listen to you? You're not even a Magician. Yanar!" he suddenly shouted, looking over his shoulder at the announcer. He pointed at Keo. "Get this dumb kid out of here. He's getting in the way of my victory."

Yanar, however, did not seem to notice Kraggan or Keo, because he was still chatting with the attractive Hasfarian lady. Oddly, she seemed to be listening to him, which made Keo think that Yanar must have had experience in talking to the ladies.

The people in the crowd, however, were starting to throw abuse at Keo, shouting things like, "Get out of there, you stupid kid!" and "You're messing with the battle, you idiot!" and "Stop trying to interrupt the duel! This is the best part!"

But Keo stood his ground and looked Kraggan straight in the eye. "No. I'm not leaving until you stop hurting her. Maryal cannot fight you anymore. There's no point in torturing her anymore, since she clearly can't fight back."

Kraggan scowled. "Are you telling *me*, the Champion of the Magician Duel Championship and a veteran of the never-ending wars against the Divinians and Restorationists, what to do?"

"I'm merely telling you that you are being excessively cruel toward her," said Keo, folding his arms across his chest. "I don't care if you're a Champion or a veteran or whatever. You will *kill* her if you keep this up."

Kraggan looked like Keo had insulted his own mother. Nonetheless, he snapped his fingers again and the fire circle disappeared from around Maryal. She gasped for air and slumped forward on the stone hand, which then dropped her onto the street, where she lay still, although she merely appeared unconscious rather than dead.

"Wait," said Keo in surprise. "Did you actually *listen* to me?"

Kraggan shook his head and raised his right hand, which suddenly burst into flame. "No. I simply dislike having my attention divided when I am going to teach a disrespectful kid like you a lesson."

Kraggan ran at Keo, his burning fist trailing fire and smoke as he ran. Keo drew Gildshine just in time to block Kraggan's attack.

But Kraggan hit hard enough to drive Keo to his knees. Then Kraggan lashed out with a kick suddenly, striking Keo in the stomach and sending him flying. Keo landed hard on the street, stunned from the attack, but still holding Gildshine in his hands. The pain in his stomach from where Kraggan had struck was intense, like he had just been kicked by a giant.

Nonetheless, Keo scrambled back to his feet as Kraggan approached, but before he could form an effective defense, something wet and sticky struck the back of his head. Taken by surprise, Keo rubbed the back of his head and looked at his hand to see a red liquid on his fingers, which he realized was tomato juice. He looked over his shoulder in time to see that the spectators were preparing fruits and vegetables to throw at him. As soon as he saw that, they started hurling their fruits and vegetables at him while also hurling abuse at him.

Keo dodged the flying food as best as he could, but there was so much of it that it was difficult to do. So Keo, in an attempt to get away from the angry spectators, ran toward Kraggan, who stopped and smiled at Keo's action.

"Stupid kid," said Kraggan, shaking his head. "But very well. Your running toward me makes this all the more easy for me to get you."

Keo prepared to slash Kraggan with Gildshine, but then the ground underneath Keo's feet shifted and he lost his balance and tripped. But Kraggan was right in front of him before he fell and punched Keo in the side of the face with his hot fist.

The blow sent Keo staggering to the right, stars in his eyes, and he fell down next to Maryal, who had still not moved an inch from where she lay. All of Keo's senses were fuzzy and his jaw felt like it had broken into shards. He still held Gildshine, but it was not particularly useful when he barely understood which was up and which way was down.

But Keo could hear and he heard Kraggan's bragging, the Magician saying, "Look and rejoice, citizens of Carrk and other towns and lands! Even when my duel is interrupted by this disrespectful kid, I am still able to deliver to him the thrashing he deserves! I am truly the Champion, no matter how you look at it!"

The crowd went wild at Kraggan's words, although Keo was less than impressed. He shook his head, allowing his senses to return to normal, but he still did not trust himself to get up.

Then he heard a voice nearby whisper, "Hey, kid, still conscious?"

Keo looked to his right and saw Maryal was looking at him. She still looked awful, with sweat on her face and her clothes somewhat blackened from the flames, but she seemed fully conscious.

"Yeah," said Keo, keeping his voice to a whisper as well. "I'm sorry, but—"

"Don't apologize," Maryal cut him off. She nodded weakly at Kraggan, who was now showing off his massive muscles to his fans in the crowd. "We're going to take advantage of Kraggan's arrogance. Together, okay?"

Keo blinked. "But isn't that against the rules?"

"I stopped caring about the rules when Kraggan did," said

Maryal. "Now, get up and distract him. Act like Kraggan broke every bone in your body."

Keo grimaced at the pain that shot through his body when he tried to sit up. "Act?"

"Just do it," Maryal said.

Even though he merely wanted to lie down and stay down, Keo decided to trust Maryal and do what she said. So he dragged himself up to his feet again, much more slowly than he would have liked, and grasped Gildshine in both hands.

He didn't even need to say anything before Kraggan noticed him, smirked, and said, "Oh, look, everyone! The kid needs another lesson from the teacher. I admit to being impressed, because most people can't take that many hits from me and still stand. But this time, I'll make sure to knock you down so hard you won't even be able to sit up for a week."

Keo said nothing. He just wondered what Maryal was going to do and hoped that she would do it before Kraggan turned him into paste, because he was pretty certain that there was no way in hell he could even hope to beat the large Magician on his own. He could, perhaps, have used Gildshine's ability, but he didn't want to kill Kraggan, because he knew that that would probably cause the crowd to turn into a murderous mob.

Kraggan ran toward Keo, a vicious grin on his lips, his fists trailing behind him. Keo still did not move. He didn't glance at Maryal, either, because he did not want Kraggan to suspect that they were working together.

Right before Kraggan's fists could hit Keo, Maryal suddenly shouted, "Move!"

Without question, Keo jumped backwards. A look of

confusion spread across Kraggan's face briefly before a sudden gust of wind exploded from the ground and sent him flying straight up into the sky. He flew high and fast, almost too fast for Keo's eyes to follow. The crowd gasped, their heads following Kraggan's procession as he flew higher and higher into the sky.

And then, when Kraggan reached the height of his launch, he fell like a rock. Kraggan screamed as he fell, but his scream was cut off when he slammed into the street. Kraggan's eyes rolled into the back of his head and he stopped moving, though the rising and falling of his chest told Keo that the Magician had somehow survived the attack.

Surprised, Keo looked down at Maryal. She was pointing her hand at Kraggan, but still looked as weak as ever.

"Wow," said Keo, looking at Kraggan again and then back at Maryal. "You took him out."

Maryal shrugged. "He didn't see it coming. Always been a flaw of his."

As for the crowd, they were all staring in utter bafflement and silence at the unconscious Kraggan. Even Yanar had finally stopped flirting with the Hasfarian lady and was looking at Kraggan like he wasn't sure if his eyes were working correctly or not.

"What …" Yanar seemed to struggle to find words. "Huh?"

As soon as Yanar spoke, the crowd started yelling obscenities at Keo and Maryal, their loud voices merging together in a confusion cacophony, making it impossible for Keo to tell what they were saying, though he caught the gist of it. Much of the crowd surged against the cord, as if to avenge Kraggan, but the Enforcers at the front of the crowd pushed them back, shouting orders at the people not to attack Keo or Maryal. Even so, Keo could tell that it was only a matter of time before the crowds broke past the Enforcers and lynched both Maryal and him.

Keo looked down at Maryal again and said, "I'm sorry, but—"

"Don't apologize," Maryal cut him off. "Just help me to my feet and help me get out of here. You can apologize later."

Keo bit his lip, but nodded and bent over to help Maryal to her feet. She was rather light, but she still had to lean against Keo in order to stand. Keo kept Gildshine out, even though he wasn't sure it would be of much use against the angry mobs that the Enforcers were trying to keep away.

"How do we get out of here?" said Keo, looking around but not seeing any possible escape routes, because the mobs had the streets packed on all sides. "Fight our way through the crowds?"

Maryal shook her head. "No. Even with my magic and your obvious fighting ability, there's no way we could get far before the crowds killed us."

"What about your flying ability from earlier?" said Keo, glancing at her robes, which were still lying on the street where she had dropped them earlier. "Can't we fly away?"

Maryal again shook her head. "Not so simple. First, I need my robes to catch the winds, but even if I had them, I'd have to carry you, and I've never glided with another person before, much less a full-grown man carrying a heavy magical sword."

Keo looked at Maryal in surprise. "How did you know Gildshine is magical?"

"I'm a Magician," said Maryal simply. "Anyway, the truth is that I couldn't fly us out of here, and even if I could, we wouldn't be able to go very far and the crowd would follow us to wherever

274 | TIMOTHY L. CEREPAKA

we landed. It would be foolish."

"Well, I'm just as out of ideas as you are," said Keo. "So unless a miracle happens—"

Without warning, Dlaine appeared out of nowhere right next to Keo, like he had formed into existence on his own. "Keo! What the hell are you doing?"

"Dlaine?" said Keo, staring at his friend in shock. "Where did *you* come from? And how did you get past the crowds?"

"Jola can teleport," said Dlaine dismissively. "Anyway, let's get you two out of here before the brave Enforcers get trampled to death by the people they're sworn to protect. Grab on."

Without question, Keo and Maryal grabbed Dlaine's outstretched arm. A second later the hot, dusty square and screaming angry crowds vanished and Keo found himself standing in a room that he had never been in before.

Chapter Twenty-One

THE ROOM INTO WHICH they had teleported was dark and dry, with a cracked floor and ceiling. A large wood stove stood in one corner, although it did not appear to be active at the moment, and there were no windows, although there was a staircase that went up to the next floor, like they were in a basement. A couple of candles on a wooden table in the center of the room provided all of the illumination, which wasn't very much, though it was enough to see by, at least.

Keo blinked as he and Maryal let go of Dlaine's arm. "Dlaine … where *are* we? And how did you find us?"

Dlaine dusted off his jacket, an agitated look on his face. "I went to the northern gates like we agreed, but when you didn't show up, I went to the town square where the charity duel was being held. Saw the massive rioting crowd and immediately knew you were probably responsible for it, seeing as you can be pretty annoying sometimes."

Keo wasn't sure whether to be offended or not, so he said, "So you and Jola teleported us away?"

"Yes," said Dlaine, nodding. "Remember how I said that Jola can teleport limited distances? She doesn't like to do it because it's very draining, but she agreed to do it here because it was the only way to get you both out of there alive."

"Who's Jola?" said Maryal, who was still leaning on Keo for

support. She coughed.

"Who are *you*?" said Dlaine, looking at Maryal questioningly. "Keo's girlfriend?"

"I am a Magician," said Maryal, coughing again, probably due to the smoke from the fire getting into her lungs. "Magician Maryal of the Wind, to be precise. Ever heard of me?"

"Nope, but I'll take your word for it," said Dlaine. Then he looked at Keo and said, "What did you do back there? Moon the people? Insult their religion? Tell them that the Carrkian government is horribly corrupt?"

Keo explained as quickly as he could what had happened. By the time Keo finished, Dlaine was shaking his head.

"Goddammit, Keo," said Dlaine, rubbing the back of his head. "I *told* you that we were only supposed to come and leave. I shouldn't have allowed you to go watch the charity duel. Should have known you would have gotten us into trouble."

"I did what I thought was right," said Keo defensively. "Kraggan looked like he was actually going to kill her."

"And get arrested by the Enforcers for murder?" said Dlaine. He sighed heavily. "Keo, I know your heart is in the right place, but Kraggan isn't the kind of guy you cross."

"You've heard of him?" said Keo.

"Of course I have," said Dlaine, running his hand through his hair in exasperation. "Everyone has. He was brutal on the war front. I heard he used his magic to incinerate whole platoons of enemy troops. He doesn't take well to getting beaten or insulted by anyone, whether they're an enemy soldier or not."

"Your friend is right," said Maryal. She coughed again. "Kraggan is incredibly vengeful and easily angered. I doubt he would have killed me back there even if you hadn't intervened, but now Kraggan will likely not stop until both of us are dead."

"Well, what was I *supposed* to do?" said Keo in annoyance. "Kraggan was still a jerk and Yanar didn't look like he was going to tell him to stop."

"Kraggan was technically *supposed* to win," said Maryal, rolling her eyes. "I was paid off to let him win. I was supposed to put up a fight for the entertainment of the spectators, but I wasn't actually supposed to beat him."

"Then why did you knock him out with your magic before we escaped?" said Keo.

Maryal shrugged. "Because he was going farther than I thought and I don't really like him all that much."

Feeling like a fool, Keo looked at Dlaine and said, "All right, all right. I made a mistake. But where are we? I don't recognize this place."

Dlaine opened his mouth to answer, but then the door at the top of the staircase opened and the voice of an elderly lady shouted, "Who's down there? Show yourselves or I'll have Ripper tear your throats out!"

Dlaine grimaced, but then turned around and shouted back, "Galy, it's me, Dlaine! I'm back and I've brought, er, a couple of friends with me."

"Dlaine?" said the elder woman in confusion. "Didn't you just leave my house? How do I know you're not some kind of mimic trying to lure me to my death?"

"Jola teleported me and my friends back in here because it was the only safe space I could think of," said Dlaine. "Besides, you old crone, you know there's not a mimic in the world that could impersonate me."

"Good point," said the elderly woman. "But who are your friends? Never mind. Let me come down and see for myself."

A second later, an elderly woman walked down the stairs into the basement. She looked much older than Dlaine—easily in her seventies or eighties—but was apparently still quite capable of walking on her own, as she made it down the stairs without any problem. She was very short, however, barely even coming up to Keo's waist, and she had large, round glasses that made her squinting eyes look ginormous.

"Ah," said the old woman when she reached the bottom of the stairs and saw them. "So it is you, Dlaine. And I see you've brought a couple of friends. Who are they?"

"He is Keo of the Sword," said Dlaine, pointing at Keo. "My friend and current traveling companion. And the young woman is Magician Maryal of the Wind, one of the participants in the charity duel. Keo, Maryal, meet Galy of the Medicine, an old friend of mine from way back when."

"Nice to meet you," said Galy, nodding at them. Then she frowned. "The young lady looks like she just escaped a fire."

"She was dueling Kraggan of the Fire," Keo said. "And he burned her."

"Then let me look at her," said Galy. She gestured at a bed that was up against the right wall. "Lay her down there and I'll take a look at her."

Keo nodded and helped Maryal over to the bed. To his surprise, Maryal went along with it, perhaps because she was too tired and weak to resist. He helped lay her on the bed and then stepped back as Galy shuffled over to them. Galy pulled up a stool next to the bed and immediately started looking over Maryal's arms, which were slightly burnt.

But Maryal was looking at all of them in confusion. She said, "While I'm thankful for your help, I realize that neither of you have introduced yourselves to me yet."

Keo looked at Dlaine. "Should we tell her?"

Dlaine shrugged. "I don't see any reason not to. Unless she's planning to go back to the people of Carrk and tell them who we are."

Maryal shook her head weakly. "I have no plans to do that. After our escape, everyone probably thinks that Keo and I are working together, that I cheated in order to beat Kraggan. And it is against the law to cheat in a charity duel."

"Even though you didn't actually cheat?" said Keo.

"They will never believe me," said Maryal. She sounded bitter about it. "Kraggan's cult of personality is so powerful that many of his followers are incapable of believing that he did anything wrong or that anyone who beat him didn't cheat. As soon as they see me again, they'll probably lynch me in the streets regardless of what Magician Enira or the Enforcers think."

"Oh," said Keo. "I'm sorry. I probably shouldn't have intervened, then. Your life is now in danger and it's all my fault."

But Maryal shook her head again. "You don't need to apologize. Kraggan might very well have killed me anyway, despite killing your opponent in a duel being illegal. At least now the smoke from his fire won't destroy my lungs."

But Maryal didn't sound like she had forgiven Keo. Instead, she sounded angry, like she was annoyed at the fact that everyone in Carrk likely believed that she was a cheater now. It made Keo feel even worse, but he didn't see any point in pushing the subject anymore, so he didn't.

Then Maryal looked at Keo and Dlaine again. "Now again, who, exactly, *are* you? A couple of mercenaries?"

Keo briefly explained to Maryal who he and Dlaine were and what they were trying to do. All the while, Galy looked over Maryal's arms and body, occasionally waving her hands over the parts that had suffered particularly bad burns and healing them, which meant that Galy was also a Magician. That made Keo wonder how many Magicians lived in Carrk, but then he realized that Carrk was very close to Capitika, which explained the presence of so many Magicians in this town.

By the time Keo finished, Maryal was frowning and looked like she was not sure whether she should believe them.

"So the demons from the old legends are going to return?" said Maryal. "And it will require the combined forces of the three factions to stop them?"

Keo nodded. "Yes. We've fought and killed two demons already. Right, Dlaine?"

"Right," said Dlaine. He jerked a thumb over his shoulder. "Fought one in the ruins of Castarious back at the Silver Falls. Killed it myself, in fact."

Keo expected Maryal to continue to express doubt about the return of the demons, as most people did whenever he told them about it, but to his shock, Maryal smiled and said, "I knew it."

Keo blinked. "Knew it? Knew what?"

"That the demons are returning," said Maryal. She tried to sit up, but Galy forced her back down and said, "Now, now, young woman, stay where you are. You need to rest after everything you've been through."

Maryal nodded, albeit reluctantly, and then looked at Keo and Dlaine eagerly. "It looks like I was right. All of those dreams … every one of them were true."

"What are you even babbling about?" said Dlaine. "What dreams? What made you think that the demons were returning?"

"Okay, let me start from the beginning," said Maryal. She tapped her forehead. "For about a year now, I've been having dreams about the return of the demons. Dark dreams, they are, with vile monsters worse than any ghost story slaughtering innocents. I've asked my interpreter what they mean and he told me they meant that the demons are returning, but no one has believed me even after I told them."

"Why are you having dreams about the return of the demons?" said Keo.

"Because I've always had dreams about the future," said Maryal. She gestured at her head. "I'm what you call a seer. That means that I can see some of the future, although only in my dreams and it isn't always obvious what they mean. It's a special ability that few Magicians are born with."

"How strange," said Keo. "Dlaine and I are going to Capitika in order to tell the Magical Council about the coming demonic threat, and then we run into you, a woman who has been dreaming about their return for at least a year now."

"It must be destiny," said Maryal. She sounded excited. "I can hardly believe it myself. I thought for sure that I was the only person in the world who even suspected that the demons were returning, but now I know that I am not."

"Well, that's interesting and all, but I don't see what this all means for us," said Dlaine, putting his hands on his hips. "Just because you dream about them doesn't mean a whole lot, if you ask me."

"Don't you get it?" said Maryal. She sighed. "Look, this *obviously* means that the four of us are destined to travel together to Capitika. I can't be the only one who sees this."

"Lady, I think we can safely say you *are* the only one who sees this," said Dlaine. "Because we sure don't."

Maryal rubbed her forehead in frustration. "Well, whether you guys see this or not, the fact is that I think it is pretty obvious that we should travel together."

"You seem awfully eager to travel with a couple of guys you just met," said Dlaine.

"Because it is obviously our destiny," said Maryal. "How many times do I have to say that? And I have made a point of *never* going against destiny, especially when it's this obvious."

"Well, I don't see the harm in letting her travel with us," said Keo, scratching the back of his head. "I think having a Magician, especially one as experienced as Maryal, on our side might make it easier for us to get to Capitika and fight any demons that might try to stop us along the way."

"Exactly," said Maryal, wincing briefly when Galy pinched her arm. "See? Keo knows about the many benefits I would bring to your team if you let me join."

Dlaine folded his arms across his chest and frowned. "It's not that I am against having a Magician on the team. It's just that I don't want anyone slowing us down unnecessarily."

"I won't slow you guys down at all," Maryal promised. "I can take care of myself. Besides, I like moving quickly, so you won't have to worry about me slowing you down."

Dlaine looked like he still wasn't enthusiastic about bringing Maryal along, but then he sighed and said, "All right. You can come with us to Capitika. Just don't be deadweight, all right?"

"Of course," said Maryal, nodding eagerly. "I'll be so useful that you won't even remember what it was like to travel without me."

"Sure," said Dlaine. "Anyway, do your dreams tell us what is supposed to happen to us in Capitika?"

"Nope," said Maryal, shaking her head. "As a matter of fact, I don't even know how we're supposed to stop the demons. But if you guys are trying to stop them, then I believe this is destiny's way of telling me to go with you."

"Sounds like destiny can be pretty vague," Dlaine said. "Anyway, now we need to figure out how to get out of this town without being caught and lynched by Kraggan's fans."

"Why can't Jola teleport us out?" said Keo, looking around the basement for their invisible friend, though he was unable to find her. "If she could teleport us in here, couldn't she teleport us out of Carrk?"

"It isn't that easy," said Dlaine, shaking his head. "Teleporting, even a short distance over a small period of time, is very difficult for Jola, and consumes a ton of her energy to boot. Teleporting all three of us plus herself out of Carrk would probably knock her out for a full week, maybe even kill her. That's assuming she succeeds; she might just end up teleporting us somewhere else in the town."

Jola, as usual, said nothing, but Keo figured that Dlaine was telling the truth, even if the truth was depressing. Yet there was nothing Keo could say or do to change that fact, so he started thinking about other ways they could escape.

"And I can't fly all four of us out here, either," said Maryal. "Well, unless you want to get carried by a tornado and risk crash landing on your skull, anyway."

Keo stroked his chin. "There has to be *some* way for us to get out of Carrk without anyone noticing. Dlaine, does Carrk happen to have any hidden underground tunnels that could lead us out of here?"

Dlaine shook his head again. "Nope. It's got a sewer system, but there's no way we can use it to get out of here, because it's too small, cramped, and narrow for anyone larger than a toddler."

Keo cursed under his breath. "Then it looks like our only option is to try to sneak out through the streets to the city gates without being noticed. Maybe we can hide our real identities by putting on new clothes or something."

"They'll have all of the gates covered," said Dlaine. "And the gatekeepers will be keeping a very close and careful eye on every person who tries to leave Carrk. We'll be found out in an instant."

"Then what do you suggest we do?" said Keo, throwing up his arms in frustration. "Sit down here in Galy's basement until everyone forgets about us?"

"Nah," said Dlaine. "We don't have time for that. I'm merely pointing out that all of your ideas just don't work."

"Well, I don't hear you offering any suggestions," Keo said. "Of course, it is easier to criticize than to come up with your own ideas, so—"

"Hey, Galy," said Dlaine, apparently ignoring Keo now. He looked down at the elderly woman, who was still treating

Maryal's wounds. "Any suggestions for how the four of us can get out of Carrk without being seen?"

Keo had no idea why Dlaine was asking Galy about this when the old lady said, without turning to look at Dlaine, "Oh, that's very simple, Dlaine. Just take the rooftops."

Keo blinked. "The rooftops?"

"Certainly," said Galy. She looked at Keo with her ancient gray eyes and pointed up at the ceiling of the basement. "No one will expect you to take to the rooftops. And what is even better is that it will make it harder for anyone to follow you, as few buildings in this town have easy ways to access their roofs."

"Okay," said Keo, "but won't people still see us jumping across the rooftops? And won't they then chase us, maybe even catch us?"

"Simply turn invisible," said Galy. She nodded at an empty spot to Dlaine's right. "Like your friend Jola."

Keo looked at the spot Galy was nodding at. He realized that Galy was actually looking at Jola, as if she could see her, but that made no sense to Keo, because he thought that no one except for Dlaine could see her. Then again, Galy was a Magician, so perhaps her magic allowed her to see Jola. It made Keo wish that he was a Magician, if only so he could have the ability to see what Jola actually looked like.

"That's a good idea and all, Galy, but I don't think it will be that easy," said Dlaine. "Jola can't turn anyone else invisible except for herself. So, while that would be a good idea under certain circumstances, here it—"

"I can turn you invisible," said Galy. "All three of you."

Dlaine looked at Galy in surprise. "What? You never told me

that."

Then it was Keo's turn to look at Dlaine in surprise. "You didn't know she could do that? I thought she was one of your old friends."

"Old, yes, but evidently not as close as I thought," said Dlaine, looking at Galy in annoyance. "Why didn't you mention that to me before?"

"Oh, I just learned the exact technique within the last couple of years," said Galy as she rose from Maryal's side. "As a hobby, you know, since I am retired and haven't had much to do except sit around all day and read."

"Well, that sure makes things easier," said Dlaine.

"The only problem is that I haven't been able to figure out how to make it last longer than an hour or so," said Galy. "Making people invisible is very difficult, at least for me. Perhaps some Magicians find it easy, but I don't."

"An hour?" said Keo. He looked at Dlaine. "Can we get out of Carrk in an hour?"

"Possibly," said Dlaine, though he didn't sound certain. "If we take the rooftops and don't waste time, then sure, we might be able to get out of town in under an hour."

Keo looked at Maryal. "Do you feel like you can come with us?"

Maryal, unfortunately, shook her head. "Not right now. I need to rest."

"That you do, young lady, that you do," said Galy. "But I believe my healing magic should have you on your feet in an hour or so. Thus, by then you should be able to—"

Galy was interrupted by the thunderous sounds of what

sounded like a large battering ram slamming against the front door of her house. Keo, Dlaine, Maryal, and Galy looked up at the ceiling of the basement in surprise as the battering noises continued without end.

"What is that?" said Keo.

"It must be the people of Carrk," said Galy. She put one hand on her head, as if to steady herself. "Of course. They must be searching every house in the area for you four. I imagine the only reason they have not yet succeeded in knocking down the door is because I have cast a few spells to reinforce it, though I don't know how long they will last."

"Then we need to leave right away," said Keo. "We have no time to lose."

Dlaine looked at Galy. "Do you think you can turn us invisible now?"

"I think so, but Maryal is not yet ready to walk on her own," said Galy, gesturing at the Magician lying on the couch. "She needs time to recover before she can go anywhere or do anything physically straining like jumping from rooftop to rooftop."

"You can't just leave me here," said Maryal. She tried to sit up, but that was apparently too much for her, because she just lay right back down again. "If they catch me, they will kill me or imprison me for life."

"I'll carry her," Keo said. "Maryal's not very heavy, so I should be able to carry her with me out of Carrk pretty easily."

"Are you sure you are up to it?" said Galy. "After all, you look rather tired, no doubt due to your fight with Kraggan. Even if she is light, it might be hard to carry her out of here."

Keo *was* tired, but he jerked a thumb over his shoulder and said, "It's all right. Back in the Low Woods, where I'm from, I've hauled much heavier things than Maryal over much larger distances. I'll be fine."

"Then what are we waiting for?" said Dlaine. "Keo, pick up Maryal. Galy, cast the invisibility spell. Then we're getting out of here before the mob breaks in here and gets us."

Without hesitation, Keo went over to Maryal and picked her up and carried her on his back piggyback style, because he figured that that would be the best way to carry her. She was still very light, but also a lot more limp than before, probably due to the healing magic that Galy cast on her. Nonetheless, Maryal managed to wrap her arms under his neck tightly, though he could still breathe and move his head freely.

"All right," said Galy, even as the sounds of the bashing against her front door above became louder and louder. "Stand still. It won't hurt, but it may feel cold for a moment."

Galy raised her hands. Bright white light shone from the tips of her fingers and the next moment an intense coldness fell over Keo's body. He shivered, as did Maryal, whose shivering he felt against his back. Dlaine shivered as well, though he did not shiver as much as them, like he was used to the cold.

In a second, the coldness was gone and Keo had returned to his original body temperature. He looked down at his body, wondering whether he could see through himself, but to his disappointment and confusion, he still saw his old traveling boots and brown pants. He looked at Dlaine and saw him just as easily as he always did.

"Hey," said Keo, looking at Galy, who had lowered her hands to her side. "I can still see myself and Dlaine. Are you sure you cast the right spell?"

"I'm sure," said Galy, nodding, though Keo noticed that she was looking slightly to his right. "The thing about the spell is that the target of the spell can still see themselves and other people who are under the same spell. While those of us who are visible cannot see any of you, you can still see yourselves and each other."

"Then does that mean I can see Jola?" said Keo, looking around eagerly, but seeing no one else standing in the basement with them.

"No, you cannot," said Galy. "Jola uses a different kind of invisibility spell that doesn't work the same way as mine. She is just as invisible to you as she always has been."

"Right, right, right," said Dlaine. "Now that I think we all understand this, let's go. Sounds to me like your admirers are not going to be held back by Galy's front door for long."

"Yes, you four must go," said Galy, gesturing at the stairs leading up from her basement. "I will try to delay them for as long as I can, but I cannot guarantee that they will not find out where you are going."

"Thanks, Galy," said Dlaine, smiling at her. "Glad to know I can still count on you the same as always."

Galy smiled at Dlaine, which made Keo wonder what kind of personal history the two had together, but decided that it wasn't worth worrying about at the moment.

So Keo followed Dlaine and Jola up the stairs, Maryal still clinging to his back, with Galy right behind them. He hoped that they would be able to escape Carrk alive, but he also had a sinking feeling that they might not.

Chapter Twenty-Two

K EO, DLAINE, JOLA, AND Maryal emerged onto the rooftop of Galy's house. The sun was still in the sky, although it had gone down somewhat since they had been in the house, and it was thus still quite hot, but Keo paid little attention to that, because his eyes were drawn to the streets.

Dozens of people—men and women alike—were gathered in the streets around Galy's house. Many were calling for Maryal's arrest, while others were calling for her death. This all seemed rather extreme to Keo, although it told him just how seriously Kraggan's fans must have taken his loss to Maryal. It just made him glad that none of the people in the streets were looking at the rooftops of the nearby houses, although even if they did they would not have been able to see Keo and the others escaping.

"Okay," said Keo, readjusting his grip on Maryal, because he was starting to feel his hands slip. "Where should we go from here, Dlaine?"

"North," said Dlaine, gesturing in that direction. "By going along the north road, we should reach Capitika within the next couple of days."

"Okay," said Keo. "So how do we get from here to the northern gates quickly?"

"Just follow me," said Dlaine, turning north. "I already see a path we can take. Try to keep up."

292 | TIMOTHY L. CEREPAKA

With that, Dlaine took off. He ran to the edge of the rooftop and jumped over the gap between Galy's house and the next building. He landed on the other side safely and then turned and gestured for Keo to follow.

Keo bit his lower lip. While he was certain that he would have been able to make such a jump himself under normal circumstances, a part of him worried that the combined weight of Maryal, Gildshine, and himself would cause him to fall into the street below. Yet he could not simply stand here and wait, either, because the spell didn't have a long time limit.

Then Maryal said in his ear, "If you are worried about falling, don't be, because I can give your jumps an extra boost with a small gust of wind. Just trust me."

Keo did not know how Maryal had known about his worry, but he did not question it. He just nodded and then ran toward the edge of the roof and, at the last second, jumped as far and as hard as he could.

When he was at the top of his jump, he felt a sudden gust of wind catch him and carry him the rest of the way. He landed gently on the rooftop next to Dlaine, who looked surprised at Keo's landing.

"Huh," said Dlaine, scratching the back of his head. "I didn't know you could use wind to do that, Maryal."

"It's simple for me to do, even in my weakened state," said Maryal. "I could even give you an air boost, if you need it."

"Thanks for the offer, but I think I'll be fine," said Dlaine. "Just follow my lead and we should get to the northern gates without any trouble."

Once more, Dlaine took off to jump over to the next building, and Keo followed as quickly as he could. With every jump, Keo was convinced that he would fall to the street below, but Maryal always helped with her wind magic, allowing him to make every jump without fail. Even so, Keo would still sometimes look over his shoulder just to make sure no one was following them, even though he had no reason to believe that anyone other than Galy even knew where they were.

Just focus on following Dlaine and getting out of here, Keo told himself, watching as Dlaine jumped over to the fifth building they needed to jump on. *As long as I keep following him, we should be able to—*

"Keo!" Maryal shouted. "Duck!"

Without asking what Maryal meant, Keo fell to the roof under his feet. A second later, a shining white light shot past where his head had been mere moments before, causing Keo to look in the direction that the light had come from.

Standing on the other side of the roof was a woman in white robes who Keo had never seen before. The woman was bald, with large ear rings hanging from her earlobes. Upon her chest was the symbol of the Magical Council—a wand sparking with energy—stitched in gold, which immediately told Keo that this woman was yet another Magician.

"Missed," said the woman, who sounded bored and who was also looking directly at Keo and Maryal despite their invisibility. "Damn it."

Keo blinked. "Maryal, can that woman see us? Or am I just hearing things?"

"That woman can see us because she is Magician Enira, the Magician of Carrk," said Maryal. Her voice trembled slightly when she spoke the woman's name. "She must be using her magic to see us somehow."

"It's an awful spell, the one used to make you three invisible," said Enira with a yawn. "I saw through it right away. Whoever cast that spell on you did an awful job, if I do say so myself."

Keo gulped, while Dlaine on the other building shouted, "Hey! Who is that woman? How can she—"

Enira immediately pointed her finger at Dlaine and another white light shot out of it. The light flew across the street and struck Dlaine in the chest. Dlaine gasped and then immediately collapsed, though he appeared to be only unconscious and not dead.

Still, Keo shouted, "Dlaine, no!" He glared at Enira. "Why are you chasing us? Why don't you just leave us alone?"

Enira looked at Keo incredulously. "Are you really that daft? I am coming after you because Magician Maryal is reported to have cheated in the charity duel and nearly killed Magician Kraggan. That goes against not only the rules of the charity duel, but also against the laws of Carrk itself, laws I, as the town's Magician, must enforce. So I am going to arrest all three of you and throw you in jail myself."

"But I *didn't* cheat," said Maryal. She patted Keo's shoulder with her hand. "I was just trying to save my own life. You can't toss me in jail, too."

"I know you didn't cheat," said Enira. "That much was obvious to me as soon as I heard the first reports about the fiasco from my Enforcers."

"It was?" said Keo in surprise. "Then why are you trying to arrest us?"

Enira gestured at the streets below, which were full of people running and shouting in confusion. "Because I know that is the only thing that will stop the people from tearing Carrk apart. If they see that the one who harmed their favorite duelist has been captured and will be judged for her crimes, they will be more than happy to go back to their normal, law-abiding laws. And that is worth jailing an innocent woman, if you ask me, because Carrkians never do things half-measure, including rioting over perceived injustices."

"Well, I certainly don't think it is," said Maryal. She tightened her arms around Keo's neck. "Especially since that innocent woman is me."

Enira shrugged. "I value peace and order above all else, because that is what the Magical Council values. But it doesn't really matter what you want. The fact is, I will arrest you three and bring you to justice, whether or not you have actually committed any crimes."

"Not unless we fight back," said Keo. "And trust me, I know how to fight. I learned from the master."

Enira smirked. "Oh? How do you intend to fight while also keeping Maryal safe? She must be weighing you down, after all. And I know that you are not a Magician, so you cannot attack me from a distance, either. Trust me, in a straight fight, I would wipe the floor with both of you without breaking a sweat."

Keo gritted his teeth, but he said nothing because he could not disagree with what Enira had just said. In order to fight her, he'd have to put Maryal down, but if he did that, then Maryal would be unprotected. Even if Maryal was capable of defending herself with her magic, the fact was that she was still recovering from her fight with Kraggan and still needed time to recover, which meant that she shouldn't be fighting at all.

"Let me make you an offer," said Enira. She held out a hand. "Surrender and I will not allow the angry throngs of people rioting in the streets to tear you apart. Or fight and see if destiny is on your side today. But if you want my advice, I find that it is generally wiser to accept offers from people who are more powerful than you, particularly from Magicians such as myself."

Even though Keo did not want to accept the offer, he knew that he didn't have any bargaining power in this situation. Enira, being the powerful Magician that she was, had all of the power and leverage here. Besides, even if Keo had some leverage, the fact was that Enira was clearly not in the mood to compromise with him, because she was more interested in restoring peace to her town than in achieving actual justice.

But then Keo felt a hand tug at his pant leg, which he glanced down at just briefly but did not see anything. Then he heard a feminine voice in his mind say, *Keo of the Sword. It's me, Jola. Please distract Enira while I sneak up on her.*

Keo had to hide his shock, because he did not want Enira to suspect that anything was amiss. *Jola? This is the first time you've talked to me. Why—*

Because Dlaine trusts you, said Jola simply. *And because that vile Magician harmed him. I just want you to know that I am going to attack her before I do so it doesn't come as a surprise to you.*

Uh, okay, Keo thought, still looking at Enira. *But what, exactly, are you going to do to her?*

You'll see, Jola told him. *Just stay where you are and don't*

move an inch. Otherwise Enira will suspect that you are planning
something, which would ruin my plan.

Then Keo felt Jola's mind disconnect from his own, like a
dark storm cloud suddenly covering the sun. He still could not see
Jola anywhere, but he decided to trust that she would do what she
said to do, which meant that Keo would have to do what Jola told
him to do unless he wanted to spend the night in jail.

"Still thinking about my offer?" said Enira. "If you keep quiet
for much longer, then I'm afraid that I will have to take that as a
yes."

Keo shook his head. "No way. We're not accepting your offer.
We're not idiots."

"Could have fooled me," said Enira. She raised her hands,
which started to glow with magical energy. "But I guess it doesn't
matter. You're coming with me no matter what—"

Without warning, a rock flew out of nowhere behind Enira,
aiming for her head. The rock almost struck her, but then she
ducked at the last second and the rock sailed over her head. She
then whirled around and unleashed a burst of light, but the light
must have missed Jola, because Keo did not hear or see her get
hit.

Then Maryal whispered in his ear, "Let's go! She's
distracted!"

Keo nodded and ran toward the edge of the roof. He heard
Enira yelling at him to stop, but Keo ignored her. He leaped
across the roof, allowed Maryal's wind spell to carry him the rest
of the way, and then landed next to Dlaine, who was still
unconscious. Keo at first did not know how they were going to
bring Dlaine with them until Jola's voice in his head said, *Don't*

worry. I've got him. We just need to keep going.

As soon as Jola said that, Dlaine immediately started floating, looking almost like a ghost. It was a strange sight to Keo, but when another light burst from Enira narrowly missed, Keo decided not to worry about it.

He dashed toward the edge of the roof of the next building, following Dlaine's floating unconscious body. He didn't look over his shoulder, so he had no idea if Enira was following them or not, but he didn't care. He just kept running, breathing hard, doing his best to keep moving, ignoring the fatigue he was getting due to the combined weight of Maryal, Gildshine, and his supplies.

But then, when they were about three buildings away from where they had run into Enira, with only a couple of buildings between them and the northern gates, something flew by overhead and then landed right in their path. Dlaine's floating body jerked to a halt, as did Keo, and Keo saw that it was Enira, who seemed to have jumped over them somehow. The Magician of Carrk looked angry, like she was getting tired of chasing them.

"Stop," said Enira, holding out one hand before her. "Or I'll *make* you stop."

Keo bit his lower lip, thinking this was the end of the road for them, but then Maryal suddenly jerked her right hand forward.

Immediately, Enira started gasping for air. She fell to her knees, grabbing at her throat, but there was nothing she could do to keep the air from being taken from her lungs, which appeared to be what Maryal was undoubtedly doing to her at this very moment. Then another rock fell out of nowhere, struck Enira in the forehead, and knocked her out cold.

Keo did not even wait for Maryal to give him the go ahead.

He just dashed past the unconscious Enira, made it across the next few buildings, and then was on the town's ramparts, which were empty of guards at the moment. The walls were high, but Keo did not hesitate to jump off them, along with Dlaine's unconscious body, which floated alongside him.

A powerful gust of wind caught Keo, allowing him to float down to the road safely. As soon as his feet touched the road, he was off, running up the road as fast as he could, never looking back at Carrk. He heard Maryal's breath in his ears and felt her breasts against his back, but he did not even slow down, because all he wanted to do was put as much distance between them and Carrk as he could.

Chapter Twenty-Three

EVEN THOUGH KEO WAS dead tired, he managed to put a good amount of distance between them and Carrk. He ran for a couple of hours, and by the time he did, it was starting to become evening and he was sweating, hungry, and tired. The activities of the day—fighting Kraggan and escaping Carrk—were starting to take their toll on his body. His fatigue forced him to slow down considerably and it was becoming harder and harder to think clearly.

Thus, he was happy when Jola's voice in his head said, *Follow Dlaine's body and we'll rest,* which he did. He followed Dlaine's floating unconscious body off the road over to a small group of hills that provided excellent shelter from the road. Here Jola rested Dlaine's unconscious body, while Keo let Maryal down and then sat down, almost collapsed, himself.

Panting, Keo reached for his flask, popped it open, and then drank as much of the cold water as he could. It was delicious after such a long, hard day, and he didn't even care that a little bit accidentally dribbled down his chin and onto his shirt. He just drank it dry, then put the flask down and lay on the soft grass, staring up at the sky, feeling as tired as if he had run a marathon, which he almost had, now that he thought about it.

Next to him sat Maryal, who was resting against the hill they hid behind. She didn't seem quite as tired as Keo, but she was sweating herself and looked like she wanted to rest.

"Wow," said Maryal. She took a deep breath, almost like she had been the one who had done all of the running and jumping, rather than Keo. "That was … amazing. I didn't think we'd make it out for a while there." She looked at Keo curiously. "Does that sort of thing happen to you guys often?"

Keo groaned. "No. Usually we're good at not angering the local Magician and having to escape her."

"Well, it certainly was exhilarating, at any rate," said Maryal with a sigh. "So much action in one day … why, I'd say this has been the most action-packed day I've experienced in quite some time. Even if this isn't an every day occurrence for you two, it was still exciting nonetheless."

Keo wondered what was so exciting about being branded criminals and avoiding capture by the local Magician before he decided that it wasn't worth arguing with Maryal over this. She seemed wholly unused to any sort of exciting adventures, which meant that she was looking at the situation very differently from Keo. Besides, he was too tired to argue with anyone at the moment.

So Keo looked to his left. Dlaine lay on his bedroll, which Jola had unrolled for him, and had not yet awoken from his unconsciousness. Dlaine's chest continued to rise and fall, which meant that he was breathing, at least.

Then, without warning, Dlaine's eyes shot open and he groaned. Sitting up, Dlaine looked around, rubbing the back of his head as he looked at his surroundings in confusion.

"Huh?" said Dlaine. He winced. "Ow, my head. What happened? Where are we?" He stopped and then tilted his head to the right, probably listening to Jola. "Oh. So we're out of Carrk, then, and didn't get arrested. Good deal."

Dlaine looked over at Keo and Maryal. "You two all right?"

Maryal nodded, as did Keo, though he had to nod more weakly than usual because of how tired he was.

"Good, good," said Dlaine. He winced again. "But I have such a *splitting* headache. What did that woman hit me with? A ten pound steel pipe?"

"It was probably a stun spell," said Maryal. "Those can really hurt, especially if they hit you in the chest. Sometimes they can even cripple you for life, depending on where they hit you and how powerful the spell was."

Dlaine shuddered. "Looks like I got lucky, then."

"Oh, Enira probably wasn't trying to cripple you for life, just take you out long enough for her to haul you to jail," said Maryal. "But you are obviously an older man and stun spells can sometimes have negative effects on older people that they lack when applied to younger people."

"Right," said Dlaine. Then he looked at Keo. "You sure look tired."

Keo rolled his eyes. "Of course … I look … tired. I've been running … carrying Maryal and Gildshine … and it's a hot day …"

"Of course," said Dlaine. "Sorry. Anyway, it looks like we're all about to get some rest soon anyway, what with the sun going down soon."

Maryal looked around at the ground they sat on. "Wait, are you saying that I will have to rest in the dirt?"

"Unless you brought your own camping supplies, yeah," said

Dlaine, nodding. "We're not exactly a traveling hotel, you know."

"I know," said Maryal. She rubbed the back of her neck. "But I didn't think that I'd have to camp out in the wilderness with you two while we're going to Capitika. At the very least I thought you'd have a tent."

"No tents," said Dlaine with a shrug. "Or anything else except for our bedrolls. You aren't going to start complaining, are you?"

"No, no, of course not," said Maryal, shaking her head. "I would complain about the hand that destiny has dealt me; instead, I will make do with what I have. I do wish, though, I could have grabbed some of my possessions from Carrk before we left."

"You're welcome to go back and try to convince them to give you your stuff back," said Dlaine. "Unfortunately, I don't think the Carrkians are going to be very thrilled to see you again."

"You are right, I suppose," said Maryal with a sigh. "But what about your friend, Galy? She was going to secure her front door when we left. Do you think she will be fine on her own against that mob?"

"I imagine she will be," said Dlaine. "Galy may appear small and weak, but she's a lot tougher than she looks. Very much capable of taking care of herself. She doesn't need us to worry about her. She'll be fine on her own."

"I hope so," said Maryal. "That crowd was awfully angry and she was such a small old lady, but she is a Magician and seemed like a very skilled and experienced one, at that."

"You have no idea," said Dlaine. "But anyway, were we followed at all by anyone from Carrk?"

Keo shook his head. He sat up, feeling a little bit more refreshed now that he had had something to drink and time to rest, and said, "Don't think so. I think we lost them."

"Good," said Dlaine. "Then that means that all we need to do now is head on to Capitika, which should only take us a couple of days to reach if we don't run into anymore delays or get caught up in any more unnecessary side quests."

"Wonderful," said Maryal with a smile. Then she frowned suddenly. "What if Enira sends people to come after us during the night, while we sleep? We'll be unprotected and easy prey for her Enforcers."

"Unlikely," said Dlaine. "Jola will stay up and keep an eye on the road for us. If she sees anyone or anything that could harm us, she'll let us know."

"Oh," said Maryal. "Well, that's good to know. Jola certainly seems like an interesting lady to me."

"She's great," said Dlaine. He yawned. "She's never failed to protect me in all of the time that I've known her. But let's change the subject, because we have more important things to talk about at the moment than Jola."

"Such as what?" said Keo, wiping the sweat off of his forehead. He wasn't in the mood to talk, but he didn't want to be left out of any important conversations, either.

"Such as what we're going to do when we get to Capitika," said Dlaine. "That seems like a pretty important thing to discuss."

"That's easy," said Keo. He patted Gildshine in its sheath at his side. "We go to Nesma, show her Gildshine, which will prove that the demons exist, and—"

"Hold on," said Maryal, interrupt Keo and causing him to look at her. Her eyes were wide in confusion. "You know Nesma of the Wand? The youngest member of the Magical Council?"

"Yes," said Keo, nodding. He grabbed his flask again, drank briefly, and then said, "We were best friends back in the Low Woods before she became a member of the Council. Have you met her before?"

Maryal put her hands on her cheeks. "No, I haven't. But I've always admired her from a distance, because very few young people, male or female, ever rise to such power and prominence so early in life. Yet you say she was your best friend?"

"Still is," said Keo. "Granted, I haven't spoken to her in a year, which was when she first joined the Magical Council. I don't really know how she's doing, but we left on good terms, so I see no reason for her not to speak to me."

"I can think of several reasons why she wouldn't want to speak with you," said Dlaine.

"What?" said Keo, looking at Dlaine again. "How can you possibly know why she would not want to speak with me? You don't know her as well as I do."

"Maybe, but I do know everything we've been through recently," said Dlaine. He started ticking off his fingers. "Escaping that jail in New Ora, getting caught up in that conflict between those two crazy sisters, fighting Old Cyclops, the demon at the Falls, and interrupting the charity duel at Carrk, though it's the last two that will really give us trouble."

"What kind of trouble?" said Keo. "I don't understand."

"Think, Keo, think," said Dlaine, tapping the side of his head. "Magician Skran and Magician Enira know who we are. They likely consider us criminals, which is technically what we are, and because we are currently traveling between towns, that means it is the responsibility of every Magician to catch us if they find us.

Wouldn't surprise me if they sent reports to Capitika telling the Magicians there to keep an eye out for us."

"You mean, if we just walked up to Capitika's gates, we'd probably be arrested by the gatekeepers for the crimes we're wanted for in New Ora and Carrk?" said Keo.

"Exactly," said Dlaine. "And even worse, they might actually succeed, because Capitika is crawling with Magicians and they aren't afraid to step in and arrest any criminals they find if the Enforcers fail to catch us."

"So you're saying that walking into Capitika might be a trap," said Keo.

"Not necessarily a trap, but it would be stupid, yes," said Dlaine. "Therefore, we need to figure out a plan of action that will allow us to enter Capitika without being seen."

"I can help," Maryal offered. "I'm a Magician, so they will recognize me and—"

"And arrest you, because they think you cheated, right?" said Dlaine, interrupting her. "Yeah, you're not going to be of much help, at least in that area."

Maryal folded her arms across her chest and pouted. "Well, I was just offering to help."

Dlaine sighed. "I know, I know, but the fact is that none of us, not even Jola, can just stroll up to Capitika's gates and expect to be let in without any fuss. So we need to figure out how we are going to get inside without being seen or noticed."

"Galy's invisibility spell?" said Keo. He looked down at his body, which was quite visible. "Isn't it still active?"

"Probably not anymore," said Dlaine. "Remember, Galy said that it only lasts about an hour, and it's been well over an hour since we left Carrk. And we can't replicate the spell on our own, either, so it looks like we're out of luck there."

Keo thought about the matter for a moment before shrugging. "I really don't know very much about Capitika, so I'm not sure how we can get in undetected or unseen."

"I think I have an idea," said Dlaine. "I've had to sneak into the city before because of … reasons I'd rather not go into at the moment. I don't know if the particular route I am thinking of is still open, but if it is, then it should allow us to get inside without anyone even knowing."

"Want to tell us about it?" said Keo.

"Not right now," said Dlaine with a yawn. "Maybe in the morning. Right now, I'm very tired and think all of us need to get some sleep so we can get up bright and early tomorrow morning. All right?"

Keo and Maryal both nodded, even though Keo was interested in hearing about Dlaine's plan right now. Still, he was so tired that he didn't mind putting it off into the morning.

Thus, about ten minutes later, Keo was lying on his bedroll, while Maryal lay a few feet away using the extra blanket that Keo had had in his pack. It was the only thing they had for her, but Maryal did not complain, even though the extra blanket was small and didn't smell very good.

And soon, Keo drifted off into sleep, too tired from the adventures of the day to even think about staying awake. Yet a part of him was excited that he would soon see his best friend in the whole world again. He didn't know how much Nesma might have changed since leaving the Low Woods a year ago, but he knew that, whatever changes she might have gone through, she was still, deep down, his friend, and always would be.

Chapter Twenty-Four

A COUPLE OF DAYS of traveling later—mostly through the wilderness, as they had to avoid the roads in order to make sure that no one saw them—the city of Capitika rose in the distance. It was early morning when Keo first saw the large city on the horizon, and at first, due to the distance and the lack of light, it looked like a collection of tall, vague objects, but as they drew closer to it and as the sun rose in the sky, he saw the city in much better detail.

Capitika was enormous; not quite as large as Castarious, perhaps, but much prettier. The buildings, which had crystalline exteriors, reflected brilliantly the morning sun's rays off of their surfaces, while the huge metallic city walls gleamed brightly, like they were polished and scrubbed clean every single day. The Hanuf River flowed beside the city, shining brightly in the sun, and from the center of the city rose the largest Tower that Keo had ever seen. It looked just like the Towers from the smaller towns, except twice as tall and large. It, too, was clean and reflective, making it look almost like a giant icicle in the sun.

The gates of Capitika were huge as well. They were the biggest city gates Keo had ever seen, and they appeared to be made out of gold and silver, although they had probably simply been painted that way. Strong-looking Enforcers, wearing beautiful crimson armor and carrying swords that looked brand new, stood before the massive gates with stern looks visible through their helmets, which were shaped like the head of a hawk for some reason. There was no way that anyone could ever hope to climb over the walls or the gates, even if the Enforcers were not there to prevent you from doing so, because their surfaces were too steep and slick to allow anyone to climb them.

But Keo and the others were not going to be climbing the walls today, nor were they going to attempt to enter through the gates.

Instead, Keo was following Dlaine along the banks of the Hanuf River. They were out of sight of the guards at the gates and walls, but still moved silently and stealthily to ensure that they would not be caught before they could enter the city. So far, no one had seen them, but that was primarily due to the low light of the morning, as well as the fog that rose from the River, though that would dissipate once the sun was high enough in the sky.

As they sneaked along the Hanuf River, Keo recalled what Dlaine had told them about how they were going to get inside Capitika without being noticed. According to Dlaine, there was a secret underground passage near the River that connected Capitika to the outside. The passageway was unknown to the Magical Council and everyone else in Capitika, and its exact purpose and origin was a mystery even to Dlaine. But as Capitika had once been a major trading port during King Riuno's reign, Dlaine theorized that the secret passageway had been built to allow important leaders to escape the city in the event it was besieged by enemy forces.

In any case, the secret passageway had been open and unprotected last time Dlaine had used it, so Dlaine assumed that it would still be open and unprotected now. He assured Keo and Maryal that the passageway would have no Enforcers guarding it, because no one in Capitika knew it was there. Even so, he advised them to be careful, because the secret passageway was old and in bad condition due to the fact that no one had bothered to take care of it since the fall of the Kingdom at least. That made Keo wonder if it would be safe to travel through, but because they had no other way to get into Capitika unseen, Keo did not object to traveling through it.

As they walked along the riverbanks, Keo glanced at Maryal. The young Magician looked a lot rougher due to sleeping and traveling in the wilderness with them over the past few days. Her blonde hair was dirtier, though a lot cleaner than Keo's or Dlaine's, probably because Maryal had used her magic to keep her hair relatively clean. The sleeves of her tunic were rolled up to her elbows and she had some cuts on her hands from where she had tripped and fallen into a patch of stickers on their second day from Carrk. Yet she had not complained about the roughness of their journey, which made Keo sometimes think that she must have done something like this before in the past, even though she claimed that she was not much of an outdoors person.

In any case, Keo was glad to have a Magician on their side. Maryal may have been a bit strange at times, especially whenever she talked about destiny, but she was obviously very magically adept and even knew a few basic healing spells, which had been handy for all of the little bumps, bruises, and cuts that they had gained during their travels. She even knew how to cook, though not as well as Dlaine, because she said that she was used to cooking in larger kitchens with a much wider variety of ingredients and better cooking tools than what they had with them. That she was a duelist was good as well, because it meant she could defend herself in a fight.

But Maryal was not perfect. As Keo had noted, she had a very strange obsession with destiny and would often declare the oddest things to be part of her (or their) destiny. Once, when Dlaine had accidentally tripped and fell flat on his face, she had claimed that his fall was an important part of his destiny. That had seemed like kind of a cruel thing to say, even though Maryal had said that she had not meant anything offensive by it and was merely offering her opinion on it (which seemed to be true, but Dlaine had refused to speak with her for the rest of the day after that anyway).

But overall, Keo trusted Maryal. Not quite as much as Dlaine or Jola, perhaps, because he hadn't known her as long as he had known those two, but well enough that he trusted her to help them. She reminded him somewhat of Nesma, except that Nesma had been far more justice-minded and less prone to apologizing than Maryal, and he was pretty sure that Nesma had been more powerful than Maryal, too, though he did not know that for sure.

"We're here," said Dlaine suddenly, his voice a whisper.

The party of four stopped and Keo looked ahead to see that they had stopped in front of a large pile of branches and dried moss on the river banks. It was somewhat hidden by the tall grass that grew out of the Hanuf River, which meant that no one traveling on the River by boat would be able to see them, but Keo did not see any doors or entrances that would take them into the city.

"I don't see anything," said Maryal, tilting her head to the side. "Just moss and grass."

"The entrance to the secret passageway is hidden under all of that brush," said Dlaine. Then he looked down to his right and said, "Jola, if you would be so kind."

A second later, the large pile of brush floated up and deposited to the left side of the entrance, revealing a rusted metal hatch built into the side of the riverbanks. The hatch had a huge handle and looked like it had not been opened in centuries, though if Dlaine was telling the truth, he had last opened it only a few years ago at most.

Dlaine, smiling in satisfaction, walked over to the hatch, grasped its handle with both hands, and pulled. At first the hatch did not budge, but after some effort on Dlaine's part, it slowly but surely opened, until soon Keo was looking down a set of ancient stone steps, with tiny puddles of water on them, leading down into a dark and dank-smelling tunnel that stretched into the shadows.

Dlaine stepped aside and gestured at the entrance. "Ladies first."

Maryal pinched her nose. "Do I have to go first?"

Dlaine rolled his eyes. "Just being polite."

Nonetheless, Maryal climbed down the steps into the dark passageway, followed by Keo, and then Dlaine. Jola had probably followed at some point as well. At least, Keo assumed so, because Dlaine pulled the hatch shut behind them once they were all inside and he doubted that Dlaine would leave Jola outside by herself like that.

When Dlaine closed the hatch shut, they were immediately plunged into deep darkness, but then a light shined in Maryal's hand. It didn't shine very brightly or extend too deeply into the dark tunnel, but it did allow Keo to see everyone else and where they were at least.

"All right," said Dlaine as he walked down the steps to join them. "This passageway is simple and straightforward. Just keep walking forward and eventually we should reach another set of steps leading up to another hatch, which will take us into Capitika itself."

Maryal suddenly yelped and jumped behind Keo, causing Keo to grab Gildshine's hilt and say, "What is it? Did you see something?"

Maryal gulped. She was now shivering in fear. "I just felt something slither by my feet."

"Probably a Hanuf snake," said Dlaine. "Because this hatch is so close to the Hanuf River, sometimes creatures from the River make their home down here. The hatch isn't exactly airtight, so sometimes when the River overflows, water will come down here, though there are vents in the floor that allow the water to drain."

"You mean there might be *more* snakes down here?" said Maryal, her voice shaky.

"Probably not very many, and they won't attack us, either, because Hanuf snakes fear humans more than we fear them," said Dlaine. "Just make sure not to step on any and you should be fine."

Maryal looked hardly comforted by Dlaine's words, while Keo looked down at the floor. By Maryal's weak light, he saw the vents that Dlaine mentioned, glistening in the light.

"Where do these vents empty out?" said Keo.

"No idea," said Dlaine, shaking his head. "I always assumed they just emptied out into the River somewhere. I don't know very much about who built this passageway or why, because I've never needed to in order to use it."

"All right," said Keo, looking up and ahead into the shadows before them. "Then let's keep going. The longer we stay here, the longer we have to deal with the awful stench of the river water."

"Good point," said Maryal. She hesitated. "Who's going to lead the way?"

"I will," said Dlaine, stepping past them. "But I need you by my side with your light so I can see where the hell I'm going. I don't expect to run into any real danger down here, but you never know and it's better to be safe than sorry in my experience."

Maryal looked reluctant to walk beside Dlaine, but she nonetheless joined him by his side as they walked. Dlaine walked with confidence, like he could take on anything that might be lurking in the shadows, while Maryal walked timidly beside him like she thought a monster was going to jump out of the darkness and get her at any moment. Keo followed behind them both, guarding the back, even though there was no one following them. He figured Jola was probably near him, but as usual, he could not see her, so he could not tell for certain where she was even in this narrow passageway.

As they walked, Keo looked at the walls of the tunnel around them. They were mostly slimy and wet and Keo occasionally saw something crawl across the surface, though they always moved too fast for him to see what they were. He noticed what appeared to be strange writing and paintings on the walls, but they were so old and faded that he could not make out most of them, though they appeared to be arrows pointing in the direction opposite they were going, perhaps to give guidance to the people coming from the other end of the tunnel.

As they walked, Keo wondered what Dlaine was thinking. Dlaine had said that he was coming to Capitika to save his daughter, who Keo still knew very little about (in fact, he didn't even know her name). Dlaine certainly seemed in a hurry to get there, but he hadn't spoken much about it. Then again, Dlaine was a naturally private person, so perhaps Keo should not have been that surprised that Dlaine had said so little about her so far.

I'll probably get to meet her soon enough, Keo thought, wrinkling his nose at the terrible river water stench that filled his nostrils. *If she's anything like her father, then she's probably a good person. It's more important that I see Nesma first, however.*

That was when Keo heard deep breathing behind him. He stopped and looked over his shoulder, but only saw darkness. Nor did he hear the deep breathing anymore. Yet Keo could have sworn that he had heard someone—no, some*thing*—breathing heavily behind him.

That doesn't make any sense, though, Keo thought. *There's nothing in here besides me, Dlaine, Jola, and Maryal. Well, maybe there are some river creatures, but that didn't sound like a snake to me.*

"Keo?" said Dlaine, causing Keo to look back at Maryal and him, who had stopped to look at him over their shoulders. "What are you doing? Did you hear something"

Keo opened his mouth to tell them what he had heard, but then Dlaine's eyes widened and he said, "Keo, watch out!"

Without hesitation, Keo dove forward, rolling across the damp stone floor just as something whipped through the air above him. Getting to his feet, Keo drew Gildshine out and held it before him as he turned to face whatever had tried to get him, but the shadows still hid it from view.

"What *was* that?" said Maryal. Her voice sounded squeaky with fear now. "A … a tongue?"

"No idea," said Dlaine, shaking his head. "There shouldn't be anything in here except for us."

A deep, harsh snarl echoed from the shadows and then something stepped into the light.

It was the most hideous creature that Keo had ever laid his eyes on. It vaguely resembled a humanoid frog, except with short, blunt horns and blood-red skin. It had a gigantic, sagging stomach, with spindly, clawed arms that clung to the walls on either side of the tunnel. Its eyes were bulging, yellow with red irises, and its body sweated some kind of ugly green slime.

Maryal was now breathing so fast that she sounded close to fainting. "Guys … what … is … that?"

"Trouble," said Dlaine. "Run!"

Before they could run, the frog monster opened its mouth and launched its tongue—black and spiked—at Keo. Keo immediately slashed it with Gildshine, causing the frog monster to yelp in pain, but when he saw Gildshine fail to cut through the frog monster's tongue, he said, "Demon!"

"Demon?" said Maryal. She staggered backwards. "That's an actual, real life *demon*? Like the ones you guys fought?"

"Looks like it," said Dlaine. "Jola! Keep it from following us!"

Without warning, a stone wall erupted from the floor in between them and the frog demon. Almost immediately, however, they heard the sounds of the frog demon beating violently against

318 | TIMOTHY L. CEREPAKA

the stone wall, which was already starting to show cracks in its surface.

"Come on, you two!" Dlaine shouted. "Run before that thing breaks through and follows us!"

Dlaine immediately ran down the tunnel, with Maryal following closely behind, and Keo taking up the rear. Even as the stone wall sank into the shadows behind them, Keo could hear the sounds of the frog demon tearing it apart and he knew that it was only a matter of time before the demon broke through and caught up with them again.

That thought gave Keo the motivation to keep running. Maryal's light was the only light that they had to see by, making it almost impossible to see more than a couple of feet ahead of them. Keo kept expecting another demon to be awaiting them somewhere ahead, but the tunnel ahead was silent.

Then Keo felt something slimy and spiky wrap around his ankle and he fell on his face with a cry. He was immediately pulled backwards, while Maryal cried, "Keo!" and Dlaine shouted, "Kid, no!"

Keo rolled over onto his back as he was dragged along and saw the frog demon pulling him toward its mouth. The frog demon's mouth was open widely enough that Keo was certain that it would swallow him whole if he allowed it, but Gildshine could not cut through the frog demon's tongue unless he activated its special ability, and he did not want to use that just yet.

So when Keo got close enough, he jabbed Gildshine directly into the frog demon's mouth. The frog demon let out a wail of pain, its tongue immediately unraveling around Keo's ankle, which allowed Keo to scramble back to his feet. But rather than run, he slammed the flat of Gildshine into the frog demon's face, sending it staggering backwards, a dazed look on its face.

Then Keo turned and ran as fast as he could back to Dlaine and Maryal and the party of four were running once more into the shadows. But now Keo heard the slapping of the frog demon's wet feet against the stone floor, could even somehow sense its anger at being denied its prey. That just made Keo run all the faster, although he was starting to get winded from running so much and would likely soon collapse if they didn't escape the tunnel soon.

"Dlaine, how much farther until we reach the exit?" said Maryal as they ran. Her voice was particularly high and squeaky, despite the breathlessness in her voice from all of the running they were doing.

"Not sure," Dlaine shouted back. "It's been so long that I can't remember exactly, but I think we're almost there. Just need to run a little bit farther and—"

Dlaine skid to a stop, forcing Maryal, Keo, and Jola to stop behind him. Keo was about to ask why Dlaine stopped when he suddenly saw the reason why: The path ahead was completely blocked by rubble. There wasn't even a hole for them to crawl through. And behind them, the slapping of the demon's wet feet could still be heard, coming closer and closer with each passing second.

"What happened here?" said Maryal. "Earthquakes don't happen around Capitika, so it can't be that."

"It's a trap," said Dlaine in anger. "Someone knew we were coming, would come through this way, and they sent this demon to stop us. I bet that the demon itself blocked off our path and has been waiting here for us for who-knows-how-long."

"Does that mean we're going to die?" said Maryal, her voice so high now that it was almost impossible to hear.

"Jola can clear it with her magic, but it will take her time," said Dlaine. "And time is the one thing we *don't* have."

Keo looked over his shoulder, but the frog demon was still nowhere in sight. "I'll hold him off, then, at least until Jola can make a hole big enough for all of us to escape through."

"All right," said Dlaine, though he hardly sounded happy about that. Then he looked down and said, "Jola, you know what to do."

Immediately, bits and pieces of rock began to remove themselves from the rubble, while Keo turned to face the darkness. The frog demon was still not in sight, but he could hear its every step as it drew nearer. Maryal was biting the nails of her other hand, but she kept the light on, at least.

Then the frog demon appeared in the light. It seemed to literally melt from the shadows, as if it was one with the shadows. As soon as it saw what they were doing, it let out an unnatural snarl and launched its tongue at them again. This time, Keo batted it out of the way with Gildshine and then ran at the demon. He swung Gildshine at its face, but the frog demon blocked the blade with its left claw and tried to swipe him with its right claw, but Keo jumped backwards out of its reach.

Stepping backwards, Keo slammed the flat of Gildshine in the demon's face. The blow hit home once again, only this time the demon recovered far more quickly than before. It lashed out with its tongue again, except this time it punched him in the gut rather than grabbing him. The tongue struck him with surprising force, almost enough to knock him off his feet.

Then the frog demon reared back with its claws, but before it could go in for the kill, it suddenly started choking. It grabbed its throat and fell to its knees, coughing and gasping for air.

Surprised, Keo looked over his shoulder and saw Maryal holding out her free hand. Though she looked absolutely terrified, she also looked determined to help Keo hold off the frog demon. Keo was glad about that, because he hadn't been sure he could beat the demon by himself.

Then Keo looked at Jola's progress on the blockade. She had already cleared a good chunk of it by now, but there was still no room for any of them to escape through just yet.

So Keo turned his attention back to the frog demon, which was still choking on its lack of air, and he swung Gildshine down on the frog demon as hard as he could, hoping to knock it out at least.

But then the frog demon's body melted into shadow and slithered back into the darkness and Gildshine hit the floor of the passageway. Keo immediately raised it back up and stared into the darkness, trying to find the frog demon, but it was too dark to see it.

"Did …" Maryal gulped. "Did that thing just turn into shadow and—"

An earsplitting yell erupted from the shadows all around them, causing Dlaine to slam his hands over his ears and Keo and Maryal to cringe. Even Jola's removal of the rock blockade halted briefly, but only for a second before she resumed tossing the debris aside in order to create a path for them.

But then the earsplitting yell faded and soon the entire

passageway was silent once more. Keo's ears continued to ring, however, and he felt the frog demon's presence somewhere in the shadows, even though he could not see or hear it.

"Is …" Maryal's voice was quieter now, almost like a whisper, yet somehow still high-pitched. "Is it gone?"

Keo strained his ears to listen for any sign of the frog demon, but he heard nothing except for Dlaine and Maryal's breathing and the sounds of the rocks in the blockade being tossed aside by Jola.

"I don't think so, but maybe … maybe it is," said Keo. "But keep your guard up, because you never know if this is a trap."

Then Keo heard the splashing of water from somewhere within the darkness. Then it sounded like water was running, which made no sense, because Keo had seen Dlaine close the hatch behind them, so he wasn't sure where the sound of running water was coming from.

"Uh oh," said Dlaine, causing Keo and Maryal to look at him. "Do you hear that?"

Maryal nodded shakily. "By 'that,' do you mean the water?"

"Yes, that's what I meant," said Dlaine. He immediately ran over to the blockade and started pulling it apart with his bare hands, tossing aside huge chunks. "Come on and help, you idiots!"

"Why?" said Keo in bewilderment. "Doesn't Jola—"

Keo stopped speaking. The sound of rushing water sounded much closer now and he immediately realized what the frog demon had done.

"Oh no," said Keo. "It's trying to flood the tunnel with the River's water, isn't it?"

"Yes," said Dlaine as he continued to pull apart the blockade. "Damn thing is trying to drown us. Come on and help!"

Keo sheathed Gildshine and immediately started helping Dlaine and Jola tear down the blockade, while Maryal continued to light the passageway with her hand. But she was now looking up and down the tunnel, while the sound of rushing water grew louder and louder with each passing second.

The rock was heavy and some of it was sharp, but Keo did not complain or slow down as he pulled the blockade apart. And then, finally, they created a hole large enough for them to slip through, causing Dlaine to shout, "Everyone through! Now!"

Dlaine crawled through first, followed by Maryal, and then Keo. As soon as they were all on the other side of the blockade, they ran, but as they ran, the sounds of rushing water were so loud now that the water sounded like it was right behind them. Keo looked over his shoulder long enough to see the rushing water flowing down the tunnel toward them. It crashed into what remained of the blockade, which was fortunately strong enough to hold back most of the water, but some of the water exploded through the gap that Keo, Dlaine, and Jola had created, and caught up with them, wetting their boots and the floor.

Yet they did not stop running. With their feet splashing in the now ankle deep water, Keo and the others ran as if their lives depended on it. Behind them, above the sound of the rushing water that was spilling through the gap in the blockade, the unnatural snarl of the frog demon could be heard, but Keo did not even look backwards to see if it was following them.

Then Dlaine suddenly pointed and shouted, "Up ahead!"

At the end of the passageway was a set of stairs, similar to the

324 | TIMOTHY L. CEREPAKA

ones from the entrance, that led up to an identical metal hatch. That had to be the exit, and its sight renewed Keo's courage. It must have renewed Maryal and Dlaine's courage, as well, because the two of them suddenly looked a lot less tired.

In seconds, all four of them were climbing up the stairs, while the passageway continued to fill with water behind them. The rapidly rising water followed them up and they just barely outran it, keeping about one or two steps ahead of it at all times.

Dlaine reached the hatch first and immediately started to turn its handle. Meanwhile, Keo and Maryal stood behind him, anxiously looking between Dlaine and the ever-rising water, which rose higher and higher every minute.

Finally, Dlaine gave a yell of triumph and pushed the hatch open. He dashed out, followed by Maryal. Keo moved to follow, but then the frog demon's tongue suddenly wrapped around his chest and jerked him backwards. But Keo reacted quickly, drawing Gildshine and slamming it into the steps, its sharp blade embedding in the stone steps and keeping Keo from being drawn into the water.

Keo looked over his shoulder and saw the frog demon standing in the water below. Its yellow eyes glowed with anger as it pulled him back with all of its might. Not only that, but it was squeezing him hard with its tongue, squeezing the air out of his lungs and making it harder to maintain his balance, especially with the river water reaching his boots.

"Keo!" Dlaine shouted from beyond the hatch.

Keo wanted to tell them to go on without him, but he was unable to speak due to how tightly the demon's tongue constricted around his body. He reached out toward Dlaine and Maryal, who grabbed his arm and tried to pull him in with them, but the frog demon was far stronger than either of them and he could feel that the frog demon was going to win this tug of war.

"Don't … give up," Dlaine said through gritted teeth. "Hang in there, kid, hang in there."

Keo tried to look brave, but deep down, he knew that there was no way that Dlaine and Maryal could pull him out. With the water rising rapidly and the frog demon resolutely holding him down, it was obvious that Keo was going to meet his end here, though Dlaine and Maryal might not if they let him go.

But then, without warning, the demon's tongue caught fire and the frog demon let go, roaring in pain. Immediately, Keo felt air return to his lungs and he yanked Gildshine out of the stone steps. Then, with Dlaine and Maryal still pulling him, he crawled out of the passageway and onto the street outside.

As soon as Keo had crawled out, Dlaine shut the hatch closed. He then grabbed a pipe lying on the street and jammed it through the hatch's handle, effectively locking it. Even as Dlaine did that, however, water leaked through the edges of the hatch and the sound of the frog demon's tongue beating against the hatch could be heard from outside of it, but the hatch must have been made out of very strong metal, because it did not even dent under the frog demon's blows.

Eventually, the frog demon's banging against the hatch ceased and all was silent again, save for the slight dripping of the river water through the cracks. Nonetheless, Keo, Dlaine, Maryal, and Jola moved as far away from the hatch as they could in the street they had emerged on, just in case the frog demon somehow made it through anyway.

"My … god," said Keo, breathing hard as he lay on the street. His lungs and chest ached. "That … was … too … close."

"That's the understatement of the year," said Dlaine, who was panting just as much as Keo and leaning on an empty garbage can. "By the way, it was Jola who set the frog demon's tongue on fire. Even though that obviously did not kill it, I guess the fire must have really hurt it or something."

Keo looked around, but as always, he did not see Jola anywhere, nor did he hear her in his mind. He just sat up, wincing at the pain in his chest and the cold wetness in his boots. He pulled off his boots and emptied the water from them into the street. He also took this moment to look around at where they had ended up exactly.

They were in some kind of dirty back alley in Capitika, right up against the city walls, which towered high above them. Behind them were large buildings with grimy surfaces and boarded up windows, which told Keo that this was probably not a very affluent part of town. There was no one else in the back alley besides themselves, though a rat scurried past them into a drain pipe and vanished.

"Well, at least we all made it out alive," said Maryal. She did not sound quite as scared as she did back in the passageway, but her voice was still very high. She leaned against the exterior of one of the buildings opposite the hatch. "And we're in Capitika, too, so it should be smooth sailing from here on out, right?"

Dlaine, however, was staring at the hatch. "No, I don't think it will."

"Why?" said Maryal. "The frog demon can't come after us, right?"

"Maybe, but aren't either of you guys wondering *why* the frog demon was down there in the first place?" said Dlaine, looking at Keo and Maryal with a serious expression on his face. He stopped leaning against the garbage can and instead stood upright. "How could it have possibly known that we would attempt to enter the city through that passageway when we didn't tell anyone that we were?"

"Um," said Keo, scratching the back of his head as he pulled his damp boots back onto his feet, "I don't know. The demons are probably watching us and probably have guards at every possible entrance."

"But why wouldn't the Magicians know about it and have done something about it?" said Dlaine, folding his arms over his chest. "I know a thing or two about Magicians and there's no way that any of them would fail to notice a demon in their city, even if it tried to hide itself in an obscure part that no one knew about."

"But *I* didn't notice it and I'm a Magician," said Maryal as she wrung water out of the hems of her robes. "It surprised me just as much as it surprised you guys."

"You mean you didn't feel anything at all before it showed itself?" said Dlaine.

Maryal glanced at the hatch, frowned, and said, "Now that you mention it, I do remember feeling something was off down there, but I just dismissed it as my nerves. Now, though, I think I must have sensed the demon's own magic, but I just didn't recognize it because I've never sense demonic magic before."

"And there are probably loads of Magicians in Capitika, such as the Magical Council, who should not only have noticed the frog demon, but investigated its existence in case it was a threat to the city's safety," said Dlaine. He gestured at the abandoned back alley they stood in. "But clearly, that is not the case, seeing as we're completely alone here."

"What are you suggesting, Dlaine?" said Keo, wiping off some of the sludge that had gotten on Gildshine from the river water in the tunnel. "Maybe the demons have a way of hiding their magical presence from Magicians."

"No," said Dlaine, shaking his head. "But let me be blunt for a moment: Someone in the Magical Council put that demon down there to kill us before we could enter the city. And, if I'm correct, I have no doubt they will try to kill us again very soon."

Chapter Twenty-Five

KEO AND MARYAL STARED at Dlaine in stunned silence for a moment before Maryal said, in a hasty voice, "Dlaine, I must have misheard you. Did you say that someone in the Magical Council put that demon down there to kill us?"

"Yep," said Dlaine, his tone as grim as ever. "You heard me right."

"But …" Maryal looked at her feet like she wasn't certain what to say. "That doesn't make any sense. The Magical Council doesn't even know we're coming this way. Even if they did, the Magical Council doesn't even know that the demons are coming back, so how could anyone among them possibly order a demon to ambush us in that passageway?"

"Because it's the only theory that makes any sense and explains anything," said Dlaine. "It explains how that demon could have possibly known we were down there and why it didn't seem shocked to see us. It explains why the Magicians of Capitika have done nothing about it, because someone in the Council is hiding the demon's existence from all of the other Magicians."

"That still doesn't make sense," said Maryal, brushing back some strands of hair. "The Magical Council can be a bit cruel sometimes, even corrupt, yes, but I don't think that anyone in the

Council would ever work with demons. That's insane."

"That theory really isn't as crazy as it sounds," said Keo. He was remembering what the demon in Castarious had said. "Back in Castarious, Dlaine and I ran into another demon. This one claimed that our quest was 'pointless,' but at the time we dismissed it as the demon trying to demoralize us. But what if the demon knew that someone in the Council works for them and that was why he told us that our quest is pointless?"

"No way," said Maryal, though she didn't sound as certain as she usually did. She slumped against the building that they were gathered before, a look of confusion and fear on her face. "If the Magical Council is working with the demons—"

"Not the *whole* Council," said Dlaine. He held up one finger. "Just one member. But hey, for all I know, there might be multiple people in the Council who are working with the demons or maybe the whole damned Council is in on it. Who knows?"

"But why would anyone in the Magical Council do that?" said Maryal. "The demons ... you guys said that they just want to kill us all, return us to the old days, before the Good King sealed them away. The Magical Council is supposed to *defend* us from threats like that."

"I don't know why anyone in the Council would work with the demons, but I see why the demons would try to get the Council on their side," said Dlaine. "It's pretty simple war tactics: If you want an easy victory, then make sure that your enemy doesn't believe you are going to attack. By taking control of the Magical Council, they can keep the rest of the country from being aware of the demons' return and thus prevent us from being able to prepare for—or outright stop—their attack."

"What a brilliant but evil move," said Maryal, putting her fist against her mouth. "Assuming, at least, that is what they are doing."

"I think it's safe to assume that something like that is going on here," said Dlaine. "The only question is, who is the traitor and can we expose them?"

Maryal looked down at Keo suddenly, like a thought had just occurred to her. "Keo, didn't you say you were friends with Magician Nesma? Do you think we should contact her and let her know about this possible conspiracy?"

Keo opened his mouth to answer, but then Dlaine said, "What if Nesma is *behind* this conspiracy?"

Keo looked at Dlaine in shock. "Nesma? Working with the demons? Impossible. Nesma would never knowingly work with monsters that want nothing more than the complete and utter destruction of humanity and everything we've created. I refuse to believe it."

Dlaine shrugged. "I didn't say that Nesma *was* behind it. I just suggested it because she's a member of the Magical Council, so we can't rule out her involvement in the conspiracy just yet."

Keo rose to his feet, despite his pain and exhaustion, and stared Dlaine straight in the eye. "Neither can we throw ridiculous accusations at her when she isn't even here to defend herself from them."

"It isn't ridiculous if we have reason to believe that the Magical Council has been compromised," said Dlaine, meeting Keo's glare with his own. "Listen, Keo, I know you are young, but one thing I've learned in all of my years of travel is that people are not always what they seem."

"But that doesn't mean that Nesma is conspiring with the demons to destroy us all," said Keo, not even bothering to hide the anger in his voice. "We're friends. Best friends. She would never send any demons to kill or even harm me or my friends."

"As I said, I don't know for sure that she's the one behind it," said Dlaine. "But I think that approaching the Magical Council now would be extremely dangerous. Even if we didn't suspect someone on the Magical Council of conspiring with the demons, the fact is that we're wanted criminals and the members of the Magical Council usually don't schedule appointments with wanted criminals."

"Then what do you suggest we do?" said Keo. He gestured at the alley in which they stood. "The whole reason we came here in the first place was to tell the Magical Council about the demons' return. According to the demon I fought back in the Low Woods, there are still six months left before they rise, so we still have time to stop them."

"I'm not sure," said Dlaine. He glanced around, like he wanted to make sure that no one was eavesdropping on them. "Truthfully, I only care about getting my daughter her medicine. If I can do that, and get her out of here before the demons rise again, well, then that's what I'll do."

"You mean you're going to just give up?" said Keo, his eyes widening in astonishment. "After everything we've been through, you're just going to run away to somewhere else?"

"Probably," said Dlaine. He nodded at the locked hatch. "Remember, Keo, that I was going to Capitika to save my daughter's life, not save the world. We only agreed to travel together in the first place because we both had the same destination and thought we would be safer traveling together than apart. And now that we're here, I don't see any reason for us to continue traveling together."

Keo bit his lower lip. "Yes, but—"

"And I really don't want to take on the Magical Council," said Dlaine. "They are a dangerous enemy to have, no matter who you are. And if this is the lengths that they are willing to go to kill us —or at least one of them is willing to go—then I frankly don't have any more time for this silliness, not if it will get me killed before I give my daughter the medicine she needs."

Keo's hands balled into fists. "So that's it, then? You're just going to leave the country, then?"

"After I heal my daughter, yes," said Dlaine, nodding. "I don't believe there's any way that we can stop the demons, particularly if the Magical Council has been infiltrated by them. I'll take my daughter somewhere far from here, maybe Hasfar or even the Upper Mountains, and never come back."

"What makes you think that the demons will just leave you alone?" said Keo. "How do you know that they won't chase you, maybe try to destroy the entire world? We have to stop them here and now, before they rise again and become a threat to everyone."

"Which we can't do if the Magical Council is wrapped around their finger," Dlaine pointed out. "Look, I agree that the demons are bad, but I've seen just how powerful they are. They can't be killed by normal means, and even magic barely slows them down. Considering I'm just a normal man, I don't think there is much that I—or anyone else who isn't a Magician, for that matter—can do to stop them."

"But—" Keo was interrupted by Jola's voice in his head

334 | TIMOTHY L. CEREPAKA

saying, *I agree with Dlaine. Sorry, Keo, but we have to look out for ourselves, which is all we can do for at this point.*

Keo tried to think of a good counterargument, but his mind kept drawing a blank because Dlaine had already answered most of his objections, and what few objections he had left were so weak that he didn't even bother to bring them up.

After a couple of seconds of tense silence, Dlaine shook his head and said, "Sorry, Keo, but this is as far as I'm willing to go. I wish you and Maryal here the best of luck in stopping the demons."

With a final nod at Keo and Maryal, Dlaine turned and walked into a side alley and was soon gone from sight.

Keo and Maryal walked along another empty and abandoned alleyway in silence. Neither of them spoke, mostly because Keo was still thinking about how Dlaine and Jola abandoned them. He supposed he should have seen it coming, because Dlaine had made it very clear right from the beginning that he was more interested in saving his daughter's life than in saving Lamaira, but it still hit Keo hard. It didn't help that there was the very real possibility that the Magical Council was corrupted by the demons, in which case the situation truly was grim beyond words.

The only upside was that Keo might see Nesma again. Even then, if Nesma truly was the one behind that frog demon from before … no, she couldn't be. Nesma was Keo's friend. She would never order a demon to kill him. Keo just had to get Gildshine to Nesma and let her read it and then she could bring this knowledge to the Magical Council, who would then prepare the country for war against the demons. And maybe this would also help them root out the traitor, whoever it was.

"So …" said Maryal, causing Keo to look at her. She seemed rather awkward around him now, probably because she had mostly stayed out of his and Dlaine's spat earlier and so was not sure if Keo was going to yell at her or not. "We need to find Nesma, right?"

Keo nodded, though he didn't smile. "Yes. Where is the Magical Council? This is my first time in Capitika, so I don't know my way around here."

"That's easy," said Maryal. She pointed ahead of them. "The Magical Council always meets at the Citadel. It's located in the center of Capitika. I've been there before, so I can show you the way if you'd like."

"Sounds good," said Keo. He frowned again. "But how do we avoid being seen and caught? We're both wanted criminals. We can't just walk up to the Citadel and ask them to let us in so we can talk to the Magical Council. We'll need to come up with disguises and false identities to get in."

Maryal tapped her chin as they walked along the street. "Visitors are usually allowed to enter the Citadel without needing to ask for permission, but you're right about the disguises. We could buy some cloaks and hoods to hide our faces under."

"Right," said Keo. "But how do we get an audience with the Magical Council, or at least with Nesma? Is there some kind of procedure we should follow?"

"Yes," said Maryal. "Actually, there are a couple of ways to gain an audience with the Council. The first is to go to the Citadel's Scheduling Office, where, for a low fee of five hundred lems—"

"Five hundred lems?" Keo repeated in shock, stopping and looking at Maryal in disbelief. "That's more lems than even Magician Skran makes in a year."

"It's supposed to keep poor people from seeking an audience with the Council," Maryal explained, stopping next to him. "Anyway, you go to the Scheduling Office, pay the fee, and then they schedule your meeting with the Council."

"How far out do they usually schedule the meeting for?" said Keo.

"A couple of years," said Maryal. "The waiting list is enormous and the Council doesn't have a whole lot of time to entertain guests, so even if you can pay the fee, you might have to wait two years before you can actually meet with them."

Keo rubbed his forehead in frustration. "We have neither five hundred lems or two years to speak with them. What about meetings with individual Council members?"

"It's an entirely case-by-case basis," said Maryal with a shrug. "Some Council members always schedule plenty of meetings with people, but others never meet with anyone outside of the Council ever, and I don't know which one Nesma fits under."

Keo scowled. "What other ways are there to meet them?"

"Being summoned by the Council to appear in their meeting room is another," said Maryal. "If you receive a summons from the Magical Council, then you always have to appear before them as soon as possible. The problem, of course, is that you can't make the Council summon you. You just have to get lucky and hope that they decide that they want to speak with you."

"Nesma doesn't even know that I'm in the city, so I can't expect her to summon me for a meeting with her," said Keo.

"Any other ideas?"

"No," said Maryal, shaking her head. "Like I said, we could disguise ourselves and enter the Citadel itself, but beyond that I am not sure how we could meet Nesma or any other member of the Magical Council."

Keo shoved his hands into his pockets, thinking about their dilemma. If Maryal was telling the truth, then he would have to rely almost entirely on luck to get a meeting with her. It made him angry, because they had come so far, come so close, to saving the country, and yet now they had run into a seemingly insurmountable object.

But then an idea occurred to Keo, causing him to look at Maryal suddenly. "Maryal, are you ready to help me break some more laws and possibly spend the rest of your life behind bars if we get caught?"

Maryal gulped, but nodded anyway and said, "Well, I believe it is our destiny to save Lamaira from the demons, so I'm open to whatever ideas you come up with no matter their legality."

Keo smiled. "Great. Now listen closely, because if we don't do this right, then we'll definitely end up in jail for sure."

Chapter Twenty-Six

ABOUT AN HOUR LATER, Keo and Maryal—wearing identical dark hoods and robes that Maryal had bought off a shady merchant a few blocks from the Citadel—stood in front of the Citadel. It was a massive building; not quite as huge as the two towers of Castarious, but it was just as magnificent as them, if not more so. It was shaped like a castle, with turrets and towers rising from its interior, and large stone walls that provided an excellent defense from outside attacks. The Citadel itself appeared to be made out of platinum, with statues of various ancient Magicians, who Keo did not recognize, set up either side of the wide steps and front door of the building. Dozens of people streamed in and out of the building, while Enforcers wearing crimson armor and carrying huge swords in their hands stood on the walls or by the entrance, their sharp eyes scanning every man, woman, and child that entered or exited the Citadel.

According to Maryal, normal civilians and visitors were not allowed to bring weapons of any kind into the Citadel, so Keo had hid Gildshine underneath his robe. He did not think he would need to use it, but he would need to bring it to Nesma, so he had to come up with a way to get the sword inside the Citadel without letting the Enforcers take it away from him.

Keo and Maryal exchanged a look with each other, nodded,

and then started walking up the steps. As they made their way past the various people entering and exiting the building, Keo quickly reviewed the plan in his mind.

An hour ago, Keo had laid out his plan to Maryal: The two of them, disguised as mere travelers who were coming to see the great Citadel of Capitika, would enter the Citadel. Maryal would then use her magic to create a distraction, which Keo would take advantage of to sneak into the Inner Chambers of the Citadel, where the Magical Council were supposed to be. In fact, Maryal claimed that the Magical Council was supposed to be in session today, so Keo would merely need to find the Council's meeting room and then he would find Nesma.

As with every plan, there were many things that could go wrong. The Enforcers might notice Keo trying to enter the Inner Chambers and arrest him, or maybe Maryal would get caught too soon and then be forced to tell them about Keo. Or maybe the Magical Council would believe Keo to be an assassin and attack him when they saw him; that wasn't such an unrealistic worry, because according to Maryal, the members of the Magical Council were very capable of defending themselves with magic, despite the presence of the Enforcers protecting the building.

But it was the only way that Keo could see that would allow him to meet Nesma and the rest of the Council quickly and easily. He just prayed that it would go smoothly, because he was horribly aware of what might happened if it didn't.

They passed by the two Enforcers at the entrance, who merely scanned them with suspicious eyes but said nothing to either of them. That was good. Those two Enforcers at the entrance had been the first major obstacle toward getting inside.

Upon entering the Citadel's lobby, Keo was surprised by its immense wide-openness. A perfectly scrubbed floor, covered with a dazzling variety of markings and paintings that Keo did not understand, spread out in every direction. Dozens of people—mostly visitors, though a handful wore Magician's robes—stood scattered around the place in small groups, talking among each other, their voices echoing off the lobby's walls and making it somewhat difficult to hear. The lobby's ceiling was a glass dome, giving them a perfect look at the blue sky outside, while a large statue of a stern-looking old man sitting on a throne stood in the center of the lobby, directly beneath the glass dome.

On the perimeter of the lobby were about a dozen doors, though Keo could not tell what was behind them. Beyond one of the open doors, he thought he saw a bunch of clerks running around with stacks of paper in their hands, and beyond another, he saw two Enforcers escorting a dangerous-looking man with shackles around his ankles and wrists and, ominously, a steel mask covering his face.

But the most important door was the one all the way on the other side of the room, a large golden door with four Enforcers, carrying spears and swords, standing guard before it.

"That's it," Maryal muttered, pointing at the large golden door. "Beyond that door are the Inner Chambers."

"All right," said Keo, keeping his own voice low, his eyes darting around the chamber for anything that might possibly cause them problems. "Ready?"

Maryal nodded, albeit shakily. "Y-Yes."

Keo looked her in the eyes. "You don't sound ready."

"No, I am," said Maryal, her voice becoming stronger. "I'm

ready for anything. You don't need to worry about me."

Keo didn't like Maryal's obvious lack of courage, but he decided not to bring it up. He would have to trust her to do what she needed to do and to do it without getting caught.

So Keo nodded and then the two split up. Keo walked along the right side of the room, doing his best to look inconspicuous, while Maryal walked along the left side, where she also tried to look inconspicuous. A quick glance at the Enforcers in the room showed that none of them were paying him or Maryal any attention, which was very, very good.

Keo stopped in front of a painting near the door to the Inner Chambers and pretended to be interested in it. The painting showed that same stern-looking old man whose statue was in the center of the lobby, except this time he was standing and his hands were glowing with light. Keo figured that the old man, whoever he was, must have been very important if he had all of these statues and paintings of him made, but Keo did not know who he was. Maybe he was the founder of the Magical Council.

In any case, Keo glanced over his shoulder. Maryal had stopped near the statue, still looking like any other visitor to the Citadel. She rubbed her hands together, which was the sign that they had agreed upon to signal that she was going to start her part of the plan.

There was an elderly man standing not far from Maryal, who was leaning on a cane and looking up at the statue. He did not seem to be paying Maryal any attention, which meant that he was a good candidate for the distraction.

So Maryal lifted her hands into the air and then brought them down. A huge blast of wind exploded from her body, knocking down everyone around her and even making the statue in the center of the lobby wobble. The elderly man who had been staring at the statue almost fell to the floor, but Maryal caught him and then held him with his arm twisted behind his back.

The Enforcers, as expected, acted immediately. While the rest of the visitors in the Citadel's lobby looked at Maryal in shock, the Enforcers from the front entrance and the Enforcers in front of the Inner Chambers moved to apprehend her.

But Maryal, still holding the elderly man hostage, said, "Don't move! Or I'll hurt this man! I'm serious. I'll do it."

Keo rolled his eyes at Maryal's nonthreatening words, but the Enforcers continued to approach her as if she was a dangerous killer anyway. Maryal started firing blasts of wind at the Enforcers, which distracted them enough to the point where they did not seem to notice Keo. The rest of the people in the lobby ran to the exit, but Keo took advantage of this moment to run up to the golden door of the Inner Chambers, crack it open, and slip inside before anyone noticed.

Now Keo found himself standing inside a narrow hallway that was just as clean and ornate as the rest of the Citadel's lobby had been. The hallway was currently empty; in fact, there did not even seem to be any Enforcers. Maryal had told him that Nesma's room was somewhere down the hall to the left, which was the direction in which the Council members' individual offices were located. The only problem was that Maryal had been unable to describe what the door to Nesma's room looked like, because she had never actually seen it herself. Still, Keo doubted it would be difficult to find. He might even bump into Nesma somewhere along the way.

So Keo walked down the hallway to the left, keeping as silent as he could so that no one would hear him. He didn't see anyone, but there were closed doors on both sides of the hall and there could be people behind them. And if those people heard him, they might go to investigate, and if they did that, then Keo would have to resort to drastic measures not to get captured.

"Hey!" a voice shouted behind Keo. "Who are you?"

Alarmed, but trying not to show it, Keo turned to see a middle-aged man approaching him from the other end of the hall. The man wore a green suit, which meant that he was not a Magician, but he still looked quite stern as he approached Keo.

Keep your cool, Keo, keep your cool, Keo thought. *As long as you don't do or say anything stupid, you might be able to use this guy to your advantage.*

"I, er," said Keo, thinking of a lie as quickly as he could, "I'm here to, uh, see Magician Nesma."

The middle-aged man stopped a few feet from Keo and glared at him. Although the man was thinner and skinnier than Keo, he exuded the kind of authority that Keo did not wish to cross.

"I don't recall Magician Nesma having any appointments today with men so ... uncouth as yourself," said the middle-aged man. He put special emphasis on 'uncouth,' like it was a devastating insult. He wrinkled his nose. "You smell like the Hanuf River."

"I, er, accidentally fell in it and did not get a chance to shower before I entered the city," said Keo, scratching the back of his head. "But I can assure you that Magician Nesma does have an appointment with me today. She's my friend."

"Really?" said the man. His eyes narrowed. "I will have you

know that I am the young mistress's personal assistant. I have complete access to her calendar and I know that she does not have an appointment with anyone today. In fact, she *cannot* have an appointment with anyone today."

"Oh?" said Keo, feeling the sweat start to trickle down the back of his neck. "Why not?"

"Because Magician Nesma is currently in an important meeting with the rest of the Magical Council and has had it scheduled for this time for three weeks," said the man. "That means you're lying to me, and if you are lying to me, then I will have to—"

Keo interrupted the man by punching him in the face. The blow made the man immediately collapse onto the floor.

Keo stood there for a moment, almost stunned by his own impulsiveness, because he hadn't thought that action through at all, and then shook his head. He couldn't stand there and stare at the unconscious man lying on the floor before him; otherwise, he risked the Magical Council or someone else finding him, and there was no way he could explain this situation to anyone without making himself look really bad.

So Keo opened the nearest door and peered inside. It was a broom closet that was almost empty, so Keo dragged the man inside. But just as he dragged the unconscious man inside, he heard voices from down the hall, voices that sounded like they were coming from the direction that Nesma's assistant had come. Alarmed, Keo closed the closet door, even though that locked him in here with Nesma's assistant, and then stood as silently as he could, even breathing quietly so they would not hear him.

As the voices came closer, Keo could make out what they

were saying. He also heard shoes clicking and clacking against the marble floor as the people who wore them walked, though the footsteps were not quite as loud as the voices.

"... And the Road Enforcers brought in a record amount of revenue this month," said one of the voices, which sounded masculine and gravelly. "Two thousand lems! That's twice what they usually bring in."

"That *is* amazing," said another voice, this one feminine and far younger than the first, which Keo recognized with a jolt as Nesma's voice, even though it had been over a year since he had last heard it. "It sounds to me like Masiz deserves a raise for having such a good month."

"True, true, I have been considering giving him a raise," said the older man, who Keo realized was another member of the Magical Council. "But I'm a little worried that the gravy train might not last. Masiz is good, but he's also arrogant and if I give him a raise right away, even for a job well done, he might slack off."

"Then give him a bonus," said Nesma. Her voice sounded the same as it always had; decisive and strong. "Tell him it's an extra for doing such a good job, and that he can get another bonus next month if he keeps up the good work."

"An excellent idea, Nesma, an excellent idea indeed," said the older man. "I must admit that having a youngster like you on the Council has to be one of the best decisions we've ever made. Your youthfulness lets you look at the world so much differently than we cranky old crones."

"Thanks, Daoli, but you don't need to tear yourself down like that," said Nesma, with the same modesty in her voice that Keo

346 | TIMOTHY L. CEREPAKA

had always remembered her having. "You 'cranky old crones' have been leading South Lamaira with your wisdom and knowledge for decades now, ever since King Riuno's death. I am just lucky to get to work alongside such wise and intelligent men and women such as yourself. As a young Magician myself, I am always on the lookout for every little bit of knowledge and wisdom I can gain from my elders."

Keo smiled. Nesma had always been a modest girl, a modest person in general, and he was glad to hear that she had apparently not changed at all. He knew there was no way that she could be conspiring with any demon to kill him or the others, but he did not step out of the closet just yet. Nesma's assistant still lay on the floor of the closet and Keo did not want to explain to Nesma or Daoli why he was hiding in a closet with an unconscious man twice his age.

"So modest, Nesma," said Daoli with a chuckle. "With an attitude like that, I believe you will be a great Magician, perhaps even go down in history as one of the greats."

"I hope so," said Nesma. "But in truth, Magician Daoli, all I want to do is serve the people of South Lamaira and defend them from all threats to their safety and well-being. If I can do that, then I will be happy regardless of what happens."

"That is a good goal to have," said Daoli. "And of course, you don't mind making a little bit of money off of the peoples' tax revenue, too, yes?"

There was a hint of greed in Daoli's voice that told Keo that he probably meant more than a 'little bit' of the peoples' taxes. Considering how fancy the Citadel was, Keo figured that the Magical Council probably got far more than just a 'little bit' of the peoples' money.

"Well, I won't say no to extra money," said Nesma with a laugh that sounded oddly forced to Keo. "But really, I would do it for free. The security of my people and my nation matter more to me than all of the money in the world."

"Certainly, certainly," said Daoli, although he didn't sound like he entirely agreed with Nesma about that. "Anyway, I am going to my office. Will you join me? We can continue our discussion in there, if you wish."

"No, thank you," said Nesma. "I need to return to my own office because I have a lot of work to get done. I received a detailed report from Captain Wrat on the northwest front about the battle against the Restorationists and I need to read it."

"Captain Wrat is hardly known for his brevity, so I guess you will be spending the rest of the day reading it, huh?" said Daoli, who sounded disappointed at Nesma's rejection of his offer to talk with him in his office.

"Unfortunately, yes," said Nesma. "But that's why the gods invented coffee, for important government officials like me who have to spend hours reading verbose reports from our men in the field."

Daoli chuckled. "Yes, indeed. Well, perhaps we can continue our little chat later at dinner."

"Maybe," said Nesma. "I'll have to ask Gers to check my schedule and see if I'm open for later."

"Very well," said Daoli. "See you later, then. Try not to die of boredom from Wrat's report."

With that, Keo heard one set of footsteps walk away from the broom closet door. Still, Keo kept his breathing low and stood motionless, because even now he did not want Nesma to know he was there just yet. He listened for any movement from her, but it sounded to him like Nesma was being very quiet and still herself.

Why hasn't she gone off to her own office yet? Keo wondered. *If she has that important report to read, why waste time standing in the hallway in front of the broom closet?*

Then he heard another door somewhere down the hall slam shut, and there was complete silence in the hallway. For a moment, the only thing that Keo could hear was his own breathing, as quiet as it was.

And then, without warning, Keo's eyes became heavy and impossible to keep open. A sudden drowsiness came over him, causing Keo to lean against the closet's door as he fought against the sleepiness.

He managed to open the door and push it open. But even as he staggered out of the broom closet, his vision turned black and he lost consciousness well before he hit the floor.

Chapter Twenty-Seven

Is he awake?" said a feminine voice that Keo did not recognize, but which seemed familiar.

"It doesn't look like it. What kind of spell did you hit him with?"

"A basic sleeping spell. It shouldn't leave him with any lasting or permanent damages, though he did knock his head against the doorknob when he fell."

Keo heard those voices talking, but his mind was at first too sluggish to understand what they were saying. He was conscious enough to register that he was sitting on a chair and that his arms and legs were tied down to the chair by some kind of rope, but with his eyes closed and his senses dulled, he found it impossible to tell much more than that. He also felt his forehead throbbing, although the pain felt like it was going away, at least.

But Keo's senses were starting to recover, and in a few seconds, he decided to try opening his eyes. Opening his eyes, he blinked several times in order to clear his vision. Once his vision was clear enough, Keo looked around at his surroundings in curiosity.

Keo was sitting in a medium-sized office, with a large wooden desk covered with papers and books and writing utensils on one end and the door on the other. Bookshelves lined the walls, a mishmash of thick tomes and slim volumes, some clearly brand

350 | TIMOTHY L. CEREPAKA

new, while others looked like they were about to fall apart any second. On the desk itself was a strange device that resembled glasses connected to some kind of glass vial, which was filled with a bubbly purple liquid that he could not identify. The room was lit by a small chandelier hanging from the ceiling, but the lights within the chandelier moved, like fireflies at night.

"Oh," said a voice to his right. "He's awake."

Keo looked to his right and saw two people in the right corner, a man who stood and a woman who sat in a comfy chair. The man was the middle-aged assistant he had knocked out earlier, the one who had seen through Keo's lie that he was here to meet Nesma. Aside from the fist-shaped bruise on the side of his face, the assistant looked well, if a bit angry. He also carried a large book under his right armpit, but what was written in it, Keo did not know.

As for the woman, she was young, about Keo's age, but her hair was much darker than his, almost as black as midnight, and her skin was pale due to a lack of exposure to sunlight. She wore black robes with a silver trim and had bright green eyes that stood out against her pale skin.

Keo blinked slowly. "Nesma? Is that you?"

"It is," said her assistant, before Nesma could reply. "But how dare you try to speak to her without her permission. So disrespectful, but then, I guess that is what I should expect from an assassin like yourself."

"Gers," said Nesma, looking up at him reproachfully. "Keo is not an assassin. He is my friend. I would appreciate it if you would not falsely accuse him of being something that he isn't."

"But Madam Magician," said Gers, looking at Nesma in shock

as he gestured at Keo, "this young man viciously assaulted me when I found out that he was lying about having a meeting with you. He is a danger to everyone in the Citadel. I believe it is foolish to treat him with any kindness, especially if he is at all related to that woman terrorist who attack the lobby earlier."

"Woman terrorist?" said Keo. "What?"

"A female Magician caused a ruckus in the Citadel lobby half an hour ago before fleeing," said Gers, looking at Keo with disgust. "The Enforcers are trying to find her in the city, but have had no luck as of yet."

Maryal got away, Keo thought. *Good.*

Aloud, however, Keo said, "I'm sorry for assaulting you, Gers, but I had to. I wasn't thinking. I thought you were going to report me to the Council, which would have messed up my plans."

Gers folded his arms across his chest, with his book in his right hand. "Hmph! I doubt you are *truly* sorry. Otherwise, you would have been quicker to apologize."

Nesma rolled her eyes and pointed at the door. "Gers, please leave. I wish to speak with Keo alone right now. You can stand outside the door if you like, but I want you to give us some privacy."

Gers looked like he thought that that was an awful idea. Nonetheless, he nodded to show that he understood, crossed the office without looking at or saying anything to Keo, and was out of the office in an instant, pulling the door closed tightly behind him on his way out.

Once Gers was gone, Keo looked at Nesma again. A powerful excitement rose in his heart when he looked at her and, despite the pain in his forehead and the fact that he was tied to the chair, he found it hard to know what to say to Nesma. It had been so long since they had last spoken that he had almost forgotten how to even talk to her.

Thankfully, it took Keo only a couple of seconds to say, "Nesma, it's been so long. You look pretty much the same as you did when you left the Low Woods, except that your robes are fancier and cleaner."

Nesma smiled, though it looked a little forced to Keo. "And you look pretty much the same, too, except you smell like the Hanuf River for some reason."

Keo cracked a grin. "Long story, that. But that's irrelevant. I'm just glad to see you because I have something important to tell you."

Nesma rested her hand on her chin. She did not look surprised. "Oh? What possessed you to come all the way from the Low Woods to Capitika? That's not exactly an easy or quick journey, you know."

"I know," said Keo. "I ran into all sorts of people and problems along the way, but that's also irrelevant. What matters is that I have some urgent news to share with you, news that will affect all of Lamaira if we don't act on it."

"And what is that news?" said Nesma, still not looking surprised.

"The demons from the old legends are coming back," said Keo. He leaned toward her as much as he could in his chair, as uncomfortable as that was. "In six months, they will rise from the pit that the Good King sealed them in and will destroy us all unless we act quickly. I came from the Low Woods to tell you this because I knew that you were the only person who could convince the rest of the Magical Council to stop the demons before they rise again."

Nesma did not meet Keo's gaze, which Keo found strange, because Nesma usually was not afraid of making eye contact with anyone, much less Keo. Yet Keo did not question it. He just looked at her, wondering what her reaction would be.

Finally, Nesma said, "That's … an interesting story, Keo."

"It isn't a story," Keo insisted. "It's the truth. Look at Gildshine. I know you can read weapons. Use your weapon reading ability to read Gildshine and see who its last victims were. I can guarantee you that they will be the two demons my friends and I slayed during our trip here." Then Keo looked down at his belt and saw that Gildshine was missing. "Speaking of Gildshine, where did it go? And why am I tied down to this chair, anyway?"

"Gildshine is over there," said Nesma, pointing to a chest of drawers near the door. Keo saw Gildshine in its sheath standing against the drawers, well outside of Keo's reach.

"Oh," said Keo. He looked at Nesma again. "Will you please untie me so I can go and give you Gildshine? Or maybe just walk over there and touch it yourself. Then you will see the undeniable proof that the demons are returning and then you can tell the rest of the Council and maybe we can save all of Lamaira before it's too late."

Keo's tone was excited and optimistic, but Nesma did not seem to share in his optimism. She looked like she was steeling herself to say something that she didn't want to say, but that she had to say anyway. Keo did not know what she would say, but he doubted it would be that bad.

Then Nesma finally looked Keo straight in the eye and said, "No."

Keo blinked again. "No? No what?"

"I will not untie you," said Nesma. "I was the one who tied you up in the first place because I did not want the rest of the Magical Council to know you were here. I was aware you were hiding in the broom closet listening to Daoli and me talk, but I didn't act because I didn't want Daoli to know about you."

"But … why?" said Keo. He struggled against the ropes, but they did not budge whatsoever. "You know me. You know I'd never harm you or anyone else. Well, okay, I did harm Gers, but I was acting impulsively, like I sometimes do. Otherwise I wouldn't have even touched him. I'm not a threat to anyone, much less to you."

"You don't understand," said Nesma. She rubbed her forehead, looking stressed out by all of this. "I can't risk you walking around Capitika or the Citadel talking about the demons coming back. I don't want the Magical Council to know, because if they did, then they might act against them."

"Wait …" The implications of Nesma's words sank in instantly. "Are you saying that *you* are working for the demons?"

"No," said Nesma, shaking her head. "What I am saying is that you are wrong. They aren't even demons at all."

"Aren't even demons—?" Keo repeated. He could barely finish the sentence before interrupting himself. "Nesma, I was told several times by these demons that they are, well, *demons*. They used that term to describe themselves to me."

But Nesma shook her head again. "I don't believe that. I believe you believe that, but the truth of the matter is that they aren't demons. You misheard them, most likely."

"Misheard them?" said Keo incredulously. "My ears are working just fine. I know what I heard. I heard them gloating about the coming Kingdom of Demons and how they are going to destroy us all once they rise again."

"Just because you think you heard something, doesn't mean you actually have," said Nesma. "I think your mind has been clouded by the ancient stories, the ancient lies, told about those who we call 'demons' but who aren't actually demons at all."

"If they aren't demons, then what *are* they?" said Keo. "They certainly aren't human, that's for sure."

"They're angels," said Nesma simply. "Angels who were attacked and sealed away by the so-called 'Good King,' who was in fact a tyrannical dictator who used his power to cement his rule over the people with an iron fist."

"Where did you get *that* idea from?" said Keo. He tried to break free of his ropes again, but they still held taut. "Who told you that?"

"One of the angels, of course," said Nesma. She cupped her head in her hands, a dreamy expression appearing on his face. "He came to me two years ago, before I joined the Magical Council. He told me the truth about what really happened a thousand years ago and he asked me for my help and I promised I would help him, because I believe in justice and freeing the angels is the just thing to do."

"What did this angel call himself?" said Keo. "And how were you supposed to help him?"

"He calls himself Love of Light," said Nesma. "As for how I was supposed to help, why do you think I joined the Magical

Council? I knew that in order to help the angels, I would need a lot of power. And Love of Light helped me by giving me unimaginable magical power. Otherwise, I would never have been allowed to serve on the Council, because I am simply too young and inexperienced for it normally."

Keo gulped. "Did this 'Love of Light' character also help you trick the rest of the Council into letting you join?"

Nesma looked down at her knees. "I didn't 'trick' them, not exactly. Just very effectively persuaded them to let me join. But even if I did trick them, it is all for the greater good, I can assure you. The rise of the angels will do far more to help Lamaira than anything else, because Love of Light has promised to share his angelic knowledge with humanity so we can rise to new, previously unforeseen heights." She looked up at Keo, mania in her eyes. "To become like gods, in his own words, gods with the power to dish out punishment to those who have evaded justice for so long."

Nesma spoke as fervently as if she were a prophet that had received divine guidance from the ancestors themselves. She rubbed her hands together and did not even seem to be looking at Keo anymore. Instead, she seemed consumed by the promises of Love of Light, promises that Keo did not believe.

"Did you send those demons after us, then?" said Keo. "Were you even aware that I was coming to Capitika to stop them?"

Nesma looked away as if guilty. "Well … Love of Light said that you and a few others were trying to stop him because you still believed in the vile propaganda that has been taught as truth for centuries. He told me that you needed to be stopped, that you had evil intent for him and his people."

"And you believed him?" said Keo.

"Not at first," Nesma admitted. "I told him you were my friend and that I knew you weren't a bad man. Yet I gave him permission to stop you anyway, because I knew that you, like most people, were misguided. I did not ask him how he planned to stop you, but I did not think I needed to, because I trusted Love of Light to do the right thing."

"His friends tried to kill me several times along the way," Keo said. "The demon in the Low Woods … the demon in Castarious … and the demon here, in Capitika. I barely escaped all three of them alive."

Nesma bit her lower lip. "I don't know that I approve of that, but I do believe that Love of Light ultimately has the best intentions for us. I don't want him to kill you, but if that's what needs to be done—"

"Needs to be done?" Keo interrupted in astonishment. "Nesma, I am your *friend*. Are you saying that you'd approve of this demon murdering me in cold blood if that's 'what needs to be done'? I thought we were best friends."

"I'm not saying that," said Nesma, holding up her hands to calm down Keo. "I'm just saying that I have seen how wrong everyone in our society has been about the angels and how I think that the angels need to do what they can to survive. I don't even know if you're telling the truth about being attacked by them anyway."

"Then check Gildshine," said Keo, nodding at his sheathed sword that still stood against the chest of drawers. "Use your magic to see the demons for yourself. I can guarantee you that you will see the true face of your 'angel's' friends."

But Nesma shook her head. "I *did* check Gildshine when I took it away from you, but Light of Love told me that the 'demons' I saw were merely corrupted angels. He told me that the seal that the Good King put on the angels has corrupted many of them and that as a result they sometimes look like monsters and may behave in ways that we normally don't approve."

Keo shook his head in annoyance. "Nesma, you have to know that that is the biggest load of dung I've ever heard. These demons were exactly like the demons in the old stories: Bloodthirsty, violent, eager and willing to kill humans, especially humans who got in their way, and insane."

"Propaganda, all of it," said Nesma, her tone becoming sharper. She sat up straight in her chair. "Tell me, were *you* there when the so-called 'Good King' sealed away the so-called 'demons'? If not, then how can you know if they really were as bad as the old stories claim? You are relying on the biased legends of a people prejudiced against the angels, while I am relying on the eyewitness testimony of someone who was actually there and experienced the events."

"I don't have to have been there to know that the demons are evil and are tricking you into supporting their agenda," said Keo, looking up at her in defiance. "They are not peaceful or oppressed or kind. They are monsters, pure and simple, and you've been tricked into believing that they are your friends."

"I haven't been tricked by anyone," said Nesma, folding her arms over her chest. "And maybe the angels are right to be angry at you. They've been sealed away for so long that I can't imagine that they or anyone else would come out of that situation nice and peaceful. I don't think they're going to slaughter anyone, but I'm not going to say that they are wrong to be angry with us humans for what we did to them so long ago."

"Are you going to be angry with them when they are finally released and start slaughtering innocent people left and right?" said Keo. "Because that's what they want to do. And once they do that, the blood of innocent people will be on *your* hands."

"There will be no innocent blood shed," said Nesma. "No one is going to die. Once the angels are freed, they will make us better. Maybe they will even make us all immortal. Don't you want that?"

"The demons aren't going to give us that or anything else," said Keo. "They are just going to kill you as soon as they don't need you anymore. Don't you get it? They're nothing more than monsters, pure and simple."

"And you are wrong," said Nesma. "But that's why I have to keep you here. I don't want you or anyone else getting in the way of the angels' freedom."

"Are you going to keep me locked up here forever?" said Keo. "Like some sort of prisoner?"

"I will keep you here as long as Love of Light tells me to," said Nesma. She looked troubled when she said that. "And he says that there should be no obstacles in the way of the freedom of his people. He said that you were the biggest obstacle to the freedom of his people, which is why I had to capture you like this. But don't worry. I'll free you as soon as the angels are free, and then you can join us in the bright and glorious future that they will build with us."

Keo shook his head. "I don't believe that, and I don't think you believe that, either. There *isn't* going to be a future for us if the demons are released. The only future we can look forward to in that scenario is death."

"Well, you're wrong about that, but it's clear that you are too brainwashed by society to even listen to me," said Nesma. "So I am going to just cast you into a deep sleep. You won't sleep forever. Just long enough for the angels to rise again."

Nesma raised her hand, but then froze. She tilted her head to the side, like she was listening to someone speak. She reminded Keo of Dlaine whenever he was listening to Jola, except Keo knew that whoever Nesma was listening to was nowhere near as kind or helpful as Jola.

"But ..." Nesma frowned. "Why ...?"

Keo did not like the shocked and questioning tone in Nesma's voice. Yet he did not speak himself. He just watched as Nesma continued to listen to whatever voice she thought she heard, telling her to do whatever it was that it was telling her to do.

Then Nesma nodded and said, "I understand. Sacrifices must sometimes be made for the common good. But Keo is my friend. Are you sure—"

Nesma abruptly stopped speaking and then winced, like she had been slapped in the face. She nodded quickly and said, "Okay, okay, I understand. I'm sorry. I will do it. For the good of Lamaira."

Then Nesma looked at Keo, but her eyes even less kind than before. "I am sorry, Keo, but it looks like I will have to make a change of plans. Love of Light told me not to put you to sleep. He says that you will be a threat to the angels even if you are asleep."

"Then what does he want you to do to me?" said Keo, although he had a feeling that he already knew what Nesma's answer was going to be.

Sparks of flame danced across Nesma's fingertips as she said, "He wants me to kill you."

Chapter Twenty-Eight

KEO STRUGGLED AGAINST HIS ropes again, but they were as solid and immovable as ever. He looked up at Nesma, trying to see any mercy in her eyes, but he saw none. She was willing to do what Love of Light asked her no matter what.

Yet Keo nonetheless said, "Nesma, this is insane. We're friends, remember? You aren't seriously going to listen to him and kill me, are you?"

"I am," said Nesma. She sounded utterly certain of that. "I would rather not, because you are my friend, but … well, sometimes you have to do things you don't want to for the greater good."

All of the hope in Keo's heart dropped when he heard that. He strained against the ropes harder than ever now, but soon gave up and said, "Please, Nesma, don't kill me. If you do, you'll never be able to live with yourself again after this."

"Maybe, but my own mental well-being isn't the only thing at stake here," said Nesma. "I also have to think about the greater good of our people and of humanity in general. And if you are a threat to that greater good—if you just want to retain the status quo—then I am afraid that I am going to have to do this."

"Love of Light is manipulating you," said Keo. Sweat was starting to run down his face, but he ignored it in order to focus on Nesma. "He's a liar. He doesn't care about you or about humanity. He's just making you do this because he sees me as a threat to his own evil plans."

"Evil?" Nesma repeated. "What is so evil about wanting to be free? What is so evil about wanting the best for your people? Trust me, Keo, Love of Light is a good being. He would not ask me to do something if it was truly evil."

"Then you are naïve," said Keo. "But you still have a choice, Nesma. You can still say no and set me free and we can tell the rest of the Council about the—"

A flame launched from Nesma's fingertips and struck Keo in the side of the face. He let out a yell of pain as the hot flame burned his face, causing his eyes to water and his skin to burn. The flame died quickly, but it still left an awful pain where it had hit.

Barely able to focus, Keo nonetheless looked up at Nesma again. She was trembling now, tears welling in her eyes, tears that she was wiping away with the sleeves of her robes.

"I can't believe this, Keo," said Nesma with a sniffle. "I never believed that I would ever have to kill you for doing such awful things. I thought you might at least be open to reason, but it is obvious now that you are not."

The flames dancing along Nesma's fingertips became hotter and larger. Keo knew that he had only seconds now before he would die. He didn't want to believe that Nesma would kill him, but he saw in her eyes that she had gone over the edge. She was willing to do anything that Love of Light told her, even if that meant killing her best friend in the world.

And even worse, there was no way Keo could escape in time.

The ropes holding him down to the chair were tied so tightly around his limbs that he believed that Nesma must have cast a spell to make them unbreakable. And the chair itself felt solid under his body, too solid for him to rock over.

So Keo could only watch as his former best friend in the world conjured a larger and larger fire ball in her hand. He said nothing because there was nothing to say.

At that moment, however, just when Nesma looked like she was about to finally burn him alive, the door to Nesma's office burst open. Surprised, Nesma looked over to the door to see who had entered, as did Keo.

Much to Keo's shock, it was Dlaine. The older man looked like he had run a mile, but he also looked like he was ready to fight. He smirked when he saw Keo and Nesma.

"Hey, Keo," said Dlaine, waving at him like he was passing Keo on the street on his way to work. "Looks like I've got to save your life … again."

"Dlaine?" said Keo. "What are *you* doing here? How did you even find me?"

Dlaine opened his mouth to answer, but then Nesma shrieked, "Die!" and hurled a fireball over Keo's head at Dlaine. But then the fireball exploded in midair halfway between Keo and Dlaine, the sparks landing on the carpet and making it smoke where they landed.

"What?" said Nesma, taking a step back. "Impossible. How did an ordinary person like you negate my spell?"

Dlaine shook his head. "Not by myself, that's for certain. But I don't think I'm under any obligation to reveal any of my secrets to you, considering how you Magicians don't share your secrets with us."

With that, Dlaine whipped out a blowpipe from his pocket, raised it to his mouth, and blew into it. A red dart flew out of the blowpipe, flew so fast that Keo could not follow it, and struck Nesma in the neck.

Nesma gasped. She slammed one hand over the dart on her neck, but it was the last action she took before her eyes rolled into the back of her head and she collapsed onto the chair behind her. Her arms hung limply, while her head lolled to her left shoulder, making her look dead, although she was clearly just unconscious.

Before Keo could even think to ask what just happened, Dlaine was at his side. Drawing a sharp, serrated knife from his side, Dlaine immediately started cutting Keo's ropes, though they were very thick and strong and so took him a little time to cut through.

"I don't understand," said Keo, staring at Dlaine uncomprehendingly. "Why are you here? Why did you attack Nesma?"

"Questions, questions, questions," said Dlaine as he finished cutting the ropes holding down Keo's left arm, immediately moving to Keo's right arm afterward. "Aren't you just grateful that Nesma didn't get a chance to turn you into burnt flesh?"

"I *am* grateful that you saved me," said Keo, raising his freed left arm and turning it to make sure that it was all right. "But I just didn't *expect* you to, which is why I am asking you these questions."

"Fair enough," said Dlaine, his focus on the ropes on Keo's right arm, which was he still cutting through. "But I will have to answer those questions on our way out. I really don't want to be here when one of Nesma's assistants comes by and finds her corpse."

"Her corpse?" said Keo in shock. He looked at Nesma, who was still breathing. "You mean you tried to kill her?"

"Unless she gets medical attention, and fast, she *will* die," said Dlaine. "That was some pretty potent poison I put in that dart. Hasfarian blue spice, actually. Said to be the deadliest poison in the world, which is why I bought it in the first place."

Dlaine finished cutting through the ropes wrapped around Keo's right arm and then immediately started work on the ones binding Keo's legs to the chair. He managed to cut through those much more quickly than the other two and then stood up and stepped back, allowing Keo to rise from the chair, rubbing his wrists as he looked at Dlaine in shock and horror.

"Why?" said Keo. "Why did you try to kill her? I don't understand. I thought you were here to save your daughter's life."

Dlaine sheathed his knife and chuckled. "Oh, right. My nonexistent daughter. I forgot how naïve you could be."

"Nonexistent?" Keo repeated. "What are you even talking about?"

"I'll explain on the way out," said Dlaine, turning and walking toward the open door. "Right now, we need to get out of here, and fast."

Keo looked back at Nesma, who was looking even paler than usual, and then turned and walked after Dlaine. He glanced around the room for Jola, but as usual, she was nowhere to be seen. He did, however, grab Gildshine on his way out, attaching its sheath to his belt where it belonged.

The two of them stepped out into the hallway of the Inner

Chambers. By the door lay Gers, who appeared to be completely unconscious, but there was no one else in the hallway, thankfully.

"This way," said Dlaine, pointing to the left. "Quickly. Don't want to be seen."

Dlaine immediately started walking down the left side of the hallway, with Keo following as closely as he could.

"I still don't understand," said Keo, glancing over his shoulder every now and then to make sure that no one was following them. "Your daughter doesn't exist?"

"That's because I don't even *have* a daughter," said Dlaine as they passed closed door after closed door. "It was a lie I made up because I was supposed to keep my *real* mission a secret. Technically, I'm not even supposed to save you. I was just supposed to go in, kill Nesma, and leave, with Jola's help, of course."

"But why?" said Keo. "And who even gave you this mission in the first place?"

"The Rebel Leader, obviously," said Dlaine, his pace quick for a man his age. "Gave me orders to kill Nesma and create chaos and confusion in the Magical Council's ranks."

"But I thought you didn't like the Rebels and wanted nothing to do with them," said Keo in shock.

"Another lie," said Dlaine as they turned a corner, which meant that they were far deeper in the Inner Chambers than Keo had thought. "Although I will admit that I find most of my fellow Rebels to be idiots, but you can't always choose your allies unfortunately and I still believe in the Rebel cause anyway."

"So the whole reason you wanted to go to Capitika was to kill Nesma?" said Keo. "Did you even know that she's the one who has been manipulated by the demons?"

"Kid, I didn't even believe the demons were real until I met you," said Dlaine. "The fact that she's a member of the Magical Council—and an important one, too, by all accounts—is reason enough to target her. But if she's also the one who sent that demon after us back in the secret passageway, that just makes her inevitable death all the sweeter."

"What about the rest of the Magical Council?" said Keo. "Are you going after them, too?"

"By the ancestors, no," said Dlaine, shaking his head. "I was given one target and that was Nesma. Besides, the rest of the Council is being guarded by the Enforcers because of Maryal's earlier stupid attack on the Citadel, so I couldn't reach 'em even if I wanted to."

"How is Maryal?" said Keo. "Is she aware that you're here?"

"I doubt it," said Dlaine. "I just took advantage of her stupid distraction to get in here before the Enforcers got everything under control. Say what you will about the girl, but she's really good at making a scene when she wants to."

Two Enforcers suddenly stepped out of a doorway on the left side of the hall near the end. When they spotted Keo and Dlaine approaching, one of the Enforcers shouted, "Halt! Identify yourself immediately or—"

Dlaine snapped his fingers and the two Enforcers suddenly slammed into each other like dolls. They collapsed to the floor unconscious as Keo and Dlaine passed them, Dlaine smirking, Keo looking back at them over his shoulder with some concern.

"That was Jola," said Dlaine, in answer to Keo's puzzled look. "It's a little trick I like to do sometimes, snapping my fingers to make Jola do something. And she always comes up with the most inventive magical tricks, too, but sometimes she goes straight for practicality, like she did now."

"Okay," said Keo. "So where are we going, then?"

"As far from Capitika as we can get," said Dlaine as they stopped in front of the golden door that Keo recognized as being the entrance to the lobby. "Because once the rest of the Council finds out that Nesma is dead, they'll shut down the whole city, which will make escape almost impossible."

Dlaine pulled open the door and stepped through it into the Citadel's lobby, with Keo following closely behind. As they entered the lobby, Keo looked around at their surroundings, just to make sure that no one was there, but the lobby was almost totally empty.

"Where is everyone?" said Keo. "The lobby was full earlier."

"They evacuated all of the visitors after Maryal's distraction because they didn't know if there was anyone else in here who was working with her," said Dlaine. "Anyway, enough talking. We have to get out of here before—"

Dlaine was interrupted by a sudden shadow appearing across the glass ceiling above. The shadow then fell to the floor like lightning, but it made no sound as it fell and was completely silent when it hit the floor in front of the statue of the old man, where it splashed like a blob.

Keo and Dlaine stopped right in front of the door they had just exited from, staring at the shadowy blob as it gurgled. Before their startled eyes, the shadowy blob started to take shape. A large mouth formed in its body, followed by arms and legs and eyes, until soon Keo and Dlaine were staring at the frog demon from the secret passageway once more.

"That thing again?" said Dlaine in surprise. "What the hell is it doing here?"

"It must have sensed you attack Nesma," said Keo. He drew Gildshine from its sheath and held it before him defensively. "The demons are working with her, so it's probably came to avenge her death and keep us from telling everyone about the demons."

"Can you kill it?" said Dlaine, looking between Keo and the frog demon worriedly.

"If I can hit it with Gildshine's ability," said Keo. "But if I use its power, I'll be too weak to run on my own. So I'll need your and Jola's help to get it into position."

"And just when I thought we'd make a clean escape," said Dlaine with a sigh. "Oh, well. Just tell us what to do and we'll get on it."

Keo nodded, but before he could say anything, the frog demon let out a croak that was almost a growl and charged toward them. Keo and Dlaine immediately separated, Keo running to the right, Dlaine to the left, but the frog demon was not confused by this tactic. It went after Keo, shooting its tongue from its mouth toward him, but Keo just barely managed to dodge it. He whirled around to face the frog demon, its eyes angry and glowing red hot as it approached, clicking its claws together rapidly.

Jola, are you there? Keo thought as he walked backwards, doing his best to keep out of the frog demon's reach.

He wasn't sure that Jola would hear him, but then he heard her familiar feminine voice in his head say, *I am. What do you need Dlaine and me to do?*

I need you to distract the frog demon, Keo said. *Or at least*

stun it long enough for me to hit it with Gildshine. I just need to
slash it once and it should go down instantly.

Stun the frog demon, Jola repeated. *Got it.*

Then Jola went silent, but Keo knew he could count on her to do her part. He would just need to survive long enough for Jola to do it.

The frog demon lashed out at him again with its tongue, but Keo knocked it aside with Gildshine. The frog demon's tongue slipped back into its mouth, but then the frog demon itself jumped at Keo with surprising speed. It landed before him and swiped at him with its claws, but Keo blocked them with Gildshine, although the frog demon continued to push down against him, making it impossible to escape.

Then, without warning, the frog demon's legs froze, causing it to roar in pain and surprise. This caused its pressure on Keo to lift, which he took advantage of to push hard against the frog demon, knocking it flat on its back.

Before the frog demon could rise again, Keo concentrated, telling Gildshine to take half his energy in order to cut through anything. And, as always, Keo felt Gildshine comply with his demand, felt his energy flow from his hands into the sword's blade, and without further ado, slammed Gildshine's tip directly into the frog demon's mouth.

The demon made a choking sound, flailed its arms about for a couple of seconds, and then went still. Its body immediately crumbled into a large pile of dust, which then sank into the floor, never to be seen again.

As soon as that was over, Keo gasped in exhaustion and leaned against Gildshine. It was almost impossible to retain consciousness now, because the after effect of Gildshine's ability had taken half of his energy. Still, he forced himself to remain awake because he did not want Dlaine and Jola to have to drag him out of the Citadel on their own.

Then Dlaine ran up to Keo, looking both relieved and surprised. "Wow. That was quick."

"Yeah … it … was," said Keo. He struggled to get out each word. "Jola … helped …"

"I saw that," said Dlaine. "Anyway, let's get you out of here. No point in sticking around any longer."

"Agreed," said Keo.

"Leaving already?" said a new voice suddenly, one that was completely unfamiliar to Keo. "Oh, where's the fun in that?"

Keo and Dlaine looked around the lobby, trying to spot the owner of the voice, but aside from themselves and Jola, the Citadel's lobby was completely empty. Yet Keo was absolutely certain he had heard someone else besides them speak just then.

"Who's there?" said Dlaine. "Are you an Enforcer or a member of the Magical Council?"

"Neither, but thanks for asking," said the voice, which sounded amused. "And you can't guess who I am, either, because none of you three have even met me before. That doesn't change the fact, of course, that I can kill all three of you just the same."

"Then why don't you show yourself, like a real man?" said Dlaine. "Or are you just going to hide from us like a coward?"

"Showing myself 'like a real man' is hard to do, considering I'm not even human," said the voice. "But I will show myself anyway, because I feel that every being deserves to see the cause of their death before it kills them."

Then, in the center of the lobby, the statue of the old man rose from its throne.

But then Keo blinked and realized that the statue hadn't moved at all. Instead, a being had somehow risen from within it. The being stepped off of the dais upon which the statue had been built and then turned to face Keo and Dlaine.

The being had deathly pale skin and snow-white hair. He looked like a human being, except for the sharpened teeth and the red eyes that reminded Keo of death. He was tall and skinny, but exuded a power that Keo had not sensed in any of the prior demons. Feathery, raven-like wings sprouted from his back, while his hands resembled metallic falcon claws.

The being grinned at their surprise. "Why are you so shocked? Did you truly believe that Smog of Wrath was the *only* demon in Capitika? Or have you already forgotten about Love of Light?"

Keo's eyes widened as he recalled what Nesma had told him earlier. "You …"

"Me," said Love of Light. "Though in truth, my real name is Plague of Envy, but that doesn't particularly matter. I've decided to step in and finish you three myself, seeing as I can't have you running around knowing about my existence."

"Who?" said Dlaine.

"The demon who … who manipulated Nesma," said Keo. He didn't want to talk, but he wanted to make sure Dlaine understood who they were fighting. "Claimed to be an angel named Love of Light."

"So he's the bastard behind all of our trouble, then," said Dlaine, glaring at Plague.

The demon held up his hands. "I am guilty as charged. You

374 | TIMOTHY L. CEREPAKA

may arrest me and judge me before your silly little human courts and then let the ancient laws of the land determine my fate. Truly, justice shall prevail this day."

"And he's sarcastic, too," said Dlaine, slapping his forehead. "How wonderful."

Plague lowered his hands. "Your own sarcasm is hardly much better, Dlaine of the Fist. But it doesn't matter. Either way, I will end your lives here."

"Why not just let us go?" said Dlaine. "I mean, sure, you hate us and have had your friends try to kill us several times already, but maybe that's just destiny's way of saying that you aren't supposed to kill us. Ever think of that?"

"I don't believe in destiny," said Plague. "And isn't it obvious why I want to kill you? I don't want you humans going around telling your friends that the Magical Council is controlled by demons. Otherwise, that would ruin my plans, and I can't very well have that, now can I? I only waited until you killed my rather dimwitted comrade because I didn't want to be killed by your sword."

"I see," said Dlaine. "So you waited to attack us until we were at our weakest. Scumbag."

Plague shrugged. "I prefer to think of it as pragmatism. In war, there is no such thing as a 'cheap' tactic, only a practical one, and attacking your opponent when they are at their weakest is certainly a practical tactic, wouldn't you agree?"

Dlaine clenched his teeth. "Well, you can try to kill us, but we're not going to let you. We've already killed three of your friends. Won't take much more to take you down."

Plague chuckled. "You *really* have no idea what I am, do you?

I'm not a mere demon like those three. You see, we demons can be divided into several different classes based upon our strengths and abilities. The three demons you killed? They are considered to be one class above the weakest class. Which is to say that they are not very powerful or smart in themselves."

"What's *your* class, then?" said Dlaine. "Do you belong to the weakest one?"

Plague smiled. He gestured at his chest "Actually, I belong to the Superior Class, which makes me one of the strongest demons around. You see, the King of Demons put me in charge of the mission to ensure the return of the demons because of my strength and intelligence. And I *will* ensure that it is completed, no matter what."

Dlaine gulped, while Keo tried his best not to look afraid, although he wasn't sure how successful he was there. If Plague really *was* as powerful as he made himself out to be, then there was likely nothing that Dlaine or Keo could do to stop him. But neither could they run, because Keo was too weak to run or even walk.

Dlaine, who was apparently trying to buy time, said, "Well, if you demons are so strong, then why haven't you broken the seal yet? What's stopping you from doing that?"

"Nothing," said Plague, shaking his head. "But it *is* starting to weaken, primarily thanks to the death of that human king, the one you call Riuno. Because he was of the lineage of the Good King, his life was what kept the seal in tact for a while, but ever since his death, it has been slowly but surely starting to weaken. Soon it will shatter entirely, along with all of Lamaira."

So that's why the demons are rising again, Keo thought. *Does that mean that, if we could get a new King of Lamaira, that it might restore the seal?*

But Keo was too weak to say that aloud. Instead, it was Dlaine who said, "If that's the case, then why are you even bothering to take over the Council? The Magical Council doesn't have much to do with King Riuno or the Good King, you know."

"Because there is always a possibility, however slight, that you humans may find another way to reinforce the seal—perhaps the legendary Rightful Heir said to have survived Riuno's death—and stop us before we can rise again," said Plague. "Besides, it is always more fun to hunt a target that is unaware that it is being hunted than one that is."

Dlaine and Keo exchanged worried looks, but neither one of them said anything in response to that. After all, what was there to say to a demon that clearly had no desire to reason with them?

"Now, then," said Plague. He held up his clawed hands, a wicked grin on his face. "I am done talking. Time to die."

One second, Plague was standing by the statue of the old man. When Keo blinked a second later, however, Plague was standing before Dlaine and him, smiling wickedly down at them both.

Dlaine raised his fists, but Plague slapped him with the back of his claw. The blow sent Dlaine flying into the wall, who then fell down onto the floor, and did not move again.

"Dlaine!" Keo shouted. "Dlaine! No!"

A sudden burst of flame exploded out of thin air and struck Plague in the side. But the flames didn't even make Plague stagger. He just stood there, half of his body burning, before whirling to the side and striking at nothing, but Keo quite clearly heard Plague's claws slam into something and also heard this same thing—which he realized was Jola—go flying somewhere. Unfortunately, he did not see where she landed due to her invisibility.

Nonetheless, Keo knew she was out for the count, which meant that he would have to fight on his own. He pulled Gildshine out of the floor and tried to wield the blade like he always did. But Keo's exhaustion made Gildshine feel a thousand times heavier than it normally did. As a result, Plague was able to knock Gildshine out of his hands easily and then, in the same motion, grab Keo by the throat and lift him off his feet.

Keo gasped for air and weakly punched Plague's arm, but his blows had no strength to them, forcing him to give up. He had only enough strength to look into Plague's red eyes, which glowed as deviously and malevolently as ever.

"Poor, pitiful human," said Plague, his tone mocking. "Believing that you, an orphan from the middle of nowhere, could somehow unite your war-torn kingdom to stand against us … what a tragic and rich joke."

Plague's grip around Keo's neck tightened, making it even harder for Keo to breathe. He knew he was going to die, knew that death was only seconds away, yet he still wanted to fight and win, even though there didn't seem to be a way to win.

Maybe … maybe I'm delusional, Keo thought. *Maybe Plague's right. There's no way I can survive. Maybe I should just let him win …*

That thought—far from draining Keo of his motivation—actually sparked something deep inside himself that he had not realized was there. It was anger, anger at coming so far only to fail, anger at Plague for manipulating Nesma, anger at how the demons had tried to kill him and his friends again and again. And anger at himself for even daring to consider dying. That infuriated him the most of all, because not even Master Tiram would have entertained such silly thoughts no matter how slim the odds of success.

A fire coursed through Keo's body, a flame that he had never known even existed. The fire burned through his veins, scorched his bones, and gave him a strength that he had never felt before, but which felt as natural as breathing.

Without warning, Keo grasped Plague's arm, earning a surprised, yet still amused, look from the demon.

"What's this?" said Plague. "Still have some fight left in you? Interesting. I thought that your sword left you a pitiable mess no stronger than a twig."

Keo gripped Plague's arm tightly and said, in a voice not quite like his own, "I still have a few tricks up my sleeve, demon. Tricks like this."

Keo, without thinking, twisted Plague's arm until he heard something *snap*.

Plague suddenly screeched in pain and let go of Keo. Keo, however, did not collapse onto the floor. He landed on both feet and watched as Plague staggered backwards, gripping his now-broken arm, a stunned look on his face.

"What … what was that?" said Plague, sounded both surprised and in pain. "No human has ever shown that sort of strength to me before. I didn't even know that humans *could* grow that strong."

Keo looked down at his hands. They looked stronger now, rougher, like they were coated in some kind of thick armor. He didn't understand it, because he had never seen anything like this before, but he decided not to question it. The fire within still burned and he was not going to ignore it. The exhaustion from using Gildshine was gone, seemingly eliminated by the fire within, for the moment at least.

So Keo grabbed Gildshine's hilt and raised it off the floor. Holding Gildshine before him, Keo said to Plague, "I am going to kill you here and now, Plague, just as you deserve."

Plague's face twisted into a snarl. "I am no weakling, Keo of the Sword. Unlike my brothers, it takes more than mere residual magic to kill me, even with your sword."

"Who said anything about *residual* magic?" said Keo.

Like Keo had always done this, he channeled the fire within him into Gildshine. And then, like a miracle, golden flames exploded around Gildshine's blade, golden flames Keo had never seen before.

Plague's eyes widened so much that they looked like saucer plates now. "What kind of magic is this? I did not know you are a Magician."

"I'm not," said Keo. "I don't know how to explain this, but I don't need to, because I now have the power to finish you off."

With that, Keo charged toward Plague with Gildshine still wreathed in golden flames. Plague raised his arm to block the blow, but Gildshine cut through his hand as easily as if it was butter, causing Plague to yell in pain again and leave his chest wide open for an attack.

And so Keo drove the burning Gildshine straight into Plague's chest. Golden flame melted away at Plague's chest and even his face, the flames distorting his features and even setting his hair aflame. Even with the stink of melting demon flesh now filling Keo's nostrils, he did not let up. He forced Gildshine's burning blade in deeper and deeper, until the tip of his sword broke through Plague's back.

Then Keo ripped Gildshine out of Plague's chest. Again, Plague stepped back, but he now looked far weaker than before. His chest was still burning and his left eye was completely melted shut. Black demon blood leaked from the hole in his chest, yet unlike his fellow demons, he did not turn into dust just yet.

"It's over," said Keo, lowering Gildshine, which continued to burn in his hands. "I win. You lose."

But much to Keo's astonishment, Plague's melted mouth twisted into the most horrifying smile he had ever seen. "Oh … really?"

With his broken arm, Plague gestured to the right. Although Keo did not trust the demon even in his weakened state, he nonetheless looked in that direction to see Nesma standing in the doorway to the Inner Chambers. She looked like she had just gotten here, her hand on the doorknob, her face even more pale and sickly than before. Keo wasn't sure how she got here, considering how the Hasfarian blue spice should have killed her, but he supposed that she was stronger than she looked.

"Love of Light?" said Nesma, staring at him in horror. "What happened to you?"

Plague smiled crookedly, but it was a sad smile. "I tried to stop him, Nesma, but I failed. Please … forgive me …"

With that, Plague gasped and coughed up more blood before his body started turning into dust. Keo could only watch, stunned, as Plague's body rapidly transformed into dust before his very eyes, starting from the demon's feet all the way up to his neck.

And right before Plague's face turned to dust, he smirked at Keo, a smirk of triumph that Keo understood completely.

A second later, all of Plague's body turned to dust and then collapsed onto the floor. And, like with the frog demon's body, Plague's dust quickly sank into the floor out of sight.

Keo immediately looked at Nesma, who was still staring at where Plague had been standing mere seconds ago.

"Love of Light …." Nesma said, her tone heartbroken. "No …"

"Nesma, I can explain," said Keo as the golden flames of Gildshine went out abruptly. "He—"

Nesma let out a yell of anguish and pointed at Keo. A ball of flame shot from her fingers and hurtled toward Keo, which he deflected with Gildshine.

"Hey!" said Keo, though he didn't lower Gildshine this time. "Aren't you going to listen to me? I thought we were friends."

"Friends? We're not friends," said Nesma, her voice full of despair and anger. "Not anymore. You killed Love of Light. You confirmed all of my worst fears. And now I am going to kill you, you son of a—"

Nesma did not get to finish her sentence, because a powerful gust of wind suddenly flew past Keo and struck her. The blow sent her flying back into the Inner Chambers, but Keo did not look to see if she was all right.

Instead, Keo looked over his shoulder and saw Maryal running toward him. She looked tired and dirty, but otherwise uninjured.

"Maryal?" said Keo. "I thought you were on the run from the

382 | TIMOTHY L. CEREPAKA

Citadel's Enforcers. What are you doing back here?"

"Came back to see if you could use some help," said Maryal as she skid to a stop before Keo. Then she glanced at Dlaine. "What's Dlaine doing here? Is Jola here, too? I thought they had abandoned us."

"Long story, which I'll fill you in on later," said Keo. "Anyway, we need to get out of here quickly. Nesma wants to kill me and she'll probably kill you, too, now that you've attacked her."

"Why?" said Maryal in surprise. "I thought you two were friends. Did you at least tell her about the demons?"

Keo looked away. "I'll explain later. For now, we just need to leave."

"Okay," said Maryal. "But how? We'll have to drag Dlaine with us and I don't think we can do that and still escape Nesma."

I can do it, said Jola's voice in their heads suddenly. *I can teleport all of us out of here, even outside of the city, but it will be tough and take a lot of my energy.*

"Jola?" said Keo. "I didn't know you were still conscious."

Just barely, said Jola. *Anyway, you two, grab Dlaine. As soon as you do, we're out of here.*

Both Keo and Maryal moved over to Dlaine, who they grabbed. Based on how warm Dlaine's body felt, Keo knew that he was still alive, which was good, although he had no idea how badly Dlaine was hurt and how long it would take him to recover from Plague's attack.

Then Nesma reappeared in the doorway, her hair and robes messed up from Maryal's attack. She spotted the two immediately and said, "Oh, no, you don't! I will destroy you all before you can escape!"

But even as Nesma shouted that threat, the Citadel's lobby disappeared around them, only to be replaced by the countryside around Capitika, with the capital city itself farther away than Keo had thought it possible for them to teleport. And Nesma was nowhere in sight.

Chapter Twenty-Nine

Upon teleporting out of the city, Keo blinked and looked around at their environment to see just where Jola had teleported them. They were once again in the countryside outside of Capitika, with the city itself a good distance away from where they stood. Trees and hills rose around them, which kept them hidden from a nearby road. The sun, as always, was out, its hot summer rays beating down on them mercilessly, in sharp contrast to the coldness of the Citadel's interior.

But Keo did not focus on that, because he soon heard Jola's voice in his head say, *I'm going out ...* and then heard a tiny body hit the ground nearby.

Maryal must have heard Jola's last words as well, because she said, "Jola? What happened to Jola? Is she okay?"

"I think she lost consciousness," said Keo, looking around for her, although Jola's invisibility made it impossible to see her. "Remember, teleportation is extremely difficult to do even for powerful Magicians. That she managed to teleport us out of Capitika at all was amazing, if you ask me. She deserves the rest."

"Oh, right," said Maryal. She looked down at Dlaine, who was still lying unconscious himself on the ground nearby. "What happened to you guys in there? Why were Dlaine and Jola in the

Citadel at all? And what's up with Nesma?"

As briefly as he could, Keo recounted the events of the last half hour to Maryal. When he finished, he said, "And now Nesma thinks that I murdered an angel, which means that there is no way that she will listen to me or let me speak with the rest of the Magical Council ever again."

"That's awful," said Maryal, shaking her head. "And here I always admired Nesma for her hard work and success at such a young age. It never occurred to me to think that she would be willing to kill her best friend at the order of a demon. Do you think she'll get better now that the demon manipulating her is gone?"

"I don't know," said Keo. "I doubt it, however. Plague had her deeply convinced of his lies. I don't think there is anything I can do now, except leave and look for help elsewhere."

Maryal crouched down next to Dlaine, looked him over once for any major injuries, and then looked up at Keo, a frown on her face. "But where will you go? The Magical Council is the highest authority in all of South Lamaira. Who else could have the power to do something about the demons?"

Keo stroked his chin in thought. "Something Plague said bothered me. He said that the reason the seal that the Good King placed on the demons is weakening is because King Riuno, who was a descendent of the Good King, died and there has been no one else in the line of the Good King to strengthen the seal." He looked at Maryal. "Do you know if King Riuno had any children who might still be alive?"

Maryal shook her head. "From what I heard, King Riuno's only child—an infant boy—died during the chaos that engulfed the Kingdom after Riuno's death."

"Where did you hear that from?" said Keo.

"The Magical Council's history books," said Maryal. "They say that there are no living descendents of the Good King anymore, that the line died with King Riuno."

"How do we know that's true, though?" said Keo. "What if King Riuno's son actually survived? Or maybe Riuno had other children who he kept a secret? I mean, the Magical Council is hugely corrupt even without the demons' influence. I can't imagine they'd want anyone to know that King Riuno has a living child, otherwise people might rally behind that kid and attempt to overthrow them."

"What are you getting at?" said Maryal. "Are you saying we should look for Riuno's son?"

"Exactly," said Keo, nodding. "Think about it. If the demons' seal is weakening because there is no King of Lamaira, then maybe, by finding Riuno's son and placing him back on the Throne, we can strengthen it again and prevent the demons' rise."

"Even if Riuno's son is somehow still alive—and I am not sure that he is—where would this child of King Riuno's even be?" said Maryal. She spread her hands. "And how can we possibly hope to find him before the demons rise again?"

Keo considered that question. He looked to the west, where the sun was heading, and then to the east. He was thinking also about the mysterious golden flames that had engulfed Gildshine, as well as that strange fire he had felt in his soul. Master Tiram had never told him about that particular ability of Gildshine, but then, Keo strongly suspected that the gold flames and the fire in his body—which he could no longer feel—were connected, though how and why, he did not know.

Then an idea occurred to Keo and he looked at Maryal. "I think I know where we can find Riuno's son. Or at least a place to start."

"Where?" said Maryal. "The Magical Council's Archives?"

Keo shook his head. "No." He pointed west. "Western Lamaira, the Old Kingdom, where the Restorationists rule. They believe in recreating the old Kingdom of Lamaira, so they might be able to help us locate Riuno's son or any other children he may have had."

Maryal made a face. "The Restorationists? Those old, backwards fools? You aren't joking, are you?"

"Of course I'm not," said Keo. "I know how you feel about them, but if finding the Restorationists will help us save South Lamaira, then don't you think we should give it a shot? What if it's our destiny to head out west?"

Maryal sighed in frustration, but nodded anyway and said, "All right. I guess you would not have suggested we head that way if destiny had not put that idea in your head."

"Then it's settled," said Keo. He looked at Dlaine, who was still unconscious on the ground. "Once Dlaine and Jola awake, we'll tell them where we're going, and then we'll head out for West Lamaira as soon as possible. We still have nearly six months left before the demons rise again, which is plenty of time to get to West Lamaira and find the answers we seek."

And the answers I seek as well, Keo thought, with a glance at Gildshine.

Continued in: Kingdom of Heirs

With his homeland falling to the demons, Keo, along with his friends, heads northwest to the Old Kingdom in search of their one possible hope for defeating the demons: The long-lost son of the last king of Lamaira, who is prophesied to return and reunite the Kingdom and save it from the demons.

Keo's journey seems to be a success when, upon arriving in the Old Kingdom, he discovers that the long-lost Rightful Heir has already returned and is about to be crowned the new King of Lamaira. But things become more complicated when Keo is revealed to also be the Rightful Heir.

To determine who the true heir to the Throne, Keo must duel his counterpart in accordance with tradition. If Keo fails, not only will he lose his right to succeed his father, but the entire Kingdom of Lamaira will fall to the demons.

Available in ebook and paperback wherever books are sold!

About the Author

Timothy L. Cerepaka writes fantasy as an indie author. He is the author of the Mages of Martir fantasy novels, the Two Worlds science-fantasy series, and the Tournament of the Gods fantasy novels. He lives in Texas.

Find out more at his website at www.timothylcerepaka.com.

Other books by Timothy L. Cerepaka

Prince Malock World:

The Mad Voyage of Prince Malock

The Return of Prince Malock

The New Era of Prince Malock

The Coronation of Prince Malock

Mages of Martir:

The Mage's Grave

The Mage's Limits

The Mage's Sea

The Mage's Ghost

Two Worlds:

Reunification

Alliance

Allegiance

Retaliation

Desinence

Tournament of the Gods:

Gathering of the Chosen

Betrayal of the Chosen

Invasion of the Chosen

Ascension of the Chosen

The War-Torn Kingdom:

Kingdom of Magicians

Kingdom of Heirs

Standalones:

The Last Legend: Glitch Apocalypse